PRAISE FOR JEAN JOHNSON AND THE SONS OF DESTINY NOVELS

"Jean Johnson's writing is fabulously fresh, thoroughly romantic, and wildly entertaining. Terrific—fast, sexy, charming, and utterly engaging. I loved it!"

—Jayne Ann Krentz, *New York Times* bestselling author

"Cursed brothers, fated mates, prophecies, yum! A fresh new voice in fantasy romance, Jean Johnson spins an intriguing tale of destiny and magic."

—Robin D. Owens, RITA Award–winning author

"A must-read for those who enjoy fantasy and romance. I . . . eagerly look forward to each of the other brothers' stories. Jean Johnson can't write them fast enough for me!"

—*The Best Reviews*

"[It] has everything—love, humor, danger, excitement, trickery, hope, and even sizzling-hot . . . sex." —*Errant Dreams*

"Enchantments, amusement, and eight hunks and one bewitching woman make for a fun romantic fantasy . . . humorous and magical . . . a delightful charmer."

—*Midwest Book Review*

"A paranormal adventure series that will appeal to fantasy and historical fans, plus time-travel lovers as well. Jean Johnson has created a mystical world of lessons taught, very much like the great folktales we love to hear over and over. It's like *Alice in Wonderland* meets the *Knights of the Round Table*, and you're never quite sure what's going to happen next. Delightful entertainment . . . An enchanting tale with old-world charm, *The Sword* will leave you dreaming of a sexy mage for yourself." —*Romance Junkies*

continue

THEIRS NOT TO REASON WHY

A SOLDIER'S DUTY

JEAN JOHNSON

ACE BOOKS, NEW YORK

THE BERKLEY PUBLISHING GROUP
Published by the Penguin Group
Penguin Group (USA) Inc.
375 Hudson Street, New York, New York 10014, USA
Penguin Group (Canada), 90 Eglinton Avenue East, Suite 700, Toronto, Ontario M4P 2Y3, Canada
(a division of Pearson Penguin Canada Inc.)
Penguin Books Ltd., 80 Strand, London WC2R 0RL, England
Penguin Group Ireland, 25 St. Stephen's Green, Dublin 2, Ireland (a division of Penguin Books Ltd.)
Penguin Group (Australia), 250 Camberwell Road, Camberwell, Victoria 3124, Australia
(a division of Pearson Australia Group Pty. Ltd.)
Penguin Books India Pvt. Ltd., 11 Community Centre, Panchsheel Park, New Delhi—110 017, India
Penguin Group (NZ), 67 Apollo Drive, Rosedale, Auckland 0632, New Zealand
(a division of Pearson New Zealand Ltd.)
Penguin Books (South Africa) (Pty.) Ltd., 24 Sturdee Avenue, Rosebank, Johannesburg 2196,
South Africa

Penguin Books Ltd., Registered Offices: 80 Strand, London WC2R 0RL, England

THEIRS NOT TO REASON WHY: A SOLDIER'S DUTY

An Ace Book / published by arrangement with the author

PRINTING HISTORY
Ace mass-market edition / August 2011

Copyright © 2011 by G. Jean Johnson.
Excerpt from *Theirs Not to Reason Why: An Officer's Duty* copyright © by G. Jean Johnson.
Cover art by Gene Mollica.
Cover design by Annette Fiore DeFex.
Interior text design by Laura K. Corless.

ISBN: 978-0-441-02063-8

ACE
Ace Books are published by The Berkley Publishing Group,
a division of Penguin Group (USA) Inc.,
375 Hudson Street, New York, New York 10014.
ACE and the "A" design are trademarks of Penguin Group (USA) Inc.

PRINTED IN THE UNITED STATES OF AMERICA

10   9   8   7   6   5   4   3   2   1

ACKNOWLEDGMENTS

My thanks to everyone who helped me with this. To Cindy and Ace Books at The Berkley Publishing Group for knowing I could write more than just romance. To my beta editors Alexandra, NotSoSaintly, Stormi, and my sci-fi pinch hitter Buzzy (beautiful, scary lady), who stepped in to be my fourth gempolisher on this task. To Dr. Ivezic, the University of Washington's Astronomy Department, and astronomers everywhere, amateur or professional—any astronomical and stellar mistakes in this book are naturally my own fault. (Alas, AAA doesn't make the right-sized map for my needs, so I kind of had to wing several things.) If you have any questions or comments, come visit me at www.JeanJohnson.net and I'd be happy to chat about my books.

My thanks also go to scientists of all types. Science fiction is the springboard for so many ideas; I hope my stories give each of you a lift toward new ideas to explore and things to create. Even if what I write is impossible or improbable, may it at least inspire you. In turn, may your efforts inspire new generations of writers to dream, imagine, and inspire yet others.

My thanks and my gratitude go out to all the military personnel who allowed me to ply them with verbal cookies and whiskey in congenially ruthless interrogations over the years, helping this story come to life. (Any errors are either my own or the result of futuristic wishful thinking.) Most important, my thanks go to every single person who has in the past or currently serves their country, regardless of nationality. You stand between the innocent and the profane, putting your lives on the line for little recognition or fame. Yet you are there. You are the big damn heroes in life, and I just wanted you to know that some of us do realize that, and deeply appreciate it.

Keep your heads down and stay as safe as you can.

Jean

THEIRS NOT TO REASON WHY

A SOLDIER'S DUTY

PROLOGUE

The Future is an ever-changing place, a point of transition between what is and what will be. Obscured by a veil of possibilities, it contains all the joys of heaven, and all the terrors of hell. You may struggle to turn your Fate into your Destiny, but the Future is inescapable; it will drag you forward kicking and screaming. But, wherever you end up, it is—to borrow from Shakespeare—a place "to be, or not to be."

That is the Future.

~Ia

JUNE 3, 2487 TERRAN STANDARD
OUR BLESSED MOTHER
INDEPENDENT COLONYWORLD SANCTUARY

It was horrible. Terrible. No fifteen-year-old—and barely fifteen, at that—should have had to face such a frightening, unrelenting truth. But she had to. She had no choice.

Her eyes *were* open. She was sure of that much. But in the grey glow of predawn, brightened occasionally by the usual morning electrical storm, her bedroom looked out of place: banal and slightly surreal compared to what she had just seen. Crowded, but banal.

There were actually two beds, a narrow one for herself and a broad one that her brothers shared in quiet sleep, with a meager aisle between them. A long counter underneath the window served as part desk, part bureau. Every toy, every book, every datachip was tucked in its place, because there was literally no room for a mess. Neat and tidy. Innocent.

Behind the evidence of her eyes, this whole building—her parents' small but prosperous restaurant—lay in smoldering ruins. Inside her head, she could see the broken plaster boards, scorched plexi tiles . . . and the body of her birthmother, sprawled and bloodied, eyes open but unseeing.

No . . . no! Covering her eyes, elbows braced on her knees, the girl on the narrower of the two beds tried to shut out the images. She couldn't banish them; she could only shove them aside. When she did . . . others took their place. Her elder brother fighting to survive, her younger brother dragged away by brute force, a laser bolt shaded in cruel dark orange arrowing for her own throat. *No! No, no, no!*

She shoved harder at the images, tried to force her way around them, but it was like wading through a muddy river, a hard, cold, murky struggle that swept her relentlessly downstream. It didn't matter which fork she chose, the flow of Time itself dragged her inevitably to the end. To the horrific images of an inevitable end, where rapacious invaders tore whole worlds to shreds. Her world, and the others. Choked by the roiling, cold waters, she couldn't see the right way to go, the best path to survive, a way to escape the lifeless, frozen wasteland lying ahead.

. . . NO!

There *had* to be a way out. She refused to accept that this . . . this *vision* was unbreakable. That it was unstoppable, inevitable. Clasping her arms around her knees, squeezing her eyes tightly shut, she forced her inner self to climb *out* of the waters sweeping inexorably onward to their ugly end. To climb onto the banks of the river—the banks of *all* the rivers in her mind, to stop herself from drowning in the ice-cold waters of Time itself.

There has to be a way out. There has *to be.*

Determined to find that way, some path that could be followed through the tangle of lives and possibilities, she searched through the stream-scattered plains. She didn't stop to check each creek; instead, she jumped from bank to bank, looking for the point where all the rivers turned into rivulets, where all of them ran into a dried, barren, hopeless desert. It was hard to see, though the more she moved and searched, the more light there was in this dark, grey, foreboding place inside her head.

Slowly, as the grey of twilight changed to the amber gold of dawn, she found a thin trickle, a single stream . . . a thread of hope that led through a tiny hole in the barrier of the desert, expanding into an oasis of triumph and beauty beyond that frightening wall of inevitability.

Here—this is the path! This is what I want . . .

But when she looked back, the complexity of the path confounded her. It stretched well past anything she herself could affect in her own lifetime—and not just her own life-*time*, but her own life-*place*, tying into yet more rivers and streams that ran through fields beyond this single, visible plain. Cautiously tracing her way back, she found nodes of influence, little nudges, artificial canals and bolstering dykes, levees built up to prevent the flooding of failure, and aqueducts bringing in knowledge from other realms. Twists and turns, knots and braids artificially plaited into the naturally woven strands of what should have been reality.

Along every centimeter of the intertwining streams she followed, images flickered in the waters, showing her meager glimpses of the way to make that one slender stream of a chance survive. *Make*, not just help.

My God . . . This will take more *than a lifetime to make happen*. She hurried back toward her entry point, only to stumble and fall to her knees, seeing the drastic changes wrought in her own future, just to make all of it possible. *No . . . no . . . No, there* has *to be a better way. Some side-stream I could take . . . some other option!*

Scrambling to her feet, straining to see through the shifting, flowing waters, she searched the currents in the meadows stretching out to either side. Time did not have the same meaning in this place as it had out there, beyond the boundaries of her mind—she knew her brothers were now awake, that they were quietly getting dressed for breakfast and for school, somewhere out there beyond the edges of her consciousness—but

she couldn't stop searching. Couldn't stop looking for an escape.
For a way out.

There wasn't one.

Not for everyone.

With eyes that were learning to skim the images rippling
and shifting in the lengthy tangle of waters crisscrossing the
plains, she saw there was no safe path for herself. No quiet life
to be led. No escape from her fate; not from what she had to
do, not with this radical of a departure from all of her childish
dreams and expectations. No avoiding what would happen to
herself, nor what would happen to her family, to her friends
and neighbors if she ignored this single, meager thread of possibility.

Worse, when she turned to look back at the future, looking
out across the other rivers and their subsidiary streams, the
way they dried into curdled, cracked mud and crumbled into
sand . . . there was no other hope for anyone else.

Not a viable one. Nothing that would bear fruit. Just the
one, rivulet-sized chance to avoid that distant, inevitable, wide-
spread desert of destruction. One chance to stop everything
from turning into nothing. One chance to avoid annihilation.

But . . . if she redirected all those streams and rivulets, goug-
ing out a new set of paths for the waters to take . . . If she
changed the riverbeds of all those lives, both here and elsewhere, fighting to redirect the course of everything, there was
hope. If she drastically altered the flow of her own life, she
could have a chance at saving the rest.

. . . *Most* of the rest. Some could be saved, she realized;
many, in fact. But not everyone.

Not everyone.

It was a horrible, terrible choice for a fifteen-year-old to
have to make.

CHAPTER 1

*Thank you for allowing me this rare opportunity. I don't
have a lot of time to spare—I've never had a lot of time, to
be honest—but there are certain things I've always wanted
to share. Indulging your request will give me the chance to
review some of the things I've done, and explain some of
the reasons why I did them. Like a stage magician revealing how the trick is done, I've wanted to communicate the
whys of my actions, but I haven't always had the opportunity before now. And, now that I finally have the time, I feel
the need to speak. So I thank you for your offer to interview me.*

*I won't waste your time with the trivial details of my
childhood. I was happy for the most part, well-loved by my
family, had a reasonably good education, and usually had
good food to eat and clean clothes to wear . . . the usual,
and therefore boring. Instead, I'll start with the day I joined
the military. That's not the moment it all began, of course,
but you could say it's the best starting point I have.*

~Ia

MARCH 4, 2490 T.S.
MELBOURNE, AUSTRALIA PROVINCE
EARTH

"Name?"

"Ia." Back straight, hands clasped in her lap, she waited for him to comment. She pronounced it *EE-yah*, not the *EYE-ah* most people assumed. "Just like it says on my ident."

The brown-uniformed recruitment officer quirked his brow and sat back at that. Light from the glow strips overhead gleamed off his service pins for a moment, allowing her to read the badge holding his name. *Lieutenant Major Kirkins-Baij*. "I know what it says on your ident, young lady. But given how the Terran United Space Force has roughly two billion soldiers to keep track of, it helps to have more than one name. Usually, a Human has at least three: a family name, a personal name, and an additional name. Some even have two family names, like myself.

"So. What is your full legal name, meioa?" he asked her. Given how it was sometimes hard for one race to recognize the genders of another, everyone in the Alliance agreed it was more polite to use *meioa* than *sir*, *ma'am*, or *hey you* when addressing one another. Originally a Solarican term, the word meant *honored one* and was most often applied in the genderless form, though one could attach a suffix for male or female if one was really sure. Ia appreciated the courtesy, given his brief chiding.

"My full legal name *is* Ia. Capital *I*, lowercase *a*. Ia," she repeated. "Nothing more, and nothing less."

The corner of his mouth quirked up for a moment. "With a name that short, I don't see how you *could* have anything less." Glancing at the workstation screen displaying her stats, he frowned a little. "Independent Colonyworld Sanctuary? Where's that?"

"It's on the backside of Terran space, close to the border of the Grey Zone. Not quite seven hundred light-years from here," she told him. "It's relatively brand-new. I'm second-gen."

"We don't normally get recruits from any I.C., not here on Earth," the lieutenant major offered. "I'll presume your Colony Charter permits its citizens to join the Terran military, and that you're prepared to sign the necessary waivers, but if your Charter was sponsored by the V'Dan Empire instead, I'll have to get out a different set of forms."

"Sanctuary's Charter was actually sponsored by I.C. Eiaven," she clarified. "That cuts the paperwork down to almost nothing."

"That doesn't make sense. Eiaven is almost the exact opposite direction from here," he pointed out, lowering his brows in a doubtful frown. "Most sponsoring worlds are next to each other, not hundreds of light-years apart."

Ia didn't let his skepticism faze her. Rather, she welcomed it as a positive sign that she was doing the right thing at the right time.

"That's true for most worlds, but most heavyworlds are sponsored by Eiaven. Sanctuary is merely the latest to prove itself viable. Article VII, Section B, Paragraph14, subparagraphs c, g, h, and j of the Sanctuary Charter—duly registered with the Alliance—state that, as a Sanctuarian citizen, all I have to do to join either the Terran or the V'Dan military is to take the Oath of Service as a recruit, and my citizenship will automatically transfer to the appropriate government. We're not so much an independent colonyworld as an *inter*dependent one. Life on a heavyworld is tough enough without adding political troubles, and both Human governments recognized this long ago. Eiaven and its sponsored colonies are legally considered joint neutral territory.

"If I choose to serve in the Terran military, I automatically become a Terran citizen, with all the rights, responsibilities, and privileges thereof, and disavowing all rights to V'Dan citizenship, should I choose to do so. Which I do, which is why I am here," she said.

"And you came all the way to Earth, almost seven hundred light-years from home, just to do so?" he repeated, still skeptical. "Exactly on your eighteenth birthday?"

"Yes, meioa," Ia admitted, reminding herself to be patient. "Provided I am a full, legal adult—which I now am—I can join up at any Recruitment Center anywhere across the Terran United Planets. I just happened to pick Melbourne, Australia Province, Earth. I'd also like to join the TUPSF-Marine Corps in specific, which is why I'm sitting here in front of you, meioa-o, instead of one of the other officers at this facility," Ia stated patiently. "You *are* the local recruitment officer for the TUPSF-MC," she reminded him, pronouncing the acronym *tup-siff-mick*. "Now, may I please do so?"

"And your name is just . . . Ia?" the lieutenant major asked dubiously. "The military needs more than that to be able to identify you, meioa-e."

"I have an ident number, duly registered with the Alliance," Ia reminded him, nodding slightly at his workstation, which still displayed her civilian profile. "Ident number 96-03-0004-0092-0076-0002. All I need to join any Branch of the Space Force is a name and a valid ident number, both of which I have provided, and to state which Branch I wish to apply for. My name is Ia, you have my ident number, and I would like to join the TUPSF-Marines."

Sighing roughly, the lieutenant major typed a command into his workstation. "It's not quite *that* easy to get into the Marines. Your background check hasn't turned up any legal troubles yet, but we'll still need to place a vid-call and confirm your citizenship status with the authorities on Sanctuary. You'll also need to take the Military Aptitude Test. You can apply for a preference in Service Branches, but depending on how well you score in the various categories, you might end up in the TUPSF-Navy, the Army, or even the Special Forces . . . though you shouldn't hold your breath on that last one. Very few are selected to join the elite Branch of the Service."

"Oh, I'm willing to take the test," she assured him. "I'm ready right now, in fact. I also know I'm well-suited for the Marines."

"We'll see." He checked her application again. "It says here you're an ordained priestess with some subsect of the Witan Order. If you're ordained, why aren't you aiming at the Special Forces for a chaplaincy?"

Ia shook her head. There was a reason why she had listed her priestess status on her application form, but she couldn't tell anyone the full truth behind it, yet. "I'm a priestess for personal reasons, not professional ones, sir. I'll be better used in fighting to save lives, not souls."

". . . Right. There is a twenty-credit nonrefundable processing fee, whether or not you pass recruitment standards, Meioa Ia," Lieutenant Major Kirkins-Baij told her, his tone just flat enough to reassure her he had said this part to a hundred recruits before her, and would recite it to a hundred more once she had gone. "On the plus side, your MAT scores are transferrable when applying for a government job, should you choose to look elsewhere."

The look he slanted her said he thought she would be smarter to look elsewhere, being a strange, one-named woman who probably wouldn't fit into the orderly categories of military life. But he didn't actively try to dissuade her. Instead, he typed in a few more commands, accepted the two orange credit chits she dug out of her pocket and handed over, then rose from his seat.

"The testing booth is this way." A gesture of his hand showed her which way to turn as they left the small room that served as his office. "I'll be placing that call to your government while you are undergoing evaluation. If you need to visit the bathroom, now is the time to go. Be advised that you *will* be tested for illegal substances from this point forward."

"I understand." She followed as he showed her to the facilities, leaving her alone for a few moments.

If I didn't have to go to a specific Camp at a specific point in time, I would've picked a more congenial recruiter . . . but this one needs to fill his recruitment quota. If I can antagonize him just enough, prick his pride, push the right buttons, he'll not try to push me into a different path, based on my testing. The last thing I need is to be thrown into an officers' academy right now. Using the facilities, she scrubbed her hands at the sink, knowing they would be subjected to sensors determining her stress and reflex responses via her sweat glands, impulse-twitches, blood pressure, heart rate, and other detection means. *A more congenial soul would be eager to help me, ruining everything I have planned.*

I cannot let him get in my way.

That was an old mantra. A familiar one, if not necessarily a comfortable one for her conscience to bear. To it, she added a new, fresh thought. *I cannot let these tests place me in the wrong Service path, either. That would be a disaster of unforgivable proportions.*

Not that it would be an easy thing. She had practiced at home with a makeshift testing center, thanks to the help of her brothers and the local chapter of the Witan Order. But the Kinetic Inergy machines the Witans had loaned her were old and most likely less sensitive than whatever the military could afford; at least, the military here on the Human Motherworld.

She would have to rely mostly on rote memorization to pass if she didn't want to trigger the wrong sensors.

Squaring her shoulders, she emerged from the refreshing room and followed the lieutenant major to the testing booths. There were three of them, hatchway-sealed rooms with their doors standing open, each one looking in on a bulky, sensor-riddled chair ringed by view screens and the like. Outside each door, a quartet of helmets hung on a hook.

"Please pick the headset size which fits most comfortably on your head, and seat yourself in the chair inside this room," he instructed her, his tone reverting to that bored, done-it-a-thousand-times tone he had used before. "Follow the instructions you are given at all times to the best of your ability. You are expected to be proficient at reading and listening to Terranglo; if you are unable to do so, you must indicate which languages you are proficient at on the tertiary second screen. Inability to follow orders in Terranglo both written and verbal will affect your placement scores.

"You will be subjected to audio, text, and spatial questioning, your reflexes and strength tested, your ethics probed, your mind monitored for KI strength and other hallmarks of psychic ability, and you will even undergo timed testing at certain steps along the way. The entire testing session will last between two and a half to three hours, depending upon the untimed portions. If you are thirsty, you may access bottled water from the dispensary, but otherwise you will not be allowed a break from the testing procedure.

"If you have any questions about the equipment, the tertiary fifth screen, the one on the lower far right, contains a diagram of what to touch and when to touch it. The pertinent equipment on the diagram will light up with arrows when you are to touch it." Gesturing, the lieutenant major pointed at the screens. "These vidscreens are arranged in the standard Terran pattern: primary is in the center, flanked to either side by secondary left and secondary right. Below them from left to right are the tertiary first through fifth screens. Please remember their positions, as they will be critical for some of your testing.

"You will also be subjected to pain threshold tests, and gravity stress tests. Please do not exit the booth during the gravity stress tests, as the gravity shear forces may cause undue injury. If you wish to end the testing at any time, simply repeat three times in a row, 'End the test, end the test, end the test,' and wait for the screens to fall dark and the door to open before exiting the equipment. Your twenty-credit fee is nonrefundable, and incomplete MAT scores are not admissible for military, civilian, or government jobs. Do you understand these things as I have explained them to you?"

Plucking one of the helmets from the rack lining the outer edge of the alcove, Ia nodded. "Yes, sir, I understand them."

"Your placement in the Service, if any, will depend almost entirely upon the machine's evaluation of your performance coupled with the current needs of the military. Some of the questions you answer may direct your career path, but placement is not guaranteed. I myself can make certain recommendations if an ambiguity shows up in your testing profile, but the Space Force has invested a lot of effort and experience in these testing centers to gauge your abilities with great accuracy. If there are no true ambiguities, I cannot sway the testing center's decisions for you. Good luck," he wished her, "and don't hold your breath. Unless the test asks for it, of course."

Ia knew he was expecting her to laugh. Most applicants did. She also knew he was serious. Settling the helmet on her head, she fastened the chin strap and climbed into the testing chair. The primary and tertiary fifth screens lit up, the former with a greeting and a list of instructions on how to strap into the equipment, and the latter with sections of the depicted chair displayed, lighting up as each point scrolled up the screen. Once her legs and right arm were strapped in, she inserted her left arm with its ident bracelet into its slot as directed, and waited while the machine pulled up her information file.

It recorded her homeworld of Sanctuary without commentary, unlike the recruitment officer. It also revved up the gravity weave built into the alcove with the warning message, "Adjusting gravity to native homeworld standards of 3.21gs for physical stress test. Please stand by, and do not exit the testing chair during the enhanced gravity phase."

It'd be rather hard for me to "stand" by and not *exit the chair,* Ia thought, letting her rare sense of humor surface for a moment. The hairs on the back of her neck prickled, accompanying a faint hum from a new machine. *Damn. They've turned on the KI sensors sooner than I expected.* Clamping down on her mind, she blanked it of all stray thoughts, and all stray abilities. Now was *not* the time to go off into an involuntary temporal fit. Not with the machine off to her left ready to record just how much Kinetic Inergy she might use, and what kinds.

Now is not *the time for the military to find out I'm a psychic. Not for a long, long time, if I can help it.*

"Meioa Ia. Are you ready to begin the Military Aptitude Test?" the pleasant audio voice of the testing unit asked.

"I am. Begin," she instructed it.

"Section One: Physical Aptitude. Grasp the blue handles and pull them down as fast as you can," the recorded voice instructed. On the secondary left screen, a question flashed in white text. "Section Two: Military Knowledge. 1) When was the Space Force founded?"

Grasping the overhead handles, Ia yanked them down, pulling hard and fast despite their pneumatic resistance. "April 14th, 2113 Terran Standard, by order of the newly formed Terran United Planets Council."

"Place both feet on the green pedals and push them far away from you," the voice instructed, while the secondary left screen printed another question. "What is the primary difference between the Space Force and planetary Peacekeeper forces?"

This one, she also knew. "Peacekeepers are civilian organizations with jurisdictions limited to a specific city, region, province, space station, and/or planet. The Space Force is a military organization with a jurisdiction limited only by the interstellar boundaries of the Terran United Planets, its sovereign territories, and its duly authorized activities."

Text and voice switched, with the voice asking the next question and the text directing her to grasp the orange handles and twist from side to side. She complied, glad she had practiced taking verbal and written directions at the same time. The cuffs on her right arm and legs measured her physiological responses to the efforts, recording without surprise her overall strength and speed. Those two things were key to survival on a heavy-world, where bodies fell faster than expected and landed harder than preferred.

Those were qualities the military liked to see, both V'Dan and Terran. Strength and reflexes were bred into the survivors of heavyworld acclimatization. For as long as she could remember, Ia had seen recruiters from both the Terran Space Force and the V'Dan Imperial Military visiting her homeworld, most with their lightworlder bodies wrapped in gravity weaves so that they could withstand the pressure of being planet-side long enough to try and encourage her fellow colonists to join the military of either government. Sanctuary was more than twice as far from the V'Dan worlds than the rest of Terran space, but the First Human Empire still sent their recruiters each year, scouting for the most physically impressive soldiers they could find. Heavyworlder soldiers, preferably from the heaviest gravitied world.

Strength and speed weren't enough, though. They helped, but they weren't enough. It would take far more to make a civilian into a competent, disciplined warrior. For the sake of everyone else, Ia had to try.

————

Lieutenant Major Kirkins-Baij studied the datapad Ia had just signed. He glanced up at her twice, each time returning his gaze to the results of her tests, then sighed and set the pad on his desk. "Well. Congratulations, Recruit. You have just signed up for a three-year attempt at becoming a Marine. *If* your test scores translate into the real world, and *if* you can pass the training, you'll make a good soldier. But only *if*.

"There is a mandatory twenty-four-hour Terran Standard cooling period. If at any time in the next twenty-four hours you wish to change your mind, you may contact me and sign the appropriate release forms." Tapping his military-issue wrist unit, he nodded at her civilian one, which chirped. "I've beamed you my contact information if you wish to do so. If you do not change your mind immediately, be advised that changing your mind after the twenty-four-hour grace period will require you to reimburse the Space Force for any and all expenses incurred for your processing, transportation, training, housing, and so forth, up until the point of your discharge, as well as being liable for any other potential legal ramifications.

"Forty-two hours from now, if you have not changed your mind, you have an obligation to be on the suborbital commuter shuttle to Darwin, on the north side of the continent. Your ticket will be downloaded to your ident half an hour before boarding begins—you will, of course, have the costs of the ticket and all other transportation, housing, equipping, and other sundry needs deducted from your recruit pay, starting twenty-four hours from now. The Space Force doesn't give free rides; we even charge the Premier of the Terran United Planets. She gets a discount," the lieutenant major allowed, "but she still gets a bill.

"In Darwin, you will be met at the terminal by one of the instructors from Camp Nallibong. He or she will be clad in the brown uniform of the Marines, and will be easy to spot. Do not delay in looking for him or her. Once you have reported in, you will then be given transportation to the base, where you will begin your training." Rising, he offered her his hand. "Good luck, Recruit. You'll need it."

Standing up, Ia squared her shoulders and lifted her hand to her brow in crisp salute, just as she had practiced for the last three years in the bathroom mirror. "Thank you, sir."

The lieutenant major quirked his brow, but returned the salute, giving her permission to drop her arm. Then he held out his hand again. "No, thank you. Thank you for being willing to serve."

Hiding her distaste, Ia clasped hands with him. She tried to clamp down on her mind, but caught glimpses of his future anyway. Snippets of his family, of him driving his hovercar, of his offer to reenlist in active duty . . . She retrieved her hand the moment he released her, glad to note that he didn't seem to have noticed what she had just done. Nodding politely, she turned and left his office, exiting the recruitment center.

The burning heat of early afternoon pressed down on her head and shoulders the moment she stepped onto the sidewalk. Turning left, she started wandering back in the vague direction of her lodgings. It wouldn't take her long to return to the salle if she went there directly, but she knew she would have to get used to the Australian heat sooner or later.

Forty-two hours, she thought, looking around at the angular buildings of the city. She wasn't far from the spaceport; every few minutes, the bone-deep *thrummm* of some transport shuttle taking off could be felt, now that she was outside. *Forty-two, and I'll be living the life I need. Praying every step of the way for success. God . . . how am I going to get everything done?*

The city looked as banal as her bedroom once had, three years ago. Blissfully ignorant, most of the people around her went about their business with mindless happiness, or at least a facsimile of content. Hundreds of millions of people. Billions and trillions who didn't know the horrors lying ahead.

No. I don't have time to wander. I have to prepare. Languid steps turning to purposeful strides, Ia headed up the street and turned right at the corner. She could have called for a hover cab, but physical exercise was as much preparation as anything mental. She had a lot of mental preparation left to do.

The moment she entered the salle several minutes later, she headed straight for the water fountain. Drinking water was a must on such a hot day. Only after her thirst was satisfied did she hear the sounds of bodies hitting mats in the training rooms off to the right. Some of the monks were giving lessons. Or maybe just practicing against each other, given the lack of vocal instructions. To her left, the chapel was an island of quiet.

What she wanted to do was retreat to the chapel and stay there, where no one could touch her. Where she had nothing to fear regarding unwanted visions of nonessential futures. What she knew she had to do was join the monks in their practices, to train her body and her mind to work together.

A few minutes in the chapel, first. Then I'll join them, she decided. Taking another mouthful of water, she left the fountain and headed for the domed hall. Like most Afaso chapels, it was based on the Unigalactan faith, which had sprung up after Terrans had reached out to the stars and found similar beliefs among the other races. Beliefs in some sort of divine Creator, beliefs in being good and kind toward one another, and the underlying tenets of wisdom stored and revered by each sentient race.

Promoted as an adjunct to every faith, *The Book of the Wise* had been at first reluctantly examined by the leaders of various religions. Philosophers and theologians had argued and debated every point being made, but could not deny that many of the words of their own holy texts were repeated in the wisdom of other beliefs. Now the Unigalactans were everywhere, promoting peace and understanding.

It was true that many practitioners of a specific faith tried to proslytize that *theirs* was the only *true* faith, and attempted constantly to argue that other beliefs were utterly wrong—including the chosen faith for about half the colonists who had settled on her own homeworld. In turn, the Unigalactans had always responded with the words of wisdom culled from their opponents' very own texts, countering such arguments.

It was very hard to maintain a religious war against people who agreed with the core tenets of one's faith.

Not that it doesn't stop the Church of the One True God, back home, she acknowledged, passing the padded pews edging the room. Her goal was one of the large floor cushions arranged around the hologram slowly rotating in the center under that beautifully arched dome. *The isolation of being on the backside of inhabitable space, coupled with the difficulties of light-worlders visiting such a heavy-gravitied planet makes it an ideal breeding ground for fanaticism to flourish without day-to-day disruption from the saner elements of overall society.*

Sinking cross-legged onto the cushion, she didn't look up at the rotating stars of the spiral galaxy overhead. Instead, she propped her elbows on her knees and slouched her chin into her hands. *Thinking of home, I should take a look at how things are going back there.*

Closing her eyes, Ia turned her thoughts inward, then out, like a gymnast flipping around a bar. She had always been able to see glimpses of the future, and sometimes even peek into the past, but as a young child, the ability had been sporadic and rarely under her control. But once she had understood that she *was* seeing the future, her younger self had struggled to control her psychic abilities. She had even sought instruction, what little there was of it on her far-flung, backwater, recently settled homeworld.

The clergy of the Witan Order—who, like the Afaso, were affiliated with the Unigalactan movement—had done their best to train her, since the Witan were one of the duly registered institutions for psychic instruction in the Alliance, as well as being a religious order. The PsiLeague was more popular, more funded, and more capable, but they hadn't made it to Sanctuary yet, mainly because of the heavy gravity problem.

That had been a lucky break for her; Ia had already seen what would happen to her carefully laid plans if the League found out what she could do. At least, if they found out any time soon. Being clergy, the Witan had sworn to keep her abilities a secret at her request, and they had kept their word.

But their training had only gone so far. For most of her other abilities, yes, they could and had helped her greatly. For this . . . no one could do what she could do. Not to her extent. Her precognition had remained mostly untrained until that fate-filled morning when she was fifteen. Now, flipping her mind in and out, she climbed out of the timestream of her own life, hauling herself onto the grassy bank of existence. Willpower and concentration were all she needed now.

The timeplains shifted under her feet, then stilled. Dropping to her knees, Ia peered into the waters of four streams. The first stream belonged to her biomother, Amelia Quentin-Jones. Ia only skimmed the surface of the water; she could have immersed herself in her mother's future, living it as if inside her mother's head like a silent observer, but she didn't need to do that. Instead, she watched her mother working in the kitchen of their restaurant, cooking for the hardworking colonists who didn't want to bother with fixing their own meals at the end of each day, struggling to carve a home for themselves on a too-heavy, slightly inhospitable world.

She watched as the curly-haired woman smiled and chatted, serving up dishes filled with meat, vegetables, and the ubiquitous Sanctuarian topado, aqua blue and vaguely potato-like, but far more tasty. There would be some dark looks sent toward the shop, but Amelia herself wouldn't receive them. Not in the near future, at any rate.

Mom will be fine . . . so let's see about Ma. Switching her attention to the next flow of life, Ia watched her mother's wife, Aurelia Jones-Quentin, smiling with too many teeth at certain of her neighbors. Ia smiled, too, albeit with more humor. *And there she goes, being polite when she doesn't want to be polite. It'll get her in trouble if she's not careful. The Church's members are slowly moving into our neighborhood, infiltrating business districts and taking over council positions. But she's always polite. Always finds the right way to tell someone to go to hell and still be socially acceptable in language and demeanor.*

But . . . I can't see any trouble she'll get into in the next year. That's good. Thorne is next. Her half-twin, as she liked to think of him. They had the same father, of course, and had even been born half an hour apart, though Thorne had been born to Aurelia and herself to Amelia. *There he is . . . ah, great. Getting into a fight on the school grounds in a few days' time. A pity he couldn't just take the scholastic tests and graduate early like I did, but then he doesn't have the advantages I had.*

At least this fight isn't his fault, and I can foresee him handling it carefully, so he doesn't hurt the other kid. And the year's almost over. Two more local months, and he can move on to business college. Most of it on the Nets, since Sanctuary is still so small. He'll need to know how to run a business, if he's going to be the anchor-stone for Rabbit's underground revolt against the Church.

Fyfer . . . She sighed mentally as she turned her attention to her younger brother. Fyfer was still young, four years younger than Thorne and her. He was her half brother, since they shared the same mother, but not the same father. Amelia, wanting another child and having Aurelia's permission to beget one, had dallied with an entertainer visiting from Parker's World, an equally new, equally heavy-gravitied colony. Fyfer had inherited his father's dark hair, good looks, and charm. *Frontman to Thorne's bedrock support. I'd warn him about the fights he's going to get into . . . except I can see that they'll teach him how to use his tongue rather than his fists to get out of conflicts. Rabbit will need his charisma in the years to come.*

A shift of her knees, a sway of her body, and she leaned over the other girl's life-stream to make sure she would be all right. Rabbit was five years older than Thorne and Ia, and already she had gotten into trouble with the law. Nothing warranting a severe punishment, but the petite girl had a habit of exploring places the government and her high-ranked, Church-fanatic parents didn't think she should. Like the caves under the capital city, where the Space Force had dug bunkers for the brand-new settlement just a couple decades ago, back when the Terrans and the Dlmvla had almost gone to war. Rabbit's predilection for amateur spelunking would serve Ia well in the years to come, as would her keen insight into what was going wrong in the local government.

Her parents were members of the Church, on Sanctuary, but Rabbit didn't subscribe to their beliefs. It would cause conflicts in the future, but Rabbit would be well-placed to hear of the Church's xenophobic plans toward the few non-Human settlers on the planet. Well-placed to warn them to get off-world before it was too late. Well-placed to sort out the nonbelievers from the believers when the Church decided to go to war against the other half of the planet.

There's that incident at the subway station she has to watch out for, but . . . yes, in the most probable time-path, she does reread my notes to her in advance, instructing her on what to do and what not to do at that moment in time. Satisfied, Ia rocked back on her heels, letting the wind of the timeplains play with her hair. *I took great pains to convince them of what to do, and when to do it. The time for action isn't now. But it will be, soon enough. I have faith they'll be able to carry out what needs to be done to protect and preserve our world for the Future.*

It was a mantra she kept repeating to herself, to stave off her doubts. She didn't have the energy to spare for those doubts, not when her own tasks would take up most of her time and attention. Dropping out of school and passing her scholastic tests early had given her some of the time she needed to prepare for the future. The rest of it, she would have to handle on the run.

So. Back home, everything is fine. I guess I should go work on my battlecognition with the monks, if they're not too busy. Unfolding her body, she rose and stretched, filling her lungs as she refilled her senses with the here and now. *Thank you, Grandmaster, for believing me, and for believing in me . . . and for spreading the word to all the chapters of your Order. Without the Afaso, my goal would literally be impossible. No one else can train the Savior, and I need you to do what I myself cannot.*

Then again, when I put my mind to it, I can be pretty damn convincing. At least, to a fellow being of faith. I have a plan for convincing the Command Staff, but . . . well, they're a tougher and far more skeptical lot. Everything she had to do, everything she needed to remember, she had to keep reminding herself about it. Too many lives could be jeopardized, if she forgot.

Leaving the chapel, she crossed to the teaching hall, the actual "salle" of the facility, pausing only for another mouthful of water from the fountain. Despite the air-conditioned temperature keeping the interior comfortably cool, the three men and one woman sparring on the padded mats were sweating from their workout. Clad in the batik-printed tank shirts and loose trousers the Afaso Order had adopted for its humanoid members' uniform, they whirled and struck, kicked and flipped. Dodging, ducking, grappling, and punching at each other, they didn't stick to just one partner, but actually flung their opponents whenever possible at the other sparring pair.

They moved quite fast, but her eyes were used to things falling at three times the gravitational pull of the Motherworld. She knew she wasn't as good at fighting as they were, but she was fast, and she had undertaken some of their training. Originally, her instructors had been costly hologram programs and her sparring partner her slightly older brother, Thorne, but for the last month, she had been a guest of the Grandmaster of the Afaso Order and had thus gained some practical experience with real teachers. She had even sparred with these particular Afaso yesterday, while waiting for her eighteenth birthday and the opportunity to join the military as a full, legal adult.

So when Sister Na'an threw Brother Tucker at her, Ia reacted as she had been taught. Her arms flung up to ward off his blows as he tumbled, straightened, and swung at her. Her knee shifted up to block his kick, and her heel slammed down, following the movement of his leg as he tried to protect his foot. And her body twisted under the arms that tried to flip her onto her back, locking their upper limbs together, thanks to the fingers he hooked into her blue flowered blouse.

Even as he let go of her shirt, she grabbed the back of his trousers, lifting and flinging him back toward the tanned, Indonesia Province woman . . . only to find Brothers Charles and T!ongun leaping her way. Her grey slacks weren't cut with the same level of give as their bright red and yellow batiks, but she managed to avoid or block most of their incoming blows. No one used their full strength, and Ia took particular care not to strike anyone hard enough to bruise; their flesh literally wasn't as heavyworlder-dense as hers.

It also helped that her gift didn't trigger involuntarily. No flashes of their pasts, no glimpses of their futures, and no involuntarily dragging any of them onto the timeplains with her.

She did focus just enough of her abilities on trying to accurately guess where each blow was coming next, and get her own limbs into position to dodge or block where appropriate, but keeping track of four opponents in a free-for-all melee wasn't easy. Sweat sheened her skin and stained the air, competing with the ventilation ducts trying to keep the air fresh as well as cool.

The scrimmage ended when Na'an slipped a blow past her defenses, smacking her fist into Ia's jaw hard enough to spin the heavyworlder around. It wasn't the blow, per se, so much as the gasp from the doorway that broke up their fight. The first of the afternoon's students had arrived, a young girl with wide blue eyes. She watched them with avid curiosity as the Afaso broke apart, bowing to each other in thanks for the practice, then moved into the salle when another student poked the girl in the back, urging her to move out of the doorway.

Na'an paused to check Ia's chin, then patted her on the shoulder. "You'll be fine, meioa-e. Do you want to join us in teaching the students?"

"I really shouldn't. I'm only a Full Master, not a Senior Master," Ia demurred. She didn't add that she didn't want to foresee the potential-possible futures of the school-aged youths now entering the room.

"The Grandmaster said you needed to practice more against unanticipated blows," Sister Na'an pointed out. "And there's nothing so unexpected as the raw attacks of a young, half-trained student. You have enough control to work with children. I think it'll do you good."

I don't want to! part of her mind protested. But duty poked at her conscience. A quick probe of her near future, more instinct than inner sight, proved that nothing she did here—provided it wasn't outlandish or unusual—would affect the timestreams adversely. Sighing, Ia nodded. "Alright. I'll be their sparring partner. But I still don't think I'm qualified to be a teacher. Not yet."

"Teachers are made, not born," Na'an countered, clapping her on the shoulder before giving the younger woman a push toward the changing rooms. "Go change into a spare set of batiks. They'll be more comfortable than those civilian clothes."

Those civilian clothes . . . For a moment, the view of the crisp, clean, uncluttered lines of the salle slowly filling with students was replaced by the shadowed, cluttered depths of a bar crammed with off-duty Service personnel. For a moment, Ia could see her reflection in the mirror on one of the walls, her long white hair cropped short, her blue and grey clothes replaced by a bloodred dress that bared her shoulders. Laughter and the chatter of scores of soldiers sharing stories and bragging rights filled her ears, including some comment about how she herself looked in her civilian clothes, but all she could focus on was her own eyes, wide and yet shuttered with the knowledge of things she hadn't done yet.

Someone clapped her on the shoulder in her vision, startling her back out of it. Grounded back in the present, the younger Ia headed for the women's locker room, blinking off her visit to the future. Most of the time, she could control such trips, but not always. Sometimes all it took was an echo of another point in time, a moment of déjà vu, to disorient her in the here and now.

I have to get better at handling those. I literally cannot afford to be caught with my attention muddled by Time itself. This entire galaxy can't afford to catch me with my psychic pants down. A glance at the chrono on the wall as she passed it reminded her that Time was not entirely on her side. *Forty-one more hours to go. These are the last hours of my freedom, yet I don't have enough time to truly enjoy them.*

I don't think I ever will, from now on.

And she didn't dare change it.

CHAPTER 2

Why join the military? Well, someone has to. Armies are formed because everyday citizens aren't trained to thwart the viciousness of hostile neighbors. They have lives of their own, growing food, manufacturing goods, selling services, doing all the things which make modern life functional, effective, and fun. Since aggression and danger are regretful facts of existence, someone needs to specialize in the training needed to protect other people. Some of that training goes into emergency services such as firefighters and medical personnel. Some go for Peacekeeper training. I went for the military because I knew I could handle it, I knew I could do it, and I knew it needed to be done.

I knew the whole universe needed to be saved. One more body placed between zones of peace and danger doesn't seem like a lot, it's true, but when it's one million and one . . . you can get a lot of things done. A soldier's duty is to place his or her skills, weapons, body, and life between all that could harm and all that could be harmed. That was always the core of what I knew I needed to do . . . and I knew I needed to do a lot of it.

~Ia

MARCH 6, 2490 T.S.
DARWIN, AUSTRALIA PROVINCE

It was easy to tell the natives from the recruits.

The natives on the flight from Melbourne to Darwin either had briefcases for business or luggage for vacation. They also headed straight for the luggage carousel with the ease and speed of familiarity. The recruits spread out, milled around, and craned their necks, checking signs and peering at the caf' shop, no doubt wondering if they had time for one more taste of civilized life before being subjected to a military diet.

"Ey. Like th' 'do."

Caught off guard, Ia blinked and looked at the young man who had moved up on her left. He sported three nose rings, grass green hair, and was dressed in skintight green fabric. Every centimeter of him was lean and muscular. He ran a tanned hand over his green locks and grinned at her.

"Like th' 'do, I do. Howja ge' it white?"

His accent was so thick, it took her a moment to understand what he meant. Lifting her hand, she touched her hair, which she had pulled back into a braid that morning. "My hair? It was already white when I was born."

"Swaggin' ey!" Rocking back on his heels, the nose-ringed youth perused her from head to toe. "Choo ain' albino. Choo got a tan, 'n neffrythin'. Born wi' it, ey?"

"Yes."

"Ey, Kumanei!" Turning, he waved at a young woman with purple and black hair, and a glitter of silver rings along the curve of each ear. "She says she was *born* wi' it!"

"That's *locosh'ta*." Sauntering over, the black-clad girl eyed Ia from head to toe. "You waitin' for the Marines?"

"Yes. Are you?" The moment she asked it, Ia saw this same young woman clad in battle camouflage, squirming her way through the underbrush of the Northern Territories. Her hair was cropped short, her light tan darkened with exposure to the sun, and she looked far more fierce than sultry, as she did right now. Ia didn't want to see any more than that. If it wasn't important to her task, she didn't want to know. She knew too much as it was.

"Tcha. It's easier 'n diggin' potatoes on some farm." She

whapped the green-clad man lightly on the arm with the back of her hand. "We're stuck on th' rehab bus."

"Perfect profile for militaristic rehabilitation," he enunciated, then grinned again. "In other words, we got into one too many spots a' trouble as kids, but we's good sorts, so rather'n chain us t' some 'tato patch, they gave us th' choice a' signin' up . . . an' th' MAT innits infinite wisdom placed us 'ere. How 'bout choo?"

"I volunteered."

"Ah. Nutcase. Them's three types wha' join up. Nutcases, poorboys, 'n rehabbers. Choo volunteered, 'n that makes fer a nutcase. Poorboys wanna get an education, onna Education Bill . . . an' a'course you know 'bout th' rehabbers like us." He flicked his hand at the purple and black haired woman, then held it out. Ia shook it briefly while he introduced himself. "Glen Spyder, from New Lunnon. That's one a' th' stations orbitin' Jupiter. Born an' bred there, but I been planet-side a few times. Got smacked down last time f' high spirits, 'n they shipped me 'ere. This's Akira Kumanei—we actually knew t'other, on th' Nets."

She offered her hand as well. "Surprise, surprise. 'M from Tokyo Underside."

"Oh, man . . . you grew up in Tokyo Underside?" one of the others hanging around the luggage area asked. He was a tall, lanky, muscular blond. "I hear that's a *crazy* place to live."

Kumanei shrugged. "It's not so bad, since they put in the new atmo-processors. Well, nobody's come down with Tuberc-73 in a while. You?"

"Casey. Jason Casey, Adelaide." He shook hands with the other two, then offered his hand to Ia. "You? Name and home-town?"

"Ia. Our Blessed Mother." At their blank looks, she allowed herself a small smile. "It's the capital city of Sanctuary, which is an I.C. on the edge of Terran space."

More blank looks. Before they could ask what she was doing all the way out here on Earth, a voice cracked through the ter-minal. "Camp Nallibong Recruits, Class 7157! *Front and center!*"

And so it begins. Nodding to the others, Ia headed for the source of that command, a somewhat short, heavily tanned man with grey-salted, fuzzy black hair and dark brown eyes. He looked like he was from somewhere in southeast Asia. She could have uncovered more, probed into his past via the timestreams, even discovered things about his family and his friends, but hadn't bothered to. All that mattered was that she knew his name, his rank, and that he would be a very tough, demanding Drill Instructor for her training Platoon. A good instructor. Ia didn't *want* to know anything more, and didn't have enough time to look.

Stopping a few meters from him, she squared her shoulders and gave him her full attention. *Step one. Survive Basic Training with distinction and honor.*

He quirked a brow at her, then scowled at the others. "I said *front and center*! That means *line up*, you sorry slags of rejected refuse! My name is First Sergeant Tae. You will refer to me as Sergeant, or Sergeant Tae. You will *not* address me as 'Sarge.' I am a Drill Instructor, selected from the best of the best in the Marine Corps, and I am here to make you sorry civilians into *soldiers*, so get your heads out of your asteroids, and *line up*!"

The others straggled into place, including one woman Ia would have sworn was a native civilian, since she was pulling an actual suitcase behind her, bumping it over the tiled floor on its caster wheels. Ia listened patiently while the sergeant berated the woman for "hauling so much junk" with her, and waited patiently some more while he nagged and commanded everyone to literally toe the line in the tiles, the same line she had stopped at.

". . . Now, when I tell you to, you will turn right, and march out that set of doors. There is a ground bus parked outside, and as I call out your names, you will stow yourselves and your gear on board in a fast and orderly fashion, filing from front to back. *Right Face!*"

Ia snapped to her right. The others followed more or less on command. She was near the end of the line, with Kumanei in front of her and Casey behind. Once they had filed out the doors and lined up again in the shaded heat of afternoon, she waited patiently while Tae went through his list of forty-five names alphabetically. Even though they were in the shade, her long-sleeved blouse, lightweight but more suitable for the cool climate of a sub-orbital flight, added uncomfortably to the warmth of the day.

Occasionally, Tae snapped orders for whomever it was to

speak up louder when answering his roll call, otherwise he spoke crisply, but not loudly. When he got to her name, he hesitated.

". . . Ia?"

"Here, Sergeant." A step to her left put her outside the half-sized line. She made sure to speak just loudly enough to qualify as obeying orders as she turned to face him. *No sense in shouting needlessly.*

"Ia. Just Ia? Where the *slag* is the rest of your name, Recruit?" he ordered, stepping up to her. He was seven centimeters shorter, and lifted his chin belligerently to look up at her. The brim of his camouflage brown hat almost brushed her forehead with the move.

She didn't flinch. "That *is* my entire name, Sergeant."

"What did you do with the rest of it, Recruit?" Sergeant Tae demanded. "*Nobody* has just one name."

"When I turned sixteen, I emancipated and legally changed it. My name, therefore, *is* Ia. Nothing less, and nothing more. Sergeant," she added, doing her best not to flinch as he swayed a little closer.

Studying her for a moment, he grunted and drew back. "You got any luggage, Recruit *Ia*?"

"No, Sergeant. Just the clothes on my back."

"Good. Get on the bus. Kaimong, Wong Ta!"

"Here, Sergeant!"

Once inside the bus, Ia claimed the next empty seat, not wanting to sit right next to anyone. It was old, a relic that had seen better days, but the bucket seats still had their cushioning, even if the overlying fabric was worn and faded with age. It also smelled of dust, heat, and bodies beginning to sweat, given the door was open to the sun-broiled air.

Kaimong took the seat across from her, rather than joining her. Ia didn't mind. What she knew of him from her trips onto the timeplains, well, she didn't see a point in making friends with him.

When the last recruit—Georgi Zpiczeznenski, whose name gave their Drill Instructor fits of pronunciation until they all heard Georgi saying, "Look, just call me ZeeZee, Sarge, it'll be easier," and heard *Sergeant* Tae ordering him to do ten push-ups for daring to shorten his title—had made his way onto their transport, the silent, brown-uniformed driver started up the engine.

The only indication it had started was the slight shiver of the vehicle's frame; hydrogenerator technology was quiet and efficient, its fuel cheap and ecologically friendly. The air vents made more sound than the engine did, hissing slightly as they worked to cool the ground bus. Sgt. Tae stepped inside, grabbed the handle on the back of the first seat, and nodded at the driver, who closed the door and pulled away from the curb.

"Welcome aboard, Class 7157! Now that we're all on board and under way, it is my sorry son of a duty to pound into your civilian heads the rules and regs of the Terran United Planets Space Force, Branch Marine Corps. Here are the very first things you sorry sons and daughters need to know: When I address you and ask you a yes or no question, you will respond by saying 'Sergeant, yes, Sergeant!' Or 'Sergeant, no, Sergeant!'

"You will preface all other answers to my questions by first saying my rank, which is 'Sergeant,' and finishing again with my title, which is also 'Sergeant.' *Not* 'sir.' If you are asked a question by someone with a command rank, you will address them by *their* rank and title in a similar manner, such as 'Lieutenant, yes, sir' or 'Captain, no, sir.' Do I make myself clear?"

"Sergeant, yes, Sergeant!" Ia snapped out. Hers was the strongest among a smattering of responses. Most of the others were neither loud nor clear. Only the voice of one of the recruits seated at the front of the bus, Arstoll, was as crisp as hers.

It didn't satisfy Sergeant Tae. "I cannot *hear* you! There are forty-five bodies on this bus, and I *will hear* each and every one of you. I said, *is that clear?*"

"Sergeant, yes, Sergeant!"

". . . You *will* work on mastering the appropriate responses during your time in Basic Training. Rest assured, we *will* pound everything you need to know into your sorry, slagging, asteroid-thick heads. You *think* you want to become soldiers, and your MAT scores *suggest* you might even make it as Marines . . . but we will see." Sweeping his gaze across the recruits on the bus, Tae grunted. "Well. You are now on your way to Camp Nallibong. The *edge* of this particular TUPSF-MC training facility lies twenty kilometers from the nearest point of civilization. It will take us two hours to drive there. During those two hours, you will listen as I explain what will happen. There will be opportunities to ask questions, but I suggest you keep your mouths shut and your ears open.

"The actual Camp comprises more than one thousand six hundred thirty-three square kilometers of Northern Territory bush," he continued. "It includes bombing ranges, live combat ranges, and the Camp itself. This is some of the toughest, most inhospitable landscape on the Motherworld. It's dry in the winter, but down here, it's now summer, and it'll be unbelievably hot and muggy, and very, very wet in certain parts of the Camp, particularly if we have a cyclone roll through. If you're thinking of going walkabout—that is, wandering off without supervision—you can and probably *will* get into trouble.

"*Some* of you are here because your psychological evaluations state that you're *good* little boys and girls, but that you just need *discipline* in your lives to become actual citizens. If you think you're gonna light out of here and go AWOL when no one's looking, sentients still *die* every year when they head out into the bush in this corner of the world. Even if they're prepared, or *think* they are. Not only is the terrain against you, but there are plenty of things that will slither, crawl, climb, and fly at you, intending to sting, bite, or otherwise eat you alive."

"Ey, 'zat mean somma th' Salik are down 'ere lurkin' inna bushes?" Spyder piped up from near the back of the bus.

His joke fell flat. Sergeant Tae glared at him. Ia tried not to think about what he had just implied. She didn't want to trigger the wrong future-echo.

"The Salik," their Drill Instructor enunciated carefully, his tone colder than the air blowing through the vents of the bus, "have been confined to their planets of origin and colonization for the last two hundred years. It is the job of the TUPSF-Navy and the TUPSF-Marine Corps, in conjunction with the other military forces of the Alliance, to see that they *stay* confined for at least two hundred more. *If* you survive being turned into a *real* Marine, one of these days you won't find that possibility so *funny* anymore!

"Now. The first thing we're gonna do is register you. Since you pansy-soft civilians have all had your twenty-four-hour cooling period to reconsider, yet you are still here, it is my sorry son of a duty to make sure you go through with your

Oaths of Service. When we arrive at the processing center, you will grab your gear, line up in alphabetical order, and march into Building A-101 to be processed. You will divide up into five lines of nine people. You will step into the processing arches one at a time, where you will place your civilian wrist units into the receptacle to verify your identity, undertake the Oath of Service as prompted by the machinery, remove your civilian wrist unit, and replace it with your military-issued ident unit. However. While the Space Force doesn't care which arm you wear your unit on in your civilian life, in your military life, you will wear it on your *left* arm at all times.

"Once you have undertaken the Oath and been issued your military wrist unit, you will continue forward to the dispensary booths, where you will present your unit for scanning, and be issued your gear. The only civilian objects you are allowed to take with you are prescription medications authorized by military medical examinations performed during or directly after your Military Aptitude Tests, education transcripts, marriage, divorce, custody, or child support documentation, vehicle operation licenses, a small vidframe with its internal maximum of memory allotment, and no jewelry beyond wedding rings. Be advised that the Marine Corps reserves the right to review and censor inappropriate vidchip materials.

"Which brings me to my next happy little lecture," Sgt. Tae drawled, baring his teeth in an approximation of a smile. "This is a mixed-gender Camp. There will be *zero* sexual fraternization with anyone while you are recruits here at SF-MC Camp Nallibong. You will be quartered together, train together, eat together, and even shower together, but the closest you will *sleep* with each other is sharing the same bunkhouse and the same tent when on maneuvers. *If* you're lucky enough to get a tent, and *when* you're lucky enough to sleep.

"Each of the meioa-es will undergo a medical evaluation during your Oath of Service to ensure that you are not pregnant, and all of you, meioa-es and meioa-os, will be administered quarterly beecee shots to ensure such things will not happen. Your training will be difficult enough without adding the stress of accidental procreation on top of everything else.

"The modern military, in its infinite wisdom, has declared rape to be one of its Fifty Fatalities. If you are *lucky*, you will receive a court-martial, cross-examination under telepathic truth-testing, and ten strokes of the cane for raping a fellow soldier. If you are *stupid*, you may end up facing twenty strokes or more, followed by incarceration in a military penal colony. Particularly if your victim is a superior officer, a civilian, or— God forefend—someone underage. You will therefore learn and memorize this and the other Forty-Nine Fatalities during the first three days of your instruction. There are plenty of other, lesser rules and regs that you might stumble over and break if you don't pay attention and keep your slagging noses clean, but you do not *ever* want to cross one of the Fifty Fatalities.

"Now. Are there any questions so far?"

A few hands rose tentatively. Their owners were told sharply, "You're in the *Marines* now, Recruit!" and ordered to raise their hands firmly. Ia listened with as much patience as she could muster. These were things she had heard before, skimming through her potential futures over and over while preparing for what she had to do. Now that she was finally here, Ia just wanted the bus to move faster. Not for time to go any faster—time wasn't something she had in surplus—but for the bus to go faster, the lectures to be shorter, and the events to move quicker.

So. I get into Camp Nallibong, and become the best soldier I can be. Better than expected of me. Graduate from Basic Training with a good, solid reputation so that I'll be placed into the right Company. Work my way up the ranks in that Company so that I can be field promoted at the right moment in time. And keep my mouth shut on everything I know, for as long as possible . . .

By the time they rolled to a stop in front of Building A-101, they had been given a brief rundown of all Fifty Fatalities, a list of what penalties and fines would be levied if they chose to quit at any point during their Basic Training and their mandatory three years of service in the military, the information that, once sworn in, they would have to refer to themselves in third person unless and until they were given permission otherwise, ". . . as a means of breaking down any pointless self-centeredness you may think you still need to cling to," and an outline of how their days would go.

The first three days would be "easy" ones, filled with

orientation and instruction on how to do things the military way, from folding and storing clothes in their kitbags to performing their daily calisthenics correctly. After that, their schedule would be crowded with lessons on everything from parade maneuvers to mechsuit drills, vehicular operations to orbital mechanics. That last one was mandatory—they were entering the Space Force, and they would be expected to know how to handle themselves in the airless, weightless void awaiting them.

Filing out of the air-conditioned ground bus, Ia followed the others into the processing center. She ended up in the middle of her line and waited patiently while the three recruits ahead of her were scanned, prompted into reciting the long-winded passages of the Oath of Service, issued their new units, and directed forward. She waited patiently, but nervously. Not because she regretted her decision to join—regret wasn't even an issue—but because this was her final moment of civilian freedom.

Listening to the others stumble their way through their vows felt like she was listening to the *clank* and *snick* of manacles being locked in place. When it was finally her turn, Ia lifted her chin and stepped forward, placing herself in the chains of military life of her own free will. *For the Future, I will do whatever I have to do. For nothing else, and for nothing less.*

Sticking her left arm in the slot, she waited while the beams swept over her body, measuring her through her clothes and probing her tissues for signs of pregnancy, drug dependency, and other potential complications.

The machine beeped, and the same pleasant neutral-female voice that had addressed the other recruits addressed her. "Please state your name, Alliance identification number, and planet of origin."

"Ia. Ident number 96-03-0004-0092-0076-0002. Sanctuary."

The machine clicked and beeped for a moment. ". . . This Processing Booth registers a Charter clause for the citizens of the Independent Colonyworld Sanctuary to join the Terran United Planets Space Force through the swearing of the Oath of Service to the Terran Space Force. Are you, Ia, 96-03-0004-0092-0076-0002 of Sanctuary, aware of this Charter clause?"

"I am," she agreed.

"Are you aware it requires foreswearing and foregoing all

citizenship of, ties of loyalty to, and benefits from your planet of origin and/or the V'Dan Empire during the full duration of your sworn Service within the Terran United Planets Space Force?"

She didn't hesitate. "I am."

"Duly noted." The sensors swept down over her body again. "Are you under the influence of drugs, alcohol, or any medication which may affect your mental capacities?"

"No, I am not."

"Are you under the orders or influence of a non-Terran government or other organization whose intent is to have you infiltrate the Terran United Planets Space Force and/or its supported government for the purposes of surveillance, subversion, sedition, or sabotage?"

"No, I am not."

"Please state your location and situation for the record."

"I am standing in a processing booth in Building A-101 of the training facilities at Camp Nallibong, TUPSF-Marine Corps, for the purpose of foreswearing my ties to my homeworld of Sanctuary and taking up the Oath of Service as a Terran United Planets Space Force soldier, for as long as I am retained as a soldier in said Terran Space Force."

"Duly noted." The machine hummed again. "Please remove your civilian identity unit and place it in the tray which will appear below the scanner slot, then return your arm to the scanner slot and prepare to take your Oath of Service. Your personal information on your civilian unit will be transferred to your military one while you take your Oath. Be advised that your wrist unit may be monitored for inappropriate materials and adjusted accordingly."

Ia removed her arm, pressed her thumb to the seals to release them, and unclasped the plain, scuffed, grey plexi unit. She didn't hesitate to drop the colony-issued unit in the slot, which opened and extended to receive it. Placing her hand back in the slot, she spread her fingers over the sensor pad.

"It is now time to take your Oath of Service. Repeat after me," the neutral-female voice instructed. " 'I, Ia, ident number—' "

"—I, Ia, ident number 96-03-0004-0092-0076-0002," she began without waiting for the rest of her prompts, "being of legal age, sound mind, and doing so of my own free will, being free from the influence of drugs, alcohol, or foreign direction, without coercion, promise, or inducement of any kind, and having been duly warned and apprised of the consequences of my Oath . . . and foreswearing all ties to my previous citizenship and the government or government-in-potential available to my planet of origin for the full duration of my terms of Service," Ia added, pausing only long enough to breathe between each memorized phrase, "do hereby solemnly swear to serve the Terran United Space Force for a term of not less than three years as contracted, and for longer should there arise legal authorized need, as a soldier and loyal citizen of the Terran United Planets, its sanctioned Space Force, and Branches.

"I solemnly swear to uphold and defend the Charter Constitution of the Terran United Planets against its enemies, within or without the boundaries of the Second Human Empire," she continued as the machine patiently recorded her words, "to uphold, protect, and defend the Chartered rights, privileges, and liberties of its citizens and other lawful residents of the Terran United Planets, its provinces, prefectures, colonies, and protectorates.

"I promise to perform, within or without said boundaries, such duties of lawful nature as may be assigned to me by any lawfully direct or lawfully delegated authority, to obey all lawful orders of the Premier of the Terran United Planets Council as my Commander-in-Chief of the Terran United Planets Space Force, and of all officers or lawfully delegated persons placed in authority over me through the chain of command, and to require such obedience from all members lawfully placed by said chain of command or otherwise delegated under me regarding my lawfully assigned orders.

"In swearing these Oaths of Service," Ia stated, meeting the gaze of Sergeant Tae as he strolled into her field of view on the far side of the archway, "I agree to abide by the laws of the Terran United Planets, its Space Force, and Branches unto my honorable discharge, understanding that with said honorable discharge I will retain all retired or reservist ranks, honors, privileges, duties, and obligations of a sworn and retired or reservist soldier, unless I am stripped of such ranks, honors, privileges, duties, and obligations by a verdict proven, sustained, and sealed by a court of my sovereign military superiors and peers. I further consent of my own free will to abide by and endure the rules of corporal discipline as set down by the regulations of the Terran United Planets Space Force, should I fail to abide by said laws, rules, and regulations.

"These Oaths I do solemnly swear this sixth day of March, in the year 2490 Terran Standard . . . so help the Future," she finally finished.

Then breathed deeply at the end of it, relieved she hadn't missed a single word of the awful, long-winded oath taking, which she had practiced over and over, back home. *There. It is done. I am now legally bound to this path by all these vows and codicils . . . even if I'll end up breaking almost half of them just to get the job done.*

". . . Duly noted and recorded. Please take the military-issued ident unit from its receptacle and secure it to your left forearm. Once it has been secured, follow the brown line to the dispensary booths to receive your standard-issue gear. Once you have received your gear, follow the blue line to the changing room and await further instruction."

Nodding, she clasped the broad Marines-brown bracelet to her forearm and stepped out of the archway. Sergeant Tae was still there, his hands braced on his brown-camouflaged hips while he studied her from head to toe.

"You have the whole Oath of Service memorized, Recruit?" he asked her.

"Sergeant, yes, Sergeant." She didn't elaborate, hoping he wouldn't press.

He did, falling into step beside her as she followed the brown line painted on the plexcrete floor. "Why would you memorize it?"

"Because it was a very long trip from Sanctuary, Sergeant."

"You did *not* use the correct mode of address, Recruit. Drop and give me ten!" he ordered.

Ia winced, but did as commanded. "Sergeant, yes, Sergeant!" Lowering herself to the floor, she braced her palms at shoulder-width, straightened her legs, and started levering herself up and down. "One! Two! Three! . . ."

It didn't take long to make it to ten. Out of shape as she was, the light gravity of the Motherworld made the task easy.

Finishing her task, she returned to her feet, squaring her shoulders and facing her Drill Instructor.

"I repeat, why would you memorize the Oath of Service, Recruit?" Tae asked her again.

"Sergeant, it was a very long and boring trip from Sanctuary to Earth," Ia repeated, careful to use the prescribed third person formula for speaking now that she was an official recruit. "This recruit didn't have anything better to do than study whatever she could of the Terran military, Sergeant."

That made him step up close and lift his face, once again threatening her nose and forehead with the stiff brim of his camouflage-patterned hat. "Do you think that a bit of *reading* while flying through space for a couple days will turn you into a *soldier*, Recruit?"

"Sergeant, no, Sergeant!"

"*I* will decide whether or not you can be turned into a real Marine. Not whatever you *thought* you learned from some history chip or an episode of *Space Patrol*. Is that *clear*, Recruit?" he demanded.

"Sergeant, yes, Sergeant!"

He flicked his hand, silently ordering her to continue to follow the brown-painted line toward the dispensary booths. Turning crisply, Ia complied. They were easy enough to find; the occupied booths were alcoves humming with light and action as the half-hidden machinery sorted out crinkling packages containing appropriate sizes of clothing from underwear to overcoats. Plexi-wrapped toothbrushes, razors, and bodywash packets spat into their vending trays. The one that her particular brown line led to was still occupied by the woman with the suitcase.

Ia watched the woman struggle with the plexi packaging, grimacing at her kitbag, which she was stuffing items into in a timid, haphazard way. After a few moments, Ia gave up and tapped the lightworlder on her shoulder.

"Need help?"

Huffing out a breath which stirred her shoulder-length, honey blonde hair, the woman eyed her. "Like *you* know what you're doing?"

"I think I can help. I'm Ia," she added.

"Forenze—go ahead give it a shot. I'm not even sure *why*

the MAT picked me for the Marines. I was hoping to get into the Navy," the other woman added under her breath.

"Here. Pack the heavy items on the bottom. Boots and so forth—you can put small stuff inside the boots to maximize storage, like socks. That stabilizes the bag so that it's easy to lift and doesn't tip over," Ia told her, pointing at the items in question. "Then in the middle you fold and stow your clothing and accessories, particularly breakables like your vidframe. Toiletries go near the top, in the plexi-sealer bag there. We'll be taught how to make neat rolls out of our clothes in the next few days and the exact places where things are supposed to go. Until then, do what you can and just expect to do a lot of push-ups for getting it messed up. Remember, absolute essentials go on the very top, the stuff you'll need to grab right away. Right now, we're headed for the changing rooms, but in the future, the most essential item will be your hat."

She picked up the plexi-wrapped hat, eyeing it. "Why the hat?"

"If we have to go outside, you'll want to put it on your head to protect it against the sun. If it's buried at the bottom of your kitbag, it'll take too long to get to it. Don't forget your sunglasses," Ia added. "Those should go on top, too. Sewing kit should be down in the middle of the bag. Here are your patches. Those go on top, since you'll need to find them to slap on your uniform as soon as we're ready to get dressed."

The other woman reworked her bag, which looked something like a backpack without a couple of exterior pockets, but gave up after she still had several items left on the dispensary table. "It won't fit!"

"It will," Ia reassured her. "Once you get out of your civilian clothes, you'll be wearing some of it. The rest will fit in your pack. Here, lace together this pair of boots and strap them to this handle at the top, then stuff a pair of socks inside, along with underpants . . . a bra . . . a T-shirt on each side . . . there. Now it's a single bundle."

The other woman eyed her. "Where did you learn all of this?"

"Survival training is an education requirement for all new, inhabitable colonyworlds. It includes camping skills, which in turn includes efficiency in packing." *Plus the dabbling of my toes in the timestreams, preparing myself for this day. They don't expect children to pack with military-grade efficiency, back home.* Fetching a half-forgotten packet of extra bootlaces from the dispensary, Ia tucked them into one of the boots. "Now you can carry everything. And now it's my turn."

"Be my guest." Stepping back, Forenze shouldered her pack with a grunt and watched Ia work.

Ia took her place in the alcove. Tapping the green reset button, Ia tucked her arm into the slot long enough for the machinery to read her profile, then started grabbing and unwrapping the packets almost as fast as the dispensary spat them out. Plexi wrappers went into the recycler, and boots went into the bottom of her bag, stuffed with quickly balled pairs of socks and spare bootlaces. Undergarments were fitted in around both pairs of boots, then shorts, T-shirts, trousers, shirts, and rain gear, each item neatly folded and rolled tight. As soon as she reached the changing room, she'd have to unpack everything to get out the required change of clothes and boots and then repack it all over again, but for now, everything got stuffed into the oversized knapsack.

On top of everything else, she fitted her hat, stuffed with her sunglasses and her freshly stitched name and Platoon patches. A moment later, she had the bag sealed shut, and swung the entire load onto her shoulder as easily as she would have swung a jacket. The next recruit behind them wasn't even done reciting his Oath of Service.

"How did you . . . ?"

"One of the keys to rolling things into a tight, tiny package is to smooth out the garments several times in the folding and rolling stages," Ia said, shrugging. "That presses out the air and makes the material that much more compressible. Come on. Let's follow the blue line to the changing room."

The two of them were joined by the purple and black haired Kumanei and one of the other recruits, a tallish, dark-skinned male. Both of them juggled their gear awkwardly, not having packed all of it into their kitbags. The blue lines on the floor converged and swerved to the right, detouring in front of a dark-skinned woman in a camouflage brown uniform similar to Sergeant Tae's.

"I am Staff Sergeant Linley. I will be your Regimen Trainer

while you are here at Camp Nallibong as members of Class 7157. That means I will be in charge of turning you soft, wet, civilian noodles into *real* Marines. You will enter the changing room here," she stated crisply, flicking the thin baton in her hand at the doorway next to her, "scrub yourself from head to toe in a maximum ten-minute shower, and change into the clothes of your SF-MC uniform.

"Today, you will wear all-brown undergarments, socks, boots, pants, T-shirt, broad-brimmed hat, and sunglasses. Do not don the mottled clothes of your camouflage uniform at this time. You will apply your name-patches to each shirt and jacket before repacking them in your kitbags; the flag patch of the Terran United Planets will go on your right shoulder, the patch for Camp Nallibong Class 7157 will go on your left shoulder, your name patch will go over your right chest pocket, and the TUPSF-Marines patch will go over your left chest pocket. If your shirt has no chest pocket, you will see the fuzz of the adhesion patches in the designated region anyway.

"If you have any questions, refer to the Dress Charts on the walls of the changing room. Refer also to the lists of local dangers of flora and fauna; pay particular attention to the posters on avoiding pools and streams while outside, and the dangers of 'salties,' saltwater crocodiles, which can and will be found in fresh water even up here on the plateau. Further instructions will be given over the next three days on all the dangers to watch for locally, and the dangers you may encounter elsewhere in the known galaxy.

"You will be expected to be ready to go twenty minutes after the last of the recruits in your training class has entered this room, and you may be quizzed at that time on the information on those charts. Be prepared and be packed. You're in the Marines now, Recruits. We do not slack on the job!"

Two more recruits approached. Sergeant Linley held up her palm, stopping them. She kept her gaze on Ia and the other three who had already been there for most of her spiel.

"When you have changed, you will pack up all your non-allotted personal belongings in the transport boxes provided, located to the left as you enter the changing room, and label them with the address of their return destination. If you have any questions regarding what you are permitted to keep, you will refer to the charts posted on the walls regarding allotted goods. Anything nonregulation which is found left in your possession at the end of this day or which was incorrectly labeled for shipping will be sent to the recyclers, so make sure you send it where you want it to go in the next few minutes. Once you have showered and dressed, all regulation and allotted items will be packed in your kitbag. You four will now move inside.

"*You* two will stay. I am Staff Sergeant Linley. I will be your Regimen Trainer while you are here at Camp Nallibong . . ."

CHAPTER 3

The first few days of any boot camp are always the toughest—not physically, since that actually happens a bit later—but emotionally and mentally. The recruits have to readjust their thinking, from "civilian" to "military." From "whatever" and "whenever" to "obedience" and "discipline." From "me" to "us."

Some would-be wit once suggested that shaving off everyone's hair isn't so much a matter of efficiency and uniformity as it is a way to give the new recruits a common traumatic experience over which to bind them together as a family. I can't say if it worked or not. I was too busy trying to get things right the first time around, so I wouldn't have to waste my time on trivial repeats.

~Ia

Ia nudged Kumanei and Forenze, getting them moving. At least they didn't seem to be required to respond to the Regimen Trainer's orders. Yet. Following behind Ia and the other women, the dark-skinned male whistled softly as they entered the changing room. "V'dayamn. She's as cold as a comet!"

"Watch your language," Forenze warned him, tugging her suitcase around the end of a gear-crowded bench. "I'm half

V'Dan on my mother's side. Don't be taking the Empire's name in vain around me."

"Then what the junk are you doin' in the Terran military?" one of the other men in the room asked. From his damp hair and half-clad state, he had already taken his appointed shower. The room smelled of soap, steam, and freshly manufactured plexi, the ubiquitous, recyclable material that had long ago replaced less environmentally friendly substances. Bunching up a sock, the recruit slipped it onto his foot. "Me? I say, if you're in the *Terran* military, you shouldn't give a V'*damn* about the V'Dan."

"You tell 'em, Akhma!" someone else called out. "We're in the Ma-*reens* now, *sojers*! Hoo-rah, *eyah*!"

"You're *locosh'ta*, meioa," Kumanei retorted, giving the speaker a dubious look as she dumped her things on the empty end of one of the occupied benches. "You've seen too many episodes of *Space Patrol*."

"Not to mention '*eyah*' is a V'*Dan* word," Forenze pointed out tartly. She found an empty bench and dumped her things on one end of it, leaving room for Ia and the man who had followed them to the changing room. "And it's '*eyah*, Hoo-rah,' in that order. It comes from when the Terrans and the V'Dan hooked up and fought together during the Salik War two centuries ago. Try to get it right."

The recruit who had joined them gave the women in the changing room a wary, wide-eyed look. "Are we really supposed to . . . change . . . in front of women?"

"Don't worry, Lackland," Forenze reassured him. "We won't bite."

"'Scuse me? Speak for yourself. *I* certainly bite," Kumanei shot back, before eyeing the men with a smirk. Laughter echoed off the plexcrete walls. ". . . But not during Basic, so you can relax, meioa-o. At least until we graduate."

Half of her attention on the others, Ia unpacked her kitbag to lay out the required change of plain brown clothes and boots, and fished out the necessary toiletries. She repacked everything else swiftly, neatly, and started removing her civilian clothes. Changing in front of mixed company had never bothered her; Ia had always shared a bedroom with her two brothers, back

home. With the military's strict views against unwanted copu-
lation, she had no worries that anything would happen.

Someone let out a low whistle right after she pulled her
lightweight, long-sleeved blouse over her head. It turned out to
be Spyder. ". . . Sweet Jovian rings! Lookit th' muscles on 'er!
Ey! Ia! Whatchoo do onna colonyworld all day, practice ferra
bodybuildin' show?"

Ia looked down at her arms, which looked like they always
had. She glanced up at Forenze, whose own arms were somewhat muscled, but not like her own. Craning her neck, she
looked back at the green-haired colonist and shrugged.

"I'm a heavyworlder. Where I come from, everyone grows
up looking like this." She paused, considered her words, then
added lightly, honestly, "Well . . . most of them are shorter than
me. But they're all just as muscular, if not more so."

"How much shorter?" one of the other recruits asked. Mendez, that was his name. Ia knew him from the timestreams.

She held up her hand at bra-level. "Most of 'em are about
this tall, on average. Very few ever reach as tall as my shoulder."

Mendez held up his own hand at about the same level, eyed
it, then lifted it to the top of her head, eyeing her dubiously.
". . . *That* much difference? If everyone on your homeworld is
so short, heavyworlder or not, how come *you're* so tall?"

She shrugged, turning away so she could have room to shuck
off her flats and remove her pants. "Good genetics, I guess."

"Whoa, looka' that! Choo an Afaso?" Spyder asked, pointing at her other arm. "F'real?"

Ia glanced down at the tattoos on her right deltoid. They were
so new, they still stung a little if she flexed her arm the wrong
way, but not so much that she noticed it. "Yeah, they're real."

The spiral galaxy was the symbol of the Unigalactan movement; the sword piercing it, point-down, was the symbol of the
Afaso Order. Below and to the left of the sword edge were two
humanoid figures. One represented the mark of the Junior Master, the other the mark of the Full Master. To the right were spaces
left for Senior Mastery and Elder Mastery, and above that would
go the tattooed representation of High Mastery, the highest rank
anyone could attain outside of the Grandmastery of the whole
Order. She might one day attain Senior Mastery rank—and thus

be eligible to teach all the martial arts that she knew—but she would never attain High Mastery. Not in this life.

She could, but she wouldn't. Ia didn't have Time for it. The best she could do was learn just enough to keep herself and those around her alive. Nor did she have the time to fuss with Order politics.

Her tattoos were plain black line art, lacking the full color found in the tattoos of someone who was a fully Vowed Afaso monk. That kept her out of the hierarchy of the Order, which would give her the freedom to give orders to the Afaso in the future, without having to take them, too. Grandmaster Ssarra would help see to that. He had helped her improve herself to the point where she had earned the second rank of Afaso Mastery, and he would help her to preserve and pass out her instructions for the future.

Without him and his successors, her plan wouldn't work.

"So, what kind of genetics?" Mendez persisted, sitting down so he could unlace his own footwear. "I'm Hispanic, from a longstanding military family, but you . . . You got white hair, but you also got light brown eyebrows. And I never saw an albino with brown *eyes*, never mind brown hair elsewhere. You also look kinda Asian, but not really."

"Sanctuary's a new colonyworld," Ia hedged, stripping off her underwear. "They're not sure if I'd been affected by something local while I was in utero, or if my hair is just some sort of random genetic quirk. All I can say is, I was born this way. White hair, brown lashes, light brown eyes, and I tan fairly easily."

"Yeah, but what's your genealogy?" Mendez pressed. "Your ethnic background? You got any V'Dan in you, or just Terran, or a mix?"

"My biomother's part Irish, part Greek, and she said my father looked Asian, possibly Japanese." Ia shrugged. She pulled the tie off the end of her braid and started loosening the plait in preparation for washing it. "Beyond that, she couldn't say."

Lackland, still looking a bit timid about removing his clothes around women, stared carefully at her face. "Your mother . . . *didn't* know what your father was? Weren't they married?"

"No, but my mothers were. My father was just some guy they met in a park one day while having a picnic to celebrate their second wedding anniversary." Selecting the cleaning gel from among her new toiletries, Ia headed for the shower stalls.

"That's . . . very different from how I was raised," Lackland stated. "Where I come from, parents are married to each other. And they don't involve outsiders in . . . in that sort of thing."

Halfway to the showers, Ia turned back and leaned over the low wall separating the dry half of the room from the damp half. "My parents were first generation first-worlders on a back-water colony so far from Terran space, it might as well have been inside the Grey Zone. They had neither the time, nor the money, nor the *resources* to get to a fertility clinic. If they wanted kids—and they did—that meant doing it the old-fashioned way. Since it was fully informed and fully consensual, agreed upon all the way around, *I* don't see what the problem is."

Spyder clapped his pale hand on Lackland's sun-browned shoulder. "Welcome t' th' real universe, yakko. Takes all sorts, dunnit? Whachoo need t' do now is t' grow up 'n open yer mind. More'n one road int' Rome an' all that, right?"

Turning away, Ia left Lackland to process his fellow recruit's heavily accented words. Grabbing a washcloth from one of the stacks on her way, she picked an empty stall, flipped on the water, and started scrubbing herself from head to toe. She was already accustomed to taking short, efficient showers, thanks to the joys of having only one bathroom for five people back home.

It didn't take her long to get clean and rinsed, nor all that long to scrub herself dry with one of the age-roughened towels waiting in neat stacks at the border between stalls and benches. Just as she returned to her waiting gear, a familiar, crisp voice called out over the noise of forty-five people trying to organize themselves, their new gear, and their efforts to be clean and dressed in a timely manner.

"Alright! Listen up, Recruits!" Sgt. Linley called out, start-ling most of the men and women in the locker room. She lifted something over her head; from the small, silvery size, it might have been an archaic stopwatch. "ZeeZee, here, is the last member of Class 7157 to be processed and receive their dis-pensary goods. Let's *move* it, people! You have exactly *twenty* minutes for everyone to hit the showers, dress in plain Browns, pack up your civvies for mailing, ready your kitbags for travel, and be lined up out in the hall, toeing the blue lines in five rows of nine each!"

Clicking the stopwatch, the tall sergeant marched back outside.

Ia grabbed at the underwear waiting for her on the bench. Her "plain" Browns were indeed a plain, dull, dirt shade of brown, unornamented save for the black stripes down the short sleeves and the long pant legs, denoting them members of the Space Force. All four Branches had their own distinct colors, brown for Marines, blue for Navy, green for Army, and grey for Special Forces, but all four Branches also shared the color black.

Black showed they were all under the aegis of the Space Force together. She knew from both the news Nets and her forays onto the timeplains that the semiformal dress uniform for each Branch was that section's color, but that full, formal Dress Blacks were what all Branches wore on special occasions. The latter wouldn't be issued until they survived and passed Basic Training, though.

For now, everything she wore would be either brown or mottled shades of brown. One day, her gear would be blue, then grey, but for now, brown. Freshly spun clothes, freshly molded toiletries, freshly minted recruits, all brown. Even her skin would end up browned by the hot Australian sun, protective lotions and all.

A glance to her left showed Lackland still seated on the bench. He had removed his shirt, but was holding it over his chest and still giving the women in the room a wary look. She hadn't probed deeply into his background since he wasn't that important to the future, but she vaguely remembered something about him coming from some conservative religious background. A fact which would hinder him, if she didn't do something now.

Shrugging her bra into place, Ia leaned over him, putting her tan nose almost against his brown one. "Get into the showers, soldier. There's no longer any room for modesty in Basic Training—now! *Move* it!"

Jumping in his seat, he hastily put his shirt down. Moving away so he had room to stand and strip, Ia finished dressing. She spent a few moments re-braiding her waist-length hair to make it look tidy—not that she'd have it for much longer, but it was one of her few points of childhood vanity—a few more minutes applying the various patches issued by the dispensary, then rolled up and repacked her kitbag. Her civilian clothes she wadded up into a bundle, stacked her shoes on top, and dumped all of it into the recycling bin by the entrance. There was no point in shipping them anywhere for storage when she wasn't ever going to wear them again.

A survey of the room showed people still chatting with each other, slow to shower and slow to change. "I suggest the rest of you get moving, meioas! You have twelve minutes to be changed, packed, and out in the hall. Get your canteens out, too. We'll probably be walking all over this place, and that means we'll need water. Move!"

"Who died and made *you* God?" someone called out from the far side of the room.

There were far too many ways she could have answered that. Picking the safest reply, Ia pointed at the doorway. "Simple logic says, the more we pay attention and the faster we cooperate, the easier it's gonna be for us. The more we slack off and the less we pay attention, the harder it'll be. It's your choice, meioa. Don't cry up a meteor storm because of the bad choices *you* choose to make, when you could be making smarter ones. Eleven minutes left. Let's move it!"

"Slag off!" "Yeah, right . . ." "*V'shakk* that!" "What are they gonna do, *spank* us?" Laughter accompanied that last quip. Some of the others moved a little faster, but most of them moved at their own pace.

Rolling her eyes, Ia finished packing her kitbag, remembering to extract her canteen from the rest and clip it onto her belt. *They'll learn soon enough.*

Forenze asked for Ia's help in rolling up her kit again. Spyder wandered over, saw how she was doing it, and requested help as well. That took up all the time Ia cared to give, though a few others did ask some questions. Exiting with her bag on her shoulder, Ia lined up with a minute to spare, toes of her brown regulation boots just touching the blue paint on the floor, facing their patiently waiting Regimen Trainer. Mendez, Spyder, Forenze, and a couple more joined her, including ZeeZee and a man named Brad Arstoll. Him, she had foreseen in the timestreams.

If she played things right, Arstoll and possibly Rigo Mendez would end up helping her career. If she played them wrong, the two could become a hindrance. But that would have to unfold when it happened. Right now, Ia kept her eyes on Sergeant Linley. The neatly uniformed woman checked her stopwatch as a few more bodies came out of the changing room, raised the archaic timepiece over her head, and clicked it.

"Time's up!" she called out, her voice echoing up and down the hall, pitched loudly enough to carry into the changing room. "I see *thirteen* people out here, on the line and on the time! That's *thirty-two* of you who can't be *v'shakked* to follow orders. For each *minute* you slags *waste* in getting out here, that number will be multiplied by thirty-two push-ups, which you will *all* have to do. *On the double! Move!*"

The others twisted their torsos and craned their necks, watching as their classmates scrambled out of the changing room. Ia didn't look behind her; she could see it clearly enough inside her head. She also didn't have to see the other woman's stopwatch to know that Kaimong was the last to amble out— amble, as in to saunter, stroll, walk at a casual pace—and join the rearmost line.

". . . Three minutes, two seconds." Sgt. Linley looked up from her watch, her dark eyes gleaming like gun oil. "Congratulations, Class 7157. Looks like Recruit Kaimong is your new best friend. He just earned *all* of you the dubious joy of doing one hundred twenty-eight push-ups."

Bodies twisted again, this time with their owners glaring rather than glancing behind them.

"Since you soft-bellied sons of slag and daughters of drek can't *do* one hundred twenty-eight push-ups in a row . . . yet . . . you will do ten now, and ten every half hour, for the next seven hours. Drop and give me ten! Count 'em out!"

Her voice cracked over the assembly like a whip. Ia dropped her kitbag and herself to the floor of the wide corridor, angling her body so she wouldn't take up too much room. Tightening her stomach, she called out the numbers. "One! Two! Three . . ."

Others copied her, but their voices weren't nearly as loud. Sergeant Linley walked down the awkward rows. "I can't *hear* most of you sorry slags counting off. Start again from *one*, and make it *loud*!"

Ia pumped herself off the floor, starting again from one as directed. Her efforts went ignored as Linley lambasted the others, forcing all of them to start over twice more, until Ia figured she personally had done about twenty-five push-ups. Most of the others had done at least thirteen or fourteen, and some as many as eighteen.

When they were all on their feet again, many of them rubbing at their arms and a few grumbling under their breath, their regimen training sergeant resumed her place in front of Ia's row. ". . . As you can see, you survived ten puny, pathetic little push-ups. Beyond that, most of you are worth less than the spit on a sidewalk. You're flabby, weak, and undisciplined. On the plus side, *if* you can survive your basic instruction, you just *might* make it as Marines. On the minus side . . . either you'll wash out, or we'll ship you off to the Army. *They* don't mind taking in losers and rejects. *This*, however, is the Marine Corps! Right Face!"

Ia turned crisply to her right, yet another thing she had practiced over and over with her brothers. The others managed to follow the direction without too much trouble, though she could hear a few extra footsteps as someone who turned left hastily turned the other way around. When they were more or less in position, Linley moved to the front of the five lines.

"In a few moments, we will proceed to the barbershop, where you will literally shed the last remnants of your civilian lives. Once you have been given your regulation SF-MC recruit haircuts, you will place your broad-brimmed caps on your heads, fill your canteens with water from the sinks at the far end of the shop, and line up outside the doors beyond.

"You are *required* to drink a minimum of seven liters a day, and that means whenever we stop to fill up your canteens, you will have already drunk them dry, or you will be instructed to do so on the spot," Linley instructed them. "Right now, I want you sorry slags to take a good look at who all is sharing your line with you. This *first* row will be A Squad. You get that distinction because you *actually* followed orders. Next will be B Squad, followed by C Squad, D Squad, and E Squad.

"You will line up in these exact rows, in these exact orders, once you are through at the barbershop—you will find five marks on the plexcrete road outside, A through E. Use them, and toe the line, filling out your ranks from left to right. That's *your* left to right, not mine. As A Squad will be at the front, I will not tell you which direction to face. I *will* tell you, however," she warned all of them, "that I have a photographic memory. For every person I find out of place, that entire Squadron will earn an extra ten push-ups before the end of this day.

"Go on. Take a good, long look at your Squad mates," she repeated, and paused to give them time to do so.

This time, Ia glanced behind herself to double-check the faces of the people she had precognitively foreseen in her line. They looked at each other and her, in turn.

The staff sergeant continued briskly after a moment. "Some activities, you will be praised or punished based on what the whole of your class does. Some, you will be praised or punished on what the whole of your Squad does. The rest, you're on your own . . . until such time as you learn how to be a *real* soldier. Move out!"

Spinning on her heel, Staff Sergeant Linley strode down the hallway. Ia followed, shoulders squared and chin level. Deep inside, a part of her dreaded this last step. For as long as she had been alive, her hair had been a distinct part of her self-identity. With locks whiter than even the most towheaded of children, her mothers had always been able to spot her in a crowd. Letting it grow long had allowed her to indulge in her feminine side even after her life had changed so abruptly three years ago.

Removing it would make this moment feel irrevocable. Irreversible. Fatal. *No, don't think about that. You have too much to do to get distracted.* It wasn't as if she could avoid it, anyway.

As the first in line of her Squad, she was the first in line for the barber chair. Not that there was much to it. The barber whipped her cape over Ia's shoulders as soon as she set down her kitbag and settled into the chair. The clippers hummed over her head in steady, almost stately passes, starting by her right ear and continuing all the way over to her left. Damp locks fell away from her face, most of them still constrained by her braid. The barber pulled it away and tossed it in the recycling bin, then ran the clippers over a few last, stray spots. The swift-moving woman set down her tool and whipped off the apron-cape almost before Ia knew it was over.

Her head felt weird. Cold, off-balance, and just weird. Grabbing her kitbag, Ia headed for the sinks by the door. Unlike some of the others, who were emerging from their chairs with bemused looks, she didn't reach up and run her hand over her fuzzy, prickly scalp. If she did that, she knew she'd cry.

I don't have time for tears. I have to get my Squad into shape . . . which is why I lined up when I did, where I did.

Mendez was still rubbing his fingers over his dark-stubbled skull when he reached her side. "V'*damn*, that's gonna take some getting used to . . ."

"Hand me your canteen," Ia ordered. "Let's get it filled up. Where's your cap?"

"In my kitbag." He handed over his canteen and crouched to fish it out. Ia leaned over, peeled off one of his patches, and reapplied it more carefully. He glanced up at her, frowning. "I know how to apply a flash patch, meioa."

"While *I* could do push-ups all day long in this gravity, not everyone in our Squad can, Mendez. Check the patches for the others as they come out." Filling up his canteen, she handed it to him, then held out her hand for Spyder's. His fancifully dyed hair—what was left of it—looked like a skimming of mottled green and brown moss on his skull. He looked about as happy to lose it as she was to lose hers. ". . . Sorry about the hair, meioa. I know how you feel."

"S'not so bad. S'*worse*," he half joked, moving out of the way as a pair from C Squad filled their canteens at the sink. "But I'll live. Erm . . . 'this recruit'll live,' ey?"

At least he was trying to fit in. In half the scenarios she had surveyed through the timestreams, she hadn't ended up with him in her training Squad. Ia handed him his canteen, then swung her kitbag around so she could fish out her own hat. Her scalp itched and prickled from weightlessness, giving her the urge to cover it. "Don't forget your cap. The sun's brutal in the afternoon. Get out there, find the spot, and line up. You, too, Mendez."

"Who died and made you an officer?" Mendez asked, wrinkling his nose. "You don't give me orders, you know."

"I speak with the authority of common sense. That should be enough reason for anyone to follow through. Unless you *want* more push-ups?" she asked pointedly. "I won't stop you if you do."

Sighing roughly, Mendez left. Spyder followed him, still gingerly touching his nearly nude scalp. Ia held out her hand for Forenze's canteen. The other woman didn't look too traumatized to lose her hair, but then hers had been only a few centimeters long to begin with. Stylishly cut, but already short.

The trill of a whistle cut through the noise of the last few recruits waiting in line, getting their hair shaved off, and filling their canteens. Sgt. Linley strode across the room, opened the door, and yelled at both groups of trainees. "Half an hour, Recruits! Drop and give me ten, loud and clear, and count 'em from eleven to twenty! Right here, right now, let's go, let's go!"

There wasn't much space inside the barbershop area, even with most of her classmates outside. Ia dropped and counted off anyway, ten fast, firm push-ups. Her kitbag bounced on her back with each stroke, since there wasn't enough room to set it down. Climbing back to her feet while the others were still only halfway through, she finished filling Sung's bottle, then bent and unclipped ZeeZee's from his belt, since he was still working on his push-ups. When both were back on their feet, she handed over their canteens.

Sergeant Linley was staring at her as she left the building. Ia could guess why, but didn't react. She just settled her hat on her head, pulled the chin cord to tighten it in place, and followed the others out to the line marked with a painted *A*. Sergeant Tae was back, patiently waiting a few meters away as he watched his freshly shaved charges file into place.

Ia didn't join the others in toeing the line immediately. Instead, she walked the line, first behind her teammates, then in front of them, checking their outfits. Sung's hat was perched a little far back on her head. The thin woman accepted her suggestion to correct it with a silent tug on the brim. Next to her, Arstoll deliberately pushed his back, tilting it up. His green eyes bored defiantly into hers. Ia quirked a brow, but said nothing. Moving to Crosp, she muttered a suggestion for him to tighten his belt, since the weight of his filled canteen was making it sag.

"Recruit Ia!"

Turning, she faced First Sergeant Tae. "Sergeant, yes, Sergeant!"

"What are you doing?" he asked, his tone crisp and hard.

Just like she knew he would. Just as she knew Arstoll would do what he did, which was to quickly reach up and tug his hat back to level.

"Sergeant, this recruit is helping ready her fellow soldiers for inspection, Sergeant!"

He strolled up to her. "So. You think you can be a *soldier*, is that it? You think you can be a *leader*, maybe?" He paused, no doubt waiting for her to answer. When she didn't—she knew better than to walk into that trap—he snapped, *"Fall in!"*

Turning crisply to her left, she strode to the end of the line and took her place next to Mendez. Tae followed her, looked her over from head to toe, then walked down the line from her at the left to ZeeZee at the right. He grunted and shifted around to walk along their backs, inspecting them from that side as well.

". . . Well. It seems you *did* get something right. Congratulations, Recruit Ia," he added, drawing something out of one of his shirt pockets. "You just got the first boot chevrons of Class 7157." Slapping the patch on her left shoulder, he grinned. It was not a pleasant grin. "Be advised that your *temporary* rank as A Squad leader comes with an *obligation* as well as a tiny modicum of power.

"For every punishment the *rest* of your Squad undertakes while you have those boot stripes, *you* will undertake them, too." His grin widened. "Consider it *motivational* training for a wannabe leader."

"Sergeant, yes, Sergeant!" Ia snapped.

He blinked a little, then moved to B Squad and started inspecting them. He found three things wrong with those recruits, and demanded that the whole line undergo three more push-ups as punishment for their sloppy dress, posture, and attitudes. Sgt. Tae then promoted "the best of a sorry lot" to B Squad leader, as he had her. C and D Squads had to do four push-ups . . . and Kaimong made his Squad mates very happy— in the sarcastic sense—earning them six extra push-ups, on top of the two earned by two of his teammates. Three of his were for having his shirt untucked and two of his patches mixed up, and three more were earned for his attitude.

As they stood out in the open, waiting for their first inspection to be over and done, the heat of the sun grew unbearable. The plexcrete under their feet was an unrelenting shade of creamy off-white, bouncing the glare of the light back up from below. Off to either side, trees and bushes helped shade the sides of the buildings, and more plants grew on the rooftop gardens dotting everything bigger than a shed as far as the eye could see.

The air was fragrant with greenery, but it was also missing something, the same something it had missed since she had boarded the first ship on her way to the Human Motherworld. There was no ozone in the air, no dusty-prickly smell of an impending daily thunderstorm. There had been too many smells in the cities, and too many things she'd needed to do while among the Afaso, for her to have pinpointed the differences until now.

A day without lightning? The Motherworld is just weird . . . She wrinkled her nose for a moment, then relaxed her expression. She tried to relax her shoulders, too. *Weird or not, I'll have to deal with it.*

The water in her canteen was still cool when she sipped from it, but it would be a little while before they would have another chance to fill the stout plexi bottles. She rationed it carefully, doing her best to ignore the trickle of sweat beginning to stain her hairline. It was a relief to more than just Ia when Tae finally told them to start marching.

No sooner did they get moving than their chief Drill Instructor enlightened them as they walked down the road under the hot summer sun. Class 7157 would now march over to the barracks and settle into their assigned "berths," and be marched off to lunch immediately afterward. Once they were fed, Class 7157 would be marched back to the barracks for lessons on how to make beds, fold clothes, pack kits, clean the latrines—not bathrooms or changing rooms or showering rooms, but latrines, he asserted—and polish everything ". . . from boots to bulwarks, since you *will* eventually get into space."

After that would come a tour of the local buildings, more lessons on the rules and regulations of the Space Force, an explanation of the orientation training classes, which would commence the next day, and a final stop in the mess hall for supper. Then would come revision in the barracks on how to fold clothes, pack gear, make beds, polish boots, and clean the place—replete with plenty of hands-on practice—and a final inspection before lights-out.

But it was a relief to be moving, even if it meant not only walking for several kilometers, but knowing those walks would be interspersed with several more sets of push-ups. Including one that came not two minutes after they started walking, with Linley blowing her whistle in between the chunks of information her fellow sergeant was imparting.

Once they were done counting off in ragged groups and back on their feet again, and Sergeant Tae had finished his briefly interrupted lecture, Linley called out a cadence-song from her position at their side as Sergeant Tae once more led the way up the road.

The Space Force is the place to be,
But I am not in its Army.
The Space Force is the place to be,
But I am not in its Navy!

The Space Force is where I am found,
I'm not some civvie on the ground!
The Space Force is where I am found,
I'm not a Special Forces Hound!

The Space Force is my special friend,
I'll fight until the bitter end!!
The Space Force is my special friend,
My government I will defend!

The Space Force is prepared for war,
Because I'm marching at the fore!
The Space Force is prepared for War,
Because I'm in its Marine Corps!

CHAPTER 4

*Going into the military as a heavyworlder, I immediately
had a number of natural advantages. Greater strength,
faster reflexes, and better stamina. Naturally, the Space
Force did what it could to level the playing field. Nowadays,
I work out every single day for at least a few hours in a
localized, stronger than Standard gravity well. Back
then . . . well, you don't have any artificial gravity weaves
lurking under the dirt of the Motherworld, so they had to
make up for it somehow. Not that I exercise in my native
gravity very often now, since it stresses a starship's hull
awkwardly, but it's much more comfortable than the "solution" they use on heavyworld recruits attending Basic
Training on a light-gravitied planet.*

*While I didn't particularly enjoy my weight suit, I did
understand why they insisted on it. Born and raised in a
heavy gravity, a native child of at least the second generation usually grows up with a naturally adapted body blessed
with greater musculature and faster reflexes. But these
things atrophy when they're not used. And, naturally, it'd
be stupid to waste those advantages in someone volunteer-
ing to fight for you. The modern military is many things,
but it is not stupid when it comes to using its greatest
resources, the men and women serving in it.*

~Ia

The sharp glare of the lights being snapped on and a voice snapping out, "On your feet and in your Browns, let's go, go, go!" jolted Ia out of an unpleasant dream of being eaten alive.

Disoriented, she rolled out of her bottom bunk, yanked open her locker, swapped her worn undergarments for fresh, and headed for the bathrooms—or rather, the latrines—on pure, timestream-guided instinct. It wasn't until she emerged from one of the stalls, still yawning and squinting at the bright overhead lights, that she realized she was literally the first person on her feet and ready for her very first full day as a Marine. Grabbing a yawning Kumanei as the other woman entered the latrines, she steered her away from the shower stalls.

"Not there, Recruit," Ia told her. "We don't get to do that until after our Regimen Training Session—otherwise known as morning exercise from hell. You don't have time for a shower right now."

"No shower is *locosh'ta*," Kumanei groused. She managed to scowl and yawn simultaneously. "Gimme a shower and a caf', stat, dammit."

"*Shakk* that," Casey muttered. The tall, blond leader for B Squad groaned as he tried lifting his arm up high enough to scratch the top of his head. "Gimme a painkiller for my arms, and another hour of sleep, *then* a shower . . ."

"*Hai*, sleeeeeep," Kumanei agreed, yawning again.

"On your feet, in your Browns, and get moving, Recruits," Ia warned both of them and the other members of their training Platoon making their way toward the facilities. "You might want to make up your bunks now, too, while you have a few seconds to spare. You all heard Tae last night. We wake up, we get dressed, we do two hours of calisthenics and fitness training, we hit the showers, we go through a barracks inspection, and *then* we get to eat. The worse our barracks looks between now and then, the *longer* it'll take for us to get fed."

"Drop dead, Ia," Arstoll told her as she headed back toward the bunkroom. He gave her a dirty look. "And what the hell kind of name is 'Ia' anyway?"

It was too early in the morning for an argument. Tossing her clothes in one of the three sonic cleaners positioned between the latrines and the bunkroom, Ia left the door open and pointed at it. "Don't forget to put your dirty clothes in the cleaner.

Everyone's sleepwear is enough to fill it, and if we fill and set it now, it'll be done when we get back from Regimen Torture."

Her deliberate choice of words made a couple of her fellow recruits snort in humor, and diffused a few retorts. It made her glad for her abrupt awakening. *Not that I mind being awoken from any of my nightmares . . . but I feel like I've woken up with the shadow of my future self laid over all of my actions. Maybe if I don't try too hard to be the perfect recruit, I'll get it right.*

Maybe. Just so long as I don't slack off, either. Returning to her bunk, Ia pulled the sheets and blankets straight, tucking them under as tightly as she could manage. Once her pillow was squared on the thin mattress, she opened her locker and dug out a pair of brown shorts. Since she had grabbed a bra as well as fresh underpants and a T-shirt on her way to the latrines, the only other things she needed to don were her socks and boots, her belt with its canteen, and her narrow cap with its bill-style brim.

Later in the day—when it finally became day—they would need their broad-brimmed hats to shade them from the sun. Right now, it was still dark outside. Dark enough, even she had to stifle a yawn as Sgt. Tae chivied them out of the barracks and onto the lawn. They weren't the only ones emerging from their white-painted building, either.

Camp Nallibong, as they had been informed yesterday, hosted a brand-new training class every single week, barring only one week in the local summer and one week in the local winter for celebrating official Terran holidays. Training Platoons ranged in size from as few as forty to as many as sixty, depending upon how many would-be soldiers were shipped their way. Given all of that, there were an impressive number of recruits filing out of their barracks and lining up on the thin row of bricks planted in the grass of the barracks lawns, their brown-clad bodies illuminated by the floodlights spaced around the area.

"It is my sorry duty to get you sons of slags and daughters of dreks *fit* enough to be called recruits, never mind Marines!" Sgt. Linley's voice snapped out, capturing their attention. "You will now space out on the lines by extending both arms to either side. You should be far enough apart that you can just barely touch the recruit next to you! Each and every morning, you will assume these positions, with each Squad rotating forward one row each week.

"This week, A Squad is in front and E Squad is at the rear. Next week B Squad will move up to the front and A Squad will fill in the rear—and do *not* make any jokes about that," she added sharply, sweeping her baton slowly in front of her, aiming it at each of the recruits like it was a weapon. "The SF-MC has a zero tolerance policy, and we are here to get your bodies into shape and your minds out of the gutter! First Recruit Ia, A Squad, front and center!"

Puzzled, Ia broke formation and strode forward. Halting in front of the taller woman, she kept her chin level. "Sergeant, yes, Sergeant!"

"Just in case you thought your time here in the SF-Marines was going to be *easy*," Linley told her, voice pitched to carry over the shouts of the other Platoons of recruits counting off their exercise movements, "I wanted you to know that I have *personally* gone over your physiology profile."

Holding out the hand wielding the baton, she pointed at a hover sled a few meters away. A hover sled which Ia had forgotten would be waiting for her this morning. Ia glanced back at the Regimen Trainer as the other woman continued briskly.

"On that cart is your new best friend: your very own gravity-gauged weight suit . . . or as close as we can get it without making it too bulky for you to use. You will strap it on every single morning and not take it off until lights-out each and every night, save only during your daily bathing needs, and when given the command to take it off for the duration of specific training exercises. You will also drink three extra liters of water every day to compensate, one at each mealtime, for a total of ten. You are *not* allowed to pass out from dehydration.

"You were born with all the advantages of a heavyworlder," Linley reminded Ia, "and you will *train* to the physical standards of a heavyworlder. Just because this is the Motherworld doesn't mean you're gonna have it easy. *Recruit Ia, weight up!*"

"Sergeant, yes, Sergeant!" Turning crisply, Ia headed for the hover sled. As she did so, Linley forged on with the explanations of how Class 7157 was expected to perform their regimen of exercises.

Listening with half an ear, Ia sorted out the well-wink of lead-weighted straps. There was a sort of long-sleeved jacket thing for her upper half which snapped across the front of her chest and down her arms once she shrugged into it—the arms of which were detachable, she knew—plus, a pair of plaid-like leggings which snapped down the outsides of her legs from waist to ankles, and a headband thing which was meant to fit around her forehead. The last four items were a set of weights for her feet, which would fit over her boots something like spats with spurs, and a pair of somewhat padded gloves, each finger individually weighted so that anything requiring fine dexterity would also be affected by the pull of gravity, not just activities that used her larger muscles.

By the time she finished fastening everything into place, her fellow recruits had already gone through one round of jumping jacks and were being instructed on the proper way to do windmill toe touches. Hurrying to join them, Ia picked up what her fellow recruits were doing. The drag of the weighted straps was fairly evenly distributed across her body, but fairly wasn't perfectly. It didn't feel like a real heavy-gravitied world would have felt. Certainly not like home.

It did make a palpable difference in her performance, though. She had known she was out of shape, compared to back home. Two whole months of living and exercising mostly in light gravity had weakened her muscles. By the end of their exercise session, including her having to do twenty extra jumping jacks ". . . to catch up with the others," Ia felt just as sweaty and just as tired as everyone else. It was a distinct relief to be ordered back into the barracks for a shower and a change of clothes.

At least she'd had the foresight to claim a bottom bunk. That made it easier to shed her weights onto the mattress, though it did disturb the tight fit of the covers. Grabbing another change of clothes and her toiletry gear, she made her way toward the showers. Rather than being first as she had hoped, she ended up in the middle of the lot, forced to wait her turn. At least being weight-free for a few minutes helped recover some of her energy.

When she got back to her bunk, still scrubbing water from her skin, she found Spyder trying to lift the leggings part of her weight suit harness. He did have some muscle on him, but the weighted straps weren't easy to hoist. Giving up, he let it drop back down.

"Whachoo got 'ere? Weighs a slaggin' ton!"

Stepping around him, Ia opened her locker and fetched out a pair of long brown pants and a shirt. Crosp came by, tossing her T-shirt and underpants onto her bed as he passed, fetched out of the sonic cleaner along with the clothes of the others.

"How much choo think it weighs, Ia?" Spyder asked. "Kinda looks like archaic armor, too."

"The legs weigh about ninety-five kilos, the chest and arms another sixty-three, the headband and gloves two kilos each, and the feet three, which makes for about one hundred seventy kilos." She nodded at the tile-shaped weights. "I counted the tiles for a rough estimate."

"*Shova v'shakk . . .*" He breathed the V'Dan epithet, staring at the web-work garments and the tile-like segments of weights attached to each and every strap. "That's gotta be, what, twice yer weight?"

She slipped into her trousers and reached for a fresh shirt. "I weigh one hundred and two kilos, so no, it's not quite twice my weight."

Crosp, on his way back from delivering laundry, stopped and stared at her, watching her sit on the edge of the bed so she could don her boots again. "You're *shakkin'* us. A hundred and two kilos? At your height? You're only, what, a hundred and seventy-four, maybe a hundred and seventy-five centimeters tall? No *way* you weigh that much. Not and look that thin! Muscular, but thin."

Mendez joined them. "I'm almost two meters tall, and I barely top a hundred kilos. How can a little thing like you weigh more than me?"

"I'm a heavyworlder. Thicker bones and denser flesh. Technically, if I'm supposed to be working out in the equivalent of my home gravity," Ia said, picking up and shrugging into the jacket portion, "there should be another fifty-five kilos spread out over this thing. But the SF-MC manufactories aren't programmed to make weight suits that heavy, because there aren't more than a handful of recruits coming into the Space Force from Sanctuary just yet. Or even from Parker's World, which is the next-heaviest colony spawned out of I.C. Eiaven. The Space Force would have to custom-make a suit just for me to wear, and they're not going to bother."

"*Ten-hut!* Fall in for Inspection!"

Caught off guard, Ia and her fellow recruits scrambled to get into position. Her top bunkmate, Sung, dropped down to stand at the end of their double bunks, while Ia moved out to stand between her and Babaga, the next top bunk dweller to her left. Sgt. Tae strolled into the bunkhouse for their morning inspection. Naturally, given this was their first day, he found several things wrong with each person. The bunkhouse quickly filled with the sounds of push-ups being counted off.

Reaching Ia, he opened up and inspected her locker, glanced at her half-webbed body, peered at the weights still bowing the springs of her bed, and grunted. "You are *supposed* to wear that weight suit at *all* times, outside of showering, sleeping, and whenever I or my fellow sergeants let you out of it, Recruit. Weight up, drop, and give me twenty!"

"Sergeant, yes, Sergeant!" Picking up the leggings, Ia snapped herself into them. The elastic sections of webbing clung to her limbs, making them feel like they were being forced to wade through mud once the weights were attached. *I am not going to have an easy time of it, until I acclimate. And even then . . .*

She strapped the weights onto her boots, tugged on the gloves, then fitted the headband and its smaller span of dense metal tiles into place. Dropping to the floor as soon as she was weighted in full by her harness, Ia started counting out her assigned demerits. She was hungry, she was tired, and she didn't *want* to be here. But she needed to be here, and she needed to play along with her superior's demands. Whether or not it was fun.

Pity.

———

Three days later, the members of Class 7157 were ordered into the training gym for their first day of basic combat instruction. Their bodies still ached from the constant rounds of physical exercise, long marches, and demerit punishments, but not quite as much as they had at the start. The large, fan-cooled hall, with its padded mats and mirrored walls, was half-filled with other training classes. Sergeant Tae led them to one of the large, blue mats, marked with five white circles reminiscent of a wrestling mat, and turned over control of the class to Sergeant Linley with a flick of his baton.

Having learned to pay attention over the last three days—and the physically exhausting consequences that came from doing otherwise—the five Squads formed their "teaching position." A and B Squads dropped into cross-legged seats on the ground, C and D Squads knelt, and E Squad stood, allowing all forty-five class members plenty of room to see whatever was about to happen. Surveying the quiet, attentive group, their Regimen Trainer began.

"Today, you will begin your training in the primary job of *any* military: how to place your bodies, your weapons, and even your lives between the civilians and the government you are here to learn how to protect, and whatever may try to threaten them. This is your number one most important job of anything you may do in the Space Force. In the future, you may find yourself assigned permanently to Kitchen Duty, based on your abilities . . . or lack thereof," Linley acknowledged wryly, "but if you pass Basic Instruction, you *will* be expected at any moment to be able to exchange your spatulas for stunner rifles, and defend the Terran United Planets and its lawfully assigned interests, and do so at a moment's notice.

"If you get *really* good," she added, displaying a rare sense of humor for them, "you may even learn how to *kill* someone with a spatula . . . and not just through food poisoning."

A handful of the others laughed at that. Ia smiled a little, but the sergeant's words had triggered the timestreams in the back of her mind. She struggled to suppress the visions of seeing someone actually slaughtering a fellow sentient with the thin, sharp edge of a metal spatula. Not in the military, and not on Earth, but in a mining colony dome several star systems and a couple decades from here.

The images weren't nearly as funny as their Regimen Trainer made it sound.

Linley addressed them again, giving Ia something to focus on. Mainly because it involved herself. Lifting her chin a little, the sergeant continued. "Now, *some* of you already come into the Service thinking they *know* how to fight. Recruit Ia! Front and center!"

Shoving awkwardly to her feet—weighted down by her tiled straps—Ia positioned herself so that she half faced the others as well as her instructor. "Sergeant, yes, Sergeant!"

"According to your file, you apparently have an Afaso Mastery rank. Is that so?" Linley asked her.

"Sergeant, yes, Sergeant," Ia agreed. She knew what the other woman wanted from her, and provided it. "This recruit is an unvowed Full Master of the Afaso martial arts system, Sergeant."

"Indeed. The Afaso," Linley informed the others, "are a militant order, as well as a religious one. Having been founded shortly before Terrans reached out into the stars, the Afaso absorbed and amalgamated all known forms of martial arts into a single training system. After the Second Human Empire joined the Alliance, they further expanded and merged their knowledge of weaponless and archaic weaponry–based combat systems. They are the *finest* warriors outside of an actual military organization, and you do *not* want to take them on in hand-to-hand combat if you yourself are not trained to a comparable level.

"In fact, we will be teaching you certain Afaso techniques for unarmed and edged weapons combat. As archaic as long blades might be in an era of stunners and lasers, you are *attempting* to become Marines, and in the tradition of Old Earth Marines, you will be learning sword fighting as well as knife fighting, ranged weaponry, personal artillery, and unarmed combat. However . . . as good as the Afaso are, the Marines are more dangerous than the Afaso. Recruit Ia, do you know *why* the Marines are better?" Linley challenged her.

Ia met her skeptical brown gaze. "Sergeant, yes, Sergeant! This recruit does know why the Marines are more dangerous, Sergeant!"

That took the Regimen Trainer by surprise. Blinking, she quirked one of her brows. "Do you? Well, then, Recruit. Explain to all of us *why* you think the Marines are more dangerous than the Afaso."

"Sergeant, while the Afaso are trained thoroughly in how to *end* a fight, they are not trained in how to *start* a fight. The Afaso are also trained to avoid killing an opponent whenever possible," Ia added, projecting her voice so that her fellow recruits could hear. "While it does take more skill to disable rather than destroy, and by that standard the vowed members of the Afaso Order are more *skilled* than the average Marine . . . they are *not* more deadly, Sergeant. Marines are trained to kill."

"Very good, Recruit. And very astute." Sweeping her gaze over the others, Linley emphasized that point bluntly. "You are here to learn how to *kill*. Your psychological evaluations during your MATs suggested that you have the intestinal fortitude to follow through when given the command to 'shoot to kill,' without the danger of a predilection for *liking* it a little too much. The modern military does not have a place for homicidal maniacs."

Without warning, Linley struck at Ia. She jabbed, swept, and kicked, arms and legs moving swiftly. Ia managed to block the attacks effectively enough, though her weight suit did slow her reactions to the point where it took effort to meet each blow fast enough to deflect it. Despite her heavyworlder reflexes and precognitive forewarnings that it would happen, the Regimen Trainer managed to distract Ia long enough with a vicious jab to her throat with one hand. That allowed Linley to grapple Ia with the other and trip her to the ground.

She landed with a heavy, rolling *whump* on the mat. No Sanctuarian survived to adulthood without learning how to take a fall with minimum injury. Doing it in less than a third of the gravity gave Ia plenty of time to curve her body in preparation for the impact; however, the grid work of weight suit tiles weren't normally a part of her practice for such things, making her grunt at the bruises caused by landing on the awkward things.

Linley gave her a few seconds to recover from her fall, then offered her hand. Ia accepted it, though it didn't make much difference against the inertia of her augmented kilos. She had to twist onto her side just to regain her feet. Once up, she resumed her attentive stance, waiting for either a dismissal back to the rest of the group, or to be used again as an example. The staff sergeant did neither, instead turning back to the others to continue her lecture.

"As you can see, Recruit Ia does have a reasonable amount of training. However, she is *not* trained to kill, and therefore will not use potentially lethal maneuvers among her opening attacks, such as my attempted throat grab. By the end of her Basic Training, *if* she doesn't wash out, this reflex will be retrained. While the majority of attack methods used by the SF-MC involve actual weaponry, you *will* learn how to kill with your bare hands. Resume your place, Recruit."

"Sergeant, yes, Sergeant!" Turning, Ia strode back to the others.

"Recruit Ia, weights off," Sgt. Linley added, pointing with her baton. "Pile them off of the mat, over there."

"Sergeant, yes, Sergeant!" Swerving around her fellow recruits, Ia did as she was bid.

"Recruits Ia, Arstoll, Shecklin, Tang, and Z'munbe all have high marks in various martial art skills, according to their files. The five of you will eventually assist the others in learning the basics as these lessons progress. You will do so when instructed to do so, and *only* when instructed to do so," Linley warned them as Ia continued to unsnap the pieces of her harness. "Until such time as I have personally evaluated your skills, you will all undertake the same basic progression in lessons as the rest. Do *not* assume that a black belt on your hips or some tattoo on your arm qualifies you as an instructor. Not by SF-MC standards.

"Now, we will begin by demonstrating several methods of escaping from being grabbed or confined by an enemy. Recruit Ia, when you're ready?"

Ia winced and quickly pulled the last of the weights from her boots. *I was hoping she wouldn't do that. Now I'll have to carefully navigate the rougher waters just up ahead . . .*

———————

"Gods! I can't believe you messed up that badly, Kaimong!" Stalking over to his locker, the member of E Squad speaking glared at his teammate. "Twenty sit-ups and push-ups, *and* we had to rerun the rope swing ten times to make sure we *all* got it right? Now we'll barely have time to shower before the inspections for lunch!"

"Slag off!" Kaimong retorted, returning his glare. "I'm doing what I can. That damned 'confidence' course ain't fair. So just slag off!"

"No, *you* slag off!" one of his other Squad mates argued,

moving up in his face. "Or rather, *slack* off. How in a K'kattan hell did you pass your MATs for the *Marines*, anyway? You should've been sent to the Army—where the *losers* go!"

Ia, still wrapped in a towel from her shower, hurried out of the doorway to the latrines. She didn't get there in time to stop Kaimong from shoving the second man or him from shoving back, but she did manage to shoulder herself between the two before their flat, pushing hands could be curled into tight, punching fists.

"Break it up!" she ordered. It was a good guess that it was the heat and high humidity that was making everyone cranky and easily irritated by each other, but there wasn't anything she could do about the summer thunderstorms plaguing the northern end of the continent. Except maybe enjoy the touch of home in the air, in those rare moments when her attention wasn't needed elsewhere. Like right now. Unfortunately, the only thing she could do was physically stop them by placing herself between the pair. "No fighting in the barracks!"

"Oh, like *you're* so superior!" Arstoll snapped from his bunk halfway across the locker room, surprising her. Jumping down, boots still unlaced, he stalked toward her as she pushed Kaimong and the other recruit apart. "Ooh, look, I'm Recruit Ia! I'm so *special*, I get picked to be first at everything. Like you're some sort of big damn hero-in-training!"

That hit a little too close to home. Hands going to her hips, making sure she stood sideways to the other two so that they were separated further by the span of her elbows, Ia met his glare. "And *you* are missing the point of *all* of this, Arstoll. Just like Kaimong and the rest of E Squad. They're not singling me out because I'm 'special,' they're singling me out—and Kaimong, and several of the rest of you—to *beat us down*. They're deliberately picking on us so they can find our weakest spots."

"Oh, really?" Arstoll challenged her, hands going to his own hips.

"What do you think the military is about?" Ia asked him. "We are *all* still civilians. We don't have the *mind-set* and the *willpower* to survive combat—do you think the Salik, if they ever broke out, would invite us over for tea and crumpets and a discussion of who's going to sleep with whom on the latest vidsoap? We'd *be* the crumpets! And you can bet as sure as hellfire and damnation that they wouldn't be *nice* to us while they're interrogating us, one tasty slice at a time! It is our instructors' *job* to be nasty to us as recruits, in the hopes of toughening us up!"

"Oh, really? Well, maybe I don't *want* to be constantly compared to some backwater heavyworlder *nobody*," Arstoll shot back, stepping forward. "The men and women on *both* sides of my family have served in one Branch or another of the Space Force since the first twenty years of its inception. I may not have the muscles or the reflexes of a heavyworlder, but *I* am tough enough for the Marines *without* heavyworlder advantages. *I* intend to get a Field Commission," he boasted, jerking his thumb at his chest. "Unlike *you*, I've studied tactics and strategies for years. I'm ready for battle!"

"I wish I could believe you," Ia stated flatly. Their own fight had diffused the tensions between Kaimong and the others, but now she had to pick her words carefully. Very carefully. Her statement caused her Squad mate to bristle, but she continued briskly. Implacably. "If you *had* taken your lessons in tactics and strategies to heart, you would realize just how *foolish* it is to antagonize someone you *know* is supposed to watch your back in the future. Military forces which are torn apart by internal antagonism are as weak as a cheap plexi net. The holes caused by internecine strife make it that much easier for the enemy to tear through them on the way to their goal.

"What you *should* be doing is seeking ways to *help* each other. To turn your fellow soldiers into a solid shield wall." She glanced to either side, taking in Kaimong and his teammates. Returning her gaze to Arstoll, who was sneering, she lifted one of her brows in return. "If you want that Field Commission, Arstoll, you're going to have to *prove* you can lead. Not just boast about it. Family connections only gave you certain opportunities to learn whatever and how much of it that you studied. Whether or not you *comprehend* it is another matter.

"And, for the record, you do not know *my* background and education level, Arstoll. Nor do I know yours. I, however, will give *you* the benefit of the doubt." Tightening her towel, she moved past him. "Prove, or disprove, that you have what it takes to lead. Don't just boast. Do."

"What, like *you* can?" Arstoll countered, sneering at her. "Just because you have boot chevrons—"

Whirling to face him, Ia cut him off. "*That* is a discussion which will have to wait until lunch. Right now, *you* are wasting everyone's time. We have six minutes left before our prelunch inspection, and *some* of us haven't showered yet." Turning around, she gave everyone pointed looks. "Well? Move! Unless you all *want* more demerits . . . ?"

They moved. So did she. Returning to her bunk and locker, Ia exchanged the towel for fresh clothes. Between the humidity and the heat, all of their outdoor activities, which took place until noon, left each of them drenched in sweat. From lunch to supper, they spent their time indoors in training classrooms, learning about the rules, regulations, history, and organization of the Space Force and its four Branches. That meant being clean and presentable so that forty-five sweat-soaked bodies didn't stink up the place.

Sung, perched on the edge of Ia's bed so that she could lace her boots, looked up at her bunkmate. "He really can't see past his own eyebrows, can he?"

Ia gave her a curious look.

"*You* just led. Good job," she added lightly.

"Thanks, but I still have a very long way to go," Ia muttered, thinking of her goals.

"Maybe . . . and maybe not. I got a cousin working in the DoI. He says people who show leadership even in boot camp get promoted real quick." Tightening the last of her laces, Sung stood and made room for Ia to don her own boots. "The Department of Innovations will have its eye on you, and soon. I don't need to be a precog to foresee that."

Funny, Ia thought wryly, though she kept that thought carefully to herself, *I had to be one, in order to see it coming.*

"So, Recruit Ia," Arstoll drawled, tearing his roll in half as he looked down the table in Ia's direction. "About those fancy *boot chevrons* . . ."

Ia chased down her mouthful of chicken with some of the water in her cup. After training hard all morning, everything looked and smelled delicious. Mostly because she herself hadn't been forced to cook it. "You're confusing temporary with permanent, Recruit Arstoll."

"Oh, really? How so?" he challenged her.

"No one in the entire history of all four Branches of the Space Force has ever kept their boot chevrons for the entire length of Basic Training. Being envious of a boot chevron is like being envious of a soap bubble. It's pretty while it lasts, but it never lasts long."

"Wait a pico," Kumanei interjected. "You don't get to *keep* your boot chevrons?"

"Ey, that's a bituva gyp, innit?" Spyder agreed, reaching for one of the pitchers of fruit juice dotting the length of their table. "Wassa point a' havin' 'em if y' don't get t' keep 'em?"

"*That's* the difference between lesson and implementation." At Spyder's blank look, Ia explained. "Giving someone a higher rank during Basic Training is a teaching tool. For the rest of you in this Squad, it teaches you how to follow orders from someone of even so much as a slightly higher rank than you. Even if you don't *like* that person," she added, glancing at Arstoll. "Or just think you don't. Learning how to take orders from others is vital to the smooth operation of any organization, and particularly a military force, because what we do can literally be deadly: to the enemy if we get it right, or to ourselves if we do it at the wrong time or in the wrong way. Therefore we *all* need to learn how to take orders from our superiors.

"For the person with the promotion, it teaches you something a little more complex. But it can be broken down into four parts," Ia said. She speared a couple vegetables and popped them in her mouth.

"Oh, really? I didn't know you were an expert in military psychology," Arstoll challenged her.

She met his green stare levelly, swallowing before she spoke. "I don't claim to be. I *know* these things because I read a lot of military and psychology texts, but that isn't the same as *understanding* what I read. Like you, I'm still trying to figure out how to put theory into real-world implementation. Part of the problem is, not everyone here has studied the same material. That makes it harder, because the others don't know what I'm trying to do. But there are four things I *do* know. First off, boot chevron promotions teach a Squadron leader what it means to live in a position of command."

"And that means, what? The heady rush and thrill of bossing people around?" Mendez asked as Ia poked at some of the vegetables on her tray.

Setting down her fork, she shook her head. "No. It means to be alienated from the others, to be disliked and envied by those who resent you for their own lack of promotion, to be fawned over by those who hope that your friendship will get them special privileges . . . envy, distrust, sycophantic fawning, all sorts of *pleasant* social interactions.

"The second thing boot chevrons teach a Squad leader is *how* to command . . . usually through trial and error. How to give an order so that others will obey, and how to re-bridge enough of that gap caused by the distancing of rank and command to soothe ruffled feelings and ease dislikes before they can turn to hatreds."

"Ha! Effective leaders *have* to keep some distance from their troops," Arstoll countered. "Excessive familiarity always breeds contempt and laziness in the troops."

"True, but they can't be too distant, either," Mendez pointed out. "Or the people they're leading won't know how their leadership will react in a given situation, or to a particular piece of bad news."

"Mendez is right about that," Ia agreed, looking at the others. "There has to be a certain level of trust in a military organization, and if your cadre is too distanced by formality, you won't *know* them, deep down to your bones . . . and if you don't know 'em, how can you trust 'em?"

"So . . . it's like a tightrope, ey?" Spyder reasoned it out. "Formal enough f' discipline, but friendly enough t'inspire trust. 'N th' more th' ranks trust you, th' better they'll be when it comes time t' poon'n'slag."

"Sweet stars, Spyder," Sung protested, wrinkling her nose. "You still say *poon*? That was last decade—my *aunt* said stuff like that."

"I'm from a *mining* station, sweets," Spyder enunciated, leaning over the table toward her. "You're lucky I know how t' say 'please' and 'thank you.'"

". . . Break it up," Ia ordered lightly, without force behind her words. She paused, then said. "And *that*, just now, is an example of how to lead under different circumstances. Compared to earlier in the barracks, this moment isn't nearly as tense as what happened with Kaimong."

"Kaimong Wong Ta should've been named Kaimong *Wrong* Ta," Arstoll muttered.

Ia ignored that. It was a problem that would deal with itself later. "Look, whatever our happy Camp instructors might do, it is *not* necessary to yell and spit each and every time you give someone an order. So the first two lessons of boot chevrons are how to put up with the distance a higher rank and status creates, and how to lead across that rank and status gap."

"So what about the third and fourth lessons?" Casey asked, leaning past Crosp so he could get at the nearest pitcher. A and B Squads were sharing the same table, and some of their nearer members seemed to be listening to Ia's lecture. Ia answered him, getting back on track.

"Right. The third and fourth lessons you learn from gaining boot chevrons always go together—and I do mean *always*. Boot chevrons teach authority *and* responsibility. You cannot have one without the other."

"Wait—isn't that th' same thing as th' second one?" Spyder challenged her. "I mean, authority 'n how t' lead th' others?"

"Nope. Authority is partly that, but it's also more. It's about giving an order and having it obeyed, yes. But if it isn't obeyed, it's about having the power to implement punishments. If it *is* obeyed, it's having the authority to praise and reward. Without going overboard on *either* end of the spectrum. That's where the responsibility comes into play," Ia pointed out. "Abuse of power, or even the laziness of not using enough of it, does not make for effective leadership. You have to strike a balance, and it's not an easy thing to do. Particularly when they're trying to beat us down, find our weakest spots, and toughen them up.

"Infractions *must* be punished, to prevent them from being repeated. Accomplishments *must* be praised, to encourage greater efforts."

These weren't just words to her; these were things Ia had tried to absorb into her bones over the last three years. Things she needed to *believe*. Not just in preparation for her career in the Space Force, but for all the preparations she had tried to make before leaving her homeworld.

"But to punish someone arbitrarily—like me ordering Crosp to do fifteen push-ups just because I feel like being nasty—isn't a good use of my authority," she continued. "Nor would giving him excessive amounts of praise, because too much of it starts to cheapen the value of that praise. There's not enough time for these four lessons of boot chevrons to really sink in during Basic Training, but you do get a taste of it, enough to maybe plant a seed of ability.

"The idea is that hopefully that seed will sink in, germinate, and start to grow. Particularly if it lands in an open, thoughtful mind. These are all the things a good leader has to remember and implement in the right way at the right time." Poking at her food with her fork again, Ia shrugged. "I myself need to learn how to lead in the practical sense, not just the theory of it. I can't do anything about my background, or my family connections. All I can do is remember what I read, try to apply it, and see how I can make it actually work. To do that, I try to think ahead of time what all the possible outcomes might be, particularly if I use or abuse my position as Squad leader.

"You can get mad at me, Arstoll, if that's what you really want. It's a free universe. But if I were you, I'd try to think about what the results will be if you keep trying to slag me just because I got a bit of *temporary* power. Of course, however *you* choose to act, *I* have to figure out how to work around that." She gave him a tight, ironic smile. "Every time you act like a pain in the asteroid, it just makes me all the more determined to win your cooperation. Your attitude is helping me figure out how to lead."

"Yeah, but what good does that do us?" Crosp asked, speaking before Arstoll could. "*You're* the one with the boot chevrons. Not Arstoll, or Sung, or even me. How does that help *us* learn how to lead?"

Sung answered for her. Ia let her, since that gave her a chance to eat and drink again.

"That's where the part about boot chevrons never lasting the whole length of training comes in. Look, we're in training for twenty Terran Standard weeks, right?" Sung asked the others. "The Drill Instructors swap 'em every two weeks or so, rotating who gets to be leader through the whole of the Squad so that *everyone* gets a chance, anywhere from ten to twenty days. Sometimes it's swapped a little sooner, sometimes a little later. It depends on the size of the training class. My cousin in the DoI told me all about it.

"Ever since they created the Department of Innovations in the modern military, and backed it up with opportunities for people to start learning and displaying leadership qualities, it's really made a difference on the effectiveness of the cadre, both noncoms and officers alike." Sung shrugged her slender shoulders. "Sure, you can get an education degree before you join up, take the MAT, and try for a shot at being an officer right from the start, but all that guarantees is a desk job at some point. A lot of *combat* officers rise through the ranks through Field Commissions. Just because you sit in classes all day at an Academy, learning about tactics and strategy, troop deployments and logistics, doesn't mean you really *understand* how to lead. Particularly in a battle zone."

Swallowing the last of her food, Ia nodded. "Exactly. A lot of the officers who go straight into an Academy after their MAT end up in noncombat positions. These positions are important—for every soldier in the field, officer or enlisted, there are at least seven or eight support personnel back home keeping them supplied, provisioned, healthy, and paid. As for how it can help you right *now*, you can always observe me, and try to figure out if the things I'm doing are good or bad, right or wrong, effective or ineffective.

"From there, you can extrapolate what thing you yourself could do, once you get your own boot chevrons. Not that my boot chevrons count for much, since we're all still learning how to be soldiers, but at least we're learning," Ia pointed out, shrugging.

"The learning's the important thing. Everyone who sits on the Command Staff has to have served in a combat zone, and specifically as a combat officer at some point during their career," Mendez agreed. "That's why I chose to start out as an enlisted soldier. Don't get me wrong; based on my MAT scores, I could've gone on to college and then straight into an Academy, but four out of the six officers in my family history started out as enlisted, and one of them made it all the way to Rear Admiral before she retired."

"Field Commissioned officers get more respect from the troops," Arstoll stated. "That's why I want to get a commission that way. FC officers *know* what it's like to be a mud-slogger. They're not going to ask you to do the impossible, because they *know* whether or not it's possible. Commissioned officers who've only ever been to an Academy aren't tested and tempered quite like we are."

"Speaking of which," Mendez warned them, lifting his chin at the chrono on the cafeteria wall, "it's almost time to be cleaning up and clearing out."

"Man, if we get more history lessons right after lunch," Kumanei muttered, "*I'm* gonna fall asleep. I don't care *how* many push-ups they assign me. I could use another hour of sleep each night . . . At least here in the military, they make sure you get enough to eat. I didn't always get that back home. That part's nice. But I miss the sleep."

"I'm still wondering how *she* manages to eat so much, and not gain weight," ZeeZee quipped, poking a thumb at Ia.

The comment amused her. "Cellular density," Ia explained, gathering up her utensils and cup on her tray. "I have more bone mass, which requires more calcium, and more muscle mass, which requires more protein. Most people require two thousand calories a day to maintain a healthy weight. People living on Sanctuary require closer to four thousand."

"Tcha . . . that much?" Spyder asked.

Rising, Ia smirked at him. "Yeah. That much. Raising food's a priority on my homeworld. But if you think *my* appetite is bad, imagine two hungry, teenaged heavyworlder boys like my brothers are, and think of how much food it takes to keep *them* fed."

He blinked. "Swaggin' ey . . ."

"Exactly. And my older brother is *bigger* than me." Nodding to her Squad mates, Ia carried her tray to the scullery window. A quick, skimming probe of the waters crossing the timeplains told her she had navigated a good chunk of Arstoll's antagonism successfully. Having Sung back her up on the duration of boot chevrons helped.

One of the recruits working in the scullery area brushed his fingers against her hand, taking the tray from her. A shock of awareness jolted up through her nerves—*fire, pain, explosive cold—*

Not now! Jerking back, she dropped her grip on the tray. Silverware tumbled from the unsupported corner as the other recruit tried to keep his hold on the metal. Stooping, Ia snatched the fork and knife out of the air before they could hit the ground. The scullery recruit gave her a wide-eyed look as she straightened and placed the implements back on the tray.

Afraid she had shown *him* that glimpse of his ugly potential future—which would be difficult to erase from his memory without touching him—she risked probing his mind. That much she could do without needing physical contact.

. . . Nothing. Thank God. He's just shocked at how fast I moved. She lifted her weight-strapped arm and hand and gave him a weak smile. "Heavyworlder. Fast reflexes."

He continued to stare at her. "Right."

Turning away, Ia breathed deeply, letting go of her anxiety with a sigh. For most psis, there were penalties for hiding one's abilities. Particularly if those abilities included any of the Pathies, telepathy, empathy, or even xenopathy, or any ability which was used to commit a crime. Most assuredly, there were severe penalties if an unregistered psi entered the military. She *was* registered, but it was hidden under the guise of her "official religion" being the Witan branch of Unigalactanism.

Membership in the Witan Order included automatic psychic training for all of its members, whether or not they had any registerable abilities to begin with—the training was included because *all* Humans had the ability to develop certain sixth senses to a small degree, with effort, though one had to be an actual psi genetically to develop anything stronger than natural gut instincts and so forth.

Psis who were willing to enter the military were too precious a commodity for most of them to be permitted to stay in the three combat Branches. Because of that, the entire Sixth Cordon of the Special Forces was devoted to psychic abilities and their potential for military application, and attached as auxiliaries to various other groupings in all four Branches. The Space Force insisted on using these abilities to the utmost. At least, according to what the Space Force believed that utmost should be.

The only problem with that was that the Special Forces Branch, the SF-SF, didn't really *train* their psis to be combat warriors, never mind combat leaders. They were too rare, too valuable, and too wrapped up in cotton wool. What Ia needed to do, she needed to do as a combat leader, with combat experience. More to the point, she needed the experience of using her abilities *in* battle, so deeply in the thick of it that they became just one more weapon in her arsenal. Not safely wielded from a sheltered distance, as the military would have it done.

I am not a gun, to be aimed and pointed and fired from a safe distance. I am the wielder *of the gun . . . and I also need to know how to turn my weapons into fists and knives when the enemy gets too close for guns.*

Turning away from the window, she jumped back, startled at how close one of her Squad mates had gotten without her noticing. Or would have jumped, if her weight suit hadn't kept her firmly on the ground. Nodding to Arstoll, she stepped around him. He handed his tray to the scullery staff, then caught her elbow. "Hey. Where did you learn all that stuff about boot chevrons and leadership? I've never heard it put quite that way."

Turning to face him allowed her to subtly free her elbow from his touch. "I might not come from a military background, but I did realize I needed to go into the military. I spent the last three years reading and studying everything I could get my hands on that was related to fighting, tactics, strategy, logistics, motivation, and leadership—from Sun Tzu to War King Kah'el, the battle tactics of Napoleon to the Dlmvla war-poem 'Room for the Dead.' If you can set aside what you only *think* you know about me, you and I just might have a lot more in common than you'd think."

He planted his hands on his hips. "Or we might have nothing in common at all."

"Except that we already do, Arstoll. We're both here, and we're both not running away." Nodding politely, Ia headed for the cafeteria counter. *That's the best I can do. The next move is up to him . . . but I think he won't rock the percentages. If everything goes as I've foreseen, he'll make a few more snide remarks, maybe grumble a bit when he doesn't get the position of Squad leader next . . . and then he'll probably settle down.* She snagged one of the apples from the fruit bin and bit into it, still hungry. *If nothing else, Hell Week—assuming I can survive it myself—should settle him down.*

Hell Week was her biggest immediate worry. While Ia could see most of the timestreams ahead of her, there were certain points that she just could not see clearly. The images in the waters were blurred, fogged over like a grey mist. Inscrutable. Nerve-wracking. As opaque as the flesh of the half-eaten apple in her hand.

Something would happen during Hell Week, something important. Either she would succeed and be able to move along with confidence, or she would sort of make it through, and have to work hard to regain lost ground. Which would be difficult, but not unattainable. But there was that one worrisome chance of failure. Of washing out of Basic Training.

Of failing the whole damn galaxy.

But that won't *happen. It's too low a probability. I refuse to fail.*

She didn't have a lot of time to get herself and everything else in place. Getting it right the first time around was her biggest concern.

The sound of the buzzer cut through the chatter in the large cafeteria. Finishing off the apple in three large bites, she tossed the core in the trash and joined her fellow recruits in lining up for the march to their afternoon classes.

CHAPTER 5

People join the military with a skewed idea of what it's actually like. We get fed images from vidshows and educational programs, but it's all been sanitized. Sure, certain games will try to imitate as much of the gore and violence as possible—to the point of gratuitous excess—but all those electronic warriors are already trained. Or, if not trained, they can be trained in just a couple of hours, or however long it takes their players to get used to the game interface.

Real military training isn't sanitized. They don't leave out the warnings of dire injury, maiming, and death by any means. But people who join the military expect to hear that. It goes in one ear and out the other. They even expect the rigorous physical training. What they aren't expecting is to be bored half to death by days and weeks of tedious, repetitive lectures and drills.

Unfortunately, it's necessary. Real combat isn't a game. You can't hit the escape code and turn it off. It'd be nice if we could, but we can't. So the military's job is to pound as much information into its recruits' heads as they can hold, and then pound it in even more, just to make sure it's wedged in tightly enough to stick. Even if most of it is stultifyingly, mind-numbingly boring to endure.

~Ia

MARCH 20, 2490 T.S.

"Congratulations, Class 7157," First Sergeant Tae drawled, surveying the men and women sitting, kneeling, and standing in an arc in front of him. They had been marched out to a new location this morning, the basic-level firing range. Sunlight angled in from the east, while clouds loomed to the north and west. "You have survived two whole weeks of the most basic, raw training. Despite my lingering reservations about the worthiness of most of you, the Marine Corps feels it is now time for you to learn how to shoot."

Flicking out his baton, the Drill Instructor pointed at the hover sled being guided into position by a buck sergeant. The woman unlocked the chest-like sled and pulled out a black-and-white, somewhat bulky rifle. Tae accepted it from her. Lifting the rifle, muzzle pointed up, he addressed the patiently waiting recruits.

"This here is the first weapon you will learn how to handle, the 40-MA, affectionately known as the 'Mama.' It is a military-grade stunner rifle, and it is designed to knock out most known forms of life via an electrosonic pulse-shock, which disrupts anything with a nervous system capable of responding to electrical and sonic stimuli. These pulses do not normally cause damage to surrounding terrain or buildings, so you will find the Mama is the most-often issued weapon in peacetime conditions.

"The Mama is not a long-range weapon, however." Lowering the weapon, he grasped a lever near the muzzle and ratcheted it, spiraling open the bulky white tip of the muzzle. Tae swept it slowly around, displaying the silvery interior. "Depending upon the width of the nosecone setting, at its widest, the Mama has an effective field width of 120 degrees, but the strength of the field at that width tapers off to uselessness after only ten meters at most."

A twist of the lever closed the cone-like tip.

"At its narrowest, it has a field width of fifteen degrees and an effective range of just fifty meters. Power settings can be set to knock out a humanoid-sized creature for as little as five minutes, or as long as a full Terran Standard hour. Because of these variations, do not make the mistake of thinking this is a simple weapon to operate. You may be able to point downrange and hit your assigned targets on your very first day, but the 40-MA has eight power settings and eight cone settings, for literally dozens of possible combinations. You will therefore learn how to gauge a situation and its appropriate settings accordingly over the length of your instruction."

Handing back the weapon, he accepted a thin, black, slightly curved box from the buck sergeant.

"The Mama is powered by a standard military energy pack, or e-clip for short. These e-clips are interchangeable with the power packs for the laser rifles." He accepted another weapon from the sergeant, this one painted in shades of brown camouflage. Lifting the weapon so its muzzle pointed into the sky, Tae displayed it as well. "This is the HK-70, military issue standard-sized laser rifle, also known as the 'Heck.' Like the Mama, it is deceptively simple to use. You will encounter several variations later on in your training, but the HK-70 is the one you will first learn to use, and use with great caution. Unlike the Mama, the Heck is a lethal weapon.

"A sustained burn from a Heck rifle can cut through most bulkheads, and its effective range is two *kilometers* in the SAC—short for Standard Atmospheric Conditions. That means you can still light the wick of a candle from two klicks away, *if* you can aim it accurately that far—and if you *can*, expect to be transferred to the Special Forces Sharpshooters division," he added bluntly. Handing back the laser rifle, Tae once again lifted the e-clip in his hand, displaying it to the waiting recruits. "The standard, interchangeable e-clip can power a Mama for roughly one hundred shots at maximum strength. It can power a Heck for one full Terran Standard minute at its highest setting of two kilocals. However, one kilocalorie per second is the normal operational setting, which will give you up to two minutes of pulsed laser fire, and of course longer in its normal operational capacity of short, carefully aimed bursts.

"Terran technology has managed to achieve a 67.19 percent energy conservation ratio in the HK-70, which is the highest crisp for your calorie you will find in a military-grade weapon this small. However, while you are still training in how to target and fire, you will be issued calorie-restricted weaponry. A full two minute's burn at ten meters *might* set a candle on fire . . . but I wouldn't count on it. The Heck also comes with a long-range scope, but constant use of the scope will drain the energy off your e-clip, so you will learn to target without it as well as with it."

Handing over the e-clip, he accepted the all-black weapon the supply sergeant dug out of the hover sled's depths. This weapon, Sgt. Tae made a visible production of checking over, first pointing it down at the ground and pulling back on the bolt lever to check the chamber, then pointing it just as carefully up in the air, never once aiming it at any particular person.

"*This* is the JL-39, affectionately called the 'Jelly.' Outside of your body and your wits—assuming you have any—it is the most versatile personal weapon you will ever use. Crafted from a composite of stainless steel and ceristeel, its gas-compression mechanism reduces the kick when firing even as it uses the force to auto-load the next cartridge, particularly during auto-fire. But it does *not* reduce the noise. When we get around to learning this one, you will be issued both earplugs and earphones to protect your hearing during practice sessions.

"The Jelly is also the most difficult weapon to learn, despite the fact that it has only two settings, single-shot and auto-fire, and thus is the simplest to operate mechanically of your three new best friends," Tae reminded them, gesturing at the other two rifles sitting on top of the hover sled beside him. "This is because the Jelly is a *projectile* weapon."

Handing it back, he accepted the handful of black boxes the buck sergeant passed to him. Lifting each one, their Drill Instructor displayed the symbols marked on each cartridge's side.

"The *versatility* of the Jelly comes from its ammunition. There are thirteen basic types of ammunition which the SF-MC uses. Most of the Jelly's cartridge clips, or c-clips for short, are preloaded at TUPSF munitions factories. The only kind that is not always found pre-loaded, though you will probably receive pre-loaded clips anyway, is what we like to call standards. The c-clips for standards have no designated markings to indicate their type.

"After that come the shotters, which are filled either with the larger buckshot or the smaller birdshot. These cartridges are modeled after shotgun ammunition and are used in a similar fashion. A laser beam or a standard bullet might hit or miss, depending on distance and aim, but a shotter shell gives you a broad range of attack which is guaranteed to put a serious crimp in the day of anything or anyone that isn't heavily armored. Shotter cartridges are marked by a scattering of white dots, small ones for birdshot and large ones for buckshot.

"Their biggest advantage is that whatever they hit, it'll hurt like a son-of-a-slag. Their biggest disadvantage is the SAC drag on each individual pellet, which reduces their effective range somewhat. Not by much, compared to the old shotguns of your ancestors, but enough to make a difference in a real fight.

"The next most common are the tracers, which can be found in *any* of the c-clip packets, as they are bullets treated with a phosphorescent coating which will flare up and illuminate the 'trace' or path of the bullets you are firing. These are usually used for nighttime activities, and the phosphorus bullets are spaced one in every four cartridges. Tracer c-clips are marked with a green diamond on the casing, which may be marked in conjunction with another identification mark for a particular type of ammunition. Once you are ready to start using the Jelly, you will be working with standard c-clips loaded with tracers so that you can see the flight-path of your shots. This means you will see a lot of these green diamonds on your clips.

"After tracers come the screamers, marked with concentric yellow arcs forming a cone shape," he continued, lifting each c-clip in question, "which whistle at a high-frequency pitch during flight, and are most often used in conjunction with echo-location scanners to provide sonar guidance in poor visibility conditions. Some of you will learn to use them in conjunction with your mechsuits. Taggers, marked with two concentric white circles, fire tracking devices, which can also be used with your mechsuit and other scanner equipment. Tracers, taggers, and screamers are all used for target location and placement purposes.

"The next group involves content-based attacks. Trankers are special darts filled with an anesthetic compound that will work on most forms of carbon-based oxygen-breathing life. Their effective range is the shortest of all c-clip ammunition, but they work for distances up to four times the length of the Mama's range, and their payload knocks their target unconscious for several hours at a time. They are marked with a blue feather. Stunners are like little beanbags crammed into a bullet cartridge; when fired, the cloth bag and its birdshot contents spread out and smack into the body of your target for a nonlethal and usually non-bloody knockback attack. I repeat, this is a knockback but *not* a knockout attack. You will recognize them by their blue-dotted rectangle.

"Trankers and stunners are followed by gassers; like the trankers, they deliver a knockout punch to their targets at longer ranges than the Mama can, but instead of a single target dart, they fire capsules which break open and spread out as a cloud, knocking out small groups of targets at a time. Naturally, gassers are marked by the green outline of a cloud.

"The last in this group are gaggers. Like gassers, they break open and deliver a gaseous payload . . . but unlike gassers, gaggers are poisonous and are capable of killing anything in their field of effect, particularly if you lay down enough of them in a small area. If they are used in thin saturation, gaggers will simply make your targets very, very sick. Feel free to question your orders if you are issued gagger c-clips, which are marked by a red *X* on the cartridge case.

"Splatters are controlled-expansion bullets; when they strike a hard surface, they spread out and stop. When they strike a soft surface, such as living flesh . . . the size of their entry hole is disproportionately small compared to their exit-hole. Unlike standards and shotters, splatters are designed to do as much tissue damage to a single target as possible without endangering too many other targets. Look for the grey mushroom shape on a splatter c-clip.

"In the same grouping as standards and splatters, we also have piercers, which are marked with a red triangle." Tae paused and gave his cadets a solemn, grim look. "If at *any* time you are issued piercers while in space, it is your *duty*, above and beyond obeying the orders of your superiors, to *question their issue*," he emphasized. "Piercers are sharp enough to pierce a standard ship *hull*, if you hit it in a thin or otherwise vulnerable spot. There may come a time when they *will* be issued deliberately; if they are and you have questioned your orders and received confirmation, make absolutely sure you, your fellow teammates, and all allied personnel within effective range are wearing lifesuits at the very least before opening fire with a red-triangle-marked c-clip full of piercers.

"Space is *not* the place for ammunition mistakes." Handing back the black c-clips with their various marks, he accepted two more c-clips. They were not black, however, unlike all the previous cases. One was a striped dun yellow and burnt orange just a little too bright to be mistaken for brown, the other a checkered bright orange and black. Lifting them, Tae displayed the distinctive cases. "The last two types of c-clip ammunition are the HEs and the SHEs . . . and as most sentient species will tell you, SHEs are more deadly than HEs."

For a moment, the normally sober, semi-grim sergeant smiled. It unnerved most of his recruits, Ia included. A few managed to chuckle, but that was all. Tae dropped the smile and continued their lecture.

"This is because HEs stand for High Explosives, and are marked by this striped yellow and orange c-clip casing. SHEs stand for Shrapnellated High Explosives, and are marked by this black and orange *checkered* casing. They are not only identifiable by sight, but also by a subtle difference in touch. Like the piercers and the gaggers, you should also question *any* orders to use these. HEs and SHEs can be used to pound through an interior bulkhead or a ship's hull, set cabins on fire, and blow up sentients, so make absolutely sure you question any orders which cause them to be issued to you while on board a spaceship. Just like gassers and gaggers, HEs and SHEs are capable of hitting not only your target, but others as well. Exploding with enough force to cover a diameter of up to nine meters in the SAC, they can hit your target's nearest neighbors, and potentially your own sweet self if you're close to your target. So be very careful where, how, and when you use 'em.

"Which brings me to the Four Fanaticals." Passing back the clips, Tae accepted the first weapon once more from the buck sergeant. Cradling the black-and-white bulk of the 40-MA stunner rifle, he met each recruit's gaze in turn as he continued. "The Four Fanaticals refer to the Rules of the Range. You will abide by these four rules at *all* times when handling all forms and sizes of projectile, laser, and stunner weaponry, whether they are rifles, handguns, mechsuit machinery, weapons mounted on your various modes of transport, or even the occasional infantry mortar.

"Rule One: Always point your weapon in a safe direction until you are ready to fire. Rule Two: Always assume your weapon is loaded and ready to fire until you yourself have personally inspected it . . . even if you just saw someone else inspect it and claim it to be safe before handing it over to you. Rule Three: Always keep your finger off the trigger until you are ready to fire. Don't mess around with it even as a joke, particularly in conjunction with Rule One. And Rule Four: Always be aware of what is downrange of your target, in case you miss. Failure to follow the First and Third Fanaticals can result in being charged with Fatality Thirteen, 'Friendly Fire,' as can failure to be aware of the consequences of Rule Four.

"Remember, the effective range of the Heck is two full *kilometers* in the SAC. If you miss your enemy in the foreground, you could end up scorching a civilian somewhere down the road. Or hitting the hull of a ship, or the edge of a dome. It's not one hundred percent likely that you may cause harm from that far way, but it *is* possible. It is *very* possible if your inadvertent target is situated somewhere close behind your missed target . . . and you *can* be held responsible for whatever you do in a misfire situation."

Accepting the e-clip the buck sergeant held out to him, Tae slotted it home in its socket on the back of the rifle. He flicked the power switch, letting the weapon warm up audibly. He also cranked the nozzle from narrow to wide, though he kept it pointed up into the sky.

"Remember: Always point your weapon in a safe direction until ready to fire. Always assume the weapon is loaded until you yourself have checked. Always be aware of what is downrange of your target. And always keep your finger off the trigger until you are ready to fire."

Snapping the weapon down, he pumped the trigger, spraying the startled recruits with a *zzzzzt* of white-flashing electrosonic static . . . all who were within the 120-degree range of the wide-open cone and its accompanying ten-meter maximum range. All who had been lulled into complacency by his long-winded display of all that weaponry.

Bodies slumped to the ground.

B and C Squads, sitting in the front rows, simply toppled over to one side or the other, since they were already seated. D and E Squads, caught kneeling behind the other two, flopped over as well. A Squadron, standing at the back of the group, crumpled from soles to heads. They landed in a tangled jumble on the dusty ground of the firing range, some on top of each other, some at awkward angles which would be uncomfortable upon awakening, whenever the effects the stunner rifle wore off.

Caught off guard by the sudden attack, Ia forgot to slump as well. Frozen by surprise, but still trapped by it, she swayed a little as Mendez's slumping body bumped against her shins. She almost dropped herself on top of him a moment later, but knew it was too late. Both Tae and the buck sergeant were already staring at her. Blushing, she cleared her throat and remained on her feet, hands clasped behind her back in the At-Ease position they had all learned in their first three days of training.

Frowning, the first sergeant checked the settings on his rifle. Lifting it, he shot her again with another flash of white. Unfortunately, it was still too late.

Knowing the damage was done—but believing it was correctable—Ia didn't bother to fake unconsciousness. She just stood there while Tae frowned, ratcheted the cone narrow enough to single-target her, did something to its power setting, and fired again, this time aiming high enough that the white pulse-beam avoided the others. The tightly narrowed field tingled against her face and shoulders as the pulse passed through her, but did nothing to knock her over.

Scowling, he lowered the weapon, pointing it at the ground. "Why the *hell* didn't you fall down, Recruit?"

Her only recourse was to tell the truth. At least a small, palatable part of it. Meeting his glare steadily, Ia gave him the portion of the truth he could handle. "Sergeant, this recruit is from Sanctuary. That's why this recruit did not fall down like the others, Sergeant."

"Explain yourself," he ordered. The wind, a soft breeze until now, gusted a bit, tugging at the brims of their hats. She could smell the faint sting of ozone, like a taste of home. Reminded of what she had given up, Ia did her best to explain.

"Sergeant, Sanctuary has a core comprised of both molten

iron and gold. This combination not only creates a magnetosphere capable of shielding its surface from the usual dangers of cosmic radiation, it also creates an *electrosphere*. An inherent electrical field," she told both sergeants. "The planet Earth, Motherworld of the Human species, averages about one thousand lightning strikes per second across its entire surface. Including that storm in the distance. Sanctuary averages twelve *million* per second, Sergeant."

The buck sergeant spoke up, her freckled brow furrowed in confusion. "How does *that* keep you from falling down under stunner fire?"

"Sergeant, by the second generation of colonization, after being constantly exposed to the prevalent static charges of the daily lightning storms, a few of us have already developed a certain resistance to strong electrical shocks. Some more than others, obviously," Ia added dryly. "This recruit is fairly certain that is the reason why the stunner field didn't work, Sergeant. At least, there is no other reasonable explanation which this recruit could offer, Sergeant."

The real truth was, the only two who *had* developed that level of resistance already were herself and her older half brother, Thorne. The others back home wouldn't develop it for another two or three generations at the earliest. *Why* she couldn't be shocked was a secret she herself had only discovered by carefully tracing the timestreams into the past. But being honest about the fact that only she and her elder brother were fully resistant would only open up a host of extremely dangerous questions right now. So Ia kept her mouth shut on that part.

"Shova v'shakk," Tae growled, glaring at her. "I haven't heard *any* such thing."

"Sergeant, this recruit is not surprised you haven't heard anything, Sergeant," Ia allowed. "Stunners have been banned from Sanctuary since our colonists first explored it more than half a century ago, Sergeant."

"Why would they be banned?" the buck sergeant asked, tugging her hat a little lower against the gusting breeze. "Stunner weaponry is standard equipment on all survey missions, in case the surveyors encounter a potentially sentient life-form."

"Sergeant, because of Sanctuary's natural electrosphere, any stunner weapon fired on Sanctuary will automatically malfunction," Ia explained patiently. "Seven out of ten times, Sergeant, that 'malfunction' manifests as static lightning striking whoever or whatever is holding the stunner gun. Two out of ten times, it will strike the target, and the remaining one in ten times, lightning will strike either both parties, or somewhere in between. The lethality of these malfunctions has caused the weapon to be permanently banned from use on the surface of this recruit's homeworld.

"Additionally, testing in the early days of colonization showed that the natural prevalence of the static field can even trigger an *indoor* lightning attack, so stunner weaponry isn't used inside buildings. It isn't allowed to be used *beneath* the surface of the planet, either, because that same electrosphere goes straight down to the planet's core," she added. The third person referencing was wearisome, but she knew she had to wade through it, or risk unnecessary demerits. "While this recruit has never before been shot by a stunner weapon, this recruit did know about the results of those early difficulties, as they were included in the standard Sanctuarian colonial history curriculum. From there, it was easy enough to extrapolate the most probable cause as to why this recruit did not fall down, Sergeant."

He stared at her. Finally, his thumb moved, snapping off the power supply to the rifle in his arms. Pulling out the e-clip, Tae handed both pieces back to his assistant. "What am I going to do with you, Recruit?"

"Sergeant?" Ia asked, not sure what he meant. She stayed where she was as he approached, unable to retreat thanks to the fallen, slumbering bodies of her fellow recruits. The tall bulk of Mendez had landed across her feet, pinning her partly in place, though she could have picked her way free had she really tried. But she didn't move.

He rested his fists on his hips, studying her. "You are *good*. In fact, you act like you've *been* a soldier before. I don't trust that."

"Sergeant . . . permission to speak both freely and directly, Sergeant?" Ia asked, mindful of the passing of time. In the distance, the thunderheads swelling along the horizon were starting to darken ominously along their bases.

"Granted."

She lifted her chin a little and spread her hands, shrugging.

"I have found the place I need to be, Sergeant Tae. I'm just doing my best to fit in. If that makes me a good soldier even this early in my training, then it only supports my theory that I do indeed belong here. To try anything less than my best would be an insult to the Space Force, to the Marine Corps, and to my own sense of duty and proper effort."

He studied her a moment longer, glanced at the buck sergeant, then sighed roughly. "You do realize I'll now have to go *three* times as hard on you with *that* little confession, just to break you down and build you up the right way?"

"That's your job, Sergeant," Ia acknowledged. "I won't hold it against you."

His mouth tightened. He looked like he wanted to say something more, but a couple of the fallen recruits were beginning to stir. Glancing at the buck sergeant, Tae sighed again. "Well. Looks like I'll have to haul out the hovercams for the days ahead."

Not sure what he meant, Ia dipped quickly into the timestreams. Not strongly enough to lose her sense of the world around her, but enough to learn he meant using a hovercamera to record everything he would make her do, to make sure there were no infractions of just what he *could* do to her, and what he couldn't, or shouldn't.

Mendez roused, shifting off her feet with a grumbling moan. He rubbed at his head, then squinted at the other bodies, more of whom were stirring. Twisting his body, he peered up at Ia. "What . . . what happened?"

Ia glanced at Tae briefly before answering under her breath. "Sergeant Tae, in his infinite wisdom, decided to stun all of us."

"He what?" Mendez accepted the hand she offered him, helping him to his feet. Others were rousing as well, most of them grumbling or groaning as they regained their senses. "He stunned all of us? That's why we all fell down?"

She didn't bother to correct the impression that she had fallen down, too. It wouldn't do to give the others—particularly Arstoll—even more reason to resent her.

After everyone had roused, while they were still milling around, trying to make sense of what had just happened, Tae spoke. His words cut through their mutterings, some of it increasingly angry for having been attacked without warning. "Back into your places, Recruits!"

His snapped command made them shuffle back into position, with the two front rows sitting, the next two kneeling, and the last standing. All of them did so quietly except for Kaimong, who continued to curse under his breath.

"Recruit Kaimong!" Sgt. Tae snapped. "Twenty sit-ups for attitude! Recruit Lackland, sit on his feet."

Glaring, Kaimong rocked onto his back while the other young man shifted over, weighting down his feet for the sit-ups. As soon as he was done counting out his demerits in grunts, Tae continued.

"Some of you may be wondering why I stunned you. That's because *most* of you don't take stunner technology seriously. It may not be a *directly* lethal weapon, but if the enemy knocks you out, they *can* and *will* use your helpless state of unconsciousness to close in and finish you off. Stunner fire can also prove lethal if it knocks you off the edge of a bridge, a cliff, or a building, or even while driving a vehicle, just to name a few examples," Tae reminded them. "Stunners are *weapons*, not toys, and you will treat them with all the care, gravity, and safety precautions that fact requires.

"With that in mind, you will move on to learning how to properly and safely handle the 40-MA. You will learn how to load, charge, operate, safely fire, disassemble, clean, and reassemble the Mama stunner rifle. These are the parts of the . . ."

Reality dropped away from her with a jolt. Dumped into the timeplains, Ia blinked and spun around, quickly orienting herself in the sepia-toned world inside her mind. Glancing down, she peered into the waters intersecting like vine-shaped rivulets. Her gifts didn't activate this abruptly unless there was something she needed to see. Something which would change the course of the future, unless she acted upon it.

There—in Kaimong's water! Leaning over his stream, she tried to make sense of what she saw.

He . . . just stepped forward with the rest of E Squad, helping the buck sergeant to pass out the black-and-white rifles . . . then people fell down a few moments later. But that shouldn't have worked; the rifles didn't have e-clips yet. I can't see from up here . . . ugh!

Gritting her teeth, Ia stepped into the water. She let the flow of his future life soak up into her senses until she *was* Wong Ta Kaimong . . . mad and hurt and vengeful.

. . . There—I'll get that e-clip while the bitch is looking the other way . . . cover it up with this . . . I've had enough of this shakk—if this is what a "respectable citizen" has to put up with, I'd rather take my chances with organized crime—and I'll grab that laser rifle along with the projectile one while I'm at it, just in case anyone decides to—

". . . Recruit Ia!"

Jolted back into awareness, Ia blinked and swayed back from the tilted brim of Sergeant Tae's hat, which threatened to knock against her own brim, given the upward jut of his chin. "Sergeant, yes, Sergeant?"

"Were you *not* paying attention to me, just now?" he demanded, glaring at her.

A lightning-fast dip into the timestreams—*her* timestream, and nowhere near the same level of immersion she had used in looking into Kaimong's future—showed that this, too, could be salvaged. "Sergeant, no, Sergeant!"

"You . . . what?" he rasped.

Carefully, she flicked her gaze to her right, where the majority of the other recruits stood, then looked back at him. And even more carefully winked, very briefly, with her left eye. The one farthest away from the others. *Come on, Sergeant,* she coaxed silently, though not through actual telepathy—she didn't possess that particular gift in any real strength. *Think. You want to be harder on me than the others, but neither of us really want them knowing what you now know . . .*

She flicked her gaze to her right again for just a little bit longer, then returned it to him. Comprehension dawned in his dark brown eyes. The merest hint of a smile ghosted across the corner of his lips then flicked down into a scowl. Reaching up, Tae ripped her chevron patch from her shoulder. "I am *demoting* you from boot chevrons, Recruit! And twenty—no, *forty* push-ups for failing to pay attention, too! Move to the far end of your Squad's line as soon as you are through. Recruit Mendez, *you* are now the leader of A Squad."

Mendez accepted the patch, then hesitated and looked at Ia, who had dropped to the floor. Over her steady counting of her demerits, she heard him ask, "Sergeant . . . does this new Squad leader have to do the same forty push-ups of Recruit Ia's demerits, Sergeant?"

It was a fair question; all of the current Squad leaders had undergone similar extended punishments.

"No. Not this time. From now on, fancy-pants Recruit Ia rises or falls on her *own*. But you will still have to undergo the same punishments as anyone else in your Squad in the future, should they be so foolish as to earn demerit punishments, too. You will learn how to evoke discipline and obedience in your fellow recruits. One way or another. Speaking of which, it's about time for the *rest* of you Squad leaders to have a change in status . . . though *you* don't have to do any push-ups."

By the time Ia finished counting firmly to forty, all of the boot chevrons had been reassigned. The thunderstorm in the distance was drifting closer, too, though it was still many kilometers off. Only the occasional flash of lightning let them know a storm was taking place at all; the clouds were still too far away for the accompanying thunder to be heard.

Righting herself, she rubbed at her sore arms around the bulk of the tile-weighted straps webbing her limbs, then accepted the stunner rifle Kumanei passed her way. It didn't take her long to walk to the far end of A Squad. Without immersing herself quite so deeply in the timestreams, Ia probed the near future as she walked. She didn't want to be caught off guard by whatever Kaimong was about to do.

A stunner rifle clattered to the ground. Tae rounded on the fumble-fingered Kaimong, berating him for dropping his weapon and assigning him fifteen push-ups. Ia caught Kaimong's glare only because she was watching carefully. It was aimed at Tae's back as the Drill Instructor moved on to the next recruit in the line, making sure she could name all the parts of the rifle in her hands.

I hate this part, Ia thought, checking over her own rifle to re-familiarize herself with the things she had learned precognitively over the last three years. *I hate the waiting, and I hate the fact that I cannot tell anyone what's about to happen. That would expose me. And if I tried to ask Tae to go easy on Kaimong, he'd go even harder on both of us.*

I have no control over how much hatred is building up inside of my fellow recruit . . . and I hate that. I hate that I won't be able to stop him. Not without drawing too many questions.

Her life was a damned tightrope walk. Damned if she didn't walk it, and damned if she did and then slipped. It didn't matter to which side; the fall would be deadly to far too many for her conscience to bear.

Fall away, Kaimong, she thought, wincing a little as Tae heaped more abuse on him for being too slow. *My only comfort is, all of this is for a good cause. I'm sorry I can't tell you that it is worthwhile, or how, or why.*

They practiced ratcheting the nozzles wider and narrower, dialing up the settings and dialing them back down, adjusting the positions of their hands for the grips and the fit of the stocks to their shoulders. They practiced fieldstripping the rifles for cleaning and maintenance, spreading out and sitting on the ground "to simulate real-world conditions," and putting them back together again. Some of the recruits were berated and assigned demerit exercises for doing things wrong, then shown how to do them the right way. Then they all stood up again and spread out to practice dry-firing the weapons.

The supply sergeant, introduced as Buck Sergeant Johannez, went from recruit to recruit, the same as Tae, offering tips and adjusting stances as they lined up along the firing range, with its holographic targeting arches, and practiced aiming down the barrels. Since the 40-MA had a limited range and a wide firing field, the rifles didn't have targeting scopes, but they were told to practice sighting down the somewhat bulky weapons anyway. The wind had gone back to gusting, making it a little harder to sight along the barrels in the face of the occasional speck of grit, but they persevered.

Ia spent slightly more than half of her attention on matching her actions to her memories of future stunner rifle use, and on pre-echoing her movements by skimming the timestreams just a few seconds ahead of what she was actually doing. She kept an eye and an ear out for the sergeants, not wanting to get caught timeplains woolgathering again, but practiced dipping into the waters of the near future all the same.

This was something that precognitive psis in the Special Forces did not do; accurate precogs were considered too important to risk in a combat situation. Unfortunately, that left very few of them capable of concentrating in chaotic conditions, where split-second choices could mean the difference between life and death for dozens, even thousands of lives. It was something she herself had tried to simulate with her brothers, but which she knew had to be tested and practiced under actual combat conditions. In the future, too many lives would depend on *her* ability to concentrate, and . . .

And anticipate problems. Tae ordered them to gather around the supply sled and accept the e-clips being handed out. She *sensed* Kaimong's decision just three seconds before he actually decided it. Though she couldn't *see* him palming the e-clip as he helpfully assisted Sergeant Johannez, she knew it was done. She didn't hear him slotting it in place, and the faint whine of the weapon charging wasn't audible over the chatter of the others cracking jokes and making comments about finally getting the chance to shoot at something.

From warning to theft to loading and charging was at most maybe ten seconds. Just enough time for her to step behind some of the others, placing several bodies between her and the angriest member of E Squad.

With the cone of his rifle ratcheted wide and the dial turned to maximum, Kaimong whirled and shot Sergeant Tae, then spun back and shot Sergeant Johannez and half of his fellow recruits. He fired again, *zzzzzt*-spraying men and women who were only just that moment realizing something was happening.

Ia dropped to the ground, rolling her spine as a good Sanctuarian should. Not that the lightworld gravity was a problem, but the tiles of her weight suit did leave bruises. Eyes closed, body slumped as limply as she could fake, she listened to the sound-sting of the stunner rifle firing a few times more. Dangling her mental fingers in his timestream, she looked for the coming impulse in his thoughts.

V'shakk this . . . I'm going to blow their slagging heads off!

Now. Straining her mind, since this was not one of her strongest gifts, Ia inserted a thought into his head.

Wait—no, if I did that, Ia coaxed, matching her thought-tone to his, *they'd* never *stop hunting me. Just stun 'em a few more times at max power. That'll keep 'em off my back long enough to get away . . .*

. . . Heh. Yeah, he thought next on his own, *I'll just* pretend *this is one of those fancy High Explosive bullets.*

Relieved that it worked, Ia relaxed further, though she kept part of her attention on the pre-echoes of his impending thoughts.

Zzzzzzt! . . . Zzzzt . . . Methodically, she heard him zapping the whole group several times over, including herself before he finally stopped. Even when he fired at her point-blank, all she felt was a tickle of energy and a lingering little buzz. Like chugging a cooled mug of caf' in one go.

"*Shakk* this," she heard Kaimong mutter out loud. She also heard something small but hard hitting the ground, and knew he had removed his military wrist unit. Removing the easiest thing pursuers could use to track him. "*Shakk all* of this! Aloha, you wastetards!"

His boots crunched across the trampled ground. Ia stayed where she was, as motionless on the outside as the others. Inside, she dipped deeper into the timestreams, looking for the possible outcomes of his AWOL attempt, and the most probable results if she just let him go, or tried any of several things to stop him.

One of the possibilities caught her attention. Not because it was the right thing to do—it was—but because of the consequences it would have on the near future. *This . . . I need to do this. This is what makes the right path run deeper and stronger for me.*

Cracking open her eyes, she cautiously checked what she could see of her surroundings, and permitted herself a tiny smile. Drawing in a deep breath, Ia sat up, worked a kink out of her neck from the fall, then started unsnapping her weight suit. Given the direction Kaimong had chosen versus the angle she had placed herself, if he tried looking back this way through the scope of one of his stolen rifles, he would only see the range targets, the fallen bodies, and the sled, the bulk of which hid her position.

Still, she took her time, readying herself for pursuit. She borrowed some of the water from Mendez's canteen since he, too, was close enough to be hidden by the bulk of the hover sled, filling hers to the brim, then carefully checked the time-plains to make sure it was safe for her to move away from her source of cover.

Yes . . . he's deep enough in the bush now, he's no longer looking back through the scope on his laser rifle to see if he's being pursued. Good. Now I can hunt him down.

Checking her stunner rifle to make sure her fall hadn't damaged it, she grabbed one of the e-clips which hadn't made it to her end of the group before Kaimong had made his move. As ready as she could be, Ia flipped up the panel hiding the comm unit on her ident and punched in the code for the emergency channel.

"This is Recruit Ia, Class 7157, out on the basic targeting range. Recruit Wong Ta Kaimong has stunned the rest of my class and taken himself and several weapons into the bush. I repeat, Recruit Wong Ta Kaimong, Class 7157, is AWOL, armed, and in the bush."

The screen on the inside of the lid flicked to light, showing a frowning man in camouflage Browns, the black-and-white lettered badge of the MPs, Military Peacekeepers, visible above the brim of his cap. "Repeat that, Recruit . . . Ia, is it?"

"This is Recruit Ia, Sergeant. Recruit Wong Ta Kaimong, Class 7157, loaded an unrestricted e-clip into his 40-MA without orders, and fired it at everyone out here on the basic firing range. He stunned the entire training class, Sergeant, the instructors included," Ia explained. She grabbed at the brim of her hat with her free hand as another gust of wind whipped across the range. "From what I can tell, he took the HK-70 and the JL-39. I don't know if he took his 40-MA, but I do know at least those two weapons are missing, along with what looks like a couple of the c- and e-clips, though I can't tell for sure which ones, just yet."

The sergeant on the other end of the comm link glanced to the side. "The security grid is showing his location is at the training grounds, Recruit. If this is a crank call . . ."

"Sergeant, he *took off* his ident unit." Crossing the ground, she picked up the abandoned curve of brown plexi and held it up to her screen pickups long enough to show the serial number stamped along the outer edge by the hinge. "Recruit Kaimong discarded his unit, the Heck and the Jelly are missing, and according to my chrono, he's been gone for at least twenty minutes now, Sergeant."

"You say he stunned your class. Why isn't your DI reporting this incident, if you're awake?"

She didn't bother to explain about her Sanctuarian resistance. They didn't need to waste time arguing about it right now. "I was behind several others when he attacked, and I only got a partial shot. Sergeant Tae and the rest are still out cold. I think Recruit Kaimong gave them a full dose. Look, the storm is kicking up, but it's still hot enough to mask his heat signature from easy spotting, if you don't know which way he went. The wind will also blow over all the traces he's making in the bush if we don't hurry, and any rainfall will wash out the rest. I'm a second-gen firstworlder, Sergeant. I can track him, and you can track me.

"By now, he's probably a klick and a half into the bush," she added. "I can at least get you a head start on narrowing down which way he went, Sergeant. Requesting permission to track Recruit Kaimong on foot."

"Second-gen firstworlder, you said?" the sergeant asked her.

"Sergeant, yes, Sergeant. Third best in my survival classes."

He leaned out of range of the pickups for a moment, then came back. "Permission granted, Recruit. Just make sure *you* don't go AWOL. We'll follow with air support as soon as we can get a team lifted—and keep your comm active!"

"Understood, Sergeant. I'm on my way."

Dropping the discarded plexi bracelet, Ia launched herself in the direction Kaimong had fled. Heavyworlder muscles flexing freely, no longer burdened by the mass of her weight suit, she cleared the west half of the firing range in a scant handful of seconds. The bare grass bordering the firing range passed by as a green blur in just a few seconds more.

Eyes fixed firmly on both the terrain and the future, Ia dove into the rough, tangled foliage of the Australian bush.

CHAPTER 6

Prior to the reform movements, which took place shortly before the inception of the Terran Space Force, discipline in the various military structures scattered across the pre-unification nations had slowly deteriorated to the point of being inadequate at best, and counterproductive at worst. After the TUPSF's inception, in order to meet the pressing need for massive enlistments which the Sulik War required, it was reluctantly decided to instigate corporal punishments as a means of keeping so many recruits carefully in line. There literally were times where there weren't enough cadre to properly oversee discipline among the new recruits by using just the usual methods from the previous military systems.

To the surprise of almost everyone—except for perhaps the most learned and philosophical of military historians, who remembered the ways of the ancient Prussians—corporal discipline was actually instrumental in shaping the Terran United Planets Space Force into the toughest, most highly effective fighting force the Interstellar Alliance had ever seen. To this day, it is mandatory for all new Space Force recruits to see at least one administration of corporal discipline as punishment for unlawful conduct before their particular Class can officially graduate. Even if the convicted soldier must be shipped all the way across the known galaxy

*to a particular training Camp, they are required to witness
it—but then again, with literally two billion people enlisted
in the Space Force, there are unfortunately enough idiots
breaking the rules and regs every day, and breaking them
badly, to supply enough examples.*

*For myself and my Marine classmates, we witnessed an
incident which didn't have to be shipped anywhere. It happened right there at Camp Nallibong, Australia Province,
at the start of our third week of training.*

~Ia

Kaimong managed to get farther through the bush than Ia would
have expected, if she hadn't had that brush with precognitive
knowledge on her side. He had also drifted a bit to the north,
and had stumbled upon a ravine sloping down toward the swamp
flats to the north and west. And he had discovered the laser
rifle had a calorie restrictor on it.

She found the proof of it at the bottom of the ravine, where
rainwater seeping through the local limestone rocks had col-
lected into the beginnings of a pool-fed stream. The skin of
the saltwater crocodile's head had been scorched in several
hastily applied lines before he had apparently switched weapons and shot it with a HE cartridge, blowing chunks out of the
animal's side.

He hadn't discarded the rifle, though. That worried her.
Unless she wanted to take the time to submerse herself in the
past through her somewhat weaker postcognitive gift, she didn't
know if it was because he feared someone finding the gun and
realizing they were on the right course to track him down, or
if he just wanted to carry it along until he could find and break
the restrictor so that he could use the rifle fully—on who or
what, she didn't know, and didn't want to know.

The uncertainty of just how dangerous he really was warred
with her trust in the timestreams. There was a chance *she* could
get shot and injured, particularly since he probably still had
the clip of High Explosives loaded in his projectile rifle. She
probably *could* avoid his attacks; Ia had trained in jungles just
as thick as this one back home, albeit in a more temperate setting than this near-tropical climate.

A faint humming sound echoed down through the ravine behind her, barely audible over the rustling of the windblown leaves. In the same moment, her precognition twinged. It didn't drop her into the timestreams, but it did warn her that the hovercamera now buzzing over the dead saltie, examining its unnatural wounds, had just been spotted by their mutual quarry somewhere up ahead.

A moment later, the humming grew louder. Sinking onto her heels to further hide herself in the bush, Ia waited for the camera. It swooped into view, circled around in front of her, and flicked on its vidscreen. The same sergeant from before appeared on the small rectangle, along with a projection of his voice.

"Good job, Recruit Ia. Looks like you've found his work. Other cameras are converging on your coordinates, and hovercars are en route. We'll take—"

"Shhh!" Snapping her gaze to the side, she peered cautiously around the hovering machine, then pulled back. "Something moved," she whispered. Lifting two fingers into the camera's view, she flicked them to the side, then out to the north. "Take it west about twenty meters, then scout ahead to the north."

The man on the screen eyed her dubiously. She kept her gaze ahead, crouching a little lower and peering more to the side. Lifting the remote-controlled craft, he guided it up over her and to her left, zooming out the requested distance. Waiting just a moment or two more, Ia started crawling through the underbrush, moving as quickly but quietly as she could manage.

Half a minute later, gunfire broke the storm-rustled forest with a *pop pop BANG BANG pop BANG*. It was followed by the sound of something heavy crashing to the ground. Grinning to herself, she scuttled forward. Two more hovercameras swooped down out of the sky, circling around the wreckage of the first one before darting forward, looking for their quarry.

More gunfire erupted, though Kaimong's efforts at shooting the now bobbing and weaving hovercameras only dented one of them, sending it wobbling through the canopy for a few meters before it righted itself. Crawling past the twisted metal and plexi of the downed camera, she reached the edge of another ragged slope, one of several terraces separating the uplands from the swamp flats in the local stretch of bush. A twist pulled her own rifle into position, a flick warmed it up, and a crank of the nozzle and dial made sure it was on its tightest, highest setting. Ia knew she would only have a couple chances at taking him down, shots that would have to take place a lot closer on her end than his own weapon's range.

There. Movement from two directions alerted her to his position. One from Kaimong himself, a blur of brown dodging between two trees, and the other from one of the two new hovercameras, angling through the canopy as it followed him. Humming from her right warned her that the third camera had oriented on her own position.

"Recruit Ia—"

"Keep him occupied, Sergeant!" Ia hissed, flicking the safety on her gun so that it wouldn't fire accidentally. Not because it would bother her if she accidentally shot herself in the leg with the stunner rifle, but because part of her was operating via the habits instilled in the future, where the soldier she would become would always flick the safety on her gun so that no one else could be stunned. She slung it down under her shoulder, out of the way, and lifted her chin at the trees below. "I think I can get a shot down there."

"Recruit, this is not your jurisdiction. You are out of range, and out—"

Ia dove into the dirt as gunfire exploded again, this time with several *pow-BANG*s from the explosive bullets hitting the hillside right below her position. The stench of explosive stung her nose and watered her eyes, mixing with the earthy scent of the dirt-covered rock giving her a modicum of shelter from below.

"Distract him!" she hissed at the hovercamera, tugging her hat lower on her head. "He *knows* I'm up here, and that *makes* me a target either way! Get him to look the other way, and I'll take him down. *You* can't do that just yet."

The camera swerved away after a moment and soared out over the next broad ledge of land. Scrambling back, Ia gauged herself in the timestreams. A deep breath calmed her mind and steadied her nerves, allowing her enough mental room to connect with the successful path for what she wanted to do. Ready, she scrambled to her feet and sprinted off the edge of the sloping cliff, leaping as hard as she could for the trees below her.

Ia fell both out and down in the light gravity. She ignored the scratch and scrape of passing foliage, focused firmly on her landing. Using the tree limbs' suppleness to slow her crackling, bush-crashing fall, Ia dropped the last twenty feet without any support from the surrounding bush.

She did so just as Kaimong stopped shooting at the battered cameras buzzing him. Clearly aware of her descent, he twisted to fire in her direction instead. Hitting the muddy ground by the bank of the stream, Ia rolled in a controlled, compact tumble to absorb the impact.

Pulling her rifle up into position the moment she uncurled, Ia flicked the safety and sighted down the barrel, popping up less than five meters from his position. Her trust in her precognition kept her rock-steady as he fired once, twice, banging shots which went just wild from the poor aim of his haste to avoid her—in fact, if she had moved out of their way in the attempt to dodge, she would have moved *into* their way, as each cartridge *whizzed* past on either side of her. Without flinching, she pulled the trigger. So did he.

Zzzzzzt—Bang-POW!

Gunpowder stung her eyes, blurring her vision. She couldn't see Kaimong, only hear him faintly over the pounding of her heart as he *thumped* to the forest floor. He had missed again, the third miniature grenade cartridge hitting the bushes somewhere beyond her in a spray of exploding leaves and dirt.

Freed from the press of Time to pay attention to the little things, Ia sagged to the ground much more slowly than Kaimong did. He flopped onto his side with a sigh; she sagged to her knees with a groan. Heart pounding, lungs heaving, she carefully switched off the stunner rifle in her arms. The last thing she wanted to do was accidentally stun herself, now that the post-combat shakes were setting in.

Not that she would fall unconscious, but she really didn't need to add any more energy to her already buzzing nerves. *And I can blame my father for* that *lovely fact . . .*

One of the cameras swooped over the clearing, recording and cataloguing the damage caused by the brief fight. The other glided up to Ia. The tiny image of the sergeant spoke again.

"Good job, Recruit. Unorthodox, but effective. You *should* have waited for the MPs to take care of the problem, however."

Lifting her hand, Ia gestured at Kaimong's quiescent form. "I had the shot, Sergeant, so I took it. If I hadn't, he would have gone on shooting at Space Force equipment, and probably at the MPs once they arrived. I'll point out, he did fire at my own location at the top of the cliff just now." Bracing her hand on her thigh, she looked into the vidscreen's pickups. "I've shot him at full stunner strength, so he should be out for an hour. Would you like me to secure his weapons, Sergeant, just in case he's faking?"

The sound of a hover vehicle approached from behind her, more of a deep thrum than a hum. The sergeant on the camera screen negated her offer. "MPs are arriving on the scene, ETA forty seconds. We will secure the weaponry. Unclip and surrender your weapon, Recruit Ia. Technically, *neither* of you are fully authorized to wield a weapon for combat at this point in your training."

"Sergeant, yes, Sergeant." Pulling the e-clip from the butt of the rifle, she waited while the Peacekeeper craft settled into a stationary hover over the tangle of bushes and trees.

There wasn't enough room for the sturdy, brown-mottled craft to land, but there was enough room for two soldiers to lower a basket stretcher out of the vehicle, then rappel down to the ground beside it. As they fell, so did several drops of rain from the approaching storm. The humidity thickened palpably, while the temperature dropped a few degrees.

Glad that the first half of this incident was over, Ia surrendered her weapon without complaint and followed the MPs' order to climb on up while they hauled Kaimong's limp, slumbering body into the basket.

———

General Tackett finished his circling visual inspection of the young woman standing At Attention in his office. "Recruit Ia. Why did you choose to go after Recruit Kaimong?"

She kept her shoulders back and her gaze forward, her words crisp and her tone respectful. "General, upon realizing that Recruit Kaimong had taken the HK-70 and the JL-39, this recruit feared for the safety of any unwitting personnel, civilian or military, who might cross paths with the AWOL recruit, sir. This recruit knew that without his military ident, Recruit

Kaimong would be difficult to track from the air, and feared that it was possible for Recruit Kaimong to get farther than anticipated, a fear which proved true. This recruit had the skills and the immediate proximity to track his progress through the bush, assisting in the rapid recovery of the AWOL recruit, sir.

"There was even a possibility that the AWOL Recruit Kaimong would be able to evade pursuit long enough to leave the Camp grounds. This recruit felt that the risk to other, unsuspecting lives was unacceptable, while the risk to this own recruit's prepared-in-advance person was proportionately small and thus negligible in the face of all the greater risks to potential others, sir."

"You are barely past your second week of training, Recruit Ia. What made you think you were 'prepared in advance' for whatever your fellow recruit might do?" the Camp commander inquired.

"General, sir, preparedness in advance meant that this recruit already knew her fellow recruit was armed and therefore dangerous. This recruit knew the general direction her fellow recruit had fled. This recruit has studied Northern Territories flora and fauna in advance of enlistment, to be prepared to deal with said local flora and fauna, sir. Knowledge, skills, proximity, and heavyworlder abilities all combined to give this recruit a clear and undeniable advantage for locating and securing the AWOL recruit for neutralization as swiftly as possible, sir."

Tackett started circling her again. Ia resisted the urge to follow him as he moved. Instead, she kept her gaze on the blue and gold seal of the Terran United Planets, depicting the main continents of the Motherworld on a grid-divided, elongated, oval map. Instead of being surrounded by the laurel wreath of peace, the Robinson projection of the Earth's surface was mounted over the crossed, curve-bladed sabers of the Marines. He seemed to be waiting for more information, so she gave it to him, eyes fixed on the golden star representing the capital of the Terran United Planets, Aloha City.

"General, this recruit was trained thoroughly in the basics of colonyworld survival principles, which are applicable to a number of other relevant, inhabitable M-class planets, sir, and which include movement through inimical surroundings of uncertain terrain features and foliage. This recruit also paid careful attention to our given instructions on how to handle and wield the 40-MA stunner rifle, and was prepared to wield it appropriately, sir. Which this recruit did, sir."

"Right. Now, explain how you ended up unaffected by the effects of fully charged stunner fire, Recruit Ia," the general directed, stopping behind her.

"General, as this recruit explained to First Sergeant Tae, this recruit is a second-generation native of the heavyworld Sanctuary. The planet Sanctuary has an iron-gold core, which creates a natural electrosphere as well as a magnetosphere. The constant high presence of static energy in the Sanctuarian atmosphere has begun to confer a certain resistance to electrical discharges in some of its native-born residents. Stunner rifles fire an electrosonic shock pulse . . . most of which was apparently absorbed by this recruit's natural high tolerance for static energy, sir."

"Yet that is not what you told the MP when you reported Recruit Kaimong's actions. You said you must have been shielded by the bodies of the others during his attack," he pointed out. "Did you lie to a superior officer, Recruit?"

Ah, yes, that. Ia nodded. "General, no, sir. This recruit was indeed partially protected by a few of her fellow recruits during Recruit Kaimong's initial stunner attack. However, this recruit felt that explaining the peculiar atmospheric nature of her homeworld to the MPs would have wasted too much time, sir. It was felt that tracking down the identless Recruit Kaimong before the approaching storm obliterated his tracks was more important, sir."

"Sergeant Tae is right. You *are* too perfect." Returning to the front of his desk, General Tackett folded his arms across his chest and studied her.

Ia remained standing At Attention in a clean set of brown recruit clothes, her gaze on what portion she could see of the stylized map behind him.

"*Why* are you in the military, Recruit Ia? Feel free to speak frankly and directly."

Finally meeting his gaze, Ia gave him the part of the truth he could swallow. "I realized a few years ago, sir, that I seem to have an aptitude for the military. I found where I was needed. And rather than sitting on my asteroid, dithering about it—if you'll pardon my frankness—I decided I would study every-thing I could about that military, so that I could be a productive, useful, effective member once I joined it. I passed the MAT successfully, met all of the standards set for entry into the Marines, and joined up. Sir."

"You met the standards well enough, you could have entered an Academy as a commissioned officer, rather than a raw recruit," Tackett pointed out. "Even without a college degree."

"With due respect, General, most officers-in-training are expected to enter an Academy with a reasonable amount of real-world experience. I *know* I lack that real-world experience," Ia stated bluntly. "I also don't know if I have what it takes to lead. The best place to find out is here, among my fellow enlisted."

"Do you think we'll just *hand* you a higher rank and pay grade if you perform exceptionally well in Basic, Recruit?" the general challenged her. "Is that why you pulled that stunt today? So you could ask for an elevation in rank?"

"No, sir. I will not ask for an elevation in rank, nor expect one to be handed to me on a platter," Ia stated, lifting her chin slightly. "If I gain a rank, it will be because I have *earned* that rank at the instigation of my superiors and the oversight of the Department of Innovations. I do *not* believe in nepotism or any of its corollaries."

"What do you want, then? A medal?" he asked, flicking one of his hands carelessly before returning it to its place across his chest. "You could ask for one, you know. You did pick up some scratches and bruises on your little jaunt through the bush. Surely that's worth a Purple Heart at the very least?"

Ia narrowed her eyes. Of all the things he could have asked her, he had to ask her *that* question.

"I will *never* ask for a medal, General. *If* my superiors feel it is appropriate to recognize my efforts and bestow upon me some commendation, that is *their* prerogative. I am *not* in the Space Force to accumulate ranks and medals like they were collectible toys. I am here to serve. To place my body, my weapons, my skills, and if necessary, my life between the citizens of these Terran United Planets and all that may threaten them. General."

Tackett narrowed his hazel green eyes. "But you *were* injured during your pursuit of Recruit Kaimong. Surely your suffering deserves recognition?"

Ia glanced down at the scrapes on her arms, mostly the scratches which she had gained on her controlled fall through the trees. "Technically, sir, these were gained *before* combat was fully engaged on my part, and were therefore not combat related."

"You may not have considered *yourself* fully engaged in combat, Recruit Ia, but Recruit Kaimong apparently did. He was already shooting in your direction, placing you squarely in the aegis of combat before you launched your little counter-offensive," he pointed out.

"If I may again be frank, General, they're just scratches. To award me a Purple Heart for tiny little scratches when so many other soldiers have literally lost their arms and legs in combat would *insult* that award. These aren't combat-gained wounds," she argued. "Don't cheapen the sacrifices fully trained soldiers have made. With respect, sir."

"I studied the vids of your descent through the trees. Inventive, effective, and even enviable, given your heavyworlder reflexes," General Tackett told her, changing the subject. "I could use a hundred recruits like you, easily. Yet, historically, getting *anyone* to join either the Terran or the V'Dan militaries from your particular pocket of independence has been notoriously difficult. Nobody wants to leave your homeworld, unless they suffer irreversibly from gravity sickness, in which case the Space Force can't use them until their bodies have adapted to life in a lighter gravity . . . which makes them only as good as anyone else in the galaxy. So. Why you? Why here, and why now?"

She carefully did not mention the main reason why so many were reluctant to leave such a difficult world: the excess of gold, which was so rare elsewhere on many worlds, but which was plentiful on her homeworld. "As I told you, sir, I found the place where I am most needed. Everyone else back home feels like they're needed there. It *is* a new colonyworld, after all. There are too many unknown locations to explore, too many dangerous life-forms to fight and tame, and too many First-worlder Family lands to stake and claim, to spare anyone else right now, General."

General Tackett snorted. " 'Dangerous life-forms' on *Sanctuary*? Try the other card trick, Recruit. Parker's World has far more 'dangerous life-forms'—more than ten times its fair share for *any* planet."

"Compared to Parker's World, that may be true, sir . . . but until you've had to face down a rampaging leafer beast, I wouldn't laugh, either."

"Leafer beast?" he asked her skeptically. "That doesn't sound very intimidating."

"It's a creature the size of a small hill, General. Average adult size ranges anywhere from fifty meters to five hundred, sir . . . with rumors of leafer beasts that are even bigger. They can lie dormant for months at a time, even years—long enough to acquire a patina of dirt and bushes, just one more hill-shaped lump in the terrain—then awaken and go on a feeding frenzy. They eat the local tree and bush variants like you or I would eat our way through a bowl of salad after a twenty-klick hike, at a speed of about one hundred meters per hour, on average. They do so in a swath ten to thirty meters wide, depending on the size of the beast and the number of its mouths."

General Tackett wrinkled his nose. "That fast?"

"Yes, sir," she asserted soberly. "There were some early attempts to tame them, sir, since they literally clear roads through the forests in an easy, swift, and ecologically friendly manner. Unfortunately, the leafers discovered that plexi was just as tasty as the local trees. Most of the buildings on Sanctuary are still prefab plexi units extruded off-world and assembled on-site. Anyone who can afford to encase their home or business in stone or brick has scrambled to do so since then. But the leafers sometimes still attack, and they will destroy anything caught in their path. What they don't eat, they can still crush."

He considered her words for a few moments, then unfolded his arms. "Right. So you entered the Space Force to serve. And you don't expect or demand any elevations or commendations, just whatever your superiors believe of their own volition you should be awarded. So. What *do* you expect, Recruit?"

She lifted her chin and focused her gaze once more on the wall. "General, this recruit expects to be trained to the exacting standards of the SF-Marines, sir. Nothing more and nothing less, sir."

"And your ambitions?" he asked.

"General, this recruit intends to serve to the best of her ability, wherever her ability may take her, sir."

". . . Right." Moving around to the far side of his desk, the Camp commander faced her. "I might wonder if you're a starry-eyed real-estater, but only time will tell if you truly are. Time, and your own funeral. Kindly do *not* go running off to the rescue if you are not the closest and best-trained personnel for that job while you are here at Camp Nallibong. You may be good even in these early days, but you still have a *very* long way to go. Recruit."

"General, yes, sir," she acknowledged.

"You will not discuss anything of what happened regarding the incident involving Recruit Kaimong with your fellow recruits until given leave to do so by your lawfully designated superiors," he warned her. "You will not be given leave to do so until after the tribunal has been arranged for Recruit Wong Ta Kaimong, its verdict signed, sealed, and sustained, and his corporal punishments, if any, have been administered. Until such time as he has been brought before the tribunal, he is still entitled to the rights of a presumption of innocence until proven otherwise in a court of law.

"Additionally, you may be called before the tribunal to testify as to what exactly happened. If you are summoned, you will do so with the understanding that perjury—lying while under oath in a court of law, civilian *or* military—is Fatality Number Forty-Three, and that you can and will be subject to prosecution and the potential for corporal discipline yourself, should you make that particular fatal error. Now, return to your Class and continue with your lessons in basic instruction. Do you understand these orders, Recruit?"

"General, yes, sir!" Ia agreed crisply. "This recruit understands her orders, sir!"

"Good. Carry them out, Recruit Ia. Dismissed."

Saluting him, she held the angle of her hand over her brow until he returned it, then spun on her heel and strode out of his office. Outwardly, Ia kept her face neutral and calm. Inwardly, however, she felt like grinning.

This little episode just gave me a really nice shortcut to my plans—I don't dare let myself get careless, she admonished herself, struggling to dampen her humor so that it wouldn't be noticed by the staff manning the front offices of the administration building. *There's far too much for me to pay attention to, which gloating might distract me from. But . . . it feels good to know I'm one step closer to my ultimate goals.*

One step out of what feels like one million to go, yes, but it's still one step closer.

———————

"Now, the *reason* why the Space Force still uses ground cars as well as various hover vehicles, hexapod walkers, and other forms of conveyance, is that different terrain can and will demand different methods of transportation," Lieutenant Billingsley lectured them as she paced at the front of the classroom. "Take the colonyworld Proxima Gamma. Some of its more exotic hybrid fruit trees are so sensitive to thruster technology emanations, yet so important to their agriculture, that hovercraft have been banned from use on the planet, particularly in its rural areas. Most people therefore still drive ground cars.

"The domeworld of Dante's Refuge is slowly being terraformed so that its atmosphere can be rendered acceptable for M-class habitation; most hover vehicles are designed more for M-class operation and lack self-contained atmospheres. Ground cars are useless outside the domes, given the coarse quality of the terrain, so self-contained hexapod walkers are the preferred mode of travel on Dante's." The lieutenant lifted her chin. "For this reason, and for the reason that the Marines are frequently sent in first as shock troops, each of you will be required to become adequately competent at guiding each of these various methods of transport. In addition, you will each learn the basics of vehicular maintenance for each type. There may come a day where you are stranded nowhere near a motor pool, and it will therefore be up to *you* to get your vehicle moving again.

"Anyone who does *not* know how to operate at least one of these vehicles . . . well, you must have lived on a resource-strapped, backwater colonyworld to not be familiar with at least *one* of them. If you were too poor to pay for the operational exams and licensing fees, well, congratulations; the military is about to train you in all of them. If you show a particular aptitude for a method of transport, or for effecting repairs, this may influence your post-training placement in the Corps . . . but I wouldn't hold my breath if I were you.

"First up, we will study the . . ." She paused as her wrist unit beeped. Flipping up the lid, she read whatever the screen said, then looked up. "Recruit Ia."

Ia quickly rose from her combination chair and desk, standing At Attention. "Lieutenant, yes, sir!"

"You are to report immediately to Major Kunaiasvatt in Building C, Room 303, Recruit."

"Lieutenant, yes, sir." Saluting, Ia left the room the moment she was dismissed.

It was raining outside Building E, the result of another tropical storm sweeping across the coast. Raining heavily at that, along with hints of lightning in the distance, though at least without the gusting winds of the last storm. She swung by one of the latrines as soon as she reached Building C, pausing at the sink to shake the excess water from the crown of her hat into the drain. Settling it on its neck-string so that it hung down over her shoulder blades, she used the facilities, unsure how long her presence at the tribunal would take. All her precognition could tell her—without immersing herself in the streams—was that it was necessary, and that she wasn't missing anything overly important in their current instructor's lecture series.

She could settle her hat behind her back, since wearing hats—particularly broad-brimmed bush hats—was prohibited indoors. However, there was nothing she could do about the rainwater soaking most of the rest of her clothes. Ia did her best to wipe her face, hands, weight suit tiles, and boots as dry as possible. Once reasonably presentable, she headed for Room 303 and knocked. Ushered inside by the corporal who answered the door, Ia was quietly directed to sit on one of the benches and await the court's leisure.

There she waited, sneaking the occasional glance at the neatly uniformed, restraint-cuffed Kaimong, slouching in one of the chairs beyond the low wooden railing, looking utterly bored by his own court-martial proceedings. He wasn't on the stand at that moment, however; Buck Sergeant Johannez was. One of the two JAG officers in the room, both clad in the grey uniform of the Special Forces, stood up at a gesture from one of the three brown-clad ranking officers seated at the judging desk. The woman started—or rather, restarted—an audio recording, asking Sergeant Johannez questions about certain points along the way.

Ia listened to the recorded sounds of Kaimong stunning everyone, of him stealing the rifles, of him choosing to shoot everyone several times more with his 40-MA, and his final out-loud comment dismissing his place in Class 7157 and the Space Force Marines. She hadn't realized all of that *had* been recorded—it hadn't seemed important to check for such things. As the JAG officer outlined her points regarding Kaimong's repeated firing of the stunner rifle on his classmates and superiors alike, Ia heard faint snapping sounds, and winced.

Damn. It caught me sitting up early and unsnapping my weight suit. And there, in the timestreams just ahead, these lovely Judge Advocate General officers will question me as to why I didn't fall down and stay unconscious. If I lie, I'll run up against Fatality Forty-Three. If I tell the full truth, and not just the half-asteroided version I've told everyone so far, I get tossed out of the Marines and straight into the Special Forces, which would destroy everything.

One *of these days, I'd love to be free to tell the truth, the whole truth, and nothing but the truth. Of course, with my luck . . . most of it will still end up being censored down into nothing more than a bland, scientific discourse on frogs . . .*

The other JAG officer emphasized the point that his silent, sulking client had been under the impression that multiple stunner shots were accumulative, when in fact they did nothing more than "reset" the starting point of how long the hour-long effect would last. His intent may have been to delay pursuit as long as possible, but he had not used the more lethal projectile weapon at that point in time. The first military lawyer argued that while stunner fire wasn't lethal, excessive exposure to the weather, both excessive sunlight and the approaching storm, could have caused problems for Kaimong's stunned classmates, if they had indeed been left unconscious and exposed to the elements for that long.

The argument went back and forth for several minutes longer, before the JAG officers were bidden by the major heading up the tribunal to sit down again. When Ia's name was called, she almost missed it. Rising belatedly, she moved over to the witness stand, saluted, and swore her oaths of truthfulness on a copy of *The Witan: The Book of the Wise*, the holy book of the Unigalactan movement and a staple of the Space Force, both for chaplaincy and courtroom needs.

Both JAG officers questioned her thoroughly. When asked why she hadn't moved immediately if stunner fire had no effect on her, and why she had started unsnapping her weight suit once she had sat up, but hadn't called for backup until after it was fully off, Ia replied with part of the truth: that she hadn't wanted to draw Kaimong's attention back to the others by moving too soon.

At that point in time, she pointed out carefully, her own weapon had no e-clip, not to mention a much shorter range than the Heck laser rifle, and she hadn't wanted to run the risk of him firing a non-stunner weapon at her. The risk of him hitting her was superseded further, Ia asserted, by the risk that he might miss her and thus hit one of the others instead. A risk she had judged to be too high to chance, in her carefully considered opinion. The same as she had considered it too risky that Kaimong would successfully lose himself in the bush, make it all the way to some civilian household, and perhaps threaten or even harm those civilians in his efforts to get away from Camp Nallibong.

The questioning went on and on. Yes, she was aware prior to facing him in direct confrontation that he had loaded the High Explosives clip into his gun, as evidenced by the sounds and visible signs of explosives in the destruction of the first hovercamera. No, she no longer had her boot chevron rank when she pursued him. Yes, she was certain he knew she didn't have that rank during the pursuit. No, she wasn't sure if he had recognized her identity and rank when he had shot at her when she had been on the higher ground.

Thankfully, she had just enough time in the pacing of each question to consider each of her possible answers against the flow of the proper future. It saved her from saying too much, or saying it in the wrong way. When she was finally dismissed, if she had been anyone else, Ia would have been hard-pressed to say what the tribunal's verdict on Kaimong's sentence and punishment would be. Other than that he *would* be punished, since the evidence was undeniable, of course.

As it was, she didn't bother to speculate. Her part was done.

This section of the dominoes was lined up, poised to give her
a small shortcut to her intended future as soon as they fell. All
she had to do right now was catch up with the rest of Class
7157 and wait for tomorrow, when the verdict would be read
and the corporal part of Kaimong's punishment carried out.

MARCH 23, 2490 T.S.

The rain had stopped, but the lingering moisture combined with
the returning summer heat left the next morning feeling oppres-
sive and sticky. After their morning regimen training and breakfast were over, Ia and the others were marched out to the parade
ground. On one side of the grassy field were the reviewing
stands, where visitors were supposed to sit when each Class
graduated. Those were filled once a week as each Class completed its training. On the other side of the damp, slightly steaming field sat the announcements platform, where the Camp
commander could address everyone in times of assembly.

It also served as the punishment platform.

Packed into tightly spaced rows so that all twelve Classes
currently stationed at Camp Nallibong could see—the other
four Classes were currently training in space at Battle Platform
Wellington, which orbited Mars—Ia and the others watched
as the projection sheets were raised on either side of the platform.

The only relief she had in the face of the muggy, rising heat
of the morning and the grim exhibition they were about to
witness was that she had been granted permission to leave her
weight suit back at the barracks. But that was the only thing that
had been left behind. Every single Class currently in progress
had been assembled, even the one training group currently
undergoing Hell Week, though from the looks on their exhausted
faces, at least their Hell Week was almost over.

The recruits weren't the only ones being assembled for this
moment. Nonessential personnel, the cooks, clerical staff, and
other enlisted, noncommissioned, and commissioned personnel who worked on the base finished filing into the grandstand
behind them. Only those who monitored vital tasks, had medical
leave severe enough to remain behind, or currently maintained

the security of the military base were allowed to be excused from this assembly.

Larger than life-sized, General Tackett strode onto those screens even as he strode onto the stage. His all-black uniform, the mark of ultimate formality in the Space Force, was warning enough of the seriousness of this moment, as was the full complement of glittery pinned to his chest, all of the ribbons and medals he had earned during the years of his military service.

Turning crisply to face the assembled recruits, he waited as the sergeants barked the command to salute, and returned it as soon as the men and women waiting on the grass had raised their arms.

"Greetings, Recruits. Assume Parade Rest," he told them, pausing just long enough for the assembled bodies to take a half step to the side and tuck their hands behind their backs. His voice, amplified by the projection system, rolled across the mist-strewn field. "This assembly is a solemn occasion. It is a *reminder* that with power comes responsibility. With destruction comes restitution. With crime comes punishment.

"We are the *finest* fighting force in the entire Alliance . . . but we are the finest because we *will* maintain discipline in our ranks. The military is not here to be soft-hearted. We trained to maim and to kill, in the defense of all civilians within our jurisdiction and protection. Loss of discipline puts not only our fellow soldiers in jeopardy, but those civilian lives as well." Grim-faced below the brim of his brown-striped black hat, the general surveyed the assembled recruits from the podium and the two screens to either side. "This is *unacceptable*. We exist to defend the laws and the lives of these Terran United Planets. *Not* to destroy them.

"Three days ago, at nine hundred thirty-two local time Terran Standard, Recruit Wong Ta Kaimong, Class 7157, broke that discipline and committed several infractions against the rules, regulations, and laws of the Terran United Planets Space Force, Branch Marine Corps."

An angled, padded metal frame levered up out of the platform behind him. It rose sideways to the assembled troops and locked into place with a *thunk* Ia could hear from her position over thirty meters away. Some of the men and women around her flinched at the sound, but she kept still. In the back of her mind, she could see a similar frame rising up out of a different platform. Blinking, she focused firmly on the here and now, not wanting her mind to be clouded by potential-possible future events.

Three figures approached from the side, one of them resisting and the other two pulling along the one struggling between them. Two more followed, one carrying a thick roll of fabric and a long, sealed tube, the other carrying what looked like a medical scanner and a small case. The struggling figure was Kaimong, caught in the grip of two Military Peacekeepers. Ia heard several of her fellow classmates inhale sharply at the sight of him, and saw a few of the backs in front of her flexing in preemptive winces.

When they mounted the stage, Kaimong caught sight of the discipline frame. He cried out, struggling, and was lifted bodily by the MPs escorting him. They lashed him to the padded frame facedown, and the man with the padded roll shook it out and wrapped it around his waist and thighs, adjusting it carefully before tightening the straps that would hold it in place.

Ia's Class had undergone plenty of instruction in what the act of corporal discipline meant: the padded roll was meant to protect the thighs and the kidneys from accidental misstrokes. The cylindrical case, which the man was now opening, contained the *rotan* cane, submerged in a mild disinfectant to reduce the risk of infection.

The person carrying both items was the caner, and it was upon his shoulders to get the caning right the first time, else the caner himself would be subjected to *twice* the misplaced or judged-excessive strokes. Additionally, men caned men, and women caned women; that was the rule, since it was judged that the strength of each gender's muscles was calibrated to what their own side could safely take, flesh-wise. Different padding was also used if the caning was to be applied against the offender's upper back, but that was usually reserved for more severe crimes.

With the caner was the military doctor, who would scan the prisoner and certify him as fit for punishment, and count out the strokes, to ensure that no more than the assigned number would be applied.

Strapped in place, Kaimong panted visibly, occasionally testing his bonds, but visibly unable to free himself. In front of him, General Tackett flipped up the screen on his command wrist unit and read aloud the charges.

"After undergoing a military tribunal to investigate the truthfulness and severity of his alleged crimes, Recruit Wong Ta Kaimong was convicted of the following offenses, which were judged severe enough to be sentenced with the following punishments: for the crimes of five counts of theft of Space Force property, which included the theft of two lethal weapons and their ammunition, Recruit Kaimong shall receive two strokes of the cane. For the crime of assaulting thirty-nine of his fellow recruits with a nonlethal weapon, Recruit Kaimong shall receive two strokes of the cane.

"For the crime of assaulting five Squad leaders with a non-lethal weapon, Recruit Kaimong shall receive one stroke of the cane. For the crime of assaulting two superior noncommissioned officers with a nonlethal weapon, Recruit Kaimong shall receive one stroke of the cane. For the crime of damaging expensive military surveillance equipment while evading arrest, Recruit Kaimong shall receive one stroke of the cane. For the crime of deliberately attacking and attempting to murder fellow Terran military personnel with a lethal weapon, Fatality Thirteen, Friendly Fire . . . Recruit Kaimong shall receive *four* strokes of the cane.

"For these combined offenses to the Terran United Planets Space Force and its Marine Corps, Recruit Kaimong is sentenced to five years imprisonment in the domeworld military penal colony of Sestus, in orbit around Proxima Gamma, deportation to take place upon recovery from the implementation of his assigned corporal punishment. This verdict was sustained and sealed by military tribunal at fifteen thirty-seven yesterday, local time Terran Standard. The sentence of a combined total of eleven strokes of the cane shall be carried out immediately, and carried out before the assembled Classes of Camp Nallibong, as an instructional reminder to all.

"The Terran United Planets Space Force *will* maintain discipline, and its soldiers, enlisted or officer, *will* abide by its rules, regulations, and laws."

Snapping the lid of his wrist unit shut, General Tackett turned and strode to the side, moving far enough that everyone would be able to see. The caner had extracted his implement, which the woman at his side scanned. The doctor then stepped up and scanned Kaimong, who started struggling again. She nodded and stepped back, her voice projecting through the presentation screen speakers as the general's had.

"The prisoner's health is in a condition suitable to receive punishment," she stated crisply, firmly.

"No!—No, I'm not!" Kaimong called out, his tone rising with increasing alarm. Compared to her, his voice was weak, but then it wasn't being projected, either. The twin screens showed a close-up of his body writhing on the frame as he tried to free himself. "I'm not in any condition for this! No!"

". . . All witnesses shall abide in respectful silence for the duration of the caning. Sergeant, are you ready?"

"Sir! I am ready, sir!"

"Is the prisoner ready?"

"Sir! The prisoner is ready, sir!"

"Administer stroke one, Sergeant," she directed. Her brow furrowed and her mouth tightened, the signs of her distress enlarged and duplicated on the twin viewing screens, but the lieutenant did not rescind her order.

Stepping up, the sergeant raised the cane in both hands, gripping it at an angle across his chest. Muscles tensing, he drew in a deep breath, and swung. Knocking Ia deep into the waters ahead.

. . . Pain cracked across her back. Her buttocks were already a searing fire that made her legs shake with the strain of staying firmly in place. Arms crossed, braced on the padded board, she endured the twenty-seventh blow, one made all the more painful by the way her upper body lacked the natural padding found below. She didn't dare bite her tongue, for fear of biting through it, but she could and did bite the sleeve of her shirt, hiding the urge to scream with each agonizing, slow-paced blow . . .

A chill up the back of her neck was her only warning—a welcome one, since it yanked her out of that all-too-vivid future possibility. Moving on sheer instinct, Ia stepped forward one pace, then to her side, moving in front of Mendez. A moment later, Casey doubled over onto the grass behind her, breaking his place in the B Squad line with the need to heave up the remnants of his breakfast. Right on the very spot she had just vacated.

He wasn't the only one rendered physically ill from witnessing Kaimong's punishment. Ia herself struggled with the fear, adrenaline, and stress churning in her stomach. The thick, muggy heat of the morning added to her distress, for there wasn't any breeze to clear the accompanying stench from the air.

The doctor finished counting out the strokes and the sergeant finished administering them, ignoring the prisoner's yelp at each blow. Stepping up to Kaimong, the lieutenant scanned him. Once again, the hovercameras focused in on her face, this time looking paler than before, and rather grim.

"General, the court-ordered eleven strokes have been administered. The prisoner has received several contusions and two minor lacerations. Damage is minimal, sir. Recovery time should be optimal," she reported.

"Good. Transport Prisoner Kaimong to the Camp stockade medical bay and monitor his recovery, Lieutenant, Sergeants." Moving back to center stage, General Tackett recaptured the attention of most of the recruits on the parade ground. "As vicious as this display of corporal punishment may have been, the rest of you *must remember*, he attacked some of *you* with the very same lethal weapons you are being trained to use on our enemies . . . and to use *only* under the lawful orders of your superiors.

"He attacked one of you with a JL-39 loaded with High Explosive cartridges—not just a lethal weapon, but a *viciously* lethal weapon. Those cartridges are meant to be used in extreme circumstances, and are normally used against terrain and other nonliving obstacles. *Not* against his fellow soldiers. Former Recruit Kaimong blatantly attempted to kill one of his fellow recruits," the general stressed. "The overall punishments assigned by yesterday's tribunal were rather lenient in the face of that singular fact, for it is the grave responsibility of the Space Force to assign corporal and penal punishments to those who break the laws, rules, and regulations of this military body.

"It is *also* the solemn responsibility of the Space Force to notice and reward meritorious effort of courage and skill which is enacted within this military body. Recruit Ia, Nallibong Class 7157, front and center."

Ia strode down the narrow gap between Class rows. She wasn't the only person who had hastily moved out of the way of their fellow recruits; thankfully, the others cleared a path for her so she could reach the nearest aisle without stepping in anything awkward. Ia headed for the platform, mounted the steps on the side, and crossed it. She carefully kept her gaze on the Camp commander, not on the discipline frame, which was being lowered back into its storage hatch.

Now was not the time to let some future possibility drag her beneath the waters lurking in her mind.

Stopping a meter away, she saluted him. "Sir."

He saluted back. Lowering his arm, he tucked it into the pocket of his dress uniform. "Recruit Ia, in the face of an unexpected attack by a presumed comrade, you displayed remarkable calm, clarity of thought, and levelheadedness. Furthermore, you assisted in implementing the location and capture of the fugitive Recruit Kaimong. You did so despite the blatant risk to your personal safety, you did so unflinchingly in the face of clearly superior firepower, and you did so with less than sixteen days' worth of training. You did so by displaying levels of comprehension and skill worthy of someone with five times your current level of training.

"It is therefore my responsibility as the commanding officer of this base to acknowledge your outstanding efforts of courage, ability, and devotion to the principles and duties of a Space Force Marine throughout yesterday's incident. In witness whereof, and with the concurrence of my fellow officers and instructors here at Camp Nallibong, I award Recruit Ia with the Honor Cross, in recognition of your outstanding acts of honor and service."

Withdrawing a small box from his pocket, he opened the lid and presented its contents to her. The small bronze medal itself wasn't much, just an equal-armed cross etched with her name and the Terran Standard date for the incident with Kaimong, wrapped in a circle with the words "Honor Cross" stamped around its rim. It hung on a short ribbon striped in shades of white and green, and came with a matching ribbon-bar, also pinned to the velvet-lined interior.

Her classes so far had glossed over honors and decorations; there were too many other things to learn first. Still, thanks to her foreknowledge, Ia knew the actual medal was meant for special occasions, such as wearing her full Dress Blacks like the general currently wore, while the ribbon-bar was for "casual" use, for those occasions when she was in any uniform requiring a jacket or a dress shirt, such as her Dress Browns. She also knew it would be highly inappropriate to wear either pin throughout most of her Basic Training.

"General, thank you, sir," Ia told him, accepting the box and its contents. She closed the lid, clasped the hand he offered . . . and tried not to shudder at the glimpses she got of his future. They weren't horrible images, just unwanted ones. Parting hands, she saluted him.

He saluted back. "Return to your Class, Recruit. Keep up the good work—but let's hope it won't be needed again while you're still in training."

"Sir, yes, sir." Turning around, she tucked the box into her pocket and strode off the stage. One unexpected step closer to her goal, but still left with too many more to go.

CHAPTER 7

Hell Week. You want to know about Hell Week? My Hell Week?

Hell Week . . . is a foundry. Recruits are the raw ore which the Space Force scraped out of the ground in the first few weeks of Basic Training, washed and sorted out, and dumped into the crucible. Hell Week is all about turning on the heat, turning it up, and up, and up, and burning away all lies and façades. Hell Week is what makes the Department of Innovations, and the Field Commissions, and the promotions based on merit actually work in the Space Force.

Hell Week is giving everything you thought you had and then everything you didn't even know you had, until you are broken and bleeding and lying in the dust . . . and then seeing if you can give ten times more.

~Ia

MAY 10, 2490 T.S.

Ia woke to the glare of lights and the banging of a baton on the metal rails of the bunk beds lining the barracks. Disoriented, she squinted and rubbed at her eyes, taking a precious moment to dip her senses into the timestreams. What she found made her grimace. *Damn . . . they're starting Hell Week a day early. I thought there was only a thirty-two percent chance of that . . .*

"Rise and shine, Class 7157!" Sgt. Tae called out in an unnervingly cheerful tone. "Rise and *shine*!" Displaying far too many teeth, he smacked his baton against the top bunk rails and poked his head over the lower bunks, grinning at the men and women trying to wake up at the unexpectedly early hour. "Guess what, Class 7157? Today is the day we start separating the *adults* from the little *kids*!

"That's right, this is *Hell Week*, and your actions and endurances over the next seven days will determine a large chunk of how far you rise in rank, and how much you will get in pay grade! The Department of Innovations is always watching, and this week—*this* week, they have their eyes on *you*!"

Bang whack clang!

"Wake up! You will dress in your full camouflage Browns from brims to boots, jackets to caps, you will pack a second change of camies and three of undies, and then you will shoulder your packs and get outside on the line, every last one of you little boys and girls, or you will *all* have one hundred push-ups and one hundred sit-ups to pay for wasting my time! Move it! You have *eight* minutes to *shakk* 'n shave—but not *you*, Recruit Ia," Tae added, poking his baton at Ia as she slipped out of her bunk. "*You* have *five*. Weight up and move out!"

"Sergeant, yes, Sergeant!" Ia snapped back. When he didn't move out of her way, allowing her access to the latrines, she dropped onto her bunk and rolled out the far side in a single smooth move. Hurrying past the others, she tapped one of the C Squad members on the shoulder, and darted past the other woman, slipping into the latrine stall.

"Hey! You're not the only one who has to *shova v'shakk*!"

"Yeah, well, just wait twenty seconds, *then* you can blow it out yer rear!" Kumanei called out from somewhere further back in the quickly forming lines for the latrines.

Inside the stall, Ia bit her lip to keep from laughing. It really wasn't a laughing matter; Hell Week was a frightening blank spot on the timeplains for her . . . but the way the woman from Tokyo Underside stood up for her was too amusing, and too encouraging, not to enjoy. Hurrying out again, she rushed through her morning routine, washing her hands and splashing water on her face, then raced back to her bunk.

"Move it, move it, move it, meioas!" Arstoll called out, voice piercing through the din of forty-four bodies rushing to get ready. "This is Hell Week! There is no slacking in Hell Week! There is no second chance in Hell Week! You want a great pay grade? You wanna be an officer? Move it, move it, *move* it!"

In the span of time it took him to say that, Ia had managed to shuck her nightclothes and don most of her camie uniform. She bent over to lace up her boots and snap on their weights—and broke a bootlace. *Dammit . . . that's going to take me a minute I don't have to re-lace it!* A furtive glance to either side showed the others scrambling to pack their gear. *I'll have to risk it.*

Reaching into her locker, Ia pulled out one of her spare packs of laces, ripped it open, and dropped one of the coils on the plexcrete floor. Stuffing the other back into its place in the inner drawer, she paused, then took it back out and dropped it on the floor as well. If one lace broke, the other was liable to break as well, so she might as well replace it. Even as it landed on top of the first, Ia pulled out her kitbag and the indicated clothes with her hands, though only part of her attention stayed with the task of packing the bag. The other half of her mind focused inward, down, and out. Not for a journey onto the timeplains, but to use one of her other gifts.

A shift allowed her to hide the fronts of her boots between the shelter of the partially open locker door and the edge of the bed. Her hands packed, and her mind worked, pulling the laces out of their holes, slithering the ends free. Concentrating on both feet simultaneously wasn't easy. Recruit Sung jumped up onto the far edge of Ia's bunk, using the extra height to tidy her own bedding. Out of habit, Ia reached up to help the other woman. At least the task of pulling the covers straight was a familiar, easy one, though she almost missed getting the last bit of lacing free before slithering the next set into place.

"I can get it. You need to move," Sung warned her.

"I got it covered," Ia muttered, smoothing the blanket and sheet into place. There was no point in fixing her own bed until her weights were on, which were currently underneath the bottom bunk, tucked into the only spot available for storage.

Sung dropped to the floor as soon as her pillow was settled and reached under Ia's bunk. "Then I'll pull out your—*ungh*—stupid weight suit. What's the point of you still wearing this thing, anyway?"

Her boots were now half-laced, with the tops of her feet and fronts of her shins feeling a little weird from the fast weaving of the corded laces through their holes. Thankfully, the noises of the others hid the rasping sounds the lacings made as they slithered into place. Ia shook her head. "Just leave it under the bed, you'll never get it out in time."

ZeeZee slapped Ia on the shoulder, startling her. She hadn't heard him approach. "You heard Sergeant Tae! *All* of us get out there on time, or we *all* do two hundred demerits. You make up her bunk, Sung; I'll drag out the load."

There! That's good enough to bend over and finish tightening them. Stepping back to give ZeeZee room, she scooped up the worn segments of the old laces and tossed them back into her locker to be recycled later, then bent over, tightened, and knotted the new ones in place. No sooner did she finish one boot than ZeeZee was there with the spat-like foot weights, ready to buckle them in place. He helped lift her weight suit pants into position as soon as her other boot was finished, snapping his way down the left leg while she caught the right. And by the time he was working on the left fitted sleeve of the tiled, web-like jacket, Sung had come over and batted Ia's hands away from the snaps so she could fastened the right one.

Slapping her on her tile-covered back, Sung nodded. "You're on your own, soldier."

"Wrong," Arstoll corrected her, hefting Sung's bag on the far side of the double bunks. "You are *never* on your own when you're in the Marines. *Eyah?*" he called out, twisting to look at the others.

"Hoo-rah!" several of the nearest recruits called back, some looking up from packing their own bags, others with their eyes still on their tasks.

"I *said*, you are *never* on your own," Arstoll called out, raising his voice once again, "when you are in the *Marines*! *Eyah?*"

"Hoo-rah!" This time, the response came from all the recruits in the bunkhouse, though some of the voices echoed out of the latrine area.

The grin Arstoll gave Ia was matched by a smile of her own. Shrugging her packed bag onto her shoulders, Ia settled her broad-brimmed hat over her weight-strapped head. "Keep *that* up, and you just might make officer yet."

"*If* we can get through Hell Week," he muttered. "Look, I may be racing you to see which of us can outlast the other . . . but only on an even start. Gimme your canteen. This one's full."

Grateful for his help, Ia nodded and swapped her empty bottle for his full one. Giving her bunk and locker a quick look to make sure everything was in order, Ia slammed the door shut and hustled outside. Sergeant Tae and Sergeant Linley waited on the far side of the exercise lawn, along with eight more drill and regimen instructors. Plus four hovercams humming quietly overhead. Twice as many as before.

Ia knew they would be watching her and her fellow recruits as much to guard against signs of severe injury and illness as to watch for the caliber of the Marine-wannabes in Class 7157. Caliber which would be revealed as Hell Week stripped away all of their bravado and false self-confidence. Trepidation twisted in her stomach.

It wasn't a fear of how far she would get before hitting the wall, that as-yet undefined point where her skills and her body just didn't want to give any more. Ia knew everyone hit that wall at some point during Hell Week, some earlier than others. Knowing that mental preparation was as important as physical, she hunted down and pinpointed her fear while the others scrambled out of their barracks in clumps of threes and fours, falling in around her on the lines of brickwork laid in the grass.

I fear not my own failure, nor any self-acknowledgment of failure, she thought, *but the military's admission of my failure. I don't dare let myself fail. I won't fail. I* cannot *fail, because I will go mad if I do. My failing is* not *an option . . . and is therefore not a problem.* It was a strange sort of reverse psychology, but she dug into it and did her best to draw strength from it. *I fear the Marines declaring me a failure, whether or not I actually am one. I will not* try *to win through Hell Week. I* will *win through Hell Week.*

Neither fire, nor flood, nor storm, not space, not Hellfire *nor* Damnation, *shall stop me from what I* will *do. And no one, civilian, subordinate, or superior, will stop me from what I* must *do.*

Sergeant Linley checked her stopwatch. ". . . On time. Every last one of you. Amazing."

"Don't worry. *That* will change." Stepping forward, Tae raised his voice. "Good morning, girls and boys. You are about to endure the single most important challenge of your noncombat military careers. From this point on out, you are hereby given permission to address your superiors with direct language. You will finally get to answer questions in the first person . . . and you will be asked a *lot* of questions. Remember all that fancy in-class lecture time you've been sleeping your sorry, slagging ways through? *This* week will be your ongoing pop quiz."

"You will do what we say, when we say it, and how we say it," the next sergeant called out. The glow of the lights on their poles combined awkwardly with the shades-of-grey of his uniform, making it hard to read the name on his chest patch. "Failure will garner either your entire Squad or your entire Class demerit training . . . not just you alone. From this moment forth, you will work as a *team*."

"For the next seven days," the fourth Drill Instructor stated briskly, "you *will* have the opportunity to back down, to say no more, to quit and walk away from the exercises awaiting your Class. *However*, if you quit at any point in time within the first twenty-four hours of Hell Week, you will be discharged from the Marines . . . and at *this* point in your training, your entire accumulated pay for the last eight weeks will total a lousy two hundred credits . . . and you will have over four *thousand* to pay back to the military to cover the cost of feeding, housing, clothing, and training you. Even if you choose to 'cash out' at twenty-three hours and fifty-nine point nine minutes Terran Standard into your very first day of Hell Week, you *will* be thrown out of the Corps, and given a bill for our services!"

"For every hour past that first twenty-four-hour mark," Tae reminded them, picking up the thread of their lecture, "you will be evaluated on your performance. Your actions, questions, responses, and reactions will be judged by the Department of Innovations, and their evaluations will go on your permanent record. Those of you boys and girls who make it only as far as the second or third day will likely spend the rest of your military career with the ranks of Private, or maybe Corporal, if you shape up and show some strength out in the real military.

Those of you who make it as far as day four or day five before calling it quits just might make it to noncom status. The rare few of you, *if* there are any, who make it to day six . . . you *might* have a shot at a commissioned career in the Space Force. But I wouldn't count on it, if I were you."

"Do *not* make the mistake of thinking this is a solo race," Linley called out. "Most of what will be gauged and evaluated will lie within you, this is true, but a true Space Force Marine is not an individual. It is a group of soldiers filled with and fired by the spirit of the Corps. You are not competing against your fellow recruits. You are competing against yourself. Cooperation will get you higher rankings in your DoI evaluations than any contention would, and your *teamwork* will ensure your survival, both right here in Hell Week, and throughout your military career."

"Those of you who do want to back out of the rigorous testing of Hell Week need only step out of formation and place both hands on top of your head at any point in time, like this," the third sergeant called out, demonstrating by placing one hand on top of the other on the crown of his hat, his feet shoulder-width apart in a sort of modified Parade Rest. "If it is past the twenty-four-hour mark, you will remain in the Marine Corps, but do *not* make the mistake of thinking you will be allowed to sit on your slagging behinds," the third drill sergeant asserted. "Those of you who step out after the first day will enter an accelerated program of *remedial* training, both physical and educational, until the end of this week."

Chong, that's his name, Ia discovered idly, dabbling her mental toes in the timestreams. *He's a member of the DoI, on permanent assignment to Camp Nallibong. That's why his uniform is grey, not brown. He's going to be watching me particularly carefully. I can't foresee everything that'll happen in Hell Week because of that damnable fog clouding the timestreams, but I know he'll be watching me all the way to day three or four, which is when the damned mist in the streams obscures* everything *from view.*

Tae barked at them to drop and give him ten. Ia dropped, kitbag still balanced on her weight-suit-covered back, and started counting off the push-ups with the others.

At least I know I make it to the midpoint . . . in most of my probable futures. I just don't think even day four will be enough to carve out the right streambed for my career.

———————

They raised the wall on her. They literally raised the wall.

Between the incident with Kaimong and the start of Hell Week, Ia's demerit punishments had been consistently doubled. Not only doubled, but if she wasn't the only one being punished, she had been expected to do them twice as fast as her fellow sufferers, or garner more physical exercises. But now, from the very start of Hell Week, where every single one of the ten instructors supervising their deployment into the bush did his or her best to find any excuse to complain about Ia's behavior, appearance, and performance, her punishments were quadrupled. And she didn't dare complain about any of it.

Her limbs ached and her ears rang from the orders they barked, often changing commands midexecution to create as much chaos as possible. But through all of that, she was able to maintain her temper. Being picked on and singled out, pushed and pulled, tested and tormented, commanded and cajoled, was expected. That was their job; each yell, each demerit, each task was carefully gauged by the sergeants to toughen up the recruits in their care, while at the same time double-checking the approach of each recruit's breaking point.

The object was to *find* that breaking point, and to get each recruit to see it coming and step down. Not to smash through it. Knowing all of this, Ia remained as calm as she could manage, whether the sergeants around her were yelling in her face, or sweetly reminding her that if she'd had enough, she could step aside. *Phlegmatic* was her watchword. *Calm* was her inner state of being.

Until they raised the damned force field wall.

Hell Week took place in a long stretch of bush running from the uplands down into the flats. It had been crafted like a combination of camping trail and obstacle course, with checkpoint stations of tents and showers, medical personnel, sonic cleaners, and clean water. Each checkpoint base was located far enough from the others that it literally took them hours to reach the next one—longer, if they lagged through the various exercises. But to *get* to each one, they had to navigate the obstacles in their path. Including leaping over two-meter-high force field walls.

The first time it was raised on her, Ia didn't realize what the pylons were doing. Instead of vaulting over the wall in a curling flip, with her loaded pack on her back and her laser rifle in her hands, she smacked into the wall. Like stunner fire, force fields were based on certain electrostatic principles developed two centuries earlier. Unlike stunner fire, the force fields didn't stun their subjects. People who ran into them could experience a tingling shock, even some fuzzy numbness should they push up against a particularly strong field. So when she smacked into the wall, she simply bounced back as the field flexed and resisted the force of her weight. It didn't actually harm her, though it did cause her to stumble and fall.

Caught by surprise, Ia rolled and righted herself. Shaking it off, she focused on the gap between the pylons, marked by the occasional, shimmering spark of energy zapping across the unseen surface. Bemused, she set herself at the wall again—and skidded to a stop the moment she saw the pylons beginning to rise up out of the ground. Scowling, Ia looked over at the next section of wall. The pylons covering her part of the fence couldn't rise very high without warping the fields connected to either side beyond sustainability . . . but they remained low enough that the other recruits were able to leap over them.

"What are you doing lagging behind, Recruit?" one of the sergeants barked at her. "You are holding up the line! Get over that wall!"

The way he pointed his baton at the troublesome force field in front of her left no doubt in her mind that if she chose a different path, she'd get in trouble for that, too. Setting her jaw, Ia backed away from the fence line. The pylons slid down. She darted toward the gap, and they shot up. Skidding to a stop, she backed up.

"Have you *forgotten* how to get over a simple, low force field, Recruit?" the sergeant demanded. "Move along, Q'iang! Use one of the other lanes, since *this* recruit feels like she can take her stars-be-damned time!"

Ia ignored both men. Walking slowly up to the force field produced the same effect as running; her proximity, not the speed of her approach, triggered it. However, over the last half meter, the pylons didn't rise any higher. Annoyed but not defeated, Ia backed up several meters, watching the pylons slide back down. The difference between their highest point and the normal height of the fence was only half a meter at most, but it was enough to present a challenge to her. If it had been a standard wooden or plexcrete wall, she could have "run" partway up the wall to reach the top, or even wrapped her hands around the top edge and pulled herself up, but force fields didn't work that way. They weren't quite solid enough to grasp.

They were the modern version of the proverbial greased pig, nearly frictionless and thus nearly impossible to grab hold of and climb. They were ideal for keeping out most intruders. They were also rather aggravating when they were just half a meter taller than usual.

A quick investigation into the timestreams gave her several options, but figuring out which would be the least damaging to her career would take too much time. The sergeant frowned at her as she stood there in thought. He frowned even more as Spyder broke out of the right-hand line. Her fellow recruit flashed Ia a grin and dropped to one knee in front of the middle field, cupping his fingers together.

"Ey, Ia! Choo wanna boost?"

His offer prompted the sergeant to yell at him. "You are *not* permitted to help this recruit—drop and give me fifteen, then get back in line! Lackland, Shinukowa, move to the other lines! Recruit Ia, you will *stay* here and *surmount that middle force field*! I don't care if it takes you all *day*, I don't care what you have to *do*, you will get up and *over* it! *Now!*"

His phrasing gave her an idea. Glancing up briefly at one of the hovercameras, the one which seemed to be permanently assigned to follow her, Ia looked over at him. "Sergeant, is that your *order*, Sergeant? Am I to get over this middle force field by any means I deem necessary, Sergeant?"

His baton jabbed at the force field awaiting her. "*Yes*, that's an order! Get over that force field *now!*"

"Sergeant, yes, Sergeant!" *Just remember you* ordered *me to do this,* she thought grimly, shrugging out of her backpack. He frowned again, then scowled even harder as she snapped out of her weight suit jacket, jury-rigging it so that it was instead snapped around her pack. She ignored him.

"What are you doing, Recruit? I did *not* give you permission to set down those weights!"

She didn't even look at him. Her attention was on the wall, trying to gauge exactly where the top of it would reach once she was close. "Sergeant, I am not setting them down. They haven't even touched the ground. I'm just redistributing the load for a moment, Sergeant."

Letting the weight-wrapped bag dangle by its straps from onc hand, she ran for the field. At the last moment, as she prepared her leap, Ia swung her kitbag back, up and around, so that the bag sailed up right along with the rest of her, rising along with the field. Her leap, even weighted down as she was, would have been enough to hook one elbow over the top edge, if it hadn't been a flexible wall of electrostatic force. But there was no well-defined edge to grasp.

There was, however, the wall itself. She snatched at the strap with her left hand just as both the bag and her leap reached their apex, and used the downward swing of the bag to slide and hook her elbows over the fuzzy boundaries of that wall. The jolt of the weighted bag jerking to a halt on the other side combined with the static sting of the force field bending and warping beneath her body, attempting to numb her flesh from ribs to elbows. Static *pzzzed* and crackled between the two pylons as the force field struggled to accept her weight.

This wasn't a starship-grade force field, designed to deflect projectile missiles and ward off the damage from micrometeors and other orbital flotsam. It was just a standard security force field fence, designed to hold back wild animals and trespassers. Using the grip of her arms where they curled over the sparking and sagging, invisible fence top, counterbalanced by her bag and its web-work of weights, Ia hitched herself higher.

Her intent was to swing one leg up and over, like straddling the back of some unseen riding animal. The force field had other ideas. Or rather, the pylons. Warped out of sustainable shape, they *pzzzted* and sparked in thin, lightning-like lines. Just as she got her leg up, boot skittering over the wall of repellant energy, the force field broke and shut off.

Yanking on the bag to make sure she moved forward rather than back, Ia *thumped* into the ground on the far side, rolling to take some of the impact. Behind her, the field *pzzzted* again, and flickered back to life, no longer stretched by excessive height, and no longer stressed by excessive weight. Regaining her feet, Ia turned to look back at the sergeant who had ordered her to climb the wall. He was just standing there. Staring at her.

Satisfied he wouldn't complain—at least immediately—she moved far enough up the trail that she wouldn't block the next recruit waiting in line to vault over it. Mindful of her orders, Ia unsnapped the jacket from her bag. Shrugging into her pack as soon as she was properly wrapped in the weights, she turned to head forward—and found Sgt. Linley blocking her way.

"You almost *destroyed* that force field, Recruit. That fence is valuable government property! *What* was going through your head?" the older woman demanded of her.

Ia met her dark brown glare steadily. Not calmly. Being cheated on like that, blatantly discriminated against in this, her most important phase of Basic Training made her too angry to entirely hold her tongue. But steadily, yes. "Sergeant. If you or any other officer puts an obstacle in my way, and then *orders* me to overcome it by any means necessary, *do not* fault me for doing so. Sergeant."

Stepping around the blinking Regimen Trainer, Ia continued down the trail.

———————

"Are you sure you don't want to quit?"

"No, Sergeant."

"Squat!"

Ia squatted.

"You know you *can* quit."

"I know, Sergeant."

"Feet!—Push-up!"

"It's okay, nobody's going to fault you if you quit."

Ia rose halfway onto her feet, then dropped onto fingers and toes, following the commands she and her fellow recruits were being given. Her attention was mostly on Sergeant Linley, who was shouting orders for various positions and regimen exercises. But it was hard to hear her, thanks to Sergeant Takna, who was being overly helpful. To the point of being obnoxious.

"Bellies up!"

Ia flipped onto her back.

"You've already survived over two days," Takna reminded her, stepping over her as Ia followed the next order to roll left. The sergeant's voice rose loud enough, it threatened to drown out Linley's commands. "You've got a good, solid career track already laid! You don't want to jeopardize that!"

Ia struggled to hear the next position command, but couldn't. She reacted instead to the movements of the front-most Squad, who were scrambling to their feet. Dipping onto the timeplains wasn't feasible anymore. She was now within that grey fog inside her mind, like a heavy mist obscuring the little valley her own timestream occupied. Too many possibilities, too many complications, not enough strength to penetrate the mist.

Plus, there was that other risk. Takna wasn't just talking loudly, she was also occasionally touching Ia on the shoulder. They were friendly touches, nothing untoward about them . . . except they were confining Ia's movements and reactions since she didn't want to hit the other woman. Aside from the whole Fifty Fatalities thing, which included attacking a superior officer, the last thing Ia wanted to do was fall victim to an accidental, deeper plunge into the timestreams. That ran the risk of dragging whoever was touching her into those waters as well. The longer she stayed away from Sanctuary, the fewer uncontrolled visions she was having, but fewer wasn't the same as none.

She tried doing jumping jacks, following orders, but Takna was being overly helpful by standing right by her side. "I think you would be *perfect* in the motor pool. Why, with those reflexes, you could easily make a great career for yourself as a shuttle pilot!"

"Sit-ups!" Linley ordered.

Ia was slow in getting down into position, because Takna was now behind her.

"Just think of it—Yeoman First Class Ia!"

"Feet! Parade Rest!" Linley snapped. Ia gave up trying to get down fully and pushed herself back up again.

"Oh, that has the most *lovely* ring to it!"

Ia shuddered. Not because it was outside the career path she needed to take—which it was—but because the sound of a Marine Corps sergeant *gushing* with enthusiasm offended her. In the next moment, she shuddered again, grunting under the impact of Sergeant Takna wrapping her arms around Ia's chest in a hug.

Enough! Grabbing and twisting, Ia flung the other woman to the ground. Takna *oofed* at the thudding impact.

"*Hold!* Recruit Ia!" Linley snapped, outrage sharpening her already hard voice. "Did you just *attack* a superior officer?"

Ignoring the recruits and soldiers twisting to look her way, Ia locked Takna's arm with her own and planted her knee on the other woman's thigh, using an Afaso hold that ensured the sergeant couldn't get up without hurting herself. It was also a hold that brought the two of their heads close together. Aware of the hovercameras orienting on her position, closing in to record everything in greater detail, she addressed the woman on the ground in a murmur meant just for the two of them. The scanners on the cameras would pick up her words, of course, but hopefully the other recruits would not.

"*You* just touched me in a manner which *could* be misconstrued as Fatality Number Fifty, Sergeant. My *reaction* may not have been unprovoked." The other woman blinked, eyes wide. Ia released her, shifting off her thigh. She even offered the other woman her hand. Takna accepted it, letting Ia haul her back to her feet. Ia pulled the other woman close as she did so, speaking just enough for the stunned sergeant's ears alone. "If you *value* your career . . ."

"Recruit Ia! I asked you a question!" Striding through the other Squadrons, Linley stopped in front of the two of them. "Sergeant Takna, do you wish to press charges against—"

"No, Sergeant," Takna quickly denied. "Nothing happened, Sergeant Linley. On *either* side."

Linley frowned, but backed off. She turned and strode back to the front of the clearing they were exercising in, passing the rows of idle, curious recruits. "Fall in!"

Ia snapped her shoulders back, eyes forward and limbs straight, At Attention along with the rest.

"Now, as I was saying about your future career," Takna stated as her colleague ordered everyone back into doing jumping jacks.

Ia snapped her gaze to the other woman even as she jumped, swinging her arms and legs open and closed. "As *I* was about to say regarding *your* career, Sergeant . . . since your time and effort are so valuable, perhaps you should go help *someone else*?"

"Windmills!—Right Face! Left Face!"

It took the sergeant a moment to catch her meaning. *If you value your career . . .*

"Jog in place—get those knees up!"

Without another word, Takna turned and made her way through the recruits jogging in place.

Ia jogged right along with them, returning her attention to their Regimen Trainer.

Off to the side, she watched a panting, flush-faced Kumanei stumble, stagger, then stop. Heaving breaths, the other woman rested her palms on her knees. Takna reversed course, approaching from her right side, while another of the sergeant-observers approached from the left. Kumanei answered their quiet inquiries while Ia dropped to the ground and did unassisted sit-ups, before being ordered to flip over.

As she did so, she caught a glimpse of Kumanei, hands atop her head, making her way off to the side. Fifteen down. Twenty-nine to go. Everyone had made it through the first day, but after less than three hours of sleep, some had faltered late on the second. More had dropped out today.

"Squad D! Start off the sound-off of the Fifty Fatalities, counting backwards from Fifty!" Linley ordered. "Bellies up! Stomach-crunches!"

Ia flopped onto her tile-wrapped back and brought her knees and elbows together in alternating efforts. She listened absently to the Fatalities being recited in reverse by those who were left in Squad D, which would be followed by Squad F, and then her own. *Twenty-nine more to go. And the near future is so foggy right now . . . not yet from lack of sleep, just from too many possibilities. I think. I can't really tell.*

Lackland flubbed his Fatality. He wasn't just one off, he was three off, and mangled even that one, in his attempt to recite it. Muttering to himself, he climbed to his feet, placed his hands on his head, and staggered off where the sergeants had taken Kumanei to await a ride to the next camp. The next recruit in his Squad quickly recited his assigned number correctly, moving the impromptu quiz further down the line.

Twenty-eight more to go. All I can do is my best. I must not fail.

"*Slag*, Ia." Arstoll slurped at the water in his canteen. "*I'm* just about ready to quit, and you're still going?"

"Shhh," Ia whispered, sweeping her arms slowly in the grand, scooping Wheel of Fire. Twisting, she leaned from one foot to the other, stretching out her legs, elbows arching up into the position the V'Dan martial artists called Yearning Birds. "I'm sleeping . . ."

"Sleeping? That's a new word for it. You're standing out here in the hot sun without a shirt!" Mendez protested. "Yet you tell me you're *sleeping*. Have you gone past the horizon, meioa-e?"

She didn't respond. He and Arstoll were the only others to survive this long into Hell Week beside herself. Recruits Q'iang and the surprisingly wiry Spyder had dropped out this morning from the simple fault of not being able to wake up on time. For all she knew, they were still sleeping, hauled bodily onto the bus by their Hell Week instructors so they could be hauled back off again to join their fellow recruits in remedial training.

"I think the sun got to her," she heard Arstoll mutter.

Hardly. The burning heat of the sun penetrated her skin with less danger than it would have seared Mendez's darker hide. Her paternal legacy allowed the bright noonday light to energize her, rather than traumatize her. If she chose. Right now, she did. It was the only way to get back more energy than food alone, since rest was in short supply. None of the three of them had enjoyed more than a single hour of continuous sleep, and no more than eight hours total in the last five grueling days.

The slow, stately moves of the Third Air Dance soothed her weary mind. Ia couldn't see anything of her own future anymore; her own timestream was a great and frightening blank wall. Not as vast or as terrifying as the wall that would come for their galaxy, but frightening enough on its own.

Moving kept her tired mind busy. It took effort to remember the martial form, effort to push her weight-suit-less body slowly yet smoothly through each pose. Not busy enough, though. Mendez's words echoed in her thoughts. *Have I gone past the horizon? Have I?*

It hurt to move. It hurt to think. It hurt even to feel. *Why am*

I here? Why am I hurting my body? Why am I pushing my self, my soul?

The golden glow of late afternoon turned a sickly amber, pushing bodies up out of the ground. Dead bodies. Seared bodies. Scorched, frozen, bloated, stripped, mutilated bodies. Eyes wide, she saw nothing but bodies and barren, lifeless dirt.

Squeezing her eyelids shut, Ia barricaded herself against the image. *I am here to* serve. *I am here to* prevent *this massacre. I am here to* stop this hell!

I have pledged my life, my sanity . . . to stop this . . .

A thread of a tune came to her, weaving its way through the desolation pressing in around her. It was an old, old melody her mother liked to hum whenever she was doing some necessary chore. Not always an enjoyable chore, but a necessary one. As an innocent little girl, Ia had happily learned the song in its original Old Earth Bulgarian, singing the pretty little melody over and over without a care in the world, until her Grandpa Quentin had taught her the true meaning of the song, how it was about the impermanence of life.

About death, and what that really meant.

She remembered crying herself to sleep, and the dreams that had followed. The melody had followed her into those dreams, too. Upon waking, she had run to her grandfather's home, still upset, and demanded to know how to stop the bad thing called death. A practical man, Grandpa Quentin had told her that all things would eventually die, but the only way to stop a premature death was to be careful, to be watchful and mindful and aware. And most importantly, be watchful and mindful not only of oneself, but of others and their needs.

The original lyrics had shifted and changed with that, wrapping themselves around her young mind like a shield. Over and over, the young Iantha had woven the new words around her psyche. She had even whispered them in his native tongue the day her family laid him in his grave after a bad fall had crushed his skull, convinced that if she had only *been* there, she could have prevented it.

That wish, that belief, had saved her crumbling sanity at the age of fifteen.

Now, as an adult, Ia shielded herself once again with the simple, short, repetitive melody, warding off the nightmares seeping into her mind. A scrap of caution kept her from singing them in Terranglo, but she could sing them in V'Dan, the language of the other Human empire. Since Terranglo was the official trade tongue these days, few people in the Terran United Planets bothered to learn V'Dan.

"Ma gla gieza vu-oul lo ma'a alkul, olnie Eltu ma'a tieh . . . Ma gla gieza vu-oul lo ma'a alkul, olnie Eltu ma'a tieh." With each repetition, she strengthened her voice, pushing back the sepia-drenched bodies with white mental light and pure, ululating sound. *"Ma gla gieza vu-oul lo ma'a alkul, olnie Eltu ma'a tieh! Ma gla gieza vu-oul lo ma'a alkul, olnie Eltu ma'a tieh!"*

"What the hell are you singing, Recruit?"

She jolted back to reality. It *hurt* to wake up fully. Eyes blurring, throat sore from not having sung in months, Ia found herself staring down at Sergeant Tae, who stood just a few inches away.

"What do you mean by singing '. . . though hell itself should bar my way,' huh? You think *this* is hell?" he demanded. "*Do* you?"

She hadn't known he knew enough V'Dan to interpret her words on the spot. "Sergeant, no, Sergeant!"

"You're supposed to be *resting*, Recruit, not standing half-naked in the hot sun, singing some silly little mantra! I wanna see you drinking a full liter right now!" he ordered, snapping his baton in the direction of her gear, then followed her when she obediently moved.

She avoided Arstoll's stunned look, crossing over to where her shirt, weight suit, and backpack lay in a tidy pile on the ground, stripped off and set aside for the duration of their half hour of allotted rest. Picking up her canteen, she drank from it, then dug out a handkerchief and wetted it. Pushing up her sunglasses, she lifted it to her face. A hand blocked her wrist before it reached her cheeks.

The hand belonged to Sgt. Tae. "Are those *tears* on your face, Recruit?" Tae gave Ia room to scrub her face clean of dust, sweat, and other things. He stayed at her side as she moved into the shade, his dark brown eyes fixed on her lighter ones. "I don't get you, Recruit Ia. We throw enough *shova* at you to choke a Battle Platform's lifesupport filters, and you take it without flinching. But a silly little *song* makes you cry?"

"What *I* want to know," Linley offered as she reached his side, "is why she's here in the Corps with a voice like *that*. I haven't heard anything that good since my last trip to Sydney. Why are you *really* here, Recruit?"

Acutely aware that the DoI observer, Sergeant Chong, was also listening for her answer, that the hovercameras were recording her every word, Ia wiped down her neck and onto her chest, scrubbing at her skin around the straps of her sweat-streaked athletics bra. "I am here, Sergeants, because I am far more useful here than I would be anywhere else. I *like* being useful. Now, if you have any problems comprehending that . . . I apologize for any tactlessness, given how tired I am, but I respectfully suggest you recheck the reasons behind your own military careers. *If* you cannot comprehend that. Sergeants."

Taking her canteen to the water pipe stationed by the latrine building for this designated rest area, she drank its remaining contents to make sure she stayed hydrated, then filled it to the brim and drank again. The water tasted bitter, but only because it was flavored with her own disappointment.

I will never *have the career I wanted as a child. All of my dreams drowned and died in the god-damned timestreams three years ago.*

With sparse, tight movements, she refilled the canteen, then marched back to her gear and shrugged back into her shirt. As tired as she was, she had to be ready to move when they ordered her back into action. Her head ached from lack of sleep, her body winced at the thought of strapping on the weight suit, and her eyes burned from her brief bout of useless tears.

All I have left are the nightmares, and the slim chance I can help save the universe. A glance at her trainers showed them conferring among themselves in a huddle. She sensed instinctively that the time to move along was almost here. *Sorry, Sergeants. Compared to the destruction of every world, every race, every* thing *in our galaxy, this Hell Week of yours is* nothing. *A mosquito-sting to a gaping gut wound.* This *is not hell. This is the only road* out *of hell.*

I will not *stop.*

———————

"Come on, you slagging slackard! Can't you do *one measly* push-up *right*?"

"You *can* quit any time you want, you know."

"Next up is the zip line, Recruit Ia. You think those trembling limbs of yours can hold on to the clip as you slide down? Or are you going to land in the bushes, or the water if you're lucky? Or maybe in the gaping jaws of a saltie—would you like that? Snap-snap?"

"I can't hear you counting to ten, Recruit! Start over from *one*!"

"Just put your hands on your heads and surrender; you've already gone farther than the rest of your classmates . . ."

"She's right; you don't have to go any farther if you don't want to . . ."

"She'll quit. She's weak."

"Back straight, Recruit!"

". . . Time!"

"Enough. *Enough!*" Sgt. Tae barked, cutting through the sudden silence. "Recruit Ia, on your feet! Fall in!"

Shaking with weariness, Ia pushed herself slowly upright. Her weight suit felt as if it weighed four times as much as it should; just balancing herself was difficult. Blinking, she focused on the shorter man waiting patiently in front of her.

Seven days of too much exercise on too little sleep had dulled her wits. She fought to focus on why he had stopped everything. The pattern should have been another . . . twenty or so minutes of regimen training, and then . . . the zip line back down from the upland zone to the salt flats, a long metal cable strung from the topmost cliff to the depths of a ravine not too unlike the one she had jumped into weeks ago, in her pursuit of Kaimong.

"About Face, Recruit! March yourself to the ground bus!" Tae ordered her.

"The General was right," she heard one of the other sergeants whisper. "If we had a *hundred* like her . . ."

Slowly, wearily, the corners of her mouth curved up. Even her facial muscles protested at having to move, but Ia couldn't resist the urge to smile. *That's what "time" meant . . . It's the end of the seven days. I won.*

I won.

Smug satisfaction gave her a tiny bit of energy. Enough to lift an arm high enough to tug off her front-brimmed cap, allowing the heat of the sun to fall on her white-fuzzed head, restoring her sapped energies just a little bit more. A tiny trickle, barely enough to allow her a deeper breath, but a trickle was enough. For now.

"Stow your kitbag and get on the bus, Recruit," Tae ordered her.

Grateful to be rid of the pack's weight, she shrugged out of it, and tucked it under the bus. Above the storage space, at the edge of her tired vision, she could see the faces of her fellow recruits pressed to the plexi windows. She smiled even more. While the timestreams were still closed to her—assuming she had the energy to reach for them—she didn't have to be psychic to know she had impressed them. Turning to head for the door, she found herself blocked by Tae's baton.

"*Why* are you *smiling*, Recruit?"

Tired but pleased, Ia smirked. It wasn't much of one, since she didn't have a lot of strength left, but she let herself smirk. "I won."

Two seconds later, she finally registered his suddenly fierce scowl. Losing her smile, Ia edged around him, heading for the front door of the bus. The blood draining from her face combined badly with her exhaustion, leaving her dizzy. *Oh,* shakk. *Maybe . . . I shouldn't have said that?*

"Where do you think you're going, Recruit?"

Confused, she turned back to face him, gesturing over her shoulder. "Onto the bus, Sergeant. As ordered."

"Well, guess what? I changed my mind. Follow me!" he barked.

Bemused, Ia followed. He didn't lead her far, just to the front of the ground bus. Unclipping the tow line from the winch frame, Tae played out about two meters, locked it in place, and re-clipped the end to the frame again. Lifting the loop of cable in his hand, he faced her.

"Congratulations, Recruit Ia. For *that* little piece of sass, you will tow this bus all the way back to the barracks!"

Eyah. *I* shouldn't *have said that.*

Too tired to grimace, Ia looked at the cable in his hands, then reached for the patch pocket on her trousers that contained her rappelling gloves. Even in her exhaustion-numbed state, she knew the cord-twisted metal would tear her skin apart if she tried to haul on it bare-handed.

"Did you not hear me, Recruit?" Tae growled. "I said *tow* this bus *back* to the barracks. That's an order!"

Tugging on the gloves, almost dropping one in her fumble-fingered weariness, she tightened the cinching straps around her wrists. Took the cable from him. Trudged forward two steps, turned, and pulled. The bus didn't budge. Drawing in a deep breath—fighting against the urge to just sit down and sleep—Ia dug in her boot heels, leaned, and *tugged*.

Her feet skidded out from under her, landing her on the dust-strewn plexcrete of the road with a surprised *oof*. Blinking, Ia stared dumbly at the cable, then at the bus. A brown-brimmed hat and a brown-tanned face interposed itself between her and the tan-hued ground vehicle.

"Are you *disobeying* a direct order? That *is* Fatality Number Five, you realize!"

Disobeying . . . oh, God . . . For a moment, the grey blankness fogging her mind opened up wide, showing her the timestreams. Not those immersed in the present or the near future, but into the cracked and barren rocks more than three hundred years from now. *Oh, God . . .*

"Do you *hear* me, Recruit? You will tow this bus all the way back to those barracks, or I will *personally* march you straight through a tribunal, plant my boot on your asteroid, and *kick* you *out* of the Space Force!"

No . . . No . . . Oh, God—no!

Horror gave her the strength her body lacked. Lurching to her feet, Ia grabbed the cable and spun, jerking as hard on it as she could. Again, her feet skidded out from under her, slamming her belly-first on the road. Gritting her teeth against the pain, Ia shoved back up and hauled again, and again. And again, and again, the bus did not move.

"Enough! That's enough Sergeant. Stop it!"

"Get back on the bus, Recruit Arstoll—get back on the bus, all of you!"

"No, Sergeant!" The voice belonged to Forenze. "You don't treat a recruit this way. You *do not* treat her this way!"

"*You* want to be court-martialed for disobeying a direct order, too? There will *not* be a mutiny in this recruitment class!"

Ia slipped and fell, again unable to budge the ground vehicle. Dazed, she rolled onto her hip and stared blankly at the parked vehicle, listening with less than half an ear to her fellow recruits arguing with their chief Drill Instructor next to the parked bus.

Parked . . . bus . . .

Parked . . .

Grunting in self-disgust, she shoved herself upright and staggered toward the front of the bus. Half careening off the corner, she hooked her hand enough to redirect herself into the steps, literally and figuratively. Ignoring the *whack* of the tiles on her web-work leggings as they hit the steps, the new bruises they gave to the older ones already mottling her shins, Ia crawled up to the driver's seat.

Parked . . .

The vehicle was powered by a modern hydrogenerator, using cheap, clean water for its fuel. But it was also a ground-based vehicle, if designed for off-road travel. A hover bus might have flown from landing pad to landing pad a lot easier, but that much thruster tech was expensive, and hovering took a lot more energy than rolling along the ground. The terrain was also a problem; in this part of the continent, there wasn't always an easy path down through the jungle canopy, even to an established clearing. Better for troop transports to be capable of following the same ground-pounding path the recruits used, which meant using a cheap, ground-supported form of transportation.

However, the *rolling* part didn't work properly if the bus was firmly parked. Which this one was. Finding the gearshift, Ia shoved it into the Neutral setting, then pulled on the release lever for the parking brake. Crawling backwards down the steps, she hauled her trembling body upright via the doorframe and edged behind Sergeant Tae, who was overseeing the recruits as they counted off their demerits.

I am not going to let you *destroy my career* . . . she thought fiercely inside her head. Tired as she was, she knew far, far better than to project that thought. *I am* not *going to let septillions be slaughtered because* I failed! I will not fail!

She tripped over the cable. Barely managing to twist in time so that she took the worst of the bruising in a slumping roll, Ia fought against the urge to cry. Mind and body were almost disconnected, she was that close to the last of her strength. She *hurt*, inside and out. For a long, pain-filled moment, there just wasn't enough left of anything within her, beyond that urge to cry.

"As for *you*, Recruit Ia—"

. . . *No.* Breath huffing through her clenched teeth, she sought for the energy she needed. Her body was used up; her muscles did not want to respond. The only thing she had left was her mind, and her mind was filling up with the horrors of whole worlds being torn apart by uncaring, rapacious hordes.

"—if *this* is the so-called best you can do—"

No. Rolling over, she grabbed the looped cable and levered herself up, hauling on the cable and jerking against the unmoving weight of the ground bus. *No! I* will *not let them die . . . I will* not *fail . . . I* will not*!*

"—then I guess I'm just going to have to—"

"—NO!!"

Screaming her denial, she threw her body, voice, and mind against the dead weight of her task . . . and lurched the bus forward. The cable fought painfully against the grip of her gloved hands, but the bus moved. Muscles straining, joints protesting, Ia hauled on the cable with sheer willpower, her weight-wrapped body leaning at an extreme angle as she fought the inertia of the vehicle. Even as a heavyworlder, even if she had been in perfect shape, free of exhaustion, it would have been difficult for her to move a ground bus loaded with recruits and instructors.

She moved it.

That was all that mattered.

Step by step, she hauled on the cable, keeping it moving, overcoming friction and inertia with burning determination, and every bit of her telekinesis she had to spare. At this point, hiding her abilities from detection was the lesser threat to the future. Being pressured to join the Special Forces Psi Division, she could work around. Being thrown out of the Corps, she could not.

The bus picked up speed from a bare crawl to a gentle roll. She forced her leaden feet to move faster, to keep her from tripping and letting the bus drift to a stop, or worse, roll over her. Not that she couldn't lie flat and clear the undercarriage, but if it stopped, she'd have to get it started all over again, and there were almost four kilometers between this spot and the barracks.

"Recruit! Recruit Ia! Dammit—somebody get behind that wheel!" she heard Sgt. Tae demand. "Chong, I'm putting an end to this—"

NO! She hauled harder on the cable, moving the bus a little faster. Faster. *I will tow it back! I will not fail!*

"*Shakk*—get on the bus! Everyone on the bus!"

His orders turned into meaningless noises. Only four words mattered to her now. *I will* not *fail!*

With that single thought burning through her blood, giving her the energy her mortal flesh lacked, Ia spun and hauled on the bus with the cable slung over her shoulder, putting her legs and her back fully into each angled step.

There was nothing left but the driving need to haul the weight of the future itself out of the grey, choiceless mist clouding her path.

I.

Will.

Not.

Fail.

———

The counter-tug on the cable, caused by the ground bus braking behind her, almost yanked Ia off her feet. Dumbly, she twisted to see why it had stopped. The oblongs of white off to either side took several seconds to register as buildings. By that point, however, she had a short, brown-clad, furious man yelling at her.

"What in the *goddamned* name of the Motherworld did you *think* you were *doing*?"

Ia blinked at him.

"Just *what* did you think you were doing, Recruit Ia?" he repeated fiercely.

"Hauling . . . the bus . . . back to the barracks," she managed, struggling through the exhaustion fogging her thoughts. "As ordered, Sergeant . . ."

Whirling, he smacked the front of the bus with his baton, then spun back to her with a growl. *"Why?"*

"You . . . You said . . . I'd get thrown out. If I didn't follow orders," Ia reminded him. "So I just . . . just followed your orders. Sergeant."

"I was trying to *rescind* those orders!" Sergeant Tae shouted, swaying so close, the brim of his hat brushed against her nose.

Ia blinked. ". . . Oh."

"What the *shakking* hell kind of Drill Instructor do you *take* me for? I expected you to *try*, yes, but I *also* expect you to *know when to quit*, dammit! I *should* court-martial you for being so stars-be-damned *stupid* as to almost *kill* yourself . . ."

His tirade floated around her like aural ribbons in an unseen wind. They flicked at her senses, but never really landed, never actually impacted. Ia just stared at him, blinked a few times, and waggled her head in vague, wearied semi-responses to whatever it was he was ranting about. Something about quitting, of course, but that didn't really make sense. She *couldn't* quit.

Whatever doubts she'd had about her own ability to carry through with what she had to do had burned away somewhere during those four or so kilometers of hauling the bus back to the barracks. Barracks which now had a bunch of men and women lining up in front of them, most with the same mix of concern, awe, and uneasiness in their eyes as she saw in Tae's. If without the ranting.

"Well?" he finally demanded.

She stared, unable to remember what he had asked. There was no past for her to peer into, and no future left to guide her. Not even a grey mist. Just the here and now. Licking her dry lips, Ia ventured the one coherent concern left on her mind. "Sergeant . . . Permission to fall down, Sergeant?"

The expletive that left his lips wasn't exactly a "yes," but it wasn't a flat-out "no," either. He didn't actually say "no." Taking that for what little it was worth, Ia closed her eyes and let the ground leap up to catch her.

CHAPTER 8

Some people . . . alright, a lot of people . . . have accused
me over the years of meddling in matters where I shouldn't.
To all of them, I'd just like to take a moment to say: "So,
what, if you catch on fire, I shouldn't inform you of it? I
shouldn't advise you to stop, drop, and roll? I shouldn't grab
for a bucket of water and douse the flames crisping their
way up your legs and your back?" Somehow, I don't think
ignoring someone if they're on fire is the right thing to do.

Parents meddle with their children's growth and devel-
opment every single day. Governments meddle in the lives
of their citizens every single day. Peacekeepers meddle in
the crimes committed by wrongdoers every single day. Even
restaurant servers meddle in your choice of meals, by making suggestions about the daily special every single day.

Don't tell me not to meddle, as if I'm some sort of god-
complexed monster. I am not the worst being in this whole
galaxy when it comes to that.

~Ia

MAY 18, 2490 T.S.

Liquid silver surrounded her. Drowned her. Ia twitched, trying to shove it away.

(*Shhh . . . shhh, little one. We're being watched, so kindly do not wake up fully, just yet.*)

Huh . . . wha . . . Sharpening her thoughts, Ia struggled to open her eyes—and felt them being kept shut from inside her own head. She shoved mentally at the other presence, but she was too weak, too sapped in strength to budge it.

(*Trust me, child, you don't want to officially wake up just yet. Not until you and I have had our own little talk, first. Afterward, we'll know how to deal with the Marines waiting to speak with you . . . particularly since I'm "legally obligated" to inform them of what I've seen inside your little white head.*)

(*Shakk!*) Fear spiked through her. She clamped down on her thoughts, on her gifts, and winced at the spike of pain that stabbed through her head with the attempt. A deep breath to stifle the pain filled her lungs with the medicated, antiseptic scents found only in a hospital.

(*Easy . . . as much as I could expose you, there's always the counterfaction threat of you deciding to expose* me *. . . ah, I see you're grasping what I am now, yes?*)

(*Feyori.*) That explained the swirling silver blinding her inner sight. With that clarity, the Feyori gave her a mental-window view into the Infirmary room where she lay, supposedly still unconscious from severe exhaustion.

A brown-haired, grey-eyed man wearing one of those ubiquitous, plain-cut exam jackets in a tastefully bland shade of grey perched on the edge of her bed. One set of his fingertips touched her brow, the other set encircled her wrist. On his shoulder was a flash patch with the Radiant Eye, marking him as a member of the Special Forces, Psi Division. No doubt he had been brought in to make sure she didn't suffer from the backlash of KI depletion, which could cause mental and emotional damage to her psyche as much as her advanced exhaustion could cause physical damage to her body.

His presence as a Psi Division soldier was highly ironic, however, because it was the fault of the Feyori that there were any psychics to begin with. Their great Game was impossibly convoluted and gave Ia a brain-twisting migraine whenever she tried to understand it. They used other races as counters and markers, they altered bloodlines and introduced abilities that should not naturally exist, and they rose or fell in their incomprehensible ranks based on the effects that they caused in the lives of the often unwitting, matter-based beings they chose to manipulate.

Like draconian players in the most complex poker game ever invented, they did not care if their actions would be considered right or wrong by the standards of their card-pawns. All that mattered was that they tried their best to behave like miniature gods, unknowable, inscrutable, and annoying as hell—particularly when their usually subtle effects exploded into blatant manipulations.

(. . . *Yes, you are a clever half-child, aren't you? And a powerful one. Your progenitor must be very pleased with your creation. Or perhaps worried. You are powerful, disturbingly so . . . and blatantly determined to do your own Meddling. If I were from a counterfaction . . . you'd be dead.*)

(*Don't threaten me, Feyori,*) Ia growled back mentally. (*I know how to kill your kind.*)

She could sense he didn't fully believe her, but he did humor her. (*And your discretion thus far is appreciated, I'm sure. But your presence, with your power and your own agenda and your determination to carry it through, threatens the Game. Thus I must decide for the benefit of all what must be done with you. But . . . I am not unreasoning; there may be an advantage for my faction in the Game, if I spare you.*)

She didn't have much energy. Of her own. Hooking her will into those fingers at forehead and wrist, Ia replied, (*My presence is the only thing which will save your precious Game.*)

Pulling, Ia dragged both of them onto the timeplains. In the real world, she was still being touched by a brown-haired man; the only visible change, had anyone been able to see that side of him, was the way his eyes had changed from grey to amber. In the golden-sepia hued realm of Time . . . he was no longer Human. With her hand submerged to the wrist in the giant, swirling silver bubble he had become, Ia dragged the Meddler over the streams to the point where everything ended. Her dreams for her own preferred future, and his dreams of continuing the Game beyond three hundred more years.

Pointing at the invaders, Ia spoke. Her words echoed across the timeplains, despite the way the wind whipped at her hair and ruffled his metallic surface. "This *is what we face. The Grey Ones called them the Soor, and they are too powerful even for you to manipulate—the Grey Ones fled from the Soor, abandoning their home galaxy in favor of fleeing to this one. You cannot stop them from stripping our galaxy, and if they strip the galaxy, you'll have no energy to eat, never mind any sentient species left with which to play your Game. In all the years I have studied this problem, I have foreseen* one *chance at stopping them, and only the one chance.*

"*Unless, of course,*" she added, turning with calculated idleness to face the Feyori tethered on her wrist, "*you would prefer to pack up all of your people to flee to another galaxy . . . as the Grey Ones have already done?*"

The Feyori's surface swirled, then stopped. (*. . . The Grey Ones are a dying race. This is not their home galaxy, and these are not their home energies. They have prolonged their own lives, but they cannot prolong their species forever.*)

"*And if you are forced to leave your own galaxy,* you *may not be able to properly digest the food of the next one, either,*" Ia agreed dryly. "*Tens of thousands of years of playing the Game, disrupted and uprooted. The pain-in-the-asteroid of having to restart the Game with whole new species, whole new parameters . . . whole new factions and counterfactions, with no guarantee of anyone's ascendancy. Or . . .*"

(*Your sub-thoughts disturb me.* We *are the Meddlers.* We *play the Game.* You *are a pawn, little half-child. You are a Game piece* we *have set in motion.*)

"*True, but* you *cannot read the future as clearly as I can. You also know what I'm showing you is true. You want your Game to continue. All Feyori, faction, neutral, and counterfaction, want your Game to continue.* I *want this galaxy to continue. Our wants are parallel, our goals complementary. I am faction to* all *of you, not neutral, and not counterfaction. Sometimes the players direct where the pieces are to be played, this is true. But sometimes the* pieces *direct where the players must play.*

"*Spread the word among your fellow Meddlers, and do as I ask, when I ask it of you . . . and you will still have a Game to play four hundred years from now,"* Ia told him. *"You have my Prophetic Stamp on that."*

(*You think you're* her? *The Prophet the Immortal One told us about? The one who supposedly will predict and guide the future for a full thousand years?*)

Ia smirked. *"Who do you think will have told* you *about* her? *Where to find her, and how to deal with her?"*

(*Self-fulfilling Prophecies—*) the Feyori snorted.

"You would have figured it out on your own," Ia said dismissively, cutting him off. *"I'm just going to speed up the process so she doesn't do any accidental damage to the timelines two hundred years from now. Which she would have done."*

(*If you know of her location in place and time, of how the Abomination gets conceived, you will tell us!*) the Feyori argued.

"So you can prevent her conception? Sorry. That would destroy all hope you have of preventing this.*"* She lifted her chin at the barren, lifeless ruin awaiting them in the future. *"If you try . . . well, as my people say, 'Vladistad. Salut.' I will not only intervene so that things happen as they should and did anyway, I will* also *intervene so that she* does *take an interest in Feyori politics. Which is what you will have been trying to prevent when you get around to tossing her back fifteen thousand years . . . isn't it?"*

That startled him, though it was more of a feeling pulsing against the skin of her hand than any actual reaction she could see, beyond the soap-bubble swirling of his silvery surface.

"Oh, yes, I can see just as far into the past as I can into the future. I know what your people did, and how, and why."

His surface roiled, agitated by her words.

(*Mind to mind, there is no lying,*) Ia projected, staring past her distorted reflection on what passed for the energy-being's surface. (*You fight me, and your precious Game will be destroyed. Vladistad, do you understand? You try to counterfaction me, and* you *will be the ones destroyed. Salut, I promise you. So. When I call for you, you will answer. What I request of you, you will do. We get* one *shot at this, Meddler. You will not disrupt my Game. Or we will* all *die . . . and I will make sure* you *as a whole* race *go first.*

(*My Prophetic Stamp on* that.)

Releasing both of them from the timeplains, Ia landed back in her body feeling more wearied than before. Most of the strength she had used had been *his* strength. Which would disturb him even more once he realized it, since to borrow another Feyori's energy was an intimacy reserved mostly for either family or for procreation. But it was necessary; she simply hadn't enough of her own.

At least I won't get pregnant off of that, Ia knew. *I'm still very much a matter-based entity.*

He shuddered mentally, though didn't seem to be enraged by what she had done to him. (*For which I am grateful. I am not counterfaction to your father, but neither am I faction. Nor am I insane enough to breed with a half-breed. I have my own lineage-pawns to establish. So kindly do* not *do that again. As for your warnings and your demands . . . they will be considered, but that is* all. *Claim all you want, we will not believe that* you *are the Prophet of a Thousand Years until it is thoroughly proven. Or disproven.*)

(*Then I invoke the Right of Simmerings. You will not interfere for an agreed-upon span of years, while my plays take shape.*)

(*You know the Rules of the Game. I find that disturbing,*) he murmured.

She smiled faintly. (*I spent most of the last three years preparing myself both physically and mentally. The Game was just one of many things I have studied and learned. I invoke the Right of Simmerings for seven Terran Standard* years,) she repeated mentally, (*or until such time as at least one of you concedes I am the Prophet of a Thousand Years.*)

He considered her offer. His mental control was good enough, she could only sense the shifting of the liquid silver still pressing against her mind. Then again, he *was* an energy-based being, for all he was currently in a matter-shaped body; thoughts were energy, and no one could manipulate energy like a Meddler.

(*. . . Until* three *of us concede you are the Prophet, or six Terran Standard years have passed.*)

(*Agreed,*) Ia confirmed, not needing to give the offer much thought.

(*I accept your Right of Simmerings. I do* not *acknowledge you as the Prophet of a Thousand Years at this time . . . but I will watch. I will also pass the word to keep an eye on you . . . but that is all. The rest will be up to you.*) He paused, then added in warning, (*Be advised, if we believe you are* not *the Prophet . . . at the end of those six years, we will destroy you and whatever pieces you have placed in the Game. You do* not *have the immunity of a true Feyori.*)

(*Understood. Don't count on being able to destroy me, though,*) she added in warning. (*I know far more than you about what you could possibly do to me.*)

From the subcurrents of his thoughts, he didn't believe her. That was alright, though; she had bought enough time for the truth to unfold. From the subcurrents in his energies, she could tell he was putting an end to the illusion that she was still unconscious.

The doctor sighed audibly, still touching her at forehead and wrist. ". . . I think she'll be waking up, soon."

"Good," Sgt. Tae muttered.

Ia had only vaguely been aware of his presence in the room before now. She also got the impression from the Meddler that her chief Drill Instructor had been waiting for her to awaken for a few hours now. The Meddler had a few more things to say before she "officially" awakened, though.

(*You want to keep your psychic abilities a secret. I want to keep my true nature and purpose for being here a secret. Since you claim to know how to play the Game, I propose a short-faction alliance of mutually beneficial silence on these two points. Agreed?*)

(*Agreed. We have a short-faction alliance of mutual silence regarding our true natures.*)

(*Good. Now, I believe it is time for you to wake up. They do know you have an incredibly high KI rating, but I will now state that I cannot say if you have any actual psychic abilities . . . which by the terms of our short-faction agreement, I cannot* say.)

Ia smiled again. This time she felt her lips actually moving, though it was a tremulous, weak effort.

"Yes, she'll awaken shortly. She's drifting in and out. She's quite strong-willed. Of course, I've given her back enough KI so that she won't suffer from depletion shock while she recovers.

The rest of it will simply be a case of waiting for her to physically recover."

"Thank you, Doctor. Now, when can I yell at her some more?"

The "doctor" chuckled. "Oh, I think she's doing enough of that to herself, mentally. Wake up, Recruit!" he asserted, raising his voice enough to make her flinch a little, startled by it. "You're not allowed to dodge the rest of your Basic Training by hiding in your dreams—wake up!"

Prying open her eyes, Ia squinted up at him. His expression was friendly enough, from his cheery bedside smile to the gleam in his grey eyes, but she knew the truth. She was just a Game piece to him—a potentially inconvenient Game piece—and while a player might have a particular fondness for the color red, it didn't guarantee a fondness in that player for every red piece and pip encountered on the board.

Withdrawing his touch, he slid off the bed and nodded to the Drill Instructor. Sergeant Tae came over to the side of her bed. His hat was resting on his back, revealing the grey-salted black stubble passing for his hair. He eyed the intravenous drip supplying her blood with nutrients and glucose, the monitors quietly scanning her body every few seconds in a soft hum, and grimaced.

"Don't you *ever* push yourself this hard again. You got that, Recruit?" he growled, though there was more concern than contention in his tone.

"Permission to speak freely, Sergeant?" Ia countered. Her mouth was dry and her throat was a little hoarse, but otherwise her tone was crisp.

"Granted."

"Don't *you* ever give me an impossible task, and then threaten me with a court-martial mere seconds later for not completing it. Sergeant." She watched his nose wrinkle in disgust and just had to point out, "The *only* thing that kept me from moving that bus right away was the fact that it had been parked and the brake set."

"Why the hell did you do it?" Tae asked. "If it was so impossible, why the hell did you do it?"

She was free of the grey-spot; she could sense the immediate pathways now. Clearer and easier than before, in fact, though she didn't have much in the way of toe-dabbling energy to spare. Answering with the full truth was not an option, but then neither was Fatality Forty-Three, Perjury: lying to a superior officer, within or without the confines of a military court. She did have the historical impact of what happened at Vladistad on her side, but the fewer lies she gave, the less trouble she would get from her superiors.

What she could do, however, was choose to misinterpret. Technically, it wasn't the truth he wanted . . . but neither was it a lie. Technically, it didn't invoke Fatality Forty-Three.

"I told you," Ia said, gazing up at him. "I wasn't going to let you win. Somewhere along the way, it feels like you took my heavyworlder strengths and my willingness to strive to be a model soldier as some sort of personal affront. I am here to *serve*, and *you* don't have the right to hate that about me, Sergeant. I will not screw up just because *you* expect me to."

Bracing his hands on the edge of her bed, Tae leaned over her. "I wasn't *expecting* you to screw up. I was *fearing* that you wouldn't *know* when you screwed up! There is no room for a starry-eyed real-estater in the Corps. If you act out of arrogance, you can and *will* get your teammates *killed*. You can go out and buy yourself a star all you want—hell, you can splatter yourself from here to Zubeneschamali, just so long as you do it on your lonesome—but you *do not* endanger your fellow soldiers!"

Ia waited in silence, knowing he had one more thing to say. He confessed it after a long, hard pause.

"And *I* do not endanger my recruits." He looked down and away as he said it, half muttering to himself. "Not if I can help it."

"I do know that, Sergeant. I was too tired at the time, and I didn't think clearly. If I had, I'd have realized that there was no way you could court-martial me for failing to obey an impossible task . . . impossible merely because the brake was set," Ia acknowledged lightly. "I *also* know, Sergeant, that it is your *job* to test us, so that we don't fail under real-world conditions. Our enemies won't be softhearted. They won't rescind orders. There's nothing you could do to us that will be as dangerous as the real risks of combat and war. Yet it is still your job to prepare us to the best of your ability. I know. And I don't hold it against you."

Tae studied her. "Just how *much* preparing and studying did you do, before joining the Corps, Recruit?"

"Once I knew where my talents were best suited? Quite a lot, Sergeant. Living on a brand-new colonyworld teaches you that survival requires preparation. The more prepared you are, the more likely you'll survive, and maybe even thrive." She gave him a lopsided smile. "And no, there *aren't* a hundred more like me back home. We can't afford to spare that many colonists just yet."

"So you keep saying—you're already a full day behind the rest of your class, Recruit," Tae warned her, straightening and changing the subject. "Dr. Silverstone says it'll take you two or three more days of recovery before you'll be fit enough to go back to duty. In the meantime, you'll be missing out on basic mechsuit instruction, which you and fourteen of your fellow recruits qualified for. The rest will be focusing on lifesuit drills and career path classes. Or did you already study mechsuit mechanics, too, in your rush to get prepared for the SF-MC?"

"Oh, I studied it, Sergeant . . . but it's all still just *theory,*" Ia temporized, giving him another lopsided smile. "Until I actually try it, I won't know how well I can shift from theory to practical application."

Sgt. Tae grunted. "Just don't overdo it. You can kill yourself by doing *too* much, just as you can by not doing enough. Learn to strike the balance, and you *might* just make a good soldier. Screw it up, and both you and a whole lot of others will die."

"Thank you, Sergeant. Believe me, I am aware of that." Tired, she watched as he gave her a curt nod and left. The man with the grey coat and the grey eyes returned. Ia quirked an eyebrow at him. "Dr. Silverstone, I presume?"

"Indeed. I'm going to get you sitting upright in a few minutes, run a couple tests of your muscle density, range of motion, and reflexes, and then hopefully clear you for real food, instead of this drip-fed junk," he agreed, bending over her bed frame so he could poke at the controls. (*I can also hear you laughing mentally over the name. It wasn't my choice. My insertion point came via a bush doctor named James Silverstone who died from a hovercar crash a thousand kilometers east of here, three and a half years ago. I discovered him, assumed his identity, and walked out of the bush as him.*)

(*With amnesia?*) Ia asked, adjusting her position on the bed as he levered the upper half higher. (*Isn't that a bit cliché?*)

(*He wasn't dead when I found him . . . and don't think those thoughts. I didn't kill him. His neural injuries were too severe even for me to heal. Since I couldn't stop his death, I scanned his mind just before he died, and assumed his identity.*) Running a palm scanner down her body, he stopped it over some of her worst bruises and *tutted*. "I'll have to do some deep-tissue biokinesis here . . . and here. And over there, I think. That'll take place after you eat, so your body has the biomatter it needs to replace what I'll be psychically encouraging your own tissues to hurry up and use."

"Thank you, Doctor." (*How many of you use dead or dying people as your "insertion points" anyway?*)

(*For a Right of Breeding? Not as often as you'd think. At least not when we're male. Like your father undoubtedly did, it's usually just a case of finding a suitable candidate, shifting shape into the appropriate type of male, swooping in, seducing, impregnating, and flying off again, to observe from afar to make sure the implantation isn't rejected, one way or another. If we're female . . . modern identity tracking methods make it harder to establish an identity long enough to stay in matter form and carry the progeny to term. Still, Belini likes being female, so "she" does it fairly often—that is, often by our terms. We do live for thousands of your years.*)

(*You should try Parker's World.*) At his sharp look, Ia smiled. Faintly, but she smiled. (*Twenty years from now, lawlessness and laziness will start pervading and perverting their original organization and bureaucracy. Bribes will become accepted practice, and false idents not too difficult to purchase. Not to mention, you'll be able to buy a new identity outright with feeble documentation in about fifty years, then you can go just about anywhere as a Terran citizen. So long as you can play the part of a heavyworlder, of course.*)

(*You insult our acting skills,*) he quipped, tapping on her knees to gauge her reflex points.

Her legs twitched. (*As the Gatsugi put it, "actor" and "liar" are one and the same thing.*)

(*And you insult us once again, little one. Perhaps I should jab you with an old-fashioned hypodermic needle, instead of a nice, numbing spraystick?*)

She could tell from the brightening of the silver sphere in

her mind that he was joking. Mostly. (*You know what they say, a soldier just calls a comet a comet. Which means I'm a half-breed, so I'm only half the liar . . . excuse me, actor . . . that you are.*)

(*Careful. Everything you say and do can and will be shared with my fellow Feyori.*)

(*Bring 'em on. Just don't violate my Right of Simmering. Even a half-breed is allowed that much leeway in the Game.*)

(*Only when the pieces are aware of it.*) Finished with his cursory exam, Dr. Silverstone straightened. ". . . I'll bet you're hungry after all that exertion, particularly with that extra heavy-worlder appetite of yours. I'll have the cafeteria bring up something right away."

"I'm *so* glad you could finally join us, Recruit Ia," Sgt. Tae drawled two mornings later. He pointed at a bulky brown packing crate as big as an extra-wide coffin, which sat in solitary splendor in a corner of the gymnasium-sized classroom. "There's your mechsuit. Since you seem to be such a good little student, so quick on the spot and so eager to study things in advance, I'm going to give you *one* chance to get into that suit, without any help . . . and if you can get at least seventy percent of it right, you *won't* have to do any push-ups today. You don't have to do it in a p-suit today, but you *will* learn tomorrow."

Ia nodded and crossed to the case. Hauling it out on its wheels, she opened the case door. The suit inside looked like a humanoid robot, silvery and silent. Opening the lid of her military ident, she powered up the suit with a few coded taps of her fingers. Powered it up, and opened it up. Since she didn't have to wear the weight suit for this drill—the mechsuit itself would become her resistance training, in a way—all she had to do was take off her boots and set them to one side, then make sure her pants were tucked into her socks so they wouldn't catch on anything.

An examination of the various parts proved they were inspection ready, freshly minted in a military manufactory. Turning around, Ia stepped back and up into the case, slotting her feet one at a time into the balance receptors, which were fitted to accommodate her feet. The pelvic joints felt like they rode a little high, but she knew she would get used to them. Closing the lid of her arm unit, Ia slotted her arms into the half-open flexor gloves, leaned back into the thoracic cavity, and flexed her fingers in the glove controls.

Hissing faintly, the legs, arms, pelvis and torso plates snapped shut, sealing themselves with a low *thrum*. A pull freed her arms from the padding. That gave her the leverage to haul her upper body partway out of the close-fitted foam, then her legs, and lastly her hips as the center-point of her balance. Stepping down and free, she tested the suit with a few steps. The floor was slightly uneven in spots, since while it was designed to accept the two hundred or more extra kilos in weight each mechsuit added to a recruit, even plexcrete could only withstand the machine-augmented force of a mechsuited soldier for so long before cracking and crumbling. Mindful of the patches underfoot, she tested her balance carefully.

"Twenty *sit-ups* for neglecting to also don your helm in a timely manner, Recruit," Tae chastised her. At her quick look, he smirked. "I only said you wouldn't have to do *push-ups*. Put on your helmet, and do your demerits *in* your suit, Recruit. Count off through your suit speakers at Volume 2 . . . assuming Hell Week didn't burn away the memory of your mechsuit theory classes."

"Sergeant, yes, Sergeant; no, they didn't, Sergeant," Ia agreed. She knew why he was picking on her again. Nobody else had needed two days to recover, and he wasn't about to retard the rest of Class 7157's advancement through their training program.

"And *don't* gouge any chunks out of the floor," Tae added briskly as she reached into the packing case for the helmet. "Fire up your helmet and run a level 1 diagnostics before your demerits, then a level 3 afterward. And *pay attention* to the rest of the class. We will not slow down just so you can bore us in the attempt to catch up."

"Sergeant, yes, Sergeant." Pulling the helm into place, she lined up the self-sealing neck flanges which would turn the mechsuit from a simple exoframe into a self-contained spacesuit, once the faceplate was sealed and a portable oxy-pack was hooked into her back. They didn't need to be that tightly self-contained just yet, and both she and Tae knew it. She just didn't want to give him any other reasons to nitpick her performance right now.

"Recruit Ia!" he barked, recapturing her attention. "One last thing. Try to remember that your own strength will *amplify* whatever you do with your mechsuit servos. That's why you're training in half-mech and not full-mech. That, and your heavy-worlder reflexes. You may no longer need to train all day in your weight suit, but you will still do so for your morning and evening regimens. That means you will still be stronger than the rest, forces which will be amplified by your suit. Don't break anything. Or anyone."

"Sergeant, yes, Sergeant."

CHAPTER 9

. . . Did I ever use any civilian or familial connections to advance my career in the military? That's a fair question. And I'll give you a fair answer.

Yes.

But that yes comes with a caveat. I never asked for any help from my family—mainly because they had zero influence on the Terran military, for obvious reasons. The only time I had a particular civilian help me, it was because he asked me what he could do. And the only reason why I told him what he could do is because I knew he'd try something anyway. Mayhem, to quote a rather long-distance friend of mine, should always be directed and purposeful. Which meant I had to guide him, or risk his interference destroying everything.

~Ia

JULY 3, 2490 T.S.

"Now, as you go forth into the stars, remember that you carry with you the pride, tradition, and training of a Space Force Marine. Each one of you has felt the call in your hearts to place yourselves, your bodies, your weapons, your skills—and if necessary, your lives—between your beloved homes and families, and all that could destroy them. You *are* soldiers. That is your duty, and your privilege.

"For that, and for all the things you are about to do, Class 7157," General Tackett stated, lifting his right hand crisply to the brim of his dress cap, "I salute you."

Snapping from Parade Rest to Attention, forty-one brown-uniformed, black-striped, sword-bearing recruits saluted him back. Three more recruits had dropped out during the remainder of their training, including poor Casey, who had suffered from an unexpected and untreatable allergic reaction to the foam lining the pressure-suits all space-traveling soldiers had to learn how to wear. Disappointed, he had been sent back planet-side after Class 7157 had been transferred to Battle Platform *Chau*.

Allergic reactions were almost unheard-of in this day and age, thanks to a modified strain of the V'Dan *jungen* virus. The microbe had allowed the ancient Humans who became the V'Dan to adapt to their strange new homeworld, thousands of years before. The original strain, while it provided immunity to almost all allergens, had also colored their skin and hair in various patterns and shades, ranging from common stripes and spots in burgundy and black, to the almost snowflake-like patterns of pale blue seen in a rare few V'Dan family lines.

Nowadays it was rare to see a V'Dan with *jungen* stripes, as rare as it was for any Human, V'Dan or Terran, to suffer from an allergy. But Casey had suffered, and couldn't don a p-suit for more than a handful of minutes before breaking out in hives. A soldier who couldn't climb into a pressure-suit within a single minute and wear it for a full two hours wasn't a soldier who could serve in the Space Force.

His trainers had written a glowing letter of recommendation to the Department of Peacekeepers, since Casey's case had proved too difficult to overcome sufficiently enough for a career in the Marines—the one thing that separated the Space Force and its Branches from the various planetary Peacekeeper forces was the word *space*, after all. For the other two recruits who had failed, one had been called back home on family emergency Leave, and the other had been unable to handle the combat simulations. Modern physical and psychological testing could weed out those most likely to fail in the first few weeks, and do so far better than any other efforts had in the past, but some things just had to be tested by actually trying them.

". . . And now, for the moment you recruits have been waiting for," General Tackett stated, smiling on the stage. "*Soldiers* of Class 7157," he stressed, "having graduated from the Basic Instruction requirements of the Space Force Branch Marine Corps . . . you are hereby dismissed for your three days of Leave, to be followed by your Service assignments to your official first duty posts. Class 7157 . . . dismissed!"

Cheering erupted from the men and women gathered on the parade ground. Even Ia smiled, relieved this part was over. It had helped that the sky was mostly overcast and the weather relatively cool, now that they were in the southern hemisphere's version of winter, but the air was still muggy enough to make their freshly issued dress uniforms borderline uncomfortable in the subtropical heat. Being free to move meant being free to remove her dress cap, allowing the wind to fluff out and dry her short-cropped hair.

Her relief didn't last long. Awareness of each passing second pressed on her. No longer would she be immersed in just her training. Now she would have to keep track of both her surroundings and the ever-pressing needs of the future. *Too much to do, too little time to do it in . . . and no time to spare for myself, just yet . . . Here come the families and friends who could make it to celebrate Class 7157's graduation.*

She searched the crowd like some of the others did, but she knew better than to expect her family to be so far from home. The person she did expect to be here was easy enough to spot. The blue-and-white batik prints were different enough from the solid hues that were currently popular that his clothes alone would have made him stand out. However, it was his physical shape that not only made him distinct, but also made some of the Humans in the audience swerve around him.

Approaching with slightly gaping jaws, but with his lips carefully hiding his teeth in the version of the smile used by his species, the Tlassian stopped in front of Ia and bowed, lacing his claw-tipped fingers over his jacket-wrapped chest. ". . . Private Ia. Congratulassionss. Did you do well enough?"

Ia bowed back. "Thank you, Grandmaster. Yes, I am satisfied with my performance."

He grinned wider, part of his split tongue poking out on one side. Spreading his arms, he waited for her to turn around, then promptly caught her in a bear hug from behind. Ia *oofed* and laughed. The feel of his yellow and brown scales sliding against her ear and cheek tickled, but she didn't flinch at the touch of his scaly skin against her smoother flesh. This, at least was one person she didn't have to fear being drawn into the timestreams with her. He had already braved it, and emerged from it with a level of equanimity she both envied and tried to emulate.

With his arms wrapped around her, he murmured in her ear, "I made ssssure to reread your advicssse before coming hhhere. Sssince I *am* sstill determined to hhhave my sssay."

"You don't *have* to . . . but it will help, thank you," Ia murmured back.

Releasing her with a chuckling, he turned his back to her and craned his neck, glancing over his shoulder. Ia returned the hug, angling slightly to avoid putting pressure on his tail—and gasped as he bent over, lifting her off her feet. Laughing from the unexpected ride, she bounced onto her toes as he straightened again. For one brief moment, she felt carefree. Having a good friend on her side, *at* her side, to celebrate the successful first step in her task was remarkably uplifting. She smiled at him—lips carefully covering her teeth—and enjoyed the rare sensation.

"Ey! Choo didn't tell us choo knew any Tlassians!" Spyder protested, working his way closer through the Humans mingling around them. "So, who's the handsome meioa-o?"

Turning to answer him, Ia spotted three figures headed their way. She held up her hand, warding off an introduction to Spyder until General Tackett, Sergeant Tae, and Sergeant Chong reached them. ". . . General Tackett, may I introduce Grandmaster Ssarra of the Afaso Order?"

"Grandmaster?" Spyder repeated, eyes widening. "He's th' Grandmaster? Choo know th' Afaso Grandmaster?"

"Grandmaster Ssarra. You honor us," General Tackett murmured, recovering quickly from his own briefly visible surprise.

Ia smiled and made the introductions, as her alien friend bowed gracefully. "Grandmaster Ssarra, this is General Tackett, commander of Camp Nallibong, Space Force Branch Marine Corps; and these are First Sergeant Ulliong Tae, my chief instructor; First Sergeant Harold Chong, on assignment to Camp Nallibong from Space Force Branch Special Forces, Department of Innovations; and my fellow classmate, Private Second Class Glen Spyder."

"An honor, meioa," Spyder asserted, bowing in Tlassian fashion with his fingers laced over his chest. "I haven't seen a Tlassian since I landed on this 'ere rock."

"Yes, it is an honor," Sgt. Tae agreed. The corner of his mouth quirked up. "Your Order trained Private Ia rather well in unarmed combat before she came here. All we had to do was sharpen her edges."

"I ssshall take that asss a persssonal compliment, ass well as a proffessional one," Ssarra returned, bowing his head. "I gave her blade, asss you put it, the fffinal pre-military polisssh myssselff. It pleasssess me to know my efffortss bore good ressultss." Turning to Ia, Ssarra laced his fingers over his chest and bowed politely. "Iff you will excusse uss, Ia, I would like to sspeak with your ssuperiorsss about your training, and your prosspectss."

"Of course, Grandmaster." Lacing her fingers, Ia bowed in return. Straightening, she nodded at the others. "General, Sergeants, please excuse me."

Subtly hooking her arm around Spyder's elbow as she brushed past him, she dragged her fellow Marine away. He stumbled, caught himself, and matched his stride to hers, grinning. "Ey. 'Zis mean choo gonna finally get all wicked 'n such on me? Since we don't gotta be asexual recruits anymore . . ."

That made her smile. "Dream on, Private. Did you get any family to drop by?"

"Nah. Jus' a vidmail from me mum, sayin' how proud she is an' all that. It's nice," Spyder added, nodding at his wrist unit. "They finally unlocked th' non-military side a' th' comm units on these things, an' there it was, waitin' in th' inbox. I figure, since I got three days, I could hop a transport. A day there, a day home, a day back . . . *or*, I could convince a certain gorgeous assortment o' meioa-es t' accompany me t' th' Mindil Beach Reserve. Ey, what choo think of that, Kumanei? Wanna go up t' Mindil Beach?"

Kumanei tipped her head, thinking about it. "You buying the bikini, space boy? 'Cause I don't recall one of those being in the standard issue in my kitbag, and I ain't wearing the asteroid-ugly swimsuit they gave me if I don't have to."

Chuckling, Spyder freed his arm from Ia's, and framed Kumanei between his outstretched fingers. "I see . . . a gorgeous, purple-flowered sarong—no, no, make it green, wi' an orchid right about . . . there. Choo'd look like a goddess what stepped outta th' bush in flowery green. An' Forenze . . . man, I'd kill t' get 'er into a nice purple outfit. As f'r Ia, here—"

"Sorry, but I'll be gone," Ia quickly demurred. "No trip to the beach for me."

"What?" Spyder squinted at her. "No beach? What kinda slaggin' idea izzat? Not go t' th' beach! Yer on Leave on th' Motherworld, f'stars' sake! S'not like th' repeller fields ain't chasin' away th' salties—in fact, I 'eard they added extra repellers jus' last week. What choo gonna do that's more important than goin' t' a Motherworld beach?"

Her rare sense of humor flashed itself in a grin and a poke of her thumb over her shoulder. "The Grandmaster's my ride. He's here to haul me back to Afaso Headquarters for the next few days."

"Nice joke, Private Ia," Arstoll quipped. "Just because you took lessons with the Afaso doesn't mean you personally know the Grandmaster."

"She does *so*," Spyder asserted, sticking up for her. "She just introduced us 'n the General to th' meioa-o. They're right over there, havin' a little confab at th' moment. Can't miss 'im, either, he's th' only non-Human in sight."

He pointed at General Tackett and Sergeant Chong, who were talking with the lone Tlassian in view. Sergeant Tae was no longer with them. Ia spotted her chief Drill Instructor chatting with . . . Dr. Silverstone. The doctor glanced up and looked straight at Ia, letting her know he was aware of her presence. He then glanced at the Tlassian, then looked back at her and quirked an eyebrow.

(*Is the Grandmaster himself one of your Game pieces?*) he asked, returning his attention to Tae.

(*Right of Simmerings,*) Ia reminded him blandly.

(*Only so long as you don't have too many pots on the stove. Too many, and things will start to boil. And if they boil over . . .*)

(*I know the rules.*) With Spyder no longer touching her, Ia dared to dip into the timestreams. She pulled out a moment later and nodded to herself. (*Come over here and offer a lift to anyone who wants to go to Mindil Beach in half an hour. Take Private Spyder and five others. You'll meet the woman who fulfils all your criteria on the north end of the beach roughly half an hour after you arrive. She'll be wearing dark red, and she'll be looking at a crab shell she picks up from the sand.*)

(*I already have a woman in mind, thank you.*)

(*That one won't be right for your needs. She'll fail to properly raise your progeny, which will damage your own Right of Simmerings. The one on the beach will do better as a mother, if you choose to vanish on her,*) Ia told him.

(*You make that sound like I should stay in this matter-based body a lot longer than it takes to select my target and ensure the progeny suits my needs,*) Silverstone challenged her.

(*You're forgetting the advantage your children . . . plural . . . would have if they were raised to understand and use their powers by their progenitor.*)

He laughed in her mind, a bark as sharp and short as a jolt of electricity. (*You're forgetting the rules. One progeny per . . . Oh. You're* that *offspring. Tell me, how did your half brother survive? Or you, for that matter?*)

(*Right of Simmerings.*)

(*Nonsense,*) he discarded. (*That would be your progenitor's Simmering, not your own, and two half-breeds at once are forbidden.*)

Ia nodded and shook her head at appropriate points, making it sound like she was endorsing Spyder's plan of convincing several others to find a hovercar for rent and taking it up to the beach. (*He made the mistake of stumbling across my mothers while they were in the mood to celebrate the idea of getting around to having a couple of children.*)

(*So? He shouldn't have mated with both of them.*)

She smiled. (*They were rather insistent.*)

(*He's a Feyori. We're only fertile in this form when we make an effort at transforming energy into matter.*)

(*He caught them while they were on a picnic . . . in a* crysium *field.*)

(. . .)

(*The crysium clouded his mind, and thus—shall we say— enhanced his efforts?*)

Ia waited for him to process that statement. It didn't take much longer.

(*That . . . is the most perverted,* disgusting *thing I have* ever *heard,*) Silverstone growled. Physically, his face remained mostly impassive, save for a pinched crease in the otherwise smooth skin of his brow. (*We've been visiting that planet for longer than your species has been sentient, and you're telling me that the* crysium *"influenced" your progenitor?*)

(*Influenced,* and *protected . . . as my progenitor found out when he realized afterward that he'd impregnated both of my mothers. He couldn't terminate either of us, though he tried. Nor could the two Feyori who came by to help him. The crysium stopped them.*)

(*It is* not *capable of doing that, little one,*) Silverstone explained patiently, coldly. (*You do not know what your precious "crystal sprays" are made of. It is* not *sentient, it does* not *interfere, and it does* not *play the Game.*)

(*Ah, but I do know what it is. I told you, I've studied you Meddlers,*) she reminded him. (*Every time you convert yourselves to a matter-based life-form, some of your energy selves remain. That's how you can communicate telepathically, and lift things telekinetically, and do all the other things we've come to associate with psychic abilities. It's nothing more than lingering traces of your energy-based abilities.*)

(*But when you revert back to your energy forms, you carry trace amounts of matter with you . . . which, to put it delicately, you eventually "shed" all over a selected planet,*) Ia recited dryly. (*Preferably a heavyworld, since that strips a higher percentage of stray matter from your forms, and preferably on a world like Sanctuary, one with its own revitalizing electrical field, so you can use it to refresh and rejuvenate yourselves with a little midflight energy snack.*

(*You haven't just been "visiting" my homeworld. You've been* shitting *on it,*) she accused.

(. . .) Ending his conversation with Sergeant Tae, Dr. Silverstone folded his arms across his dress jacket. He was too canny to look directly at her, but he was also too upset not to scowl. Proof that he had learned to act Human quite well by now. (*I find it disturbing that you know so much about us. I find your claim that the crysium interfered even more unsettling.*

I would far more believe that you *intervened, even as a tiny squidge of barely fertilized pre-sentiency, than that a pile of crystalline* shit *intervened. How much* do *you know?*)

Ia figured it was wisest to admit the truth to him. Hopefully, the truth from her metaphysical lips would convince him she did, indeed, know how to play the Game.

(*Crysium dust—the lingering, energy-infused particles of matter you expel—either gets absorbed into the local life-forms, both the plants and the animals that eat them, or it absorbs water, electricity from lightning storms, and certain minerals from the indigenous rocks, until it grows into a crysium spray. The dust ingested by the plants and animals helps both kinds grow larger than they should on a world with as high a gravity as Sanctuary's. And when it accumulates in the bones of sentient beings, it not only strengthens those bones, it increases the native-born settler's chances of developing psychic abilities.*

(*You don't have to* breed *a progeny to develop a bloodline capable of Meddling in matter-based affairs,*) Ia pointed out, listening with only half her attention on the conversations of her fellow Humans. (*Roses will grow in a carefully tended garden, yes, but they'll also grow on a compost heap, given the right conditions. Even seemingly random ones.*)

(*Yes, but the fertilizer doesn't* plant *the flowers. Something else does that. The wind, the rain, a stray dog carrying a seed. Not the fertilizer.*)

(*We'll see, won't we? Take my advice, either way. Offer them a ride, leave in half an hour, and roughly half an hour after you get there, you'll find a woman in dark red looking at a crab shell on the north end of the beach—if nothing else, consider it a preliminary test of my prognostic abilities,*) Ia told him.

(*And what if I'm at the south end of the beach instead? What if I go into the water?*) he countered.

(*Have you ever stepped on a lionfish before?*)

(*No.*)

(*Don't be in the water at the south end of the beach at the half-hour mark. You may be a Feyori, but you're also in a matter-based body. You can feel pain just like anyone else,*) Ia warned him. (*As for the lady in dark red, it would be no fault*

of yours *if* she *were releasing two eggs at the moment of procreation.*

(*My "advice" isn't illegal interference . . . barely. You only
have my "word" that such a thing could be possible, never
mind true. And the odds of you procreating at the right moment
in time to "accidentally" take advantage of such a thing . . .
well, I'm not going to tell you* when *to actually do that part,
so my words couldn't be considered a factioning of your efforts.
Particularly since you don't think I'm the Prophet of a Thousand Years . . . but also because I* do *know how to play by the
rules. I haven't given you enough information to give you an
illegal faction-boost.*)

". . . Wha' *choo* don't understand, Private Arstoll, izzat I
don't *wanna* speak educatedly," Spyder argued tartly, recapturing her attention. "If I wished to do so," he enunciated carefully,
"I could speak as clearly as the rest of you. But we New Lun-
noners take great pride in our local 'color' and its slang. From
the ancient, pick-dug coal mines of Newcastle to the drone-
gathered gas mines of Jupiter and Saturn, my ancestors take
great pride in being generation after generation of miners." He
dropped the precision of his speech as he continued. "I'm only
here 'cause I got caught messin' wi' th' equipment an' th' Nets,
and a freight-load a' other stuff one too many times, an' the
psychologists said I needed 'a better outlet' for my energies.

"Right now, that outlet sez take me 'n a bunch a' pretty
meioa-es t' th' beach. Now, choo wanna come along, or choo
wanna sit here an' pretend choo don't wanna see Forenze in a
teeny-weeny bikini? 'Cause if you say that, *we're* all gonna call
you a liar!"

Arstoll crossed his arms over his chest. "If I wanted to see
her naked, I could have done so at any point during Basic
Training. We *did* share the same latrines, after all."

"Neh-yah-veh," Kumanei argued, waggling her hand to
accompany the V'Dan slang for "more or less," literally "no-
yes-maybe." She winked at Forenze, who bore a mildly insulted
look at Arstoll's words. "If you ask me, it's all in th' *packaging.*
Naked is okay, but draped in something that covers just the
right spots, and a tiny bit more, that's a whole 'nother matter.
Now, if we put you out there naked? No interest, meioa-o. But

wrap you in a Samoan *lavi-lavi*, with that chest of yours all muscled and bare on top, but only your calves and your feet showing down below? *Mucho irropoi*."

"Did I hear something about a *lavi-lavi*?" a new voice interjected. The Human-shaped Feyori had approached while they were talking, and now nodded at the former recruits. "Captain James Silverstone, paraphysician."

"Sir!" Arstoll said, snapping to Attention.

"Relax, Private, you're on Leave. If you're looking for a *lavi-lavi*, there's an excellent little import shop at the Mindil Beach Market." He glanced briefly at Ia, then aimed a smile at the other ladies. "They also sell civilian swimwear and other goods. I'm headed there in about half an hour for a couple of hours of relaxing on the beach; my hovercar has room for five or six more. If you're interested . . . show up outside Building D-400. Will you be joining us, Private Ia?"

She managed to keep her smile polite, rather than smug. "No, I can't, though I appreciate the offer, sir. I'm headed across the Indian Ocean with my friend. We have to leave shortly, so I'll say this now, and I mean every word. It was an honor to survive Basic with all of you."

Arstoll smirked. He held out his hand. " 'Survive' is right. Good luck, Private Ia. May you get a good duty post. You have some good leadership potential. Rough in places, but I know you'll polish it once you're out there."

Clasping his hand, she shuddered internally, sensing his soon-to-be disappointment and frustration at his own first post. If he didn't lose his temper, he would have a good shot at advancement through the ranks and a decent enough career for the next few years . . . but she didn't want to see all the way to the inevitable end of his life, and freed her fingers. "Thanks for showing us all those fine qualities of your own. You'll make a good officer, Arstoll, noncom or commissioned. Once you get there."

Silverstone held out his own hand to her. "Private Ia . . . try not to be so stubborn about carrying through an impossible mission. Next time, I won't be around to patch you back together." (*Though we* will *keep an eye on you and your Simmerings.*)

"I'll keep that in mind, sir." Shaking his hand briefly, she didn't bother to reinforce her reply telepathically.

The others offered their hands, too. Sharing a round of firm handshakes, and an abrupt, friendly hug from the irrepressible Spyder—whose fate she mercifully didn't sense—Ia moved away and found Ssarra just finishing his own conversation a few meters away. Crossing the grass to join him, she guided him toward the exit from the parade grounds.

"If you're about ready, I just need to get my kitbag from the barracks and to take a moment to stow my mechsuit case with the Supply Department at the Camp here, then I'll be free to go. I'll also need to be back here in three days to pick up my orders."

The Grandmaster nodded. He waited until they were out of earshot of the others, beyond the grandstand, before speaking. "My sssuborbital ssship is at the landing padss eassst of here. Ah—I meant to tell you, now that we are alone, the planss ffor the Vault have been approved by the Order Counssil. But winning the fffunding for it through the Lottery ssseemss like a cheat. When I opened that envelope and sssaw what the insstructionss were . . . it sstill leavess a bad tasste on my tonguess. I fffollowed your insstructionss . . . but it iss a bad tasste, none-thelesss."

"I carefully picked a ticket that wouldn't harm the future if it went 'missing' from the unaltered version of time," she murmured back, eyes and ears alert to any chance of being overheard. Dr. Silverstone didn't count, of course; she could feel his extra senses blanketing the area, pricked to pick up anything of interest to him. This was just part of her Simmerings, though. "I told you I wouldn't ask you to start such a huge, costly project as the Vault without paying for it. Since I don't have any other funds available, this was how I chose to pay for it."

"But, a lottery ticket . . . Aren't precogss fffforbidden to usse their abilitiess fffor . . . ?" He fell quiet as she lifted her fingers, silently urging caution.

Ia waited until they passed the knot of graduated recruits and family members stopped for a chat on the grass next to the path. A training class jogged by; from their plain brown T-shirts and their huffing breaths, she didn't have to peek into the timestreams to know they were still in their first couple of weeks. She continued once they were out of earshot.

"We aren't allowed to *personally* profit by them for more than a set amount of money per year—I believe an average year's wages, whatever that's considered to be right now. I haven't ever exceeded even half that amount personally, I'm sure, and not at all in the last half year. Nor are we allowed to let any family member profit by more than that amount, unless it's tucked into a managed trust account or they hand all of it over to a nonprofit entity. Nor can it benefit any corporation or other for-profit entity. However . . . the Afaso Order isn't a for-profit entity."

Not that it'd stop me if I had to give the money to a non-charitable cause or whatever else I may need to fund . . . and I will have to fund things at some point, she added silently, but only silently.

"Nothing stays our hand legally for a proven good cause, other than that we shouldn't exceed a certain, much larger amount per year. Which I have not yet done. Technically." Shrugging, she added, "For that matter, I'm also technically required to undergo yearly psychic evaluation scans. Which I'll be doing as soon as a certain trio of priests from the Witan Order back home arrive at the Afaso Headquarters tomorrow. But I don't have to *tell* anyone I'm a psi, so long as I am scanned by authorized telepaths and the results are filed with a duly authorized psi organization. Which they are."

Ssarra smiled humorlessly, showing hints of his teeth. "You should have been a law-sssayer."

That amused her. "Yes, but I want to *save* the galaxy, Ssarra, not destroy it."

Her dry counterargument delighted the Grandmaster; he let out a staccato hiss, the Tlassian version of laughter. Smiling wryly herself, Ia led the way to the cluster of white-clad, green-roofed barracks sitting in the distance.

CHAPTER 10

What did I think of my first command officers? Well, Lt. Ferrar was very quick on the mark. Intelligent, efficient, and possessing a nose for trouble. I haven't seen instincts like that outside of longtime combat personnel, the occasional battlecog, and the Peacekeepers, but he'd only held his position for a year and a half when I encountered him. Then again, he was a Field Lieutenant, promoted out of the rank and file for his combat leadership skills.

Lt. D'kora . . . she amused me. The woman never asked a question if she could instead make it a statement. I think she asked maybe two, three questions the entire time I knew her. She was tough and efficient, too. The tough was easy to explain since she was from Eiaven, the heavyworld that colonized my home. Not quite as quick-minded as Lt. Ferrar, but smart all the same. The efficient? That one's obvious, too. She was an officer in the Marine Corps.

~Ia

JULY 30, 2490 T.S.
TUPSF *LIU JI*, DOCKED AT BATTLE PLATFORM *HUM-VEE*
GLIESE 250 SYSTEM

Dropping her kitbag at her feet and setting her rolling case upright on its end, Ia saluted the blue-clad officer waiting on the gantry. He looked up from the datapad in his hand, no doubt expecting to handle only an inventory of supplies arriving on the courier ship, and quirked a brow at her. "Yes, Private?"

"Sir! Private First Class Ia, TUPSF Marine Corps, assigned to Ferrar's Fighters, requesting permission to come aboard, sir," she reported crisply. He returned the salute, letting her drop her arm. Fishing a datachip out of her pocket, Ia handed it to him. "Here are my transfer orders, Lieutenant."

The lieutenant stuck it into his datapad and checked her orders. Nodding, he extracted it and gave it back. "Everything looks in order. Take the airlock behind me, turn right, go straight through three more airlocks, the lift will be on your left. Take it down to Deck 8. When you emerge, turn left, go to the second . . . no, sorry, third door on the left, and report to either First Lieutenant Ferrar or to one of his junior officers. I'll have Supply deliver your mechsuit case to the flight deck. From there, you'll have to get it to the right prep bay yourself, depending on which Platoon you're placed in."

"Thank you, sir." Hefting her things once more, Ia headed for the first set of airlock doors.

She hadn't really needed to be told where to go; for the next two and a half years, the TUPSF *Liu Ji* would be her home, which meant she had studied its layout, routines, and missions as thoroughly as possible on the timeplains. Still, the courtesy was appreciated, if unneeded for navigating the multiple levels and airlocks of the modest-sized battleship.

Reaching the correct door, Ia pushed the buzzer, announcing her presence. Two Marines strode up the corridor, dressed in casual Browns. She turned to nod to them in greeting as they eyed her, and the door opened behind her.

"You're the new transfer. Good, come in," the woman in the doorway stated. Ia turned back to face her, meeting the other woman's assessing green gaze. "The Lieutenant wants to see you."

Nodding, Ia followed her inside. "You must be Second Lieutenant Lucille D'kora, sir," she offered, nodding politely to the shorter woman. It earned her an arched brow. Ia shrugged. "I checked over the roster of Lieutenant Ferrar's Company on my way out here. I thought it would be smart to get to know everybody in advance."

"Yes, your record did indicate you like to prepare yourself. The DoI has already flagged your file with a few things," D'kora added. "The Lieutenant wants to discuss them with you. Call me D'kora. I don't answer to my first name. Neither does the Lieutenant."

"Of course, sir. I'd say, neither do I, but I only have the one name."

D'kora smiled briefly and gestured for her to follow. Ia had already foreseen this meeting. Depending upon her replies to his questions and his own internal thoughts—whatever those might turn out to be—the Lieutenant would assign her to a handful of different positions, most of which would progress her career. There weren't too many ways she could mess up this interview, thankfully.

"That's the Company Sergeant for Ferrar's Fighters, Master Sergeant Brickles," D'kora introduced, nodding at the freckled man seated at the desk in the front office. He lifted a hand briefly from his workstation console but didn't look up. It was just as well; D'kora didn't pause for anything more, just reached for the button on the frame of the next doorway. "He'll be retiring in a few months. You'll get a more formal introduction to the rest of the Company later. *Lieutenant D'kora and Private Ia to see you, sir.*"

"Come in," a male voice said over the door's comm unit.

Touching the button to open the door, D'kora led Ia inside. The man seated behind the desk had dark brown hair like D'kora, but his was very short and crinkled, and only a few shades darker than his face. He rose at Ia's approach, waited for her to set down her kitbag and stand her case next to it in the corner of the smallish cabin, then returned the salute she offered.

Ia offered him her datachip as soon as the brief formality was over. "Private First Class Ia reporting as ordered, sir."

"Welcome aboard, Private. Have a seat," Ferrar added, gesturing at the two chairs in front of his desk. Ia took the one on the right, and Lt. D'kora took the one on the left. Lieutenant Ferrar reseated himself, plugged her datachip into his workstation, and studied the file for a long moment. He nodded and touched a control that sank all four of the workstation screens down into his desk. "Everything's in order, and the same as the advance copy I received from Personnel. *And* from the DoI. But we'll get to that in a moment.

"In the last year, my Company has seen an increasing number of border violations, ranging from ordinary smuggling attempts to ship hijackings, to what look like possible supply runs attempting to circumnavigate the Salik Blockade. We are not officially a part of that Blockade," Ferrar added bluntly, "but it is definitely beginning to feel like it."

"In the last four months, we've seen our border encounters increase to at least once a week," D'kora stated, supplementing his claims. "And in the last three weeks, we've had border encounters five times. Three of them have involved the SF-MC in combat."

"As good as we are, we've taken some hits," Lt. Ferrar continued. "The Personnel Department knows that this Company is four bodies short. Three bought a star due to sabotage on a smuggler's ship, and the fourth I sent back home on the last supply transport so he can get a higher level of medical care than what the Navy doctors on the *Hum-Vee* can provide. Now, I need two privates, a corporal, and a sergeant to fill out my ranks. The Department of Innovations seems to think that *you*, a Private First Class, would make an appropriate replacement sergeant. But you're fresh out of Basic."

Pressing a button on his workstation, he raised up his far right screen. A touch of his hand angled the screen so that it faced Ia and D'kora, though the lieutenant had to shift in her seat a little bit to see it comfortably. Hands flicking over the keys, Lt. Ferrar called up part of Ia's record.

"So. I have a few questions. The incident with Recruit Kaimong. Why did you go after him?" Ferrar asked her.

"I was there," Ia stated simply. The look he leveled her said that wasn't enough. She shrugged. "I knew I could track him."

"Just that?" the Lieutenant questioned her.

Ia shrugged again. "It's all in my report to the Camp Command Staff. I knew he was armed, and I knew he was dangerous.

The priority of the moment was catching him before he could encounter any unsuspecting personnel, or worse, innocent civilians. I knew I could track him through the bush, finding him that much faster. It made sense to offer."

"You were barely trained. A raw recruit. A *civilian*," D'kora scoffed.

"I'm a second-generation firstworlder, sir," Ia retorted levelly, glancing at the other woman. "I may not have been trained by military standards before my enlistment, but I went into the Marines with far more training than the average civilian ever gets. You're from Eiaven. You know what it's like on a new but inhabitable colonyworld. It takes at least five generations to tame a world enough that survival is no longer the education system's first priority. I knew I had the training to be useful in that particular situation. Keeping quiet made less sense than offering."

"Right . . ." Ferrar muttered. "Moving along, we have another blip on your files. This time during your vehicular training sessions. The cameras caught an incident where you spent time calming Recruit Kumanei when she lost control of her hexawalker during maneuvers, and almost fell off a cliff. You successfully talked her through her predicament," the Lieutenant pointed out. "How did you know what to do?"

"I did pay attention to our instructions on hexawalker operations, sir," she countered dryly.

"I meant, how did you know how to explain it in a way that Recruit Kumanei understood?" Ferrar corrected. "You weren't using the standard explanations and terminology the Terran military gives to its recruits."

"She's from Tokyo Underside, sir," Ia explained. "They use a lot of public transport, a few hover vehicles, some ground cars, and a lot of wall-crawlers. Of those four, the wall-crawlers are probably the closest to a hexawalker. Where I grew up, we have numerous kinds of vehicles for wilderness explorations, both for surface and subterranean. I've manned both hexawalkers and wall-crawlers back home," she confessed, shrugging. "I took a chance that she might know how to operate one—I've heard they're popular among teenagers down in the Underside. Luckily, she did."

"Your reaction time on your fellow recruit's crisis was also commendable. How did you know she was in trouble?" the Lieutenant asked next.

This was an easy question to answer. "I was keeping an eye on my Squad mates as well as on the exercise objectives, sir. Kumanei just happened to be next in line when I looked up and saw that she didn't look right. Knowing her background, it was easy enough to guess that she'd mixed up her control commands."

"Yes," Lt. Ferrar murmured, brown eyes flicking between her and his workstation screen. "Your profile suggests you're rather quick in many things." Bracing his forearms on the edge of his desk, Ferrar laced his fingers together and gave her a look of polite interest. Not quite a smile, but polite and attentive. "Alright. *You* tell me why I should make you a Buck Sergeant."

"You shouldn't." Ia watched him blink, and guessed he had made the offer to see if she was the kind of glory-hog who would take the promotion. She didn't wait for him to respond beyond that, but laid out her logic. "I'm a wet-behind-the-ears recruit fresh out of Basic, sir. No one in your outfit would be willing to take a sergeant's level of orders from someone like me. Corporal, you might be able to get away with. It's a higher rank than PFC, but not that much higher in responsibility and authority. It would be a challenge since I *am* fresh out of Basic, but that level of promotion wouldn't stir up anywhere near the same degree of resentment and resistance as making me a sergeant would, sir. Not even a relatively lowly Buck Sergeant."

"So you think I should make you a Corporal? Or even a Lance Corporal?" Ferrar asked her.

She wasn't going to fall into that trap. "The easiest course, Lieutenant, would be to keep me a Private First Class, see how I do, and then promote me based on merit, as is standard, sir."

He studied her a long moment, then opened up one of the latched drawers in his desk. "I don't 'do' the easiest course. Your new assignment is under Lieutenant D'kora's command, 2nd Platoon, position A Squad Alpha. Your teammate is Corporal Angela Estes, and your shared quarters are on Deck 7, Section D, Corridor 4 Foxtrot A Alpha." Ferrar stood and held out the two objects he had extracted from the drawer. One was a fist-sized box stuffed with the patches and pins bearing the two chevron stripes and one curved rocker of her new rank. The other was a datachip. "The chip has the protocols and operations manual for this Company on it. Study it. As the senior-most enlisted for your Squad, you'll be expected to help enforce it.

"Welcome to Ferrar's Fighters, *Lance* Corporal Ia," he stated firmly. "The DoI says you can do the job. Don't prove them wrong. Go and get familiar with your new life. Our next call to arms could come any day, and you'll need to be ready for it."

She stood as well, accepting the box and chip with a salute. "I'll do my best, sir."

"So we've heard. Don't disappoint us," Lt. D'kora murmured. Rising, she nodded at the door. "I'll show you to your quarters and introduce you to your Squad mates, Corporal. They're in the gym right now."

Pausing just long enough to unsnap her left jacket sleeve and slot the manual chip into her arm unit for download, Ia grabbed her belongings and followed the other woman back into the corridors of the ship. Her promotion didn't entirely surprise her. Either the rank of Lance Corporal or Private First Class she knew she could manage, and manage well enough to guide her future along the best path. Being promoted to Buck Sergeant would have stirred too many resentments to overcome easily. Without that as an issue, Ia could turn more of her attention to the reality, and not just the theory, of life on board a military starship.

Psychological studies had proven ages ago that Humans needed certain things to remain healthy, including when serving in the military. If you didn't require privacy, the best places to socialize, work on projects, and relax were usually the commons, large rooms with couches, chairs, tables, general access workstations, and entertainment facilities. The Navy had their own designated relaxation areas on higher decks, while the Marines had three commons, one for each Platoon. Standard crew quarters contained a head, a bedroom with two bunks, and a living area that was the size of sleeping quarters and head combined. Neither overly cramped, nor overly large.

The corridors were also designed just wide enough for three people to pass, though narrow enough that one could reach out and grab the maneuvering rails if necessary. The internal safety fields, visible as black-paneled nodes spaced every two meters both down by the floors and up by the ceilings, would actually save the crew from a truly bad shake.

The most interesting visual effect belonged to the frames holding the placards naming everything. If it was on a forward wall, facing toward the bow of the ship, the top and bottom edges were rimmed with blue. If it was on an aft wall, top and bottom were yellow. The starboard-side edge was always marked with green, and the port side was always edged in red. Since there were no portals peering out into the depths of space this deep inside the ship, it wasn't always easy to tell fore from aft, port from starboard. The same rules applied to the bulkheads and doors when one faced starboard or port: facing starboard, top and bottom were green, with the left side blue and the right side yellow, and if one faced port, blue and yellow were reversed, with top and bottom edged in red.

It was an important, if subtle clue. The regularly spaced section doors didn't help, for they were all uniformly bulky, rounded at the corners to improve their sealing ability and gear-wheeled in the middle, capable of being opened or closed manually if the ship lost all power. The three passenger ships Ia had taken to get to Earth had boasted more friendly looking doors, with the section seals spaced farther apart, but then they weren't expected to be spaceworthy under battle conditions.

Most of these corridors were painted in bland, easily cleaned shades of beige, blue, and grey broken up by the glossy black safety field nodes, silvery rails, color-coded placards pointing out the various door, facility, floor, sector, and corridor names, lockers stuffed with emergency gear and other equipment, engineering access panels, so on and so forth. However, someone had taken the effort to hang flatpics of landscapes from various planets, mostly of inhabited M-class worlds—the designation for habitable planets was an old in-joke among planetary scientists, who had given up centuries ago on trying to name such worlds anything else in the face of persistent popular culture. All those images of various homeworlds brightened the view and broke up the institutional-style monotony. There were even prints of old silk paintings in the boxy cabin of the lift, providing something to look at as they rode up one level.

The closer they came to actual living quarters, the more

such pictures could be seen, setting apart the practical sections of the battleship from the domestic. As they approached, D'kora pointed at a junction marked on the right-hand side, one made slightly more memorable thanks to a flatpic print of a pastoral picnic set in ancient China.

"All forward-to-aft corridors are numbered. All port-to-starboard corridors are lettered phonetically. To reach the 2nd Platoon Commons, you take Corridor 4 aft-ward down to the double doors on the right, just past cross-corridor Juliett. To reach the 2nd Platoon Cafeteria, you take Corridor 4 aft-ward to the double doors on the *left* just past Juliett, directly across from our commons. To reach the gym facilities used by the Marines, you take Corridor 4 forward to the lifts located at cross-corridor Echo, ride up to Deck 5, take Corridor 4 aft-ward to the double doors just past cross-corridor Juliett, and use the facilities on the right. The gym on the left is reserved for Navy personnel.

"The *Liu Ji* has a larger crew complement than we do, but the Marines have the same size gym facilities, as we are expected to maintain ourselves in greater physical shape. We are also expected to get out of their way when it comes to shipboard maintenance, drills, and emergencies. Study your manual to learn all the zones to stay out of or head into during a ship emergency," D'kora lectured, taking a side passage marked as Corridor Foxtrot. She stopped at the first door on the forward side of the hall, designated by the bluish trim at the top and bottom of the plate, with red on the left and green on the right. "These are your quarters. I'll sync your wrist unit to the privacy lock now. Only yourself, Corporal Estes, myself, Lt. Ferrar, ranking medical staff, and the Command Staff of the *Liu Ji* will have access to that locking code.

"Command Staff access requires probable cause with their reasons broadcast through the comms either to you, your roommate, or into your quarters beforehand. Medical staff has the right to enter any quarters in a medical emergency at any time, with or without prior warning. Inspections are held every duty shift morning cycle after breakfast; you will follow the Lock and Web Law at all times. As I do not currently have a Platoon Sergeant to oversee such things, I will be handling the inspections for 2nd Platoon myself. Other than these instances, your private quarters are private. The only person you cannot lock out under any circumstance is your roommate. If you have any questions, speak up now, or save them for later."

"I did pay attention in Basic, Lieutenant," Ia reassured her. Lifting her wrist unit, she flipped up the display and waited while D'kora did the same. A few quick taps synchronized their units, allowing the Second Lieutenant to download the code. As soon as her wrist unit *blipped*, Ia put her left hand on the access panel. The proximity to her wrist unit slid the door open, revealing the living area. The lieutenant's voice stopped her from entering.

"2nd Platoon is scheduled for gym exercises at this hour." D'kora checked the chronometer on her unit. "In forty minutes, they will break for a half hour of cleanup, followed by mechsuit drills in the 2nd's prep bay, which is located down on Deck 10, Sector F, Corridor 3 Kilo. By that point, the Navy should have your mechsuit case delivered to the combat lockers, which are located Deck 10, Sector F, Corridor 3 Golf."

Since her immediate superior was still talking to her, Ia remained in place. The door slid shut automatically, sealing off the room with Ia still outside, patiently listening to her Platoon commander's instructions.

"Be advised that the cross-corridors correspond to distances on board this ship, and do not necessarily follow the standard progressive alphabetical order," D'kora continued. "Deck 10 only has five cross-corridors, Bravo, Golf, Lima, Quebec, and X-Ray. Marine personnel are not permitted access to any section of the ship forward of cross-corridor Bravo, or aft-ward of cross-corridor Sierra unless given specific orders. Study your manual in full; any infraction after the leeway of your first three days in this Company will be punished accordingly. You will not like being assigned demerit duties under me." She paused for a few moments, then continued briskly. "Since you have no further questions, I will see you in the gym in twenty minutes."

Nodding briskly, D'kora turned and left, headed back the way they had come.

"Sir, yes, sir," Ia murmured, watching her go. Palming the door open again, she wheeled her case inside, kitbag balanced on her right shoulder, and nudged the light switch panel inside, illuminating the cabin.

The contents of the room were both familiar and new to her. The personal touches which Corporal Estes had given to the otherwise bland, grey-walled room included a row of folding fans spread out and clipped to the bulkheads via magnets, a poster of some vid star Ia was only vaguely familiar with, and the shifting images of a flatpic frame. Some were of various locations around the *Liu Ji*'s patrol zone, but most were of the absent corporal's friends, family, and home colony dome on what looked like Mars. Or maybe it was Dante's Refuge. Ia didn't know, and didn't care.

She knew enough about her teammate to know how to influence the other woman at key points in the upcoming months. Beyond that, she couldn't afford to care; there were far too many future possibilities for Ia to risk foreseeing the unnecessary ones, and far too little time in her life to peer into someone's past if such things weren't necessary.

And they're not, Ia reminded herself, wheeling her case past the beige, padded couch bolted to the floor along one side of the smallish living room. Across from it was a flatpic screen, currently dark. At the near end of the couch was a workstation desk, and in the corner across from it, over by the front door, was a locker with pressure-suits, emergency rations, and other goods in case anyone needed to wait out a hull breach or other containment problem. In the corner on the other side of the flatpic screen was a small dispensary with a caf' machine, sink, miniature fridge, and storage cupboard, while the far end of the sofa held a second workstation desk.

Taking the door opposite the entrance, she maneuvered the case down the short hall past the head, archaic nautical term for the bathroom, and tucked the wheeled carry-all into the corner between the bunk beds and the built-in cupboards and drawers. She unpacked her kitbag first, pausing to apply her new rank patches to the various shirts and the pins to the collars. Most of her clothes went into the drawers below, and her dress uniforms, her Browns and her unused Blacks, went into the locker with her spare boots and training shoes.

The smallest of her few personal belongings tucked into the bedside drawer built into the underside of the upper bunk, a flatpic frame and a couple of data crystals memorializing her visit to the Afaso Headquarters. Her toiletries went into the

equally sturdy, latching cupboards in the head, following the
Lock and Web Law of shipboard life. If it didn't go into a locking drawer or cupboard, it got tucked into a pouch or lashed in
place with a security web. Sudden jolts, accelerations, and
ship-wide losses of gravity meant that anything could become
a hazard, or even a lethal projectile.

Changing out of the brown camies that served as her travel
uniform, she stuffed them into the dirty laundry drawer, donned
plain brown pants and a T-shirt, fresh socks, and her trainers,
and opened up the rolling case. During her brief Leave between
Basic and this assignment, she had picked up a special portable
workstation, which combined a keyboard, folding screen, and
archival-quality printer, plus a sturdy lockbox and two cartons
of contiguous paper to feed through the machine. That, too,
ended up in a locker, the second of her two allotted storage
lockers. Below the boxes of paper, she had packed the individual cases containing her weight suit.

The artificial version of gravity keeping everyone clinging
to the deck plates and aware of a distinct sense of "down" could
be adjusted on board a ship, but it was a delicate balance. Gravity weaves had a limited radius field, tapering off to negligibil-
ity after only thirty or so meters. Thankfully, the K'katta who
had invented the things had also figured out a way to make
them monodirectional, projecting their field only on one side.

Each deck was lined with the weave under the floor plates
pointed up, and in the case of the cabin, beneath the carpeting.
But with the next deck not quite four meters up, the weaves
didn't actually run at full strength. They could, in case of damage or even routine maintenance needs. Technically, a gravity
weave could run up to 8.5gs if fully engaged, and the internal
safety fields were based on a similar principle.

The lowest decks—crawl spaces, really—ran at very low
gravity, allowing the decks to build up in their pull so as not
to stress the hull. The highest decks also ran weakly, but more
to allow the cumulative effects of the lower areas to taper off,
so that projectile missiles and space mines couldn't be pulled
into contact with a ship's hull by sheer proximity to the fields.
And while the ships were designed to be rugged and durable
in zero gravity as well as standard, they weren't designed to
permit a lot of local variation. Which meant the gyms would

be running at a combined total of 1g, and that meant she had to strap on the weight suit in order to get a decent workout.

As soon as the packing cases were loaded back into their carrier and the carrier hung from a hook inside the second locker, she strapped on the weight suit, but didn't head for the gym. She had almost ten free, unobserved minutes. Hauling her portable writing station and a box of paper back out of the locker, she turned it on, fed one end of the paper into the machine, closed her eyes, composed her thoughts, and reached her mind into the tangle of electrons that served as the machine's programming.

The keyboard wasn't necessary, though she could and would use it in the years ahead. Several days of practicing during the trip from Earth out to Battle Platform *Hum-Vee*, where the *Liu Ji* was docked, had given her some skill in manipulating the machine electrokinetically, but not a lot of skill. In fact, typing would have been faster, but she needed the practice. One day, she would do this literally as fast as a thought. For now, it was an effort to write up even a simple note, since what she thought in her head had to be translated into a format the workstation could understand.

DATE: TERRAN STANDARD 2513.08.14, SANCTUARY, PAS-SAGE WARREN, LOCAL TIME 13:14 +/- 2 MINUTES MAX.

LOCATION: SANCTUARY, PASSAGE WARREN, NORTHWEST HUB 5TH TIER, 3RD WING, APARTMENT 325.

RECIPIENT: ALMA "STUTTER" SUVRAMANYA (DARK BROWN EYES, DARK BROWN WAIST-LENGTH BRAID, BLUE BLOUSE, GREEN SLACKS, BEIGE SANDALS, RED AND GOLD CLOISONNÉ CHRONOBRACELET ON LEFT WRIST). RING DOORBELL, STATE "MESSAGE FROM CENTRAL, IA'N SUD-DHA," DELIVER MESSAGE TO RECIPIENT, MAKE SURE SHE READS IT, THEN LEAVE.

That was the first page. A nudge of her mind scrolled the sheet upward . . . and an extra sheet as well. Rolling her eyes, Ia firmed her concentration, rolled it back by one sheet, and thought the body of the text at the machine.

Stutter,

Hugo is not the best partner for you. Tell him he deserves someone who has more in common with him, and that you are moving. Take the job offer in Capsicum Warren; it will lead to something better. Ignore the job offer in Greenleaf, it's not as good as it looks. Make sure you have moved by no later than TS 2513.10.02. Once you do, look for the man with two earrings in his left ear. Forgive him on the second date, ignore the incident on the third. Avoid the trip to Halfway Warren TS 2633.04.23-27 at all costs, extended family included. The disaster would be restricted to your family, but with far-reaching consequences. Do not go. Otherwise, live long and well.

Ia

Tearing the sheet free, Ia scrolled it up out of the machine, separated the two pages, and tucked one note inside the other. Putting workstation and paper back into the locker, she pulled out the lockbox. The lock was an expensive DNA model, keyed to the genetics of just two people, herself and Grandmaster Ssarra. The only things currently inside the largish box were a bundle of silver sealing wax sticks and a custom wax stamp. The other time-sensitive letters she had crafted on the voyage to the *Liu Ji* had been mailed on the Battle Platform just before boarding.

Selecting a stick, Ia ignited it with a thought and dripped a small puddle onto the folded sheets. A press of the seal marked the wax with the symbol she had chosen to represent herself, an arrow drawing a line from the right, wrapped in a circle. To her, it represented the way she drew upon the future to inform and shape the present, wrapped within the arms of the Milky Way galaxy. That, and she wasn't an artist; drawing anything more complicated than an arrow-and-line within a circle for the company that had made the seal would have been beyond her capabilities.

The wax stick was snuffed as easily as it had been lit. More easily, since it simply required drawing back the heat-based energies into herself. She wasn't a full-blooded Feyori—if they could be said to have blood, since they didn't have anything of the sort in their natural state—but manipulating energy was a part of her nature. A headache-risking, hunger-stirring part of her nature.

No time for food right now, she reminded herself, locking up the letter and tucking the strongbox back into its cupboard. *I'm going to be late by three or more minutes, then it's an hour or so in the gym, a shower to freshen up, a tour of the prep bays, and the installation of my mechsuit in its designated storage alcove, plus there's that sixty-five percent chance Lt. D'kora will insist on a full diagnostic of the suit to make sure it's battle-ready.*

Which it had better be, Ia added, shutting off the lights with a swipe of her hand as she left the cabin. *I have just three days until my first official combat as a TUPSF Marine.*

CHAPTER 11

In the military, your teammates—Squad mates, Platoon mates, shipmates, whatever—are the single most important resource you have, outside of your own body. Getting along with everyone is vital for the survival of your group and the successful completion of your missions. It is also one of the hardest things to do, because in the military, people come from hundreds and thousands of different backgrounds, cultures, social standings, interests and creeds.

The person fighting next to you on the line of combat may believe in a completely different god, or in none at all. They may prefer comedy over horror or action-adventure. They may think lettuce is disgusting but munch their way through fried squid strips with glee. But that's the thing about a good, effective military. None of that matters . . . because they're fighting at your side, with you, protecting your hide. The same as you're doing for them.

Ethnicity, culture, creed. None of it matters. At least, none of that matters once you're out on the line. Until you've proven yourself in combat, however, getting along is not the easiest thing in the universe.

~Ia

Ia studied her teammates, familiar with their faces and some of their personality quirks from the timeplains. They eyed her back, not at all familiar with their newest Squad member. A stray thought flitted through her head. *They say Merlin aged backwards, which was how he knew everyone. Maybe he was just a precog like me . . . sort of like me . . . and just remembered everything in advance. Just one difference: none of these will be a future King of England.*

Given the white and steel gleam of the exercise equipment bolted to the deck of the gym, nothing could have been further from a sword-stuck rock in a Motherworld forest. Amused, she let herself smile slightly. "Hello."

". . . Right."

That came from the biggest, most muscular male in D'kora's A Squad. D'kora had introduced them to her before abandoning her to make her way. Only Estes was a corporal, the rest were all privates, either first or second class. This one was Jamil Eimaal-Elelle, lead member of A Squad Beta, nicknamed "Double-E" by his teammates. He towered over her by nearly forty centimeters, with muscles to match, and flexed. Given he was wearing a sleeveless brown shirt, the effect was no doubt meant to be intimidating. He just wasn't as muscular as her older brother.

"You're supposed to lead us? I heard you were coming straight from Basic," Double-E challenged.

"You're from Mars, aren't you?" Ia countered, changing the subject. "My biomom has relatives in the Thessaluna Dome area. I've seen pictures; it's nice. You from around there?"

"Nah. South Pole. Closest I ever got to Thessaluna was Rainbow Rock. You ever been there?" he asked, distracted from his posturing by her interest.

She shook her head. "I wish. Closest I ever got to Mars was a flyby on my way to Earth." She turned to his teammate, Tom Harkins. The man was almost as tall as Double-E, but skinny by comparison, and pale where Jamil was dark in complexion. "You're 'Happy' Harkins, and you're from . . . don't tell me . . . ah . . . Beaumonde, in the Lalande System. Space station in orbit around the third moon, right?"

"Right. What's with the funny outfit?" Happy asked her, lifting his chin at the tile-covered straps of her weight suit.

"I'm from a heavyworld. I wear the extra weight to keep in shape when I work out," Ia explained.

"And they put you in a half-mech team? Shouldn't a heavy-worlder be in full-mech?" The question came from a curly-haired woman with skin somewhere between Ia's light honey and Double-E's chocolate hue, Angela Cooper. Her question was understandable, given how she and her teammate wore the heavily armed, oversized suits, and how both of them had the wiry muscles to match. She poked her thumb at him, addressing Ia. "Guichi and I are both heavyworlders. I'm from Tau Ceti Gamma, and he's from Theta Five."

Happy Harkins snorted. "Theta Five's a heavyworld only by a thousandth of a G-point."

Guichi grinned. "And only that if you stand on a mountain." He bumped knuckles with his tall teammate, then lifted his chin at Ia. "Which world or satellite are you from?"

"Sanctuary." Blank looks met her gaze. "It's the heaviest heavyworld, on the backside of Terran space. Second-gen first-worlder."

Thom Estradille, the second team member in A Squad Delta, mocked her. "Ooh, we got a firstworlder here, an honest member of the planetary squatocracy! Why the hell aren't you at home, grubbing in the dirt?"

"Because I'm not a dirt-grubber, I'm a ground-pounder. And they put me in half-mech because they didn't want to waste my reflexes," she added to Cooper. "Full-mech is meant for standing, taking, and giving a pounding. Half-mech is for maneuvering and outmaneuvering the enemy, and I'm far better at outmaneuvering."

". . . In other words, your aim is *v'shakk*," Cooper translated. She grinned and shared another fist-bump with her teammate Yoishi Guichi.

Ia smiled slightly, not offended by the other woman's quip.

"Gentlebeings." Coming from the far side of the gym, D'kora's voice cut through not only their conversation, but the clanking of weights and the humming of treadmills. Her words turned several heads among the members of the other Squads, aimed first her way, then theirs. "The Marine Corps does not pay you to stand around talking. We pay you to keep in shape. Do so."

"Sir, yes, sir." Gesturing at the machines, Ia let the others settle back into whatever routine they had been doing before her introduction, then opted for one of the empty treadmills.

With roughly fifty people in the room, there weren't many machines open. She found herself next to the last member of A Squad, Oslo Knorrsson. He wasn't much taller than her, had a stocky build, tanned skin, and a shock of light blond hair. He was also wearing wraparound sunglasses. She didn't know why, though; that was one of those unnecessary details Ia figured she didn't have to learn in advance. If she never learned in the course of the next two or so years, then so be it.

The moment she stepped onto it, the treadmill beeped and scrolled a message across its display screen. "*Excessive weight detected in single occupant. Report to the infirmary to implement weight removal regimen.*"

She burst out laughing, startling the Marine jogging at her side. Knorrsson stumbled, recovered, and lowered his shades long enough to look at her with his pale blue eyes, bouncing smoothly in place with each running step. "What's so funny?"

"It wants me to remove my excess weight. The funny thing is, so do I." Chuckling, she synched her wrist unit with the machine, downloading her exercise routine into the treadmill's programming. There wasn't much that made her laugh anymore, but that had done it. Ia grinned as she began jogging, savoring the good feeling for as long as it lasted.

The voice of her teammate wafted out of the head. "You know, I don't get it. I just don't get it. I know I can't do a damn thing about it, but I just don't get it. Why *you*? Why did *you* get the Lance Corporal rank fresh out of Basic? I'm up for review and promotion in just three more weeks! Why *you*, Ia—and what kind of name is 'Ia' anyway?"

"What kind of name is Estes?" Ia shot back, tucking the last weighted strap back into its carry case. She kept her tone light, not wanting to antagonize the other woman. "It's just my name."

"Yeah, but usually there's more." Swinging her upper body around the corner of the wall, she started to say more. Ia jumped back, startled by her teammate's appearance.

The green goop on her face was unexpected. Nothing

foreseen in the timestreams. Cut off by her sudden movement, the other corporal blinked, then blushed. Or rather, some of her face blushed, the parts uncoated by whatever-it-was Estes had smeared over her forehead, jawline, and chin.

". . . I get acne if I don't clean up right after I sweat, okay? It's the late twenty-fifth century," Estes added tartly, swinging back into the bathroom, "and you'd *think* modern medicine could come up with some sort of cure for pimples, but *noooo*. I even keep a jar of this stuff in my armor locker so I can pre-coat my face if it looks like we'll be suited up for more than an hour. So. You got any bad habits, Ia? Aside from being promoted straight outta Basic? By the way, you have to take the top bunk. I don't care if you outrank me, I have the senior-ity time-wise in this cabin, and I want the bottom one."

"I prefer the top bunk, actually. I don't like being touched when I sleep. Particularly when it's unexpected." The face-goop was unexpected. Ia didn't like the unexpected. She cautiously probed the nearest fringes of the timestream, then offered a little bit more. "My only big 'bad habit' is writing a lot of let-ters. And . . . I sing."

"What, like in the shower?" Estes asked, voice echoing once more from around the corner.

"Sometimes." Fetching her writing materials from their locker, Ia hauled herself into the upper bunk. The ship swayed around them, undocking from the Battle Platform. They wouldn't be back to the *Hum-Vee* for a good two weeks. They would, however, reach Battle Platform *Johannes* in one week, since it lay on the far side of their circuitous patrol route.

"Well, singing's not so bad. It's part of being a Marine and all. But if you sing off-key, I'll have to shoot you." Splashing noises followed, before Estes added, "Nothing personal. So just make sure you sing quietly, and keep the door shut." She poked her head around the corner again, this time pink-scrubbed and damp around the edges of her hairline, making her brunette hair look even darker. "You're also gonna have a hellish time convinc-ing everyone in A Squad that you can lead us, fresh from Basic."

Ia spread her hands in an eloquent shrug. "Blame the DoI. They actually thought I should be D'kora's new Platoon Sergeant."

Estes stared at her. "You're *shakking* me."

"Only if the Lieutenant was *shakking* me," Ia returned. "He gave me the option. I pointed out I'd never get anyone to follow me, not fresh from Basic, so he made me the A Squad leader instead. His idea, not mine."

"Yeah, but it's up to you to pull it off." Ducking back inside briefly, she did something in the head, then came out again. "Where'd you put your gym stuff?"

"Laundry bag, in the locker by the head." Her own ablutions had been quick; a wipe down with a damp cloth and a change of clothes were all Ia needed to freshen up at this point.

Estes opened it up briefly, eyeing the mesh bag. "Not quite enough to go to the sonics yet. I've filled it up twice by myself, since . . . Corporal Suvrapati was a good woman. A good Marine."

Since there wasn't anything Ia could say, she kept her mouth shut and focused on typing her next letter to the future. There were only so many minutes in a day she could spare for these precognitive directives, and far too many years they had to cover.

AUGUST 2, 2490 T.S.
DEEP SPACE, NOT FAR FROM CETI CETI 126 SYSTEM

A sandwich was a deceptively simple thing. Layered of meat, greens, sauces and sprouts, a slice of cheese and two of bread, it represented a complete meal, save only for something to drink. Which Ia had yet to consume, being a glass of orange juice. The Navy crewmembers assigned to feed the Marines on board the *Liu Ji* made simple fare, but they made it well, with ingredients assembled as fresh as modern transportation and a small hydroponics garden could manage to procure. In fact, she had two sandwiches, which was appropriate given her daily caloric requirements as a heavyworlder.

There was just one problem.

"You gonna eat that?" The question came from the lead private of Delta team, Harry Soyuez, affectionately known as "Ticker" by his fellow Marines. Why, Ia didn't know. Given his fondness for food, she would've thought "Tucker" would have been a more appropriate nickname. How he kept his figure, she didn't know, either, other than perhaps though the route of spending plenty of time in the ship's gym.

Since she couldn't confess the real reason, Ia shook her head and pushed the tray with its plate of sandwiches and glass of juice away from herself. The ship's alarm blared just as he reached for it, making the man jump in reaction, as if the sandwich was the cause.

"Attention, all personnel. This is Captain Davanova. We have received a distress call from a Gatsugi merchanter, and are altering route at best speed. ETA is forty-five minutes. Ferrar's Fighters will be briefed by Lieutenant Ferrar in the lower boardroom in five minutes."

"You heard the Captain. Lock and web—take care of your dishes—then lock and load," Ia ordered her tablemates, grabbing her tray and rising from her spot on the bench. "You have four minutes, forty seconds to get to the briefing."

Leaving them to handle their own half-eaten meals, she carried her tray back to the serving line and offered it to the nearest of the three Navy men working in the galley.

"Can you put this in the fridge for me? I'll be back for it later," Ia added.

"No problem. If it's gonna be a fight, better not to go in with a full stomach. Or a full bladder," the crewman quipped, taking the tray away.

A hand clapped her on the shoulder. Had she been lightworlder-dense, it might have staggered her, but Double-E didn't even rock her physically. His words were meant to rock her mentally. "If it's a fight, what makes you think *you'll* be coming back for that? You're raw meat—no offense, of course, Corporal. But you've never been in combat."

"None taken." Slipping out from under his fingers, Ia headed for the boardroom. "Lock and load, Private. Make sure *you* survive, if this comes to a fight."

The lower boardroom wasn't far. The upper boardroom was big enough to hold almost the entire ship's complement, which she knew from studying the ship's schematics, but the lower one was just large enough for their Company.

The room was shaped like a small auditorium, and the cushioned seats lining it came with restraint straps and could be used as acceleration couches if needed. They faced a broad table at which the Platoon's cadre could sit, and a quartet of screens on the back wall, a large primary one, two secondaries to either side, and a narrow one along the top, all of which could stream information for whoever needed to view it.

Claiming one of the seats in the front row, Ia waited as the others filed in and took whatever chairs they wanted. The 3rd Platoon had been asleep when the call came through; most of them were fully dressed, but some were still dragging bootlaces and looking like they needed a cup of caf' to wake up. Ferrar and his three Platoon lieutenants entered with the last few to trickle inside. Everyone stood out of respect.

"At Ease. Sit down," he added as soon as he reached the head table, dismissing them back into their seats. "Here's the situation. The comm officers have received a distress broadcast from a Gatsugi merchant vessel, the *Clearly-Standing.* They had enough time to report their location, dead-stop in an ice field, and that they were under attack from another vessel, but that was it. From the way the signal was cut off, either their hyperrelay dishes were damaged, or the enemy in question is working with the criminal elements intent on circumventing the Blockade. If they are, we are under standing orders to find their jamming equipment and bring it back intact. Which means the Marines will be going in on this one, and not sitting back so the Navy can take their usual potshots."

A touch of his command wrist unit, twice as long as the standard issue one Ia and the other Marines wore, called an image to the main screen. Chunks of grey, barely lit ice filled the screen, floating slowly in space. The left-hand screen lit up with a view of the galactic plane, showing the time-frozen whorl of stars forming the Milky Way. One of those pinpoints of light had a circle around it

"This is Ceti Ceti 126, a star system on the zenith leeward edge of the Vela Ridge, at the border of Terran/Gatsugi space. It is also on the far edge of long-range for flights from Salik space. Because of this, patrols sweep through here twice a day, including us. Normally, we'd be arriving on the other side of the system. And while there are plans to build an official refueling station in the system within the next three years, since the ice fields in the seventh orbit make it an ideal refueling stop . . . well, budgets are budgets, particularly when it comes to intergovernment budgets, and budgets don't budge very much.

"Currently, it is most commonly used by those long-range

ships carrying the right equipment for midflight ice skimming, or by ships who are willing to stop, grapple, and haul on board chunks of ice for processing into purified hydrofuel. Most ships can usually make it from port to port without having to stop, but a few of the shipping lanes do route awkwardly enough that a midflight stop can be considered justified by some captains. For whatever reason or need," Ferrar stated, "the *Clearly-Standing* decided to stop and take on fuel. That's when they ran into trouble."

"Sir." The interruption came from the 3rd Platoon leader, Lt. Nguyen. He showed Lt. Ferrar something on his wrist unit, and the Lieutenant nodded. Nguyen transferred it to the right-hand screen.

"Lt. Nguyen is relaying ship schematics received from the Gatsugi government regarding the ship class which the *Clearly-Standing* is registered under. There may be differences, as merchanters like to rearrange things internally," Ferrar warned them, dipping his head in wry acknowledgment, "particularly as time and patchwork repairs take their toll. Be mindful when boarding. There's no telling what damage their attackers have done at this stage, nor how fragile the ship's hull may be. We do know there was a second ship involved, but whether the Gatsugi came upon them unexpectedly or whether they decided to ambush the next merchant freighter in the system, we can't say.

"We don't have much more information than that, but we will know at least a little more as soon as we come into the system. Updates will be scrolled to your mech HUDs. We could be dealing with a crippled hulk, a tail- or a tow-chase, two ships still dogging each other in combat, or two ships grappled together." Another tap of his wrist unit changed the main screen to a computer-projected view of the last known coordinates for the Gatsugi freighter. "We'll be coming in at system nadir, same as the most plausible plotted vector for the *Clearly-Standing*, but skimming the disc from the other direction.

"Captain Davanova says we'll be coming in within ten minutes' insystem flight from their coordinates, but no closer than five; navigation will have one minute thirty from the moment we hit the system's far edge to determine how close we can safely get. There's no way of telling if these attackers have damaged, destroyed, or altered the navigation beacons in the system, though the *Clearly-Standing* should have reported any discrepancies within minutes of entering the system, so I doubt their attackers took the time to alter the projections. Regardless, expect it to be a bumpy flight, particularly if the unknowns are still in the system and not grappled to the freighter. They may take objection to the Space Force's presence.

"3rd Platoon, you're on prep and standby for this fight; get some rest while you can, but no falling asleep at your post. 1st and 2nd, you'll be our boarding parties this time around. Lt. Cheung is more familiar with Gatsugi ships and their layouts than Lt. D'kora, so his team will board the merchanter. If there is an enemy vessel, D'kora and the 2nd will take them on. If not, you'll be backup to the 1st. Your two Platoons will suit up in full, and be ready to seal up and move out as soon as we know if it's a boarding situation. Lock and web, lock and load. You have less than thirty minutes. Dismissed."

Bodies scrambled out of their seats. Rather than wade through the crowd heading for the two exits, Ia remained in place, studying the schematic of the Gatsugi ship. A hand came down on her shoulder from over the top of her seat.

"Scared, Corporal?" Double-E asked her.

"You just might break your hand if you keep doing that." Slipping out from under his palm, she stood and faced him. Most of A Squad was still there, clustered in the seats behind her. Guichi and Cooper had gone on ahead, along with Estes, but Double-E, Harkins, Ticker and Estradille, Knorrsson and his teammate Hooke were all there. All of them eyeing her like a combination vidshow and meat counter. "Is there a reason why you aren't eager to follow the Lieutenant's commands?"

That stung most of them into straightening. Harkins twisted his mouth, suggesting his nickname "Happy" was sardonically meant at best. "Just wondering why *you* aren't so eager."

Ia, mindful that Lt. Cheung, leader of the 1st Platoon, hadn't yet left the table behind her, took a moment to pick the right reply. But looking into Harkins' brown eyes held her tongue just long enough for a wave of time to reach up and drag her down into *laser fire, shrapnel, exploding hand grenades, the ship rocking beneath her feet, the sight of Harkins impaled through the chest by a chunk of hydrofuel pipe . . .*

No. I will not let that happen. He will not *be in that corridor. I need him to be alive five years from now.*

"Or are you afraid of buying a star out there?" Double-E asked dryly. His deep voice gave her something in the here and now to focus on, to pull herself out of the cold, cold waters.

"Death and I are already well-acquainted. Trust me, I don't need to shake his hand." Shifting her gaze to the back of the boardroom, she lifted her chin. "The crowd has cleared. We can get to the prep bays now."

Leaving them to follow—or not—Ia headed for the doors. From the wisps of sound, they had chosen to follow her.

Seven minutes later, she was stripped and clad in the dark, silvered, tight-fitted p-suit that every mechsuited member of the Space Force wore into combat while in space, a brown headband covering her brow to absorb any perspiration. This was her first combat, and she wanted to get it right, without distractions. Once her helmet snapped into place, she wouldn't be able to scratch her nose, let alone wipe sweat from her eyes.

Familiarity had gotten her into the suit, but not from precognition; every single member of the Space Force, regardless of Branch, had to don and strip the suits five hundred times, and don them in less than one minute flat, blindfolded, by the five hundredth try before they could pass out of Basic Training. Pressure-suits were located in every section, every cabin, every corridor on board a Space Force vessel; with o-ring sealed boots, gloves, and helms and an emergency air pack, they were the default survival tool for interstellar travel.

The airtight plexweave had a peculiar, foam-like inner layer that, when depressurized, would expand much like a marshmallow in a vacuum chamber. The foam was designed to press against the pores and dimples of her skin, preventing them from inverting painfully, something which had been a severe annoyance in the earliest space-faring days. Unlike the training suit she had worn back in Basic, the trunks of this one were designed to capture and contain any leaks from the occupant's bladder—which was why she hadn't drunk her juice at lunch. And instead of solid boots, her feet were covered in thin, fitted booties.

Stepping up into her suit, she stooped and made sure her feet were cushioned comfortably in their sensory shoes, with nothing pinching her flesh. Mechsuits were hard-suits—even the light-weight version known as half-mech—which meant no part of the wearer's body was exposed to the outside. Nothing contacted the world directly. That meant tactile feedback sensors were vital for successful operation. Strapping her legs into place, she sealed the lower torso, methodically checking sensor lights as she went. Not that it would be airtight just yet, but the seals had sensors on their inner edges that green-lit as they made full contact, visual confirmation that everything was right.

Next came the somewhat thin, fitted gloves. These weren't the standard p-suit gloves; these gloves came with feedback sensors that would plug directly into the flexor gloves of her suit. In its wisdom, the Space Force had figured out that its recruits learned best in increments. The first week of mechsuit drill did not include the glove feedback sensors, specifically so that the operator could get used to the simple, awkward chore of walking and maneuvering. By adding in the sensory gloves, she could literally pluck a flower out of midair with the larger robotic hands extending beyond her own by a quarter of a meter, and not crush the delicate petals. If she didn't want to.

If she wanted to, Ia could crush a brick in her mechsuit hand. A brick, a blade, a skull . . .

A twist of her wrists locked the wrist-rings into place, hooking her wrist unit, sensor gloves, and flexor gloves into a single unit. Flexing her fingers, she leaned her head back and closed the rest of the suit, lifting her chin to clear the O-ring that formed at the base of her throat and merged with the one on her p-suit. The helmet came down and locked in place, forcing her head back to level.

The interior lit up, wires projecting the HUD, heads-up display, into her eyes and onto the half-silvered faceplate. The faint hum of the power cocooned her from the clanks, whines, and thumps of the others in A Squad's section of their Platoon's prep bay. Focusing on the menu floating to one side, Ia blink-commanded a level 1 diagnostic; the wires, tracking the focal points of her eyes, directed the onboard computer to comply.

A model of her mechsuit rotated in front of her eyes, lighting up from the feet to the crown with first yellow, then green pin-points, green-lighting the suit for combat. Beyond the floating representation of herself, the tactical software outlined and identified the approach of an unarmored male, zeroing in on his name patch and face: Lance Corporal Vic "Viper" Dunsby, her counterpart from the 3rd Platoon.

Ia politely stepped down out of the alcove to meet him. The redhead looked like he needed a shave and at least another three or four hours of sleep, but while his green eyes were hooded and his jaw cracking with repeated yawns, he didn't miss a step in checking her visually, slapping panels, poking joints, testing connections on those few cables that couldn't be completely concealed. She watched the flexing of the serpents tattooed on his deltoid muscles, clad as he was in a sleeveless brown shirt, and knew she'd be doing a similar task all too soon.

Ferrar likes to keep one Platoon in reserve, resting and on double-check duty for battle prep. If they have to get called into armor, it's potluck as to how prepared they are, particularly since they have to be up and mobile in mere minutes. But this careful prebattle prep does pay off in fewer accidents, complications, and casualties overall.

I'll have to remember to implement it when I get my own Platoons.

Just as he had done for Estes in the next alcove, he fetched the c-clip and e-clips for her own forearm-mounted guns. Ia flexed her fingers and blink-coded the suit, popping the guns out so they could be loaded. Just as they had both been taught to do in Basic, he carefully displayed each of the disk-like objects before slotting them into place.

Mounted on her left forearm was a stunner turret; it received one energy pack. Its remote-controlled nosecone wasn't quite as flexible as the Mama's, but it was more of a holdout weapon. There were slots in her upper arms on both sides for five more e-clips each. Her right forearm took a c-clip, hiding a miniature, holdout version of a Jelly. He lifted the c-clip for that one last, giving her a chance to read the identifying marks.

"Grey mushrooms with green diamonds," Ia dutifully noted aloud, knowing her wrist unit would record anything she said from this point forward. Standard ammunition for a routine space boarding; unless they were boarding a true derelict, it was unlikely the soft-metal slugs would puncture even a standard bulkhead, let alone the hull of whatever vessel they encountered. Still, she had to acknowledge aloud what she was being handed. "I have been issued a single c-clip of splatters with tracers for my right forearm gun."

Nodding, Viper slotted the magazine into her right forearm. "Anything else? Grenades, tranks, in-flight magazine?"

She wouldn't need grenades, this trip. "Explosives scanner, and a knife."

He gave her a sardonic look. "Paranoid much?"

She blink-raised the volume of her suit speakers two notches, echoing it down through the prep bay. "There are old Marines, and there are bold Marines—"

"—But there are no old, bold Marines!" Estes called back from her alcove. *"Eyah?"*

"Hoo-rah!" everyone else answered, Viper and Ia included. He grinned and slapped her on one metal-plated thigh, then went to fetch the requested gear. He came back a few minutes later with a knife in a clip-on sheath that fastened to the front of one thigh, and a thin box with four antennae, which slotted into the pauldron covering her left shoulder joint.

She started a diagnostic of that as well, noting the floating lights targeting and outlining the c-clips in the room, the e-clips, and mechsuit power packs. In twos and threes they lit up, then faded from her HUD view, identified and labeled as ally-controlled components. Once that was settled, she stepped back up into the alcove, bumping her metal-covered backside into the power plugs to conserve internal energies. A blink-code unsealed her helm, lifting it back out of her way so she could breathe unfiltered air.

She wasn't the only one to retreat and attempt to relax, nor the only one to unseal their helm to conserve lifesupport power. The noises of the others died down as well. While they rested, the members of the 3rd Platoon attending the 2nd padded out of the prep bay, no doubt to find the nearest acceleration seats. That left them in near-silence as the minutes slowly ticked away.

Someone spoke up from further down the bay. "Well. That's the military for you—"

"—Hurry up and wait!" several others catcalled back. Chuckles broke out. From his position two alcoves over, Double-E called out to her.

"Hey, Ia. You bored, yet?" he asked. Then joked, "Want me to tell you a story?"

"You want me to sing you a song?" she countered, unfazed.

"Oh, please, *do* sing us a song," Private First Class Hooke catcalled from the alcove across from Ia's. "Double-E's stories always start out with 'No *v'shova*, there I was . . .' and always end with the rest of *us* saying 'bull*shakk*!' "

Others joined her in laughing at Double-E's expense. He chuckled, too. "Okay, okay . . . fine. You sing us a story, Corporal Ia. A good one, with action and plot and stuff. Prove you got what it takes to be a real Marine while you hurry up and wait."

"A song *and* a story? Don't push your luck," she countered. "But if you ask nicely, I'll sing you a simple, easy song right here, right now. Something even you would know."

"Alright then, I'm askin' *nicely*, Corporal," he drawled. "Sing us something, pretty please?"

The others chuckled, and a couple more muttered and joked with their neighbors.

"As you wish." She would rather have been in her quarters, filling out letter after precognitive letter. But that wasn't an option. "Like they say, *Lock and Load . . .*"

Out on the battlefield,
Your weapon, you gotta wield
Out on the battlefield
You gotta bear your load.
Out on the battlefield
The enemy ain't gonna yield
Out on the battlefield
You gotta lock and load!

A couple of catcalls mixed with several whistles as she began the opening verse slowly and steadily. Ia ignored them, launching into the carefully paced first round of the chorus.

Load 'em up
And rack 'em up
And put 'em in the chamber
Load 'em up
And rack 'em up
You gotta lock and load!

Load 'em up
And rack 'em up
And put 'em in the chamber
Load 'em up
And rack 'em up
You gottta lock and load!

The next verse picked up pace minutely, just a subtle increase in tempo.

When you're in war
And you don't care what you're fighting for
When you're in war
Your captain, he will goad
When you're in war
Blood and death you may abhor
When you're in war
You gotta lock and load!

Load 'em up
And rack 'em up
And put 'em in the chamber
Load 'em up
And rack 'em up
You gottta lock and load!

Load 'em up
And rack 'em up
And put 'em in the chamber
Load 'em up
And rack 'em up
You gottta lock and load!

Again, she increased the pace. With each new verse, followed by the twice-repeated chorus, the tempo quickened. This was an old song, but still a favorite in the Space Force. Particularly when sung drunk, but just as difficult when sung sober.

Your gun on your shoulder
You sure ain't gettin' older

Your gun on your shoulder
Move 'em down the road
Your gun on your shoulder
You gotta do it bolder
Your gun on your shoulder
You gotta lock and load!

Feet planted on the ground
Chamber up another round
Feet planted on the ground
It's the soldier's code
Feet planted on the ground
Concentrate through battle sound
Feet planted on the ground
You gotta lock and load!

Other voices joined her on the chorus, then fell silent again. They listened, anticipating the increase in tempo, the flawless patter of words. Ia did her best to not disappoint.

When foes use greater force
You gotta stay the steady course
When foes use greater force
You gotta hit their node
When foes use greater force
Hit 'em in their battle-source
When foes use greater force
You gotta lock and load!

When foes go on attack
You gotta really hit 'em back
When foes go on attack
Make 'em all explode
When foes go on attack
Their bodies you will have to stack
When foes go on attack
You gotta lock and load!

Out on the battlefield
Your weapon, you gotta wield . . .

The double chorus flew from her tongue and lips, cycling back around again to the start of the song and the first few verses, racing through the beginning all over again. She all but bounced through the tune, hitting the notes as true as she had started. If she couldn't sing on a stage, at least she could still sing her best, even if the audience was small. Unfortunately, she couldn't keep up the pace indefinitely and, a few verses into the second round, fumbled the rapid-fire words.

> *Load 'em up*
> *And flak 'em up*
> *And pug 'emmububl—*

Her tongue tangled and knotted itself. Wincing and chuckling, Ia broke off.

"Sorry, meioas. I rarely make it to the fifth verse!"

Her chuckled apology was met with cheers and whistles, and an appreciative, "*V'dayamn*, woman!" from Double-E. "Most people drop out by the *first* verse!"

"Normally I'd do better, but my mouth is a little dry," she quipped back. With the helmet unsealed and tipped back, she didn't have access to the sip-straw that would provide her with a ration pack of water.

His teammate Harkins called out, "Hell's bells, meioa, I'd like to see you try that when you *aren't* sober!"

"I'll even buy you the first drink," Double-E agreed. "*If* you survive your first bloodbath."

She shook her head, though she knew he couldn't see it. Hooke and Knorrsson could, though Knorrsson had his helmet down and was either viewing something on his HUD, or catching a covert nap. "Sorry. I don't drink."

"*Sonova'shova!*" she heard Soyuez exclaim. "You're in the military, and you don't drink? What in th' galaxy is *wrong* with you?"

"My family line has a risk factor for genetic alcoholism . . . and before you ask, no, I didn't get any gene therapy to correct it. You don't get any fancy medical procedures for the nonfatal stuff on a new colonyworld. Too many other problems have a higher priority."

That silenced him. Technically, the risk factor was very

small, something which hadn't cropped up in a handful of generations, but it was more convenient than telling the truth: if Ia ever drank herself silly, she might lose control over her psychic abilities. That would be bad.

For a given value of bad, she thought idly, *insert the death of the entire Milky Way galaxy as my one shot at saving it goes careening off wildly into dust . . .*

"Attention, Ferrar's Fighters. ETA to system Ceti Ceti in two minutes. ETA two minutes."

Footsteps *chung-chung-chunged* up the length of the prep bays. "You heard the bridge!" Lieutenant D'kora called out, checking for herself that her Platoon was suited and ready to go. "Two minutes! I want everyone secured in their alcoves and on their chargers before we break out of FTL, helms down and ready to go! Lock and web, lock and load!"

They settled into place. Ferrar's Fighters was a full combat Company; everyone went into combat, privates, corporals, sergeants, lieutenants. Some Companies had noncombatant Squads, even whole Platoons of personnel whose primary job wasn't infantry in nature. They served by making repairs, doing routine maintenance, even handling the simplest things like cooking and cleaning.

However, the *Liu Ji* was merely a frigate class battleship, almost a corvette, designed more for speed than for size. There wasn't room for extraneous bodies, not when the Navy half of the ship's complement already carried the personnel for maintenance, logistics, and support services.

A new voice intruded over the comm system. *"This is Chaplain Benjamin. As it says in* The Book of the Wise, *'Soldiers do not go into battle expecting to kill, or expecting to die. They are prepared, but they are as mortal as you or I.' May whatever deity or faith you hold safe in your hearts this day in turn hold you safe and sound. Keep your heads down, and make sure this is my only prayer for the day. Blessed Be."*

Ia lowered her helm, sealing it in place. Not just the clear inner faceplate, but the silvered blast plate as well. That left her one more anonymous soldier among the dozens in the 2nd Platoon's prep bay, save for the nametags installed in embossed, silvery-grey letters on her shoulder guards, chest plate, and helm, spelling out in terse symbols and code her name and rank.

The helmet's HUD lit up, and the captain's voice projected into her ears, echoing slightly through the mechsuit's external speakers as they picked up the comm system broadcast.

"Entering insystem speeds in three . . . two . . ."

The ship swayed. That was the only visible, tangible effect of crossing the barrier between faster-than-light and insystem speeds. Wrapped in a peculiar field that "greased" the laws of physics around the ship's immediate environs, the *Liu Ji* could travel at speeds of roughly one hour to the light-year; the bigger the ship, the longer it took to speed up and slow down, but all FTL vessels traveled at roughly one hour to the light-year. The ship shivered as the FTL field's greasiness eased back, allowing the ship to be slowed by the insystem thruster fields. Ia swallowed, popping her ears. The air pressure hadn't changed, but the trick was the only thing she could do to counteract the slight well of nausea stirred by the braking turbulence.

Data spilled across her HUD. The *Liu Ji* had arrived very close to the ships in question, feeding them nearly real-time data from the ship's passive sensors. She skimmed it as it scrolled up her field of view, knowing most of what it said in advance.

The *Clearly-Standing* was locked in a grappled, boarded embrace with a vessel that looked like several ships had been pried apart, crumpled up, and then patch-welded together. The only thing keeping both vessels still within the ice fields of the seventh orbit was the damage visible on both ships' faster-than-light panels. With nothing else to do, Ia sunk a corner of her mind into the timeplains and walked a few steps upstream, peering into the postcognitive waters of the Gatsugi crew. Not enough to lose her awareness of the prep bay, but enough to satisfy that slight itch of curiosity.

The *Clearly-Standing* had dropped out of FTL to pick up ice, and dropped out very close to that pirate ship, who was already there, lurking and scooping up fuel. They didn't see the pirates until after they had started their own fuel-snagging efforts.

Confronted with the risk of being identified, the pirates had flipped on their jammer and attacked. They caught the merchanter midtransmission, relaying their coordinates to the rest of their commercial fleet, and that had given the alien vessel the small break it needed. The density of the ice field had also muffled some of the jamming, allowing the hyperrelay on the Gatsugi vessel to fire off a partial warning before the pirate vessel had moved close enough to sever the connection and destroy their ability to flee.

The first set of damage was to the *Clearly-Standing*, done by the pirates. They didn't want their prey slipping away. Since it was an older vessel, the Gatsugi had some of their crew suited up and waiting outside, ready to clear the ice scoops if they jammed. The pirates didn't know this, and so the p-suited crew were able to float around both ships and plant their incendiaries—normally used to break up the largest blocks of ice—on the hull of the pirate ship. That allowed them to cripple its own FTL panels, and hopefully give them time for a rescue attempt from outside.

If their message had gotten through, which it had. Mindful of the seconds ticking by on her HUD chronometer, Ia pulled her thoughts fully into the present. A few moments later, the Lieutenant spoke through her headset speakers.

"Ferrar to the 2nd Platoon, looks like you will get to play after all. You will be boarding the enemy vessel at three points of entry. Lt. D'kora will split you up. 1st Platoon, you will be boarding the Gatsugi vessel at two points of entry. Lt. Cheung will split you up. Be very careful when aiming; we're still downloading the official crew and passenger roster from the Gatsugi collective.

"2nd Platoon full-mechs, be doubly careful what you aim at; I don't like the looks of that hull. Priorities are comm systems, bridge, engineering, and any gunnery stations. 2nd Platoon top priority is securing the bridge, particularly the comm equipment, and any chance of finding an intact, functional jamming device—comm ops says they're picking up some interference on the relays. 1st Platoon, top priority is securing the Gatsugi crew, bridge, engineering, and gunnery pods.

"Here we go—official word, if it has four arms, give it the benefit of the doubt before you shoot. If it doesn't, the Collective has the ship registered as an all-Gatsugi crew, zero passengers, I repeat, all-Gatsugi crew, zero passengers, so if it isn't Gatsugi or Space Force, presume it's a pirate. Priorities are capture over kill, disarmament over dismemberment.

"One more thing. You all heard Bennie. Nobody buys a star

on this one, so you be careful. No glory-hogging, either; that's just another form of deadly real-estating. By the book and stay sharp, soldiers. Line up for the Liu Ji's boarding shuttles, lock and load."

"Sir, yes, sir," Ia murmured, stepping forward and down from her prep alcove. Not on an active link, of course, but enough to let her suit know she had heard her commander's orders.

Her mechsuit and wrist unit would record whatever she said, regardless of whether it was an active link or not; that was part of the suit's "black box" systems, designed to record everything for potential analysis in the event of injury, death, or an infraction of the TUPSF's stringent bylaws, for as long as she wore the suit. Removed from the suit, the wrist unit had to be manually activated to record anything, which was also per TUPSF regulations, the ones regarding personal privacy rights.

Falling into line behind D'kora, Ia reminded herself of that fact. *Everything I do, everything I say, for the next few hours has to seem normal in every way.* Like the lieutenant in front of her and the lead corporal of B Squad behind her, she used her mechsuit hands to grab one of the HK-114s off the weapons rack waiting in the corridor on their way to the launch bay. A quick check made sure the mechsuit-sized rifle was unloaded, and a whirring shrug of servos slung the carry strap over her helmed head. *I am perfectly normal. I am a Marine.*

A moment later, a ghost of a smile curved her mouth. *Of course, there are those who say that "perfectly normal" and "I am a Marine" are two statements that contradict each other.*

They bypassed the airlock leading to the transport shuttle reserved for the 2nd Platoon, one of the vessels which could be converted to carry mechsuited soldiers, suitless soldiers, cargo, or light vehicles. It was also designed to be able to cross into an atmosphere. The boarding shuttle was the next stop down, and it was designed specifically for boarding hostile ships in space.

The central trunk formed the core of the shuttlecraft. They entered through the rear airlock and marched up to the side airlocks, peeling off according to Squad. D'kora stayed in the corridor, gestured for Ia to duck into the right-hand boarding pod. Carefully stepping on the rib at the corner of the hexagonal-walled oblong, Ia moved past the first two padded alcoves slanted to either side, and picked the left-hand niche.

A twist and a crouch allowed Ia to lower herself into place. Swinging her legs into the alcove, she could see Estes entering. Lying back, she let the gravity of the *Liu Ji* snap her onto the same sort of prongs serving as both chargers and acceleration restraints back in the prep bay. They attached at her ribs and down by her heels, and there were optional prongs for her wrists as well. Since she needed to keep her gun from dangling free, Ia cradled it against her armored chest, and popped out one of her e-clips. Slotting it into the rifle, she turned it on, but didn't release the safety, yet. Over her suit's speakers, she could hear the faint whine as Estes did the same.

Moments later, Double-E and Harkins thumped and clanked into the pod, taking their positions on the other two cushions, locking themselves into place. The pod's internal comm beeped and a neutral-female voice stated, *"Pod one rotating in five . . . four . . ."*

On *zero*, the entire semi-cylindrical room swiveled up and around, then jerked to a halt. That left Ia lying sideways, locked in place. Teams Gamma and Delta entered, taking up four more slots in the hexagonal chamber, then the same voice gave its warning and rotated the boarding pod. Now she dangled more or less facedown, if at a slight angle. The last pair then entered, followed by D'kora. Like Delta, team Epsilon and the lieutenant had to maneuver past the bulk of team Gamma in their full-mechsuits, which overflowed their own alcoves by several bulky, silvered centimeters.

The inner airlock sealed shut, leaving them in the soft glow of the guide-lights rimming each alcove. Ia rested while she could. Her p-suit was constrictive, the air in her helmet smelled dull, and she had nothing but the whine of charging laser rifles for company, since no one was talking. *Hurry up and wait . . . hurry up and wait.*

D'kora spoke up, broadcasting to her Platoon. The different links showed up as blinking lights on the edge of Ia's HUD, each hue corresponding to a broadcast channel so that a listener—or a speaker—knew which group of people he or she was conversing with at any point in time.

"A Squad will board with me at midship, looking for the bridge. B and C Squads, you will stack your pods and take the aft airlock. D and E, you will stack and take the bow. B, your

priority is engineering. E Squad, disable any hyperrelay systems they may have, then sweep for the comm system jammers. Such things are usually found at the front of a ship, but don't count on it. C and D, look for gunnery pods, weapons lockers, and pirates, but be mindful of your fellow Squads, and be ready for backup."

The voice of their shuttle pilot was next. *"This is Yeoman Lutzoni to the 2nd Platoon. The* Liu Ji *has found and neutralized the enemy's broadside external gun pods. Ops reports minimal damage to the hostile vessel. All systems are ready; all pods are secured. We are green for go. Departing in thirty seconds."*

Ia closed her eyes, skimming the timeplains for her immediate future paths. The shuttle lurched around her, swaying her sideways inside her armor. Then the pull of downward gravity ceased with a stomach-twisting, sideways-squishing flip, and only acceleration held her that way. Two more minutes passed; the second minute involved maneuvers that altered her sense of up from down, based on which way the shuttle swerved.

"Launching pods two and three in five . . . four . . ."

The shuttle jerked on either side, shoved by the launching of the pods containing C and D Squads.

"One of you gets to volunteer for point," D'kora stated in her question-avoiding way. "Make up your minds, fast."

"Launching pod one in five . . . four . . ."

"I lead from the front." The words escaped Ia without conscious thought.

The pod lurched headfirst away from its shuttle. Acceleration shoved Ia onto her feet, then swung her sense of down shoulders-up as the craft braked abruptly. They touched with a shivering *thump,* and the automatic grapples *chunked* into the side of the enemy craft. Despite knowing—or perhaps because—what was about to come, Ia felt her heart leap into her throat.

Oh, God. Help me.

CHAPTER 12

I've been asked many times about that song—the very first one. A lot of people have wanted to know about it over the years. A lot. So. Was any of it actually true?
Every damn word.

~Ia

She levered herself off of the restraint struts with her elbows, then kicked her heels free. Before she could float across the smallish chamber, Ia twisted and grabbed the airlock wheel near her head. Curling up her legs, she touched the keypad that unlocked the wheel and cranked it open electronically. The wheel could be unlocked and turned manually, in case of a power failure, but didn't need to be, this time.

Beyond the door lay the second airlock, opposite the one she and her Squad mates had entered. She could now hear through her helmet the faint *thrum* of the sealers welding the two vessels together with a special type of plexgel. The lights around the outer airlock door glowed amber, indicating a tenuous contact at best. She didn't have to enter the airlock; she was now close enough to feel the tug of artificial gravity from the ship. It was weak even at this close range, since she was sideways to the weaves, but it did pull her toward the outer door.

Blinking and focusing to activate the module attached to her shoulder, Ia waited impatiently for the results. As soon as they scrolled up her HUD projection, flashing red in chunks too large to ignore, she activated her comm link on the Platoon-wide channel. *"2nd Platoon, all boarding parties—all stop, all stop! I repeat, 2nd Platoon all boarding parties, all stop, all stop!"*

"—Corporal Ia, you had better explain yourself!" D'kora snapped.

"This is Corporal Ia, A Squad, I am detecting explosive charges placed around the midship enemy airlock. Estimated volume . . . eighty-five cubic decimeters of cubane. I repeat, the doors are armed with cubane. That's enough to rip the back *doors off the boarding pods, and cream anyone inside. Presume all airlocks are rigged. Stand by."*

Her heads-up display warned her of D'kora's approach. *"I want confirmation, Corporal."*

The catch-release for the sensors plugged into her shoulder required fingers to remove it, not bulky servo-digits. Ia brought her arm up to her shoulder. A blink-code and a twist of her wrist opened up the panel hiding her hand. Air hissed out of her torso, but not her helmet. The foam lining her p-suit expanded, pressing against her constricted flesh. It still stung a little, like having every little hair on her body from the neck down tugged upon by tiny imps, but once the suit's inner layer expanded against her hide, it was bearable. The cold of the pod's airlock was the worse discomfort, by comparison.

Pinching the connectors with grey-gloved fingers, Ia disengaged the device, then twisted a little bit further. D'kora wedged her own half-mechsuited body closer, giving her just enough reach to push the attachment into place. *"Scan it for yourself, sir."*

"This is Lt. D'kora, confirmed. Midships airlock is rigged to explode. Assume all airlocks are so rigged until confirmed otherwise. Unless we can figure out the right code to open the airlock, we'll have to back up and cut our way through the hull."

Ia tucked her hand back into the arm of her suit and sealed it again. It didn't take much air to re-pressurize the interior of her suit, or much time to warm her gloved fingers.

"This is Sergeant Pleistoch. We already looked at opening

the door with the controls, but they were warded with a force field, sir."

"A force field on top of a booby trap makes no sense, Sergeant," D'kora returned.

"I know, sir."

Ia switched to a private channel, contacting D'kora. *"Lieutenant, it doesn't make sense for common pirates to rig the controls with a force field. The field would make it harder for us to depress the buttons, and harder to set off the explosives. Not impossible, since the fields are compressible to an extent, but harder all the same."*

"You have an idea." It wasn't a question.

"I say these aren't common pirates, sir," Ia stated. *"The force field ensures that anyone but a Salik would have to press hard to activate the buttons . . . but all a Salik has to do is make enough contact to suction the buttons, and lift them for activation. Not depress them. The force field would simply keep them from setting it off. Either these pirates are using old Salik tech and the tools to simulate their capabilities, or . . ."*

"Estes!" D'kora barked. *"Break out the sucker hand!"* She switched back to broadcasting. *"This is Lt. D'kora to 2nd Platoon. A Squad has the lowest casualty risk. We're going to try something. Stand by."*

"Good luck, Lieutenant." "God bless." "Bennie said buy no stars, so take no careless risks, sir," someone else said, standing out among the brief babble of well-wishes.

Silence followed, broken only by the *clakk* of metal on metal from Corporal Estes hauling herself partway through the inner airlock opening. She passed up the requested apparatus. D'kora took it, and found Ia holding out her suit hand. The older woman paused, then passed it to her. If she had wanted to do it herself, she would have had to maneuver awkwardly, juggling the bulk of their suits as they traded places.

Ia pushed up the cover on the control panel, meant to protect the buttons against space debris. The black field-projection ring surrounding the niche was subtle, but her HUD sensors picked it up, registering the energy field as a pale blue mask with a brighter blue outline. Unfolding the sucker hand, she checked the position of the mechanical tentacle, then laid it down over the opening. Pressing carefully, she suctioned the cups on the underside to the grid of buttons. There were only three buttons to worry about, but that was still a large risk of getting it wrong. Except she couldn't; she could only pretend to be worried about the outcome.

"Standard Salik pattern, sir?" Ia offered.

"I don't know the standard pattern," D'kora countered.

"I studied a lot of old military and history files. The Salik 'hand' would wrap from outside to inside, lift the middle button, then the inner one, using a light touch if it wasn't an emergency. The closer to the macrojuncture, the stronger the suckers would be; they'd rig the outermost button for self-defense, and then automated guns would pop out and fry whatever they were programmed to identify as an enemy target."

"I'll take your word for it, Corporal. And your advice."

Tapping the controls, Ia lifted the middle button, then the one closest to the doorframe.

The ship's airlock cracked open. No explosions. Both women sighed audibly over their external speakers.

"Thank you, Ia." The heartfelt mutter came from Estes. A few more drifted through the pod from the other members of A Squad.

D'kora switched back to broadcast. *"2nd Platoon, break out the sucker hands, middle, then inner buttons. Soft and easy, but be quick and lively about it. They'll know we're getting through by now. Salik tech and Salik treachery may indicate an actual Salik presence on board. If so, I want proof."*

"I'll bring you their stomachs, sir," Ia quipped.

A servo-hand on her other shoulder stopped her, as did the cold broadcast words accompanying it. *"That was uncalled for. Corporal."*

Oh. Shakk. *I didn't just . . . ? Yes, I did.* Wincing, Ia cleared her throat. *"I apologize, sir. My sense of humor is a bit skewed, at best."*

"I will settle for a visual confirmation. An intact *visual confirmation."*

Nodding, Ia pulled herself into the empty airlock. Greenish white light met her eyes, oddly hued for Humans, who were used to either a more golden or a more bluish hue, but comfortable for amphibians. Gravity righted her in relation to the ship, weak compared to Human Standard, but definite in its sense of *down*. The inner controls didn't have a force field on them, and no prescience of danger lurked in the timestreams. Ia readied her HK-114 in her right hand and used the sucker hand on the same middle and inner buttons with her left, closest to the doorframe.

Nothing happened as it cycled open, but she knew they were there, lurking behind cross-corridor cover, just waiting for the first Marine to show his or her armored face. Folding up the hand, she fastened it into her now empty shoulder socket. Breathing deeply, twice, thrice, she reached for her own timestream, psyching herself up for what was about to happen. Fingers curling inside her flexor gloves, she bent her knees, balancing on the sensors under the soles of her feet, and nodded, switching back to her comm link, this time dropping down to her Squad's comm channel.

"Let's do this."

Her mechsuit slammed into the far wall of the corridor, launched hard and fast through the airlock door. Two searing shots of bright orange missed her. Two of deep red light scored, one on the armored figure to the left and, as she whirled around, the other on the armored figure to her right. Most of that shot seared a charred line in the paint of the bulkhead rather than the armored body ducking back for cover, but she knew she'd tagged the bastard.

Neither of her shots was lethal, but her abrupt entrance and accurate attack had rattled both would-be foes. Estes peered around the corner, then darted into the corridor, followed by the tall bulk of Double-E and Harkins in their own half-mechsuits.

"Humidity eighty-five percent," Harkins announced, his own left shoulder socket bearing a set of atmospheric sensors. *"Gravity .73gs. Temperature averaging 28C. Amphibious country, sir, either Salik or Choya."*

"Amphibious atmosphere," D'kora ordered on the Platoon channel. *"Everyone stay suited. No sweating allowed."*

The corridors here were a singularly uninspiring shade of muddy beige, oddly mossy under the green white glow of the overhead lights. It was something which might be considered soothing to Choyan or Salik eyes, but which unfiltered would send a Human twitching within an hour. Ia fired a short burst at a grey shadow on the far wall of the side corridor joining this one. The source of the shadow jerked back, unharmed but no longer sneaking up for another attempt at a counterattack. Paint smoldered on the bulkhead, charred black from her laser fire.

A couple chuckles came back on the comm. Even Ia smiled, though she didn't take her eyes off her target corridors, the ones straight ahead and the one to the left.

"Corporal Ia, take Alpha and Beta straight ahead and find a way down. Gamma, Delta, Epsi, you're with me. If this is a Choya ship, the bridge will be located somewhere on or near this deck. If it's Salik, it'll be down below. If we're lucky, it's just Choya. Salik is a shakk-*load of paperwork."*

"Sir, yes, sir." Dashing across the opening, Ia fired twice as she spun, putting her back to the bulkhead on the far side of the opening. Shots streaked out of the corridor. Estes, taking up Ia's former position, squatted down and fired back from a low crouch. Double-E joined her, firing over her head. A *fzzzt . . . fzzzt . . . fzzzt* approached from both directions, growing rapidly louder.

"Shakk. *Force fields, sir! They're pinning us down,"* Harkins announced. *"They might intend to blow the airlock anyway!"*

"Pirates who are rich as well as paranoid?" Estradille asked. *"They can't have the* whole *ship sectioned off."*

Turning to face the forward corridor, Ia aimed at the corner of one of the panels. A sustained burn cut a smoking, glowing-hot line diagonally into the bulkhead and ceiling. The faint glow of the nearest force field sputtered and vanished. *"Burn through the conduit cables. Use a thirty-degree angle, about a palm-length from the fields, and just pick a corner,"* Ia called out, shifting up and lasering through the upper left corner of the next one. *"Most ship-built fields are vulnerable at corners and midpoints. It's faster to cut out the midpoints, but you do more structural damage at the corners. Cut enough corners, and they can't blow the airlock without the risk of cracking open the ship."*

"That's devious, Corporal. I'm glad you're on our side. Do it," D'kora ordered the others.

As she burned through the bulkheads, cutting through each force field in succession, Ia blink-programmed her comm channel for Alpha and Beta teams alone. *"Okay, people, listen up. Elevators are death traps. But if this is a Choya ship, we won't fit down the emergency ladder ways in our mech. If it's Salik, they'll have stairways. They don't do ladders. We'll take this corridor, up here."*

"Salik, sir!" The shout was broadcast on the Platoon channel. *"PSC Jundran Pzettisva, D Squad Beta, bow boarding party, I have visual confirmation of a mechsuited Salik on board. Repeat, visual confirmation! Salik on board, armed and armored!"*

"Find that bridge, A Squad!" D'kora ordered.

"Harkins, you're with me. Estes, take Double-E," Ia ordered, lascring through the power conduits for the last of the force fields slowing them down.

"Platoon policy is to keep teammates paired together, Corporal," Estes reminded her.

"You and I are short enough to crouch in front of them for a firing line, Corporal," Ia shot back. *"They can't say the same. Start opening doors left side. I'll take right. Kill all sensors you see. If a room is clear, shoot it shut as we go."*

"—Choya on board, sir! PFC Juno Dexter, E Squad Beta, I have visual confirmation of Choya on board, armed but not armored!"

The interior doors they encountered were controlled by simple rocker switches. Storage closets, crew cabins with oddly shaped furniture meant for bipedal but otherwise non-Human bodies, some with signs of hasty evacuation since some items had been left out on tables and such.

"Where are all the crewmembers?" Double-E asked quietly after a few minutes of searching.

"Split between the two ships," Ia offered, sealing the latest door shut with a stuttering blast from her rifle. *"They'll be hoarding any Gatsugi prisoners for shield-hostages, and protecting the engines, lifesupport systems, and the bridge."*

"Those they haven't eaten, you mean," Harkins offered grimly.

"This is either a door to a section seal, or hopefully a stairwell, since that looks like a set of lift doors up ahead," Estes observed, reaching a heavy metal door with a crank handle.

Ia positioned herself across from the door, opposite the hinge.

She gestured for Harkins to take point on her far side, watching the cross-corridors. Aiming her gun, she nodded at Estes. *"Crank it open, Corporal."*

Nothing met her but a stairwell, with treads big enough for Salik-sized feet. Plenty of room for mechsuited Marines to descend.

"Harkins and I go first. Estes and Double-E, watch our backs. Wait for us to descend two turns before you follow, and scan as you go. I don't want all of us caught in one trap." Stepping carefully, Ia descended.

The leg-joints on a Salik were odd. They had a thigh that bent backwards, and a rear-facing, hock-style knee, like the legs of an Earth ostrich. Below that was a long shank for a shin, and then their oddly shaped feet. Despite the length of their lower limbs, Salik never stood up completely straight; their legs were always bent, ready to flex and bounce. The accordion-folds of joints made them prodigious leapers in open terrain. The relatively low ceilings of a spaceship would prevent any of the enemy from leaping down upon her team, but facing them on a planet's surface would be a whole different matter. Backwards knees and meaty thighs weren't the only oddity, however.

Ankle and foot attached to that calf-shank backwards, so that a Salik's clawed, webbed toes trailed the foot, rather than led them. Salik young were born in water and breathed through gills, spending the first seven to ten years of their life almost completely underwater. It took Salik adolescents roughly an additional five years to fully develop their lungs and be comfortable breathing air, so long as it was humid. Their big flipper-feet were essential for movement through water, if somewhat cumbersome on land despite the way they pointed backwards.

In the water, there was no sentient species faster than a Salik, not even a dolphin. On a ladder, the Salik were slow and clumsy, thanks to their version of feet. Those feet were flippers designed to send them darting through the water after their prey, which they preferred to eat alive. Cooked food was an affront to their digestive systems, and fire had been one of the last technologies the Salik had mastered in their ancient past, long after the wheel, lever, and even writing had been developed.

The oddness didn't end with their legs. Their heads were bulbous, with almost no neck, and their eyes projected out of their heads on either side, giving them a wide field of view with a modest but useable amount of depth perception. Big mouths concealed sharp incisors meant for rending and tearing flesh.

Their arms were the strangest of all; while they did have a stout upper arm bone like most sentient races, their lower arms were boneless, muscular tentacles that split twice, forming four tips at the shank-long ends. They were also suckered down the undersides, starting from the first split about one fourth of the way from the ends. Naturally, they took advantage of this fact in their technology. Toggles and switches and buttons which could be depressed did exist, but all sensitive equipment was designed to work by *pulling* on buttons, not by pushing them down.

In contrast, the Choya were fully amphibious throughout their lives, born with lung structures that worked as gills and thus had to be kept moist at all times. The Choya were also more bipedal with somewhat normal-looking legs, webbed hands and feet, if with six fingers and toes instead of the Human five. They did eat cooked food, but didn't hesitate to eat their meat raw. Their eyes were set more on the sides of their heads than forward, and their ears had crest-like fans which could spread up and out or flick down and in. Unlike the Salik, they had a finned tail when born, but it shrank and vanished around what passed for their version of puberty, leaving them to walk and swim bipedally.

Stairs were no problem for the Choya, either, though they wouldn't have bothered to accommodate the other amphibious race. This was a Salik vessel.

"*Estes, Double-E, seal the door and follow.*"

"*I thought I heard something,*" Double-E replied. "*I should check it out.*"

"*Seal the door and follow, soldier,*" Ia ordered. "*Our priority is the bridge.*"

"*I'd have checked it out,*" Harkins grumbled. They could hear Estes and Double-E closing, cranking, and lasering the door shut. "*You don't leave an unknown force at your ba—*"

BOOM—KLANG!

The ship rocked with the force of the explosion. Everyone grabbed for the railing or the wall. The stairwell reverberated with the sound of whatever metallic object had struck the section seal door. *Hit by the fuel pipe that would've impaled Harkins, if I hadn't dragged him down here . . .*

"Headcount!" D'kora's voice snapped through the full Platoon channel. *"I want a headcount!"*

As the lead soldier in A Squad, Ia's HUD lit up in a grid of ten names. She blink-toggled her own box green, and watched the other nine light up with verdant health as well. Though she couldn't see it, she knew D'kora was seeing all fifty-three names on her own heads-up grid.

"Thank the gods, we didn't lose anyone. It seems they took exception to our presence and blew the airlock anyway. Entry-point deck and the decks above and below for that section appear to have vented to vacuum. A Squad, find that bridge and lock them down, meioas! B and C, find engineering, cut them off cold!"

"Enemy fire, sir! I think we found engineering. This corridor's heavily guarded!"

The conversation dropped off the Platoon channel, leaving Ia and her three teammates in the silence of the stairwell. Estes spoke up. *"Now what?"*

"I'm looking at a Choyan number right now. At least, I think it's a number," Ia added, wanting to sound uncertain. *"If I remember it right, that's their symbol for 8. We go down five more decks, and we should be on Deck 3. Most Salik ships have their bridges on Deck 3."*

D'kora's voice cut through their link on the Squad channel, echoing Ia's words. *"A Squad, no sign of a bridge on this deck. Proceed downward. Salik-designed ships usually have a bridge on the third or fourth up from the bottom. Stay paired; watch your backs."*

"Why would the Salik build a ship and put Choyan numbers on it?" Double-E asked Ia as she started down the stairs again.

"For that matter, why would the Choya build a ship in the Salik style?" Harkins quipped.

Estes came to her rescue. *"You saw the hull. They probably just grabbed an old Salik wreck out of some battle junkyard and slapped together whatever repairs they could manage on it. And then the Salik somehow got ahold of the Choya pirates and apparently cut a deal."*

"Keep alert, meioas," Ia interjected, easing down another flight of steps, rifle at the ready. There was an eighty percent probability they would make it down the stairs just fine, but

twenty percent was still enough to worry. *"We're headed down, and the Salik are built to look up. We need to be ready if they spot us coming."*

Red light lanced down over the railing, blackening a tiny box in the corner of the next turn. *"What, like they won't notice us shooting out their cameras?"* Harkins asked sardonically. *"They know***ing."*

"Wh**? You're br***up," Estes asked. Or tried to ask. A burst of static came across the comm from her link, vehement enough not to need a translation.

Damn, indeed, Ia thought, grimacing. *Onboard jammers. That was low on the probability chart.* Stopping Harkins on the landing between Decks 5 and 4, she beckoned the other two down to meet them. Once Estes and Double-E were in range, she triple-tapped all four of their helms, and triple-tapped Estes' helm a second time. Estes levered up the silvered outer layer of her faceplate, meant to protect her from laser fire, as did Ia, though neither unsealed their suits. The two women looked into each other's eyes, Ia's amber brown to Estes' hazel green.

"Either they want to overhear this," Ia stated slowly and clearly, "or they want us to unseal. Stay suited and switch to hand signs. I repeat, switch to hand signs."

Her helm buzzed faintly with Estes' reply, conducted between the two helmets. "Hand signs, got it."

They pulled apart and Ia touched helmets with Harkins, repeating the command to him as Estes did the same for Double-E. Separating, she gestured at Harkins and herself to move forward, further down the stairs. All of them lowered their blast plates, locking them back into place.

The door to Deck 3 cracked open. Alien muzzles aimed up in their direction. Ia crouched and shot through the railings while Harkins aimed over their tops. Double-E hurried down half a flight and burned into the metal plate forming one of the steps directly over the hatch. Dark orange ricocheted off Harkin's silvered armor, scoring a dark line on the plates covering his arm, but not doing enough damage to slow him down. Had it hit the elbow or wrist joint, it might have been a different matter.

Ia fired back, just as Double-E burned through. The armored figure on the other side of the door retreated hastily from the dual attack. Ia didn't hesitate; punching the air with her left fist even as she moved, she threw herself down the stairs at that door. Jerking it open, she dove through, clanging across the deck in a screeching tumble. Harkins followed a beat and a half behind, obeying her command to charge.

Just like every time she had practiced in the timestreams, Ia blink-opened her holdout gun on her right forearm even as she slammed upright against the far wall, rifle extended as she aimed. A split second later, a single bullet launched itself at the retreating, multijointed mechsuit. Electricity sparked and crackled across the alien's silvered back.

Red streaked overhead, coming from Harkins' Heck as he took out the sensor nodes in the corridor. Jerking her rifle back into her shoulder, Ia seared laser fire into the cracked panel, destroying the delicate conduits the splatter bullet had exposed. Based as it was on old, smuggled designs, Salik ceristeel was inferior to modern Terran manufacture, and it showed.

The Salik jerked to a stop, teetered, and toppled. The lumpy oval on its back smoldered, limbs and joints frozen from the destruction of its power pack. Orange light streaked past her left shoulder. Whipping around, Ia fired, scoring on the hock joint of the other armored Salik. That forced the alien to lumber awkwardly back around a corner as it retreated. With everyone armored, only the shapes of the armor and the nameplates embossed on shoulders, helms, and chests identified friend from foe.

Hand-signing to Harkins and Double-E, she gesture-ordered for both men to go check the downed alien and guard the back corridor. Moving up beside Estes, Ia traded potshots with the alien around the corner, inching forward. This corridor was broad, wide enough for two half-mechsuits side by side, though it would've been a tight squeeze to fit two full-mechs. It was also brightly lit, and turned a corner up ahead, angling to the left.

The Salik charged, firing. Estes plastered herself against the wall, scored on her shoulder-joint by the wild laser fire. Ia turned sideways and fired back, a steady stream that targeted the alien's silvered head. Orange fire scored along her forearm and the black paint of her rifle, scorching it clean. She didn't flinch. The tip of her Heck wavered in time with the alien's charging footsteps, searing the left-hand side, until the mechsuited warrior stumbled. Ia swapped her aim to the other side and the alien turned protectively, trying to protect his or her undamaged eye.

Estes raised her right arm and fired a single shot from her forearm gun. The bullet shattered the laser-weakened helm, splatting into the head of the Salik inside. A quick check behind showed Beta Team doing the same with the other Salik, killing the warrior to ensure he or she couldn't squirm out of the armor and attack them from behind.

Inching up to the corner, Ia crouched and peered around it. Nothing but empty muddy beige corridor lit by greenish white light, a couple of cameras . . . and two heavy blast doors, one on the left and one on the right, both sealed and secured against entry.

Raising her left hand, she sign-spelled "bridge" for the others, then beckoned them forward. Harkins kept his weapon trained on the corridor behind them. Pulling back, Ia triple-tapped Estes on the shoulder, raised her blast plate, and touched their helms together.

"The Salik always build a false bridge door on their warships. We need to get them to open up the real one. Any ideas?" Ia asked her through the conducting buzz of their touching faceplates.

"They'll come out for live bait, but I am *not* un-suit . . ." Estes trailed off, frowned a moment, then grinned wickedly. "I have an idea. Cover me, and be ready to move."

Nodding, Ia pulled back and lowered her blast plate again. Estes didn't lower hers. Switching to external speakers, she strolled into the corridor, HK-114 gripped muzzle-up in her right mechsuit hand, left hand on her hip. Ia followed in a half-crouch, her own mechsuit rifle held at the ready.

"Yo! Frogtopuses!" Her amplified voice echoed down the hall. "Are you all so toothless, you have to hide like jellyfish behind those blast doors? What do you do, *gum* your prey until it dies from *laughter*?"

Hidden behind the silvered blast plate, Ia allowed herself a grin. Estes was just as inventive in the here and now as she'd predicted the woman could be in the timestreams.

"Were you born with defective flippers? Are you faster on *land* than you are in the sea?" she scorned, turning around in a circle that took in both blast doors. "Let me guess. You've given up on eating flesh and are hiding inside, sucking on *roots*!

You're not warriors! You're not hunters! You are *food*! *I* could hunt and eat you! Hell, you'll probably stand still so I can sear off one strip of toadish calamari at a time!—You know what? I feel *sorry* for you!"

Ia pointed her gun at the ceiling, affecting a bored pose of her own. Her body was on the near side of the right-hand door, blocking its occupants from getting shot by Harkins or Double-E, but that was alright. Her position and seeming unconcern would encourage the Salik to open up and fight.

"Yeah, *that's* right!" Estes shouted, turning again and again, facing each door in turn. "You heard me! I feel so sorry for your pathetic frogtopodic asteroids, I'm just gonna stand here until you eat me! You hear me? Eat me!" she yelled at the right-hand door, then smacked her lips together. It was the way the Salik themselves mocked their prey, smacking their lips in chilling *pwop-pwop-pwops*. She turned back to the left one and smacked her lips at it, too. *"Eat me!"*

The right-hand door hissed open and a tentacle-hand lashed out, unwrapping and hurling the dark object caught in the purple pink flesh. Ia was faster than that flicking limb. Spinning into the doorway, blocking it from being thrown, she grabbed the alien grenade with her left servo-hand and shouldered the door panels wider with her armored right arm. The doors tried to shut again automatically, but she was too fast, too strong, and already through, live weapon in hand. Everything was perfect, exactly as it should be.

"Thank you!" Ia finished her spinning dash and her speech with an elbow-check to the Salik's head, ripping the grenade free . . . which yanked up on the activation button as the sucker covering it was jerked free.

Behind her, Estes jammed one armored foot in the doorway, poking the muzzle of her rifle into the opening, giving her some cover.

Ia had half a second to pick the largest group of bodies, some wearing their own versions of pressure-suits and others clad in their deliberately damp version of uniforms. Some were Choya, thin and yellow-skinned, moisture-packs strapped to their chests and throats; the rest were Salik, who didn't need to keep their gills constantly wet.

Several had laser pistols in their hands, but her entrance had rattled them, and none scored a hit on anything vital. Tossing the grenade to the right of the biggest knot, she sidestepped to her left, away from the sudden scramble of bodies desperate to get away from the weapon. It exploded in a spray of fiery shrapnel, shredding through five or six bodies and wounding a handful more. Blue hemocyanin from the Choya mixed with red hemoglobin from the Salik, painting the front half of the bridge in disturbingly colorful ichor.

Even knowing it was coming, Ia flinched as a chunk of something struck the right side of her faceplate, along with a peppering of shards and fluids. It plopped onto her right shoulder and dangled halfway down her back, caught on her armor. She didn't bother to wipe it off. Darting forward, she dodged a couple of wild shots from deeper into the bridge, with its workstation seats canopied in overhead screens better suited for Salik-style vision and control panels designed with buttons meant to be pulled as well as pushed.

Her goal was a keening, grey-mottled, multi-armed figure strapped to one of the chairs flanking the captain's station. The Gatsugi prisoner, captain of the *Clearly-Standing*, was a bloody mess, with chunks of flesh literally bitten out of his limbs. The bloodied lips of the Salik captain proved who had been feasting on this particular war-prize. He hissed at her and charged in a near-horizontal leap, yanking something from his belt. Ia dove forward, hitting the deck in a clanking skid that flipped into a roll, using her momentum to twist up and around onto her feet, facing the landing alien.

Behind him, she could see Harkins and Double-E prying open the blast doors wedged open by Estes' foot, and see the red streaks of the other woman's weapon, tagging and scorching the few surviving unarmored occupants of the bridge standing up to take potshots at the Human in their midst.

"Hhheww die, Hhhumans!" Hissing the words through both his broad mouth and his nasal flaps, the captain whipped around, grenade caught in the curled-up vee of his front microjuncture. The moment he faced Ia, he lashed the supple, cephalopodic limb at her. Ia, ready for him, clamped down hard with her mind. Startled, the alien stared at his limb, still tightly curled around the now charged device. Telekinetically curled. Crushed, almost. Gurgling a curse, he frantically shook his

limb, then turned and scraped it against the nearest workstation seat, desperately trying to release the explosive.

She had just enough time to step between him and the Gatsugi captain, shielding the wounded alien, before the captain exploded, spraying crimson chunks across the back half of the bridge. Dripping with blood, Ia brought up her rifle, aiming it at a pair of Choya crewmembers who were hesitantly rising from behind a computer console, weapons in hand.

"Surrender and live; fight and die," she warned them. One of them, a female by the duller yellows and browns of her skin, hastily tossed her gun onto the ground and crossed her arms over her chest, webbed palms cupping the moisture packs over her neck gills in symbolic surrender. The other gave in, dropped his weapon, and copied her move. On the other side, the three remaining Salik charged, firing. Ia whipped her gun around and shot one of them in the upper knee, toppling him with a screech; Estes shot the other two in the chest, slicing a sustained pulse from one alien to the other.

The corporal hurried inside, gun trained on the downed Salik with the injured knee . . . but the alien was faster. Still holding his pistol, he—or she; it was hard to tell with their species, particularly as they could literally change genders when needed, though the male form was preferred—turned the weapon on himself and seared his own brains. So did the two remaining injured Salik by the now-closed entrance, startling the trio of Marines. Death before capture, indicating this was no ordinary Blockade breakout. Which Ia already knew, but now Estes and the others did, too.

Double-E finally looked up across the carnage, spotting Ia. "Oh, holy . . . Ah, Corporal," he called out hesitantly, using his suit speakers. "You, ah . . . have . . . oh, God . . . *body* parts on your . . . uh . . ."

She was well aware of just what, exactly, dangled off her shoulder plate and clung to her torso and helmet. The part of her that dealt with her nightly nightmares had locked down her emotions the moment the first bodies had splattered across the room. As much as she wanted to scrub and scrub and scrub until she was clean . . . she didn't have time. That was the worst Ia had to face. She did not have the time.

"Unseal your helmet if you're going to vomit, Private," Ia told him. "If you're not, help Estes disarm and secure the prisoners. Strip and zip. Don't forget to check the Choyas' gillpacks. If they resist or fight back, shoot them, but try not to kill. Harkins, your file says you have field medic training. Tend to the Gatsugi captain and make sure he doesn't die from his wounds. Keep your armor clean around him; I don't think he's too mentally stable right now."

"What are *you* gonna do?" Estes asked her, aiming her rifle in wordless threat at one of the three shrapnel-wounded Choya bleeding in blue streaks at the front of the room.

"I still have the sucker hand, and some rudimentary knowledge of Choyan and Salhash," Ia stated. "I'm going to see if I can figure out the bridge controls so I can get those doors open again. If they're code-locked, we might be stuck in here for a while. That, and see if I can do anything to cut the jammers and maybe help the others on the ship."

"Just don't blow us up by suckering up the wrong keys," Harkins muttered, fetching a set of plexi ties from one of the small compartments built into his thigh armor.

Stowing her rifle behind her back, Ia stepped away from the whimpering Gatsugi. She eyed the chair at the captain's workstation, then sighed and crouched, pulling her weapon forward again. A bit of lasering broke the furniture free from the floor, allowing her to toss it aside. Bits of the dead dropped from her armor with the move. Mouth tightly clamped shut, she inhaled the self-contained, relatively clean air of her suit in slow, deep breaths, grimly mastering the urge to be sick.

Once it was out of the way, she had room to step under the overhead screens and crouch down. Locking her armor into a balanced crouch with another blink-code, she unhooked the sucker hand from her shoulder slot and studied the console with its splayed buttons and controls. The combination of having to look up to see the alien characters and symbols displayed on the screens just above her forehead and needing to look down to see where to put the sucker-lined device was going to be a literal pain in her neck.

As much as she wanted to cheat and just go straight to the ship functions she needed to access, she knew she had to make a show of hunting for and suckering up each command. Quick checks of the timestreams allowed her enough knowledge to position the hand over the correct controls on the console, bringing up the current operations controlled by the bridge.

Ia took her time puzzling through the alien script, double-checking the timestreams not just for the language, but for the next four hours, making sure everything was on track. Only then did she unlock the door. By that point, she also had the commands for the ship's internal comm system figured out.

Activating the comm, she broadcast to the whole ship. *"Attention, Salik and Choya. Your captain is dead, his top crew have been captured, and the bridge is under Terran control. You are accused of interstellar piracy, and in violation of Alliance Blockade Sanction against the Salik government, all of its citizens, and any other persons assisting them in breaking those sanctions. Blockade law is strict, but fair. Surrender and live; continue to fight, and die."*

"Human/Terran/Female . . . My ship/vessel/crew?"

Ia looked down from the overhead screen. The Gatsugi captain had recovered somewhat. His skin was still more a mottled grey than any other hue, his dark, round eyes wide with shock, but Harkins had used the emergency first aid kit all mechsuits carried, binding the alien's wounds against further blood loss. He gestured with one of his two unbitten arms, gesturing her closer, a faint brownish flush coloring his four slender fingers.

"Captain," Ia acknowledged. "We don't know/are blocked from communicating/finding out, but/yet the Marines have boarded/are helping your vessel/crew. Are you/will you be alright/functional/stable?"

Gatsugi almost never approached a conversation in Terranglo with a single set of terms. Their language was literally an amalgamation of language, gesture, and skin-changing colormood. It was an awkward way to talk, and a bit lengthy, but diplomatic. She knew the alien was on the edge of his version of sanity, given what he had just endured.

"Yes/no/yes. I live/survive/will suffer/have nightmares/terrors." He flicked his hand again, the tips now turning reddish. "The Salik/leader/effluence used/touched the yellow/bright/scared buttons/keys to lock/seal/secure the bridge/this place, and

another effluence/beast/monster approached/used the olive/
dull/morose console/panel/controls over there/to the left to seal/
stop/interrupt communications/broadcasts."

"You are a brave/watchful/coherent being/meioa, keeping your
wits/eyes open like that/as you did," Ia praised him. Shifting the
sucker hand to the right-side controls on the captain's console, she
prodded and pulled on several of the buttons. The doors beeped
after several seconds. "There. They should now be unlocked."

"Good job. Can you get those jammers off, too?" Estes asked
her. "We're all working blind, if we can't communicate with
the others."

"I'll try." Carefully disengaging the hand, she unlocked her
armor and shuffled back out of the captain's alcove. It didn't
take long, once she lasered away the seat so she could fit into
the workstation, to figure out where to place the vacuum-
suckered device. The workstation controlled three sets of jamming devices. Two were active, the hyperrelay jammers, and
the internal radio-based jammers. The insystem jammers
weren't working, mainly because the explosion back at the
midship airlock had wiped out the necessary equipment.

The hyperrelay jammers were code-locked; there was no
way she could crack them without proving she was a psychic
of some sort. The internal jammers were simply a matter of
manipulating the control menus to shut down the program. As
soon as she did so, Ia activated her command link to D'kora.

*"This is Corporal Ia to Lieutenant D'kora. Can you
hear me?"*

"Corporal! You got the jammers shut off!"

*"Just the internal ones, sir. Radio wasn't code-locked. It'll
take cryptographers who are a hell of a lot better at reading
Salhash than I am to break the codes on the hyperrelay jammers."*

"So they do have one. Good work."

"Thank you, sir." Head craned up to look at the screens, Ia
skimmed the information, leaning heavily on the timestreams
to read what she was looking at. *"This control also has some
operations sensors . . . what few we haven't shot to hell, of
course. Ah . . . the hyperrelay jammers are located in the hangar bay . . . forward bulkhead. I can't tell if there are any Salik
or Choya present in the hangar, but given how all of the sensors are still active, I think it's safe to say yes, sir."*

"*Noted.*" D'kora switched channels to the Platoon-wide link. "*This is Lt. D'kora. All combat frequencies are now clear. B through E Squad leaders, report.*"

The link for A Squad lit up. "*Private Hooke to the bridge crew, I've got your location on my scanners. We're tracking several armed and armored Salik headed your way. I repeat, A Alpha, A Beta, you have several armed and armored Salik heading your way!*"

"*Acknowledged, Hooke. I can see you on the internal sensors,*" Ia added, depressing a couple of the controls. "*You're headed . . . yes. Split up and half of you take the next junction on the right. You're one floor above us. There are two stairwells down. One is the one the Salik are headed for. The other is just below the damaged section, but I know the seals are still good.*

"*The group taking the damaged stairwell will come in from the right of the bridge as you face into it, and the group trailing the enemy will come in on the left. We'll be ready to attack from the bridge when you get here.*" She paused, then added, "*Be advised the bridge is intact, but currently a mess. Don't look too closely at anything.*"

"*What does that mean?*" she heard Knorrsson ask.

"*It means I made a mess. Hurry up, the Salik won't wait long to attack.*" Moving back to the captain's station, she relocked the double doors into the bridge, then switched to her external comm again. "Estes, get the captain a gun. Captain, come here/take refuge/shelter."

Wounded but no longer bound in place, the Gatsugi limped her way. He accepted the gun Estes passed to him with grim but pleased shades of blue and red; beyond that much, his colormoods were too complex to be discerned without dipping into the timestreams. Ia didn't bother. Easing out of the confined space, she moved around to the front of the console and stooped, pointing with a servo-finger at the sucker hand.

"Touch/press/manipulate the buttons/controls on this hand/ device in this/this pattern when I tell you/command it," she instructed, repeating "this" so he recognized it as emphasis. Showing the alien the pattern to unlock the doors, she made sure he practiced it, fingering the controls lightly. A bang on the bridge door startled both of them. The alien flushed a muddy shade of beige, fear-mood, and tightly gripped the laser pistol

Estes had liberated from a dead Choya. "You will survive/get home," she murmured. "I promise/swear."

It was hard to tell what a Gatsugi was looking at, since their pupils and irises were nearly the same, multispectrum-absorbing black, but he did nod. Or rather, bobbed his inverted teardrop of a head, on a neck with two more of what passed for its vertebrae than what a Human possessed. She couldn't bob her own head in reply, but flexed her wrist, bobbing her left servo-hand in Gatsugi third-gradient agreement.

"They're beginning to burn through, Corporal," Double-E warned her.

"I will count down/reduce from/at 5 to 1," she instructed the alien. He bobbed his head again. Pulling away, she swung her rifle back into her servo-hands and took two steps forward, facing the doors. The position would put her armored body, with its ceristeel coating, between the captain and the enemy. "Lock and load. Double-E, you're on the right. Estes, on the left. Harkins, keep an eye on the prisoners. If they move, shoot them."

"They/The Salik will perish/die. Not/Not me," the captain of the *Clearly-Standing* asserted softly, clutching the gun. The door banged a second time, but held.

"*Shakk* that," Harkins muttered, and flexed out his left-forearm gun, stunning the five surviving prisoners. Sealing up the holdout stunner, he swung his own HK-114 into position. "I'm with the good captain. We fight, and *they* die."

"*A Alpha, Beta, this is Hooke, we're in position.*"

"*Be mindful of cross-fire. A Epsilon, stay under cover. Fire only if they retreat to you. A Delta, open fire on my mark. Heads up,*" Ia warned the Squad members in the bridge, blink-coding her helmet to broadcast the countdown to both them and the rest of A Squad. "5 . . . 4 . . . 3 . . . 2 . . . 1, mark!"

The doors successfully opened. Ia aimed and fired the moment the crack between the two blast panels was wide enough for the streak of light. More crimson shot from the left, countering the deep orange of the Salik weapons. Two of them whirled to fire at the bridge, but Estes and Double-E were right there, cross-firing through the opening from each side.

Harkins fired at something gripped in one of their servo-tentacles. A grenade. It exploded, banging chunks of mechsuit arm into the other Salik. The proximity of the explosion ripped a chunk of protective casing off the power pack in the back. Ia smiled grimly, watching as fire from Soyuez, or maybe Estradille, lanced into the sparking gap as the alien lost control and spun around. Cranking her external speakers up, she shouted a warning.

"FIRE IN THE HOLE!"

Estes and Double-E instinctively flinched back at her shout, spinning away from the opening. Harkins crouched reflexively. Ia stood her ground, though she lowered her rifle. The damaged power pack exploded with a *bang*, releasing all of its stored energy. Pieces flung everywhere, knocking the other Salik off their servo-flippers.

A large chunk of chest plate and what had sheltered behind it flung into the bridge, slamming into Ia from head to chest. It knocked her back a step, but only a step. Had she taken cover, it would have bashed through the captain's station, damaging too many of the bridge controls and possibly killing the Gatsugi taking shelter behind it.

As it was, the armor *clanged* to the ground, and the flesh it had protected slid down her helm with a *glop* onto her armored foot. The crimson mess rendered her faceplate useless, leaving Ia with only what her HUD sensors could pick up and display. She lifted her rifle and fired again, based on its telemetry, until the outlines of the different mechunits dropped from red-lined Salik to green-lined Terran. Only then was she free to manipulate her servo-hand to scrape some of the gore from her helm. Some, but not all.

Quiet descended. Ia drew in a deep breath, focusing on the recycled, dry scent of her sealed mechsuit's air. *"Corporal Ia to A Squad, is the enemy neutralized?"*

Several replies came back at once. *"Aye, Corporal!"* *"Indeedy."* *"Splattered to goo."* On-mike groans met that last one.

"Delta, Epsilon, remain on alert. Guard both corridors against further incursions. Beta, keep an eye on the prisoners, and on the good captain. Estes, you and I get to check to see if anything is still alive, and clear a path through the mess." Switching frequencies, she contacted D'kora. *"Corporal Ia to Lieutenant D'kora, the bridge is once again secure. A Squad excluding Gamma will maintain a perimeter watch and hold the bridge until further notice."*

"Good work, Corporal. We're experiencing some resistance in the hangar bay. I'm keeping Gamma Team with me for the extra firepower."

"Understood, sir." Scraping again at her faceplate, reducing the crimson blur to streaks of reddish brown smears, Ia moved forward to help Estes sort through the firefight debris.

Double-E turned to face her, then did a double take. "Holy . . . ! I think you got even *more* . . . stuff . . . on your armor this time! You're covered helm to boot in that stuff."

Ia didn't bother to scrub at her faceplate a third time. The flexor gloves inside her suit could imitate many of the moves possible by a Human hand, but the servo-gloves on the outside were only covered in the plexi version of flesh on the palm-side of her mechanical hand. Plexflesh which was growing sticky from the drying blood already scraped onto it, and which would only smear around the remaining mess at best.

She shrugged at him. "Unless we stumble across a cleaning supply closet while we're down here, Private, I'm just going to have to stay 'painted' from helm to boot."

"It doesn't bother you?" Estes asked her. "Your first combat, and none of this bothers you?"

"I've seen worse," Ia stated flatly. She didn't have to see through their silvered faceplates to know her Squad mates were looking at each other. Mindful of their reactions, she added, "Not much worse, but the only thing I can do at the moment is clean up what I can, and deal with my nightmares later. Right now, we have a job to do, which is taking care of this mess. I'd like to focus on *doing* it, and being useful, for my sanity's sake."

CHAPTER 13

Fighting in real life isn't like the way they show it in the entertainment industry. They show you the tensions leading up to it, they show you the excitement and the horror of it . . . and then the heroes just walk off into the sunset or whatever. They never show you the literal hours and hours—and sometimes days and weeks—of cleanup which is required, post-battle.

With good reason, of course. It's hard, it's gross, it's messy, it's depressing, and it's boring. Usually.

~Ia

"Bloody Mary!"

Stopped in his tracks, Lieutenant Ferrar stared at Ia. Just stared. He wasn't the only one, but his exclamation and his sudden halt in the middle of the 2nd Platoon's prep bay captured the attention of the rest.

Since all three of the airlocks had been blown on the offside of the enemy ship, the *Liu Ji* had been forced to hook up to the far side of the *Clearly-Standing* to transfer troops and crew to the larger starship, first the injured and the prisoners, then the rest. Members of the Navy half of the ship had taken their place, swarming over both vessels to see what could be done to make both of them spaceworthy. A Squad, holding secure the vital bridge area, had been the last to evacuate.

That meant the prep bay was filled with Marines who were climbing out of their suits, cleaning them up, and checking them over for repair. Plenty of ears to hear the Lieutenant's loud exclamation, and plenty of eyes to seek out the source of his shock. Plenty of mouths to drop and gape, too.

"Corporal Ia and the remainder of A Squad reporting in, Lieutenant," Ia stated, staying sealed and keeping her blast plate down. By now, the gunk on her armor had congealed into a sticky brown crud which she didn't want gumming up the helmet's works.

"Bloody Mary!" he muttered again, eyeing her from head to toe. Craning his neck, he peered at the others lined up behind her. "Are you injured?"

"Sir, no, sir. All of this came from the enemy. Nor were any of the rest of my Squad, beyond some minor damage to Private Cooper's armor during the hangar fight with the lieutenant, sir. The Salik bridge has been surrendered to the command of Ensign Brakk and his crew," she reported. "Requesting permission to clean up and perform the necessary battle repairs before our debriefing, sir."

"Permission granted." He eyed her bloodied armor a moment more, then shook it off. "Since you don't have a sergeant, gather the reports from your Squad mates and report directly to Lieutenant D'kora for your debriefing. And make sure your armor is scrubbed and sanitized thoroughly before you leave this bay."

"Sir, yes, sir." Turning to face the others, she gave her orders. "A Squad, you heard the Lieutenant. Clean up, repair what you can, file any replacement forms, then fill out your battle sheets. I want them in my inbox folder in three hours. Dismissed."

They scattered. Ia headed for the decontamination stalls. The auto-scrubbers would get the worst of the gunk off of her armor, which would allow her to unseal and step out so she could hand-clean the remainder. Estes, who had gotten a bit messy herself in clearing up the bridge enough for the Navy to have room to work, followed her. She, however, was free to unseal and tip her helmet back; most of the stains on her armor were from the chest down.

" 'Bloody Mary,' *eyah*?" Estes asked her teammate.

"Bloody Mary, *hoo*-rah," Ia quipped back, drawling her reply through her suit speakers.

"Shyeah," one of the members of C Squad retorted as they passed him. "*One* battle. *One* fight. A nickname like that, you gotta *earn* it."

Ia carefully did not reply.

———————

Polishing her armor was necessary. As was repairing it, though Ia's mechsuit only needed a few touch-ups with a filler compound where it had been scratched by flying debris. Polishing it slowly, buffing every single inch of the hematite grey composite of ceramic and metal until she could see her white-haired head in the shine, was overkill. She had already cleaned and polished her knife and its clip-on sheath, and had made sure even the Choya blood, which dried into a hard-to-see clear paste, was no longer present anywhere on her gear.

Further down the prep bay, she could hear two of her fellow members of the 2nd Platoon, Dexter and Adams, discussing repairs that had just been made to Dexter's mechsuit. She could hear the slight hum and hiss as Dexter flexed his elbow joint. A third, Hmongwa, was using his suit to store heavy equipment used to make needed repairs to his own half-mech.

Even knowing it was coming, when it sounded, the klaxon startled her.

"This is Captain Davanova. We have intruders on the Clearly-Standing. *I repeat, intruders on the* Clearly-Standing. *Several Choya have grabbed Navy personnel as hostages and are fighting their way back to the Salik vessel. All hands, report for battle! All hands, report for battle!"*

Grabbing knife and sheath, Ia slammed the blade home and tucked the sheath in the waistband of her camouflage brown trousers. "Adams! Hmongwa! Dexter! Lock and load, we're going in!" Tapping the comm link on her wrist unit, Ia spoke into it, sprinting down the bay toward the weapons lockers. *"Ia to Lt. D'kora, I need the weapons lockers released. Adams, Hmongwa, and Dexter are still in the prep bay with me; we're on first response!"*

Skidding to a stop in front of the cabinets, she waited

impatiently for the red locked lights to turn green on the security panels. Thumping noises showed the two mechsuited Marines following her orders.

"Move it, Adams! Forget your armor! Grab a weapon and go!"

"We need to wait for our Squads," Hmongwa pointed out, reaching her side with thumping strides. "You're A Squad, I'm B."

"Potluck of war, meioas!" she snapped, making sure her voice carried to the back of the bay. "When you're caught with your pants down, you grab any and all personnel—*move it*, Adams!"

The lights finally changed. *"Corporal Ia, I've released the weapons lockers. You are green for go. We'll be right behind you. Remember, we like the Navy. Don't get them killed."*

"We're on it, sir." Yanking up the largest cabinet doors, she flung two HK-114s at the two mechsuited men, who hastily caught them, then pulled up the doors to the e-clip cabinet and tossed a trio of e-clips at Adams as he came skidding up to them. He fumbled one to the floor as she opened a third locker, grabbing a smaller-seeming HK-70. "Pass those out, Adams! The three of you, follow me!"

She turned and ran—jogged, so they wouldn't fall behind—up the corridor leading to the launch hangars. Rather than turning right toward the boarding pods, she turned left, taking the nearest gantry tube still attached to the *Clearly-Standing.* A tap of her comm link controls linked her to the *Liu Ji.*

"Corporal Ia to Captain Davanova, we're responding to your distress call. What is the known location of the enemy?"

It wasn't the Captain who answered, but rather the comm officer on the bridge. *"Uh . . . Corporal Ia, last position was Deck 3, Mauve Sector. That's the section with the purply pink walls . . . Who the hell paints their walls purply pink?"*

Ia grinned. She knew that last comment wasn't meant to be on-mike. *"The Gatsugi, of course. Deck 3 Mauve, got it."*

"Mauve Sector is . . . midships starboard, close to the Salik vessel."

"Got it. Ia out." Closing the link, Ia led the others into the *Clearly-Standing.* The airlock was white, but beyond that, the corridors were a soft shade of aquamarine. She ran lightly, mindful not to go too fast for either the unarmored Adams or

the burdened Dexter and Hmongwa behind her. "I studied the ship schematics we were given at the debriefing. We're entering on Deck 5. Mauve Sector is on the far side of Lemon Yellow, which is the central core on these vessels."

"If you ask me," Dexter muttered through his external speakers, following Ia at a deck-plate-shuddering jog, "the Gatsugi are insane. Painting their corridors weird colors?"

"Yeah, well, at least they don't *eat* people," Adams retorted. "Did you hear what those frogtopuses did to this ship's captain?"

"I didn't have to hear it," Ia muttered. "I *saw* it—Yellow Sector—forest green doors, that's the lift service!" Dashing forward, she slapped the lift controls. "Up we go."

It took a small eternity, six or seven seconds, for the lift to reach their deck. Ia and Adams ducked inside and plastered themselves against the front wall in each corner, allowing the two mechsuited men room to enter. The last thing either of them wanted was to have a foot stepped on by a half ton of moving machinery.

"Deck 3," Adams muttered, twisting to punch the buttons. "Uhh . . . there, that should be it. Top down, left to right?"

"Correct," Ia confirmed. "Their number 3 kind of looks like an incomplete four-point star."

"Got it." The doors closed. The elevator lurched upward, straining under the weight of the two mechsuits, then chimed and opened up again. Ia darted out, oriented herself, and took off to the right. Dexter and Hmongwa followed, and Adams trailed behind.

They heard the sounds of shouting, hissing, and the sizzle of laser fire striking something, though there were no screams of pain, yet. They also encountered a knot of Gatsugi, wringing their four-fingered, fourfold hands in hues of muddy yellow distress, or gripping their version of laser pistols grimly in shades of rage-mottled red. Two blue-clad Humans were there as well, one clearly dead, the other gasping in pain as a grim-brown Gatsugi did her best to bind his bloodied leg.

Ignoring him, Ia squeezed past the other aliens so she could crouch and peer around the corner. She could just make out four Choya and two hostages, one a blue-clad Human, the other a beige-clad Gatsugi. It looked like they were keeping watch both on this corridor and on the airlock into the Salik ship. Pulling back, Ia hissed at the aliens around her.

"Back/back/back! Clear/exit this corridor/hall!" she ordered, shooing them with rolling flips of her hands, Gatsugi-style. They blinked their black mouse eyes at her, then scattered. Some helped the injured Navy man retreat into a side cabin. "Hmongwa, Dexter!" she ordered in an undertone. "Four of them, just around the corridor. Two hostages, one Navy. Keep them pinned down. Don't let them escape this way, but definitely get their attention focused on *you*. Adams, you're with me."

"*We're* not armored," Adams reminded her as he hurried after her, following her back up the corridor.

"No, we're not." She beckoned for one of the Gatsugi to follow her. "But if I remember the schematics right, there's a service access panel in the bulkheads just behind where their rearguard is stationed. You, show us!"

"Access/hatchway, behind/near them?" the crewmember asked, blinking. She thought a moment, then tipped her head and gestured in affirmation. "This/This way!"

"Sneak attack?" Adams murmured, figuring it out. Grinning, he warmed up his rifle and followed. Then caught Ia by the elbow, jogging at her side. "You don't have a weapon, Corporal!"

She shrugged off his touch. "Don't worry, I brought a knife."

"To a *gun*fight?" he scoffed.

The Gatsugi led them into a cabin before she could form a retort. It was a private cabin, crew quarters with a table, a pair of chairs, and two bunk beds. While the shapes of the furniture were normal enough, the sheer clash of colors made both Humans wince. Everything was painted, tinted, or plastered with hues both bright and pastel, and none of it arranged according to Human aesthetics. Prisms cast rainbow reflections on the walls from where they hung around the edges of the recessed overhead lights, and a strange-scented incense lingered in the air, making Adams sneeze and Ia rub hastily at her nose.

"This way/Here," the Gatsugi told them, manipulating the locking mechanism on a slim rectangle of wall. The space beyond was narrow for a Gatsugi, and very narrow for a Human. Ducking and squeezing in sideways, Ia worked her way after the alien, following the female through the mesh of bundled wires and pipes.

The crewmember did something to another panel, creating a crack of light on the left, then edged further along between the conduits. Ia hissed at her as she passed. "Stay/stay/stay, or go back/retreat!"

The alien tipped her head side to side quickly, her version of nodding. Satisfied, Ia moved. Contorting down into the opening, Ia stuck her hand out first, quickly signing a cautionary gesture in Gatsugi for the crewmembers she couldn't see but knew were off to the left, so they wouldn't shoot.

Only then did she ease her way out as quietly as she could manage. Adams followed, managing a credible level of silence, though the noise from their two fellow Marines, shouting orders at the Choya to set down their weapons and let their captives go, helped cover the few wisps of sound they made. Just as Ia had foreseen.

She didn't want the rearmost of the Choya to have enough time to glance back at the Gatsugi crewmembers pinning them down with their pistols, and shout a warning. Sprinting forward, she caught up with the yellow green male just as he glanced back down the corridor her way. Her palm snatched at his throat, yanking him forward into the side hall with her. Spinning both of them around to pull them out of immediate enemy view, Ia grabbed his face with her left hand, palm cupped over nasal slits. She snatched at his left shoulder with her right hand and twisted. The short, sharp *crack* was lost in a reply shouted by the Choya around the corner, responding to her fellow Marines.

Lowering her victim to the deck, she laid the body on the floor against the wall and eased up to the corner. A probe of the future showed none of them likely to glance her way in the next five seconds. Slipping her knife free, she eased around the corner, then dashed forward. Her left hand cupped over the next Choya's mouth and nostril slits to keep the alien silent; her right hand sawed the blade across his throat, slicing deeply above the edge of his moisture-packs. Blue gushed from the wound. His webbed hands tensed, then slid free of the blue-clad Human in his grasp.

One of the other Choya glanced back, the female holding the Gatsugi crewman. Ia flung the dead Choya free and leaped at her, slamming her into the rose purple bulkhead, one hand on the alien's shoulder, the other stopping her knife a mere centimeter from one of those yellow, slit-pupilled eyes. Shocked, the Choya didn't maintain her grip on the other alien, who freed himself with a wrench, diving behind Adams for cover.

"Surrender!" Hmongwa thundered through his external speakers. "Your hostages are freed and your crewmates are dead!"

Behind him, several more Marines appeared, unarmored but taking cover behind his and Dexter's mechsuits. The plethora of Heck muzzles pointed their way convinced the last of the Choya to carefully drop his weapon to the blue-bloodied floor and clamp his palms around his throat in surrender.

"You got her?" Ia asked Adams, whose own rifle was poking over her left shoulder.

"I got her," he promised.

Easing back and to the right, out of his field of fire, Ia released the alien's arm. She stepped back with careful deliberation, misplacing her foot . . . and slipped, falling flat on her back, elbow banging into the corpse of her previous opponent. Her body rolled with the fall, partly from expecting it, partly from lifelong training in how to fall safely in heavy gravity, but it still knocked some of the wind out of her.

Two of the unarmored Marines hurried forward to secure the last prisoner. Ia pushed up onto her elbows, watching them work. Her backside was soaked from shoulders to hips with Choya blood, still warm and slightly greasy-feeling. They couldn't regulate their body temperature quite as efficiently as a mammal, but more than any Terran amphibian or reptile could. Her skin wanted to crawl with the urge to scrub herself clean, but she had to wait for permission to go get cleaned up again.

"Situation under control, Lieutenant!" she heard Dexter call out. "They killed one man, but the others look like they'll live, sir."

"Good job, meioas," Lt. Ferrar called back. Ia rolled up onto her hip and her hand, and pushed to get up . . . and faked another pratfall, landing on her side with a soft *oof*. Ferrar frowned and stepped forward. He stopped before reaching the edge of the puddle on the floor. "Corporal Ia? Is that you? You're . . . ah . . ."

That was her cue to stand. Rolling onto her knees, Ia got

one foot underneath her. She pushed to stand up and face her commanding officer—and her foot caught on the slick ichor the wrong way.

Knee twisting painfully, Ia slipped for real and *splapped* onto the deck. She caught herself with her forearms, absorbing most of the impact, but still thumped chin-first into the hemocyanin. Only the twisting of her neck and the clamping of her lips kept the bitter stuff out of her mouth.

A quick check of the timestreams relieved her. It was the only relief, though. Now she was coated up the front of her body from toe to chest, mostly on her right side, and her knee throbbed, warning her of the need to visit the Infirmary. Self-disgust warred with a tiny spark of her twisted sense of humor. *Bloody Mary, indeed . . .*

The smell clung to her, subtle but coppery and, well, alien. Not like Human or even Salik blood. Keeping her expression confined to a wrinkled nose and a grimace, Ia—carefully— pushed back up onto her feet.

Lieutenant Ferrar was waiting for her. Staring, rather. He blinked twice, swallowed, blinked again, then met her stiff salute with a salute of his own. "Corporal . . ."

"Lieutenant. I apologize we didn't get here fast enough to save the Navy one of their own, sir," Ia stated, lifting her chin and doing her best to ignore the cooling liquid staining her cheek, hands, and brown casuals. She stood mostly At Attention, not wanting to put too much weight on her right knee, and waited for the comment she knew was coming.

He stared at her, dragging his gaze down to her brown leather boots and back up again. "Are you *that* determined to earn your nickname, soldier?"

"Sir, *no*, sir. I fell and twisted my knee, sir; I wouldn't do that deliberately." She grimaced, showing some of her pain. "In fact, it hurts like hell right now. Permission to report to the Infirmary, sir?" she asked.

"Granted—*after* you run through decontamination on your way back to the ship, if that's your only injury," the dark-skinned man added, pointing a finger at her bloodied clothes. "I don't care how deep you wade into it in future battles, Corporal; you *will* be cleaned up and ready for inspection within an hour after each Stand Down. Dismissed . . . 'Bloody Mary.' "

"Thank you, sir." Slowly, carefully—her knee twinging with each step—Ia picked her way out of the mess smeared across the floor, limping back toward the *Liu Ji*. No one offered to help her, wary of the inky mess making her clothes cling to her body, but a few did offer her grins.

She knew why they grinned. Bathed literally in the blood of combat, she was now officially one of them: a Space Force Marine.

"Please, sit down, Corporal," Chaplain Christine Benjamin urged Ia. "Would you like something to drink? Water? Caf'?" The redheaded woman gestured at the dispensary in the corner of her office. "I just put in a fresh packet a few minutes ago. It should be hot by now."

"Water would be fine, thank you." Ia sat in one of the cushioned chairs across from the chaplain's desk and waited while the other woman dispensed a mug of water for her and a cup of caf' for herself. Accepting the plain white plexi cup, she sipped from it while the chaplain settled herself into the other chair and crossed her legs. She was clad in the Dress Blues of the Space Force Navy, but her trousers bore a grey stripe next to the black one, indicating she was part of the Special Forces. The Special Forces weren't just about Sharpshooters, Troubleshooters, the Department of Innovations, or even the Psi Division; they were the catchall for various nonstandard, highly trained groups.

"Well . . . I suppose you know why you're here, Corporal— actually, do you mind if I just call you Ia?" the older woman asked. "Please call me Bennie. Everyone does."

"No, I don't mind. And yes, I do know why I'm here," Ia added.

"Well, it *was* your first combat, and the medical divisions, the Department of Innovations, your superior officers, so on and so forth all want to make sure you came through it okay," Bennie stated. "Not to mention me, as both your chaplain and the ship psychologist. You had an extraordinary day, you know."

"You could say that again," Ia muttered, sipping again from her cup. It gave her hands something to do. She knew this interview was necessary, but knew it was also a minefield of potential career traps. "This session is being recorded, right?"

"Yes. Anything you say here will be held in confidence, and will not go on your permanent open record against you. But it will be a permanent part of your sealed files," Bennie explained candidly. "Those are only opened in case you, oh, go absolutely insane and start murdering everyone in sight. Then the psychologist and parapsychologists would obtain permission to crack them open and pick through your past to see where things started to unravel. But unless you do that, they remain sealed. Not even Admiral-General Christine Myang, the highest-ranking military officer of the entire Space Force, can crack them open casually."

Ia nodded. It was good to know what she was about to say would be a part of her permanent record . . . but not easily accessible. Depending on how she phrased things, she could cover her asteroid legally here in these sessions. There were rules and regs regarding those with psychic abilities to hedge around, after all.

"I understand. And I'll be as candid as I can, since I know you want to make sure I get any help I might need," she stated.

"You put that rather conditionally," Bennie observed, pouncing on Ia's phrasing. "Do you feel you don't need help?"

Ia smiled wryly. "Sir . . . Bennie," she amended, "I have already been parapsychologically evaluated. Repeatedly, through the years. I grew up as the second child of the second generation of a nearly brand-new colonyworld. A heavyworld, where literally falling down the wrong way could kill a grown man. I saw . . . things . . . as a child. Things that children from more developed, more civilized worlds shouldn't ever have to see.

"My parents made sure that the Witan Order—they had the cheapest rates—evaluated me fully on all levels. Psychologically, parapsychologically, even psychically. I've had my head rummaged through on multiple occasions to make sure I was—and am—mentally stable, and I have received their stamp of approval for my sanity, stability, and morality in *all* categories."

Her next evaluation wasn't due for almost a full year. Still, Ia had already made arrangements to "meet up with old friends" on board the *Hum-Vee*, her friends being a trio of registered telepathic evaluators. All psychics had to undergo morality and ethics checks at least once a year. They could keep their abilities private, but they had to be registered, and they had to be scanned, to reassure the rest of the galaxy that a particular psi wasn't using the abilities illegally.

Her own actions could very well qualify as illegal at times, except for two special words protecting her.

"Were you, now?" the chaplain asked her, sipping at her mug of caf'. The drink was a hybrid between the Terran and V'Dan versions of coffee, without the acrid bitterness of the Terran kind, and with more stimulants than the V'Dan. Ia liked the beverage, but didn't want the caffeine running through her system so close to her bedtime. "Are you stable?"

"Once the parapsychologists and I figured out how best to work through my nightmares . . . yes. And I do mean work through them," Ia added, knowing she had to turn the session to her advantage.

"Please, explain," Bennie urged, gesturing with her free hand.

"I'm good at helping people. Because of the things I saw as a child, I developed the urge to help others. But I'm also good at fighting. Combining the two, helping people, fighting to defend others, striving to stop other people from being violent . . . these things soothe my psyche. I'm stable in combat because I know I'm helping save innocent lives. Put me behind a desk . . . and, well . . ." Ia shrugged. "The memories start to eat at my soul. I cannot *not* help people."

"You saw . . . things . . . as a child, but combat as an adult doesn't bother you?" Bennie asked. "The blood, the gore, the screams of the dying?"

Ia gave the chaplain a level look. "I never said it *doesn't* bother me. I said I figured out how to work past all that. For the record, it *does* bother me. I want to make it stop. More than that, I want to make it stop happening to other people. And it makes me want to try harder the next time. My reflexes, my skills, my grasp of tactics, these things make me a natural warrior. My will to place these things between innocent lives and whatever threatens them, *that* makes me a natural soldier."

Her claim to natural warrior skills was a lie; she had forced herself to work hard at training everything for over two years before joining the Marines. By now, the habits were ingrained into her muscles, but it hadn't been easy, let alone natural, at the beginning.

"I have certain abilities which the average person does not," Ia continued. That statement was the absolute truth, counterbalance to her lie. "It would be wasteful if I didn't use them, particularly if I could help others," Ia pointed out. "Someone has to stand between the innocents of the world and anything that might try to harm them. To not use these abilities when I know I can, and I know I should . . . *that* would be the real nightmare."

Absolute truth.

Bennie considered her words. She mulled them over, sipping at her caf'. Ia sipped at her water, letting the silence stretch between them. Eventually, the chaplain nodded, coming to whatever conclusion was in her thoughts. "And if you fail to save someone?"

If she failed to save the *future*, which might and could turn on the saving of a single life, that was a nightmare Ia didn't ever want to have to face. Far more rode on the outcome of her actions than this one woman could even dream existed. But the question demanded a reply. Setting her mug in the clip on the end table next to her, Ia shrugged. "Then I'll acknowledge my failures, make whatever reparations I can, and try even harder the next time. It's called maturity. Taking responsibility for your actions. I'll be more cautious. I'll develop better skills. I'll work smarter, and harder, so I won't fail the next time."

"And if you still fail?" Bennie asked quietly.

Ia met her gaze levelly. "Then I'll have died trying."

"And the people around you?" the chaplain asked her next. "While you're so busy trying so hard that you die?"

She braced her elbows on her knees and clasped her hands, staring at a spot somewhere past nowhere. Not quite onto the timeplains, but definitely seeing the faces of the lives that surrounded her. "They're the people I'm trying to save."

"Save them from what?"

Ia looked up, mouth twisting in a lopsided, wry smile. "Wrong question."

The chaplain arched one of her reddish gold brows. "Is it, now?"

"It's easy to find something to fight *against*, sir. I'm sure you've seen that time and again, as a chaplain. Warriors who get so caught up in the fighting and the dying, the hatred and the misery, they can see nothing but the wounds scarring their bodies, the blood coating their floor. What a soldier needs is something worth fighting *for*. A goal. Something beyond the war . . . because all wars come to an end, one way or another," Ia told her. "It's what comes after that you have to focus on, that you have to pull through the mud, and the blood, and the gore."

Bennie lifted her chin at Ia. "So, tell me. What comes after? What are *you* fighting for?"

Ia looked down at her clasped hands. "It's not words. It's a moment. Dusk. On my homeworld, in the summertime. The evening lightning storms are flickering off to the east, bluish white against the deep purple of the mountains. Off to the west . . . sunset over the ocean in the distance, and the deep oranges and reds of the fading light. The barking of a stubbie— that's a kind of heavyworld-adapted dog," she added in explanation. "The laughter of the children as they play in the sandpit, happy and content . . ."

Her words filled the quiet of the chaplain's office, painting the picture found in her heart.

". . . The sleepy chirps of the rauela perched in the trees, their rainbow hues subdued in the shadows. The spicy-sweet scent of the plimka bushes in bloom, and the buzzing of fritteries as they feed on the sap. The crisp, hunger-inducing scent of fried topadoes, blue and bright, and the seared sweetness of sunsalmon imported from the planet Scadia, all of it still lingering in the air. A father calling out to his children to come eat their dessert. A mother pouring glasses of milk. A hovercar humming past, skimming on its way to who knows where. The soft bounce of the plexcrete underfoot as you walk up the path to your home."

Pain welled up inside of her, forcing her to close her eyes and calm herself, or risk crying for what she could not have. Bennie waited patiently. As soon as she felt safe enough, Ia concluded the scene with the truth, with the deepest longing in her heart.

"Just . . . one moment of peace."

Silence filled the room once more. Ia sat back and waited for the results of her honesty. Bennie studied her for a few moments more, then nodded slowly.

"I think we've talked enough for one day. I'd like to chat with you after your next few combats as well—and you can come to me at any time in between and talk about anything. But you're stable enough to go on, for now. It's also just about your Platoon's bedtime, isn't it?" she asked the younger woman.

Ia nodded, relieved the future wasn't mucked up too badly. She had found mostly the right words. This time. Following the future wasn't always like following a script; sometimes there were just too many just-good-enough options to pick out the absolute best. "I know I can come here, sir."

The chaplain smiled wryly. "Bennie, please. The only reason I have bars on my collar is so I can officially sit on the *un*stable members of my flock, and legally get away with it."

Ia smiled back. "I'll try. Sir."

Bennie grinned at the teasing, and gently shooed her out of the cabin. Ia grateful retreated with a lighter feeling held inside than when she had entered. Not truly light—not a moment of peace—but lighter.

———

"Hhheww will die, Hhewmanss!"

Frantically, Ia reached out with her mind, but nothing happened. She flung her hand down as well, as if she could crush the grenade in the alien's pseudopodic hand several meters away, but it hurled through the air at her anyway. She ducked and twisted, diving out of the way, but couldn't avoid it. The grenade exploded, ripping her apart in pain-filled chunks that splattered all over her unshielded face as she stood there, facing the hate-filled alien, paralyzed with the need to get *out* of the way—and the grenade hit her a second time, this time with the exact same impact as landing face-first on the floor with a jarring, wakening *thud*.

"—Whuh?" On the bunk next to her, Estes shot up quickly. So quickly, she smacked her head on the bottom of the upper bed. *"Ow!"*

Glad the cabin had only lightworlder gravity, Ia rolled over onto her back, nursing her battered nose and shoulder. She covered the former with the hand of her uninjured arm, then quickly covered her face as well when Estes hit the switch for the cabin lights.

"Ia? What are you doing on the *floor*?" Estes demanded.

Several options raced through her mind. The pain in the bridge of her nose made it hard to think. Ia rolled away from the bed, facing the lockers. Grabbing her nose, she pulled, resetting the bone with a gasp. Her psi countered with a flood of numb heat. She couldn't heal as fast as some biokinetics—not without a source of energy to feed upon—but her nose would look more or less normal by morning. No questions would be asked, provided she kept her back to the other corporal.

"Ia? Are you alright?" Estes asked.

With the numbness soothing the pain, Ia could think. A quick skim of the immediate future showed her a little humanity would go a long way. "Nothing . . . just a nightmare."

"Nightmare?" her teammate asked. Ia could hear her sitting up more cautiously this time. "About what?"

Ia pushed herself upright and gestured vaguely with one hand. "You know . . . the fight, today." Opening her locker, she pulled out her writing equipment. "I can't get back to sleep, right now. I'll go do something in the front room until I'm tired again, so I don't disturb you. Only one of us needs to be awake right now."

"If you want to talk about it . . ." Estes offered.

"Yeah, I know; I can go see Bennie," she quipped, stacking papers and equipment in her arms.

"I meant you could talk with *me*."

The soft chiding touched Ia. It was an offering of friendship. One she didn't dare accept too closely. She knew what would happen to the other woman in the most probable futures ahead of them. Everything that *had* to happen hurt too much as it was. Nodding, keeping her gaze averted, Ia closed the locker and headed for the door. "Thanks . . . but I think another time. I need to get my mind off of it and onto something more useful right now. Sleep well. Or at least better than me."

Sealing the door between them, she padded through the near-dark of the room, lit only by the faint yellow and green glows of various indicator lights. Flicking on the lamp by her desk, Ia set up the portable writer and bent her mind away from splatters of red and blue.

If I can't sleep, I can't afford to waste my wakefulness.

Hands hovering over the keys, she cleared her mind firmly, focusing down and in to get onto the timeplains. *I have everything in the near immediate future covered for most of the galaxy . . . but I have too many things to write out for my homeworld. And far fewer years to guide its future than to guide everyone else's.*

So . . . let's find the next locutus in the streams I need to dig around and guide just right . . .

As horrific as the possible futures would be if she failed, they at least were concrete possibilities, potential chances she could work with. Nightmares were nebulous horrors she felt powerless to prevent. She hadn't lied to Chaplain Benjamin about what kept her sane, of how she needed to help others to work through the pains and horrors of each day.

Frowning in concentration at the keyboard, she caressed it with her fingers, but didn't type; instead, Ia stimulated the circuits with her mind. She picked out a seemingly innocent message, one which would actually affect her own lifetime, and began composing it electrokinetically.

ATTENTION: AFASO SENIOR MASTER KILLA JAMBE'A. YOU'LL BE ON YOUR WAY TO TERRA VERDE. YOU'RE THE CLOSEST PERSON WHO CAN HELP ME WITH THIS MATTER.

DATE: TERRAN STANDARD 2491.01.03, <u>PARKER'S GATE</u> STATION LOCAL TIME 13:50 +/- 5 MINUTES

LOCATION: PARKER'S WORLD, <u>PARKER'S GATE</u> STATION, SECTION C, 15TH DECK, A DIVE OF A BAR NAMED JINN'S LAST STAND. ORDER A BOTTLE OF K'VASSA, UNOPENED, BUT DON'T DRINK IT OR ANYTHING ELSE. YOUR STOMACH WON'T HANDLE IT.

TARGET: DREK THE MERCILESS. HUMAN, DARK HAIR, GRIZZLED BEARD, BLACK VEST, RINGS WITH SPIKES ON HIS FINGERS, AND A NOSE-RING CONNECTED BY A CHAIN TO HIS LEFT EAR. METALS SHOULD BE MOSTLY SILVER OR STEEL. HE WILL GO UP TO THE BAR AND ORDER A DRINK. ORDER YOURS AT THAT MOMENT, TOO.

**MESSAGE, TO BE DELIVERED MURMURED IN HIS EAR
WITHOUT LOOKING AT HIM, WHILE THE BARTENDER
IS BUSY FETCHING THE DRINKS:** "A CERTAIN, SPECIAL
SOMEONE SENDS HER REGARDS. SHE RESPECTFULLY SUG-
GESTS YOU PICK YOUR MENU CHOICES FROM COLUMN B
INSTEAD OF COLUMN A, NEXT TIME YOU'RE IN CHAN'S.
SHE ALSO SENDS A REMINDER. YOU OWE HER QUITE A
DEBT BY NOW. BE READY TO REPAY IT ONE DAY."

ACTION: ACCEPT YOUR BOTTLE FROM THE BARTENDER
AND LEAVE. GIVE THE UNOPENED BOTTLE TO THE
CRESTED TLASSIAN JUST OUTSIDE. HE'LL TAKE CARE OF
ANY FOLLOWERS. JUST MAKE YOUR WAY BACK TO YOUR
SHIP, AND CONTINUE ON YOUR JOURNEY. THANK YOU FOR
YOUR HELP IN THIS MATTER.

With that letter finished, she printed it out, signed and sealed
it, and set it aside to work on the next one. This message was
intended to affect the lives of two people who would otherwise
never meet, nor affect the future generations waiting to be born.

ATTENTION: CENTRAL AGENT INSTRUCTIONS 7809-35-A.

DATE: TERRAN STANDARD 2522.02.03, SANCTUARY,
RIVERVIEW WARREN, LOCAL TIME 05:02:17 +/- 2 SEC-
ONDS. TIMING IS CRUCIAL. BEGIN WALKING ACROSS THE
BRIDGE AT EXACT TIME, AND PACE YOURSELF TO REACH
BRIDGE MIDPOINT WITHIN 35 SECONDS. PRACTICE THE
WEEK BEFORE.

LOCATION: SANCTUARY, RIVERVIEW WARREN; THIRD
SOUTH BRIDGE, FIFTH TIER, LEFT-HAND SIDE HEADED
OFF-TOWN, 2 METERS FROM THE RAILINGS.

TARGET: WOMAN IN RED DRESS, LIGHT BLONDE HAIR,
AGE APPROXIMATELY EARLY THIRTIES.

ACTION: BUMP INTO HER HARD ENOUGH TO MAKE HER
DROP HER BAG AND BREAK ITS CONTENTS, AND KEEP

WALKING. DO NOT STOP TO HELP. LOOK BACK ONLY AFTER
IO FULL SECONDS HAVE PASSED. MAKE SURE A DARK-
HAIRED MAN IN A BLUE SHIRT AND DARK TROUSERS, LATE
TWENTIES, HAS STOPPED TO ASSIST HER, THEN EXIT THE
AREA. IF HE IS NOT CROUCHED AND CHATTING WITH HER,
CONTINUE TO ALTERNATE INSTRUCTIONS 7809-35-B OR,
FATE FOREFEND, 7809-35-C . . .

Slowly, the memories of her useless nightmare faded,
replaced by the intense needs of the futures she could foresee.

CHAPTER 14

So that's how I got my nickname. Drenched from head to foot, repeatedly, in my enemies' blood. It wouldn't be the last time, either. As for how it spread through the Corps, never mind beyond . . . well, you kind of had to be there.

~Ia

AUGUST 6, 2490 T.S.

From the outside, Battle Platform *Johannes* looked like a giant prickle-burr. All around the outer edges of the massive structure, docking gantries competed with gunnery pods and force field projectors on long, silvery ceristeel struts, which could be extended when parked or retracted when moving. Battle Platforms were not space stations; they were not set in a planetary orbit.

If they orbited anything, it was the local sun, parked in an L5 orbit either preceding or trailing a particular planet. Designed to move occasionally from sector to sector, they were the interstellar equivalent of a portable, defendable, military-run city. Size and shape didn't matter all that much in space; only the energy requirements to move something of that much mass mattered. The *Johannes* could move, but it took a while to get up to speed, and another while to slow down, and a vast amount of hydrofuel to do either. As a result, Battle Platforms often took up orbit near ice worlds or comet fields on the edges of systems, and this one was no exception.

On the egg-shaped inside, in the sections not dedicated to purely military matters, Ia thought the place looked like an indoor shopping mall. Or perhaps more like the visions she held for her own homeworld—the sane half, at least. There were clothing stores, shops selling fresh, frozen, and packaged groceries for those who had the free time and facilities to cook for themselves, purveyors of personal items and other sundries, even hobby shops for those off-duty who were bored. Given it was "home" not only to a plethora of Navy personnel, but also enough TUPSF Army Companies to form its own Legion, as well as various SF-MC contingents like Ferrar's Fighters, *Johannes* had numerous such services.

Naturally, it had a post office, which she had visited on her shopping trip to drop off her lockboxes of temporal instructions and to mail a physical copy of her application to a Net-based college. Ia needed to earn a degree in military history to prepare for the future, and taking correspondence classes via the Nets would suit the mobility of her life in the Marines. The mobile battle station also had a branch office for the Alliance Sentient Aid Service, which could get military personnel in touch with civilian loved ones and vice versa, the best medical facilities found outside of a well-established world, retail shops, restaurants . . . and bars. Taverns. Pubs. Establishments filled with games, sports-vidshows, food of dubious but snackable quality, and alcoholic beverages. No uniforms allowed, of course.

Though her pay as a Marine was supposedly generous, in reality, the military deducted all manner of costs from each cheque transferred to her bank account. Including an ongoing fee for the cost and maintenance of her mechsuit. It didn't leave much for personal purchases, but she'd earned enough, fresh out of Basic, to afford a couple of civilian outfits.

She was on her way back to her quarters from the gym when Double-E and Soyuez met her in Corridor 4, just as she reached cross-corridor Foxtrot. The tall, dark-skinned Marine flashed a grin at her. "There you are!"

"Meioas," Ia acknowledged, since they were officially on twenty-four hours of Leave. She edged around them to reach her cabin door. Soyuez briefly caught her by her unburdened, brown-clad elbow.

"Hey—you got any civvies?" he asked.

"A couple," Ia replied.

"Good. Get into 'em and meet us in the 2nd's common room in five minutes," he told her.

"Don't be late," Double-E added, lifting his chin at her. "You don't want the party to start without you."

Feigning a mix of curiosity and ignorance, Ia gave both men a questioning look, but they just waved and moved on down the hall. Unlocking her quarters, she moved into the back and stripped out of her exercise clothes, taking barely enough time to wipe off the worst of her sweat. Just as she was squirming into the dress she had bought, Estes came into the bedroom. She, too, was wearing civilian clothes, though she had opted for a pair of knee-length shorts and a crop top, both decorated in shades of purple and blue.

"There you are. And you're in civvies. Good. Everyone's gathered in the common room—Ferrar has a tradition. All newly blooded Marines in his Company get taken down to Frostie's Bar when we're here on *Johannes*, or to The Scottish Cactus when we're on the *Hum-Vee*. They're the favorite watering holes among the jarhead set." Estes looked her up and down, then gave Ia a lopsided smile. "You do realize you'll be in for a lot of teasing in *that* outfit."

"I know," Ia said wryly, glancing down at the crimson fabric clinging to her arms and breasts, and draping down to her knees. "But all things considered, it's not a bad nickname."

Adjusting the thumb-wide straps stretching across her shoulders and down her arms, Ia opened one of her lockers and checked her reflection in the mirror affixed to the inside. Her hair needed a bit of finger-combing, now that it was beginning to grow longer than a buzz cut, and her lips needed a bit of crimson moisturizing gloss to match the dress, but that was all. Once her mouth was slicked and ready, she tossed the tube and her military clothes inside, closed the door, and lifted her chin at her teammate.

"Lead on."

It didn't take them long to reach the common room, though they weren't the only ones lining up to enter. The moment Ia came into the room, whistles and cheers greeted her entrance. Lieutenant Ferrar, standing near the middle of the room, raised his hands for silence. "Enough! . . . Enough. Looks like everyone is here. Form up, meioas, let's go. The first round of drinks is on our new corporal!"

The others started to cheer, until Ia's voice cut through her Platoon mates' celebration, cracking like projectile fire, ringing off the bulkheads of the large room. "Like *hell* they are!"

Everyone stopped cheering and Ferrar stopped in his tracks, checked in midstride for the doors. He arched a brow at her. "Oh, they're *not*, are they? Are you countermanding one of my orders, soldier?"

"Are you on duty?" Ia shot back, hands going to her scarlet-clad hips. A small handful of men and women choked on their laughter, some even hastily turning away and mock-coughing to clear their throats.

Lt. Ferrar grinned at her, and swept her a mock-bow. "A hit, meioa, and square on-target. You're quite right. We're *all* on Leave at the moment, and I can't order you to do a thing." He leveled a finger at her. "But you still owe me a drink at the very least, for being rude to a superior. On-duty *or* off."

Ia lifted her index finger. "*One* drink." Stepping to the side, she gestured at the double doorway. "After you, meioa . . ."

Still smiling, Ferrar led the way off the ship.

It was a bit of a hike; the gantry attached to the side of the *Liu Ji* itself was a quarter of a kilometer long. The group, which seemed to comprise most of the 2nd Platoon and several more from the 1st and the 3rd, laughed and chatted among themselves as they made the trip. Following directly behind the Lieutenant meant Ia wasn't entirely a part of the camaraderie behind her. She idly studied the dozens of flatpics mounted on the walls of the gantry, each bearing hundreds of rotating images taken from the various homeworlds and hometowns of the beings serving on board the *Johannes*.

Not all were Human, though the vast majority were. There were aliens living on Terran-controlled worlds, of course, and some did offer to serve in the Space Force. Because of the sheer differences in biology—carbon-based, oxygen-breathing, and blood-bleeding similarities aside—they were usually shunted off to specific Cordons in the SF-Army and the Navy, replete with their own ships for biological and psychological comfort. The Chinsoiy . . . were too different to serve, requiring daily doses of radiation which would kill a Human in the long run. The Dlmvla were methane-breathers. Only the V'Dan-born were lumped in among the Terrans.

Her own homeworld wasn't represented. Yet. A lot of the images were of domeworlds, and many were from Earth. But one shot showed a lightning storm, four writhing bolts caught lancing between ground and sky. A lump of homesickness formed.

The recycled air of the station, while clean and fresh thanks to the Terran plants imported for the residents to enjoy, and better-smelling than the smaller confines of the *Liu Ji*, didn't smell right. The steady faint whoosh of the lifesupport fans weren't the same as actual gusting breezes, and the lightning in that one image didn't move. It was static. Far away.

"Rumor has it you don't drink, Corporal."

"What? Sorry, sir. No, I don't," Ia confirmed, looking up at Ferrar. He had slowed just enough to pace beside her. "A history of genetic alcoholism in the family."

"Pity. But that's alright," he allowed. "Someone needs to be the designated pilot; I guess that's you, tonight. The real question is, are you going to force *me* to drink something non-alcoholic when you buy me that drink?"

She smiled wryly. "Hardly, sir." Risking a glance over her shoulder at the Marines following them, their casual and cam-ouflage Browns traded for a plethora of civilian hues, she added half under her breath, "I have a sneaking suspicion they're going to be ordering me Bloody Marys. I'll need to pass word to the bar staff to make sure they're Virgin Marys. If they slip up and serve me something fermented, *you* can have it."

He wrinkled his nose. "I'm not fond of tomato juice. I'm more of a bourbon man."

"Duly noted." Behind her, someone called out a question for the Lieutenant, which sparked a running conversation that carried them all the way to the white-walled, plant-filled, multi-leveled atrium that served as park and commerce sector for the Platform.

The wave of off-duty Marines spilled down the stairs and across two balconies, past a lawyer's office advertising special-izations in both military and civilian laws, an ice cream shop—

where they promptly lost nine or ten members of the group who clustered with all the fascination of young children around the chilled display cases inside—and into a faux-brick fronted, shadow-steeped pub. Tables and chairs filled over half the bar, which was deeper and larger than it seemed. What looked like a good sixty or seventy off-duty Marines lurked, drank, and played, some throwing darts, others taking potshots at holographic enemies with toy laser pistols in the back corner, and a couple playing pool at the billiards tables across from the bar.

"Hey, Frostie!" Ferrar called out, striding between the tables with the confidence of familiarity. He clapped his hand on Ia's shoulder, pushing her forward. "We got a new one!"

The bald, spectacle-clad man behind the bar, with a chest-length, blue-dyed beard and muscles almost as big as Ia's brother's, looked up at the tide of men and women flowing into his establishment. He grimaced and lifted his chin at a woman with bright cerulean hair who was serving drinks a few meters away. "Hey, Rostie, we're being invaded. Quick, call the Marines."

"We *are* the Marines!" Ferrar catcalled back. *"Eyah?"* he added over his shoulder.

"HOO-RAH!" The call-back came not only from his own Company members but from most of the other Marines in the pub as well.

Pushing Ia forward, Ferrar stopped her at the bar and introduced her. "Frostie, this is Corporal Ia, 2nd Platoon A Squad Alpha . . . and a hell of a good fighter. She is *also* on permanent Designated Pilot Duty. Show 'im your unit, Corporal."

Ia obediently held out her left wrist and her military-issued ident. She knew it was so that he could put her ident and its bank account on permanent file in his records, running a tab for her.

"'Zat right?" Frostie asked her, picking up a scanner wand and tapping the brown plexi housing on the back. "No alcohol?"

"None whatsoever," Ia confirmed. "I don't like it, and I don't want it. I'll take a dark ginger ale in a mug, though."

"Got it." He thumbed the controls on the wand, then set it down. "One permanent DPD on your bar bill. And one frosted gingersnap on tap, coming up," Frostie muttered, fetching a cold-misted mug from the cold locker under the bar.

"She's also paying for my drinks tonight," Ferrar stated. Behind them, the other servers were taking orders, each one with a different shade of blue hair. It was the only way to tell which ones were the servers, since Ferrar's Company had clustered around them like bees in a hive.

"*One* drink," Ia retorted. She lifted her chin at the bartender, who she knew was also the owner. "Make it a bourbon. The most pretentious-sounding bourbon you've got."

"Gingersnap and a fancy-pants, got it," Frostie acknowledged, handing over Ia's drink before moving off to fetch a liquor bottle from one of the back shelves.

"Why, Corporal, are you trying to be nice to me?" Ferrar asked. The woman Rostie slipped behind the bar and started helping Frostie pull drinks from the spigots. This was an old-fashioned pub, not an automated commissary. "Or are you trying to bribe me?"

"Nah. Just trying to shut you up," she quipped back. "If I bought you something cheap, you'd grind your gears all night about it. Be honest, you would."

Chuckling, the Lieutenant took his drink from the bartender and nudged her ahead of them. Together, they squeezed a path away from the now crowded bar. "True. I would. Thank you for the good stuff. By the way, this first drink, you drink with the officers, meioa. Every fresh-blooded newbie in my Company gets that right."

One of the Marines they passed—not one of Ferrar's—looked up at that. "Hey newbie, you earned a nickname yet, or should we just call you Red?"

He grinned, and his companions chuckled. Ia stopped and faced the man, free hand going to her hip. "*Yeah*, I earned a nickname. Do you actually want to hear it, or do you just want to laugh into your drink?"

He smirked and sipped at his beer. "Only if it makes a good story, meioa."

"Hey, Double-E!" Ia's shout cut across the babble of voices in the pub. "You asked me for a story before the mess on the *Clearly-Standing*. You want that story now?"

"If you can tell one even *half* as good as you can sing, hell yeah!" the tall, dark-skinned Marine called back, lifting his mug over his head. He worked his way closer, as did several others, until three dozen of Ferrar's Fighters crowded around the other Marines' table. "Lay it on me, Corporal. Make it a good 'un."

The one who had asked her about her nickname craned his neck, looking up at the crowd, and lifted his brows in surprise.

"You must be one helluva newbie, if you're already a corporal, an' they ain't giving you *shakk* 'bout your first combat," the Marine told her, brows quirking.

"Maybe they're just waiting for her to fall flat on 'er face," one of his friends snickered.

Ia didn't bother to respond. Instead, she lifted her free hand for silence, or as close as she could get to it in the now crowded pub, and took a quick sip of her ginger ale to wet her throat. Her fellow Company mates shushed and nudged each other, grinning at her in anticipation. When she had an acceptable level of quiet, she lowered the frosted glass and began, pointing at her would-be hazer.

"Pay attention and draw near, for the story you will hear is one you would have more than liked to see," she stated, tightening her gut so that her voice carried the patterned, rhyming words without her having to shout each line. "It's about a call for distress, some pirates in a mess, and a TUPSF battleship called *Liu Ji*. We were out on patrol, just taking a stroll, when the Gatsugi gave a distress ring. The story unfolds with the pirates in their holds . . . and a Marine whose praises you will sing!"

"Yeah, but you ain't singing," her catcaller muttered. He got nudged from behind by Estradille, and subsided. Ia continued, looking over his head at not only her fellow members of Ferrar's Company but the other off-duty soldiers in view.

"We answered their call by speeding one and all, to get to the scene of the crime. The pirates had boarded, their cargo to be hoarded, but the *Liu Ji* got there in time. I suited with my friends, and we attacked from several ends; the Lieutenant said that we would split apart:

"The 1st Platoon would go and help them overthrow, with the 2nd set to carve the pirates' heart." She winked at Ferrar, lifting her glass in brief salute. "We set off in our shuttle—their ship was fit to scuttle—and grappled to the side of their hold. Our entrance was too easy; it made me slightly queasy, and the tactics set to trap us were quite bold. The pirates on the ship were going to give us all the slip, and they'd set up force fields to make us slow. The moment we unsealed, their plan would be revealed—the hull had been charged and set to blow."

One of the women at the table in front of Ia lifted her brows. "'Zat true?"

"Word for word, soldier," Ferrar told her. "I don't know if she can keep up this rhyming stuff, but truth is, it was Corporal Ia, here, who first scanned the explosives. She was—"

Ia held up her hand, cutting him off. "I'm telling this one, Lieutenant. At Ease."

That earned her a frown from Ferrar, and more than a few astonished stares from her fellow Marines. Ferrar didn't protest, though. In fact, he grinned into his drink, sipping at the bourbon she had bought him.

Tapping her lips with her finger, indicating silence, Ia continued. "Their bombs we neutralized, but then we realized that we weren't dealing with your standard scum. The ship was moist and dark, Choya writing for their mark . . . but from the Salik worlds some had also come. Our lieutenant split our might, some went left to go and fight, and she told me 'take your Squadron straight ahead.' So, knowing from the ship and its heat and moisture drip, I knew that down below was where they'd fled."

Her hazer wrinkled his nose. "Salik. *V'shakk*. Pond-sucking scum!"

Someone else shushed him, gesturing for Ia to go on.

"We came down by the stairs, working group by group in pairs, and I set my plan in motion with my team. We'd ambush and have fun, when they came all at a run, brought from their bridge by my teammate's taunting scream." Ia raised her mug at Estes, who gave a little head-bow from her position at the far side of the table. Acknowledgment made, Ia continued. "Two came at her demand, one with a grenade caught in his hand, and he yanked upon its safety-holding pin.

"I grabbed it from the guy, said 'thanks' and went bye-bye, and ducked into their bridge to do them in." Ia grinned as that earned her a couple chuckles. "I threw the charge inside—well, they had nowhere to hide, and when it went, it splattered half the crew. Unfortunately for me, I was caught by the debris, and painted helm to boot in bloody goo."

That earned her more than a few grimaces, though the few noises of disgust were hastily hushed. "Their captain, who was sound, prepared another round . . . but the thing went off while still wrapped in his grip. So again I was in style with all manner of things vile, adhering to my armor with a drip." She paused again to take a sip of her drink, wetting her throat.

The Marine who had started this eyed her askance. He then looked at Ferrar, standing behind Ia's right shoulder, and lifted his chin. "You're kidding me, Lieutenant. This couldn't have happened like that. Not word for word!"

Ferrar shrugged and nodded. Ia went on with her rhymed tale, carefully sculpted for this moment in the handful of days it had taken the *Liu Ji* to reach the *Johannes*."We captured all the rest; I put the comm system to test, and announced that we had seized the bridge's crew; then the rest of my Squad, out on cleanup promenade, announced we had more battle left to do. Some pirates on their way were going to spoil our fray, so I ordered a pincer team attack. Someone hit a spot that got the Salik hot, and blew up one of their mechsuits' power pack."

Estes, not quite opposite from Ia on the far side of the crowd-ringed table, mimed a *BOOM* explosion with her hands and her lips. That earned her a few chuckles from the other members of A Squad who had been there.

"So again I was designed in blood and gore that made me blind as it smeared across the front of my faceplate. But we got our enemy, and went back to the *Liu Ji* . . . and the Lieutenant said 'Bloody Mary!' at my state." Turning, Ia saluted him with her mug. He lifted his shot glass of bourbon in return. With that acknowledged, she returned to her tale. "I'd washed off all the goo—you'd think I had *enough* to do—when the klaxon came resounding down the hall. Some pirates had been stashed, so back to war I dashed, answering the Navy's distress call.

"I gathered up three men and went back inside again, and we split up once more to take them out; Hmongwa and Dexter, the enemy, they vexed 'er, their armor—"

"—Hmongwa and who did *what*?" someone spluttered, laughing over the names.

"Hey, that is *not* easy to rhyme!" Ia shot back, pointing at the woman, one of the non-Ferrar Marines at the fringe of the crowd who had drifted closer to hear her story. "Where was I? Ah, yes, here we go . . . Hmongwa and Dexter, the enemy, they vexed 'er, their armor and their weapons set to rout. With I and Adams in like mind, we got ourselves around behind, and I grabbed the nearest Choya by the throat. I broke his scaly neck, dropped him softly to the deck, and went for the next alien of note.

"He had grabbed a Navy man—I didn't like his plan, so I took my knife and severed half his neck. We pinned the other two, our reinforcements coming through as the dead one's blood began to slick the deck. I released my captive's arm, with no more intent to harm, but *didn't* realize that that wasn't all. You see, I stepped into the blood that had spilled out in a flood . . . and I slipped and took a really *stupid* fall."

She paused a moment, giving them a grimace of embarrassment, then finished the tale.

"Well. I lay there on the floor, amidst the blood and gore, then pushed to get back up onto my feet. I slipped *twice* more and fell," she complained, waggling her finger at the others, "and damn it all to hell, but if 'Bloody Mary' wasn't my defeat!"

Roars of laughter filled the pub. A couple of hands reached through the crowd, some slapping her on the back, others gripping her by the shoulders. Ia clamped down hard and tight on her psi, to the point of an ache behind her temples, and lifted her mug in salute.

"To Bloody Mary!" Hooke shouted, raising her own mug.

A forest of arms, some slopping still-full drinks, shot up into the air, echoing her cry. *"Bloody Mary!"*

The crowd started to disperse. The nameless Marine who had started it all—just as she had foreseen—lifted his half-empty mug at her in salute. "That's one helluva tale, meioa. An' if it's true . . . welcome to the Marines, Bloody Mary."

Giving him a little bow, she turned and followed Ferrar and the others to a table off to one side. D'kora was now there, as well as Lt. Cheung and Staff Sgt. Blakely of the 1st Platoon, Lt. Nguyen of the 3rd, and Staff Sgt. Chirol Kulo'qa. Cheung offered a seat to Ia while more sergeants gathered. By now, she was known to the other Squad Sergeants in her Platoon, Pleistoch, Buddanha, and Culper. She, of course, knew them all too well, already.

Buddanha would retire in half a decade after several fierce battles, losing most of his legs, half of one arm, and facing years of regenerative surgeries. Culper would be listed as CPE, the military's shorthand for all individuals lost behind Salik enemy lines; the acronym meant, "Captured, Presumed Et."

Pleistoch would earn a Field Commission before dying on his second posting, while Cheung would die somewhere around his fourth promotion. Kulo'qa would serve as an adjunct to the V'Dan military, earning honors from both sides.

Ferrar . . . she couldn't quite see. There was a grey spot coming up in a few months; too many possibilities emerged from its far side to be easily calculated. Most wouldn't harm her path, so she hadn't tried to push through the mist cloaking that knot in the waters. A few of those potential-possible paths would strengthen her goals, but she didn't know how to achieve them. Yet. As for the last two, Nguyen might or might not be transferred shortly after that masked point in time. Blakely would earn her own Field Commission, and rise to be a general on the Command Staff many years from now.

D'kora . . . would recover. Provided Ia played her cards right.

Ferrar lifted his glass once his cadre had settled into place around the table, squeezed elbow to elbow with their newest member. Ia obligingly raised her mug, listening patiently to his praise. "To Lance Corporal Ia . . . and to the brand-new legend of our very own Bloody Mary. You did an outstanding job on the *Clearly-Standing*. Meioa-e, I salute you."

I'll drink to that, she thought, lifting and clinking her mug, then sipping from it. *And I'll salute the whole galaxy, too.*

CHAPTER 15

Everyone knows what a soldier does during times of war. We place our skills, our weapons, our bodies, and even our lives on the line, protecting the innocent from all that which would threaten them. We fight, so that others do not have to fight. We take the risks, because we know the price.

What people tend to forget is how much we also do during times of peace. We are the supporting arm, the helping hand, the strength of a friend coming to save you from the monsters that plague you in the middle of the night. We aren't always big damn heroes demanding big damn parades; most of us are nameless, faceless, and interchangeable . . . and for that reason, we are indispensable.

We serve in many ways. It is our duty, and our right.

~Ia

DECEMBER 13, 2490 T.S.
HASKIN'S WORLD
JOINT COLONYWORLD, GLIESE 505 SYSTEM

Rain lashed into Ia's eyes as she turned, struggling to carry her burden against the rib-deep muck flowing through the trees. Cold and soaked as she was, she didn't shiver nearly as hard as the child whimpering in her arms. The boy struggled, holding out his arms to his father, who was still clinging to the purple bark of the sheltering tree. He didn't see his mother waiting in the low-hovering van, her own arms held out in desperate need, until Ia lifted him high enough for her to grab her son.

She didn't bother to seek a translation in the timestreams for the babble of V'Dan as mother and son reunited with squeals and cries. They were no different than the other words exchanged by the seven others crammed into the vehicle struggling to stay aloft on the unsteady surface of the floodwaters.

"Suloc v'sulo kei'il?" she half shouted, returning to the man trying to pick his way through the branches. *Are you ready?*

"Ya, ya!" He pointed at the van, straining for his son. *"Nii c'mosuloc, v'shail!"*

Ia grabbed him around the waist as he started to fall, losing his grip. His lips were tinged blue from having picked a lower resting point than his wife and son, his body icy through the cold fabric clinging to his skin. Hefting him so that she could get her arm under his knees, Ia slogged through the mud, forcing her way against the current with mind as well as muscle.

"Hyu . . . Hyu are very . . . st-st-strong," the colonist managed to say, stumbling over the Terranglo words.

"Neh-ya-veh," Ia grunted, hefting him up toward the hands extending out of the side door. The other rescued colonists hauled him inside, then reached for her. Strong as she was, she was cold and tired from three hours of nonstop flood rescues. Accepting their help, Ia let them pull her inside. Squirming over the damp Humans crowding the cabin, Ia tapped Estes on the shoulder. "Gimme the scanner, I want to do one last sweep!"

Estes handed over both the scanner box and Ia's headset, taken off so it wouldn't be lost if she went under. Ia fitted the curve of wires over her hair, scraping her dripping white bangs back from her eyes. Clicking it on, she synched with the scanner unit, aiming it in a slow arc to extend the signal. It didn't take her long to pick up what she wanted to see.

"Fifteen degrees east, and fast! I'm picking up another signal!"

"You want fast, tell that to the muck under our thrusters!" Estes shot back, guiding the hovervan further out across the flooded valley. "Much more weight than this and we won't—"

The voice on both their headsets interrupted her.

"D'kora to all teams. The Plistek Dam is breaking. I repeat,

*the dam is breaking. The engineers say you have five minutes
at most before it dumps the entire reservoir on top of you. All
teams in the Plista Valley are ord—"*

"—Human!" Ia shouted, drowning out what their superior
was saying. "I'm getting a Human reading! Hurry it up! We're
a full twenty minutes downstream, we can save them!"

For a moment, it looked like Estes was going to obey that
half-heard order to return to base. Ia waited, holding her breath.
Her fellow corporal gripped the steering wheel and gunned the
thruster. The van sped forward incrementally faster, kicking
up a spray of water behind them.

Ia probed the timestreams . . . and winced. There was
more trouble up ahead than she had anticipated. Ia swore and
dumped the scanner onto the lap of the V'Dan-born colonist
occupying the front seat next to Estes. "There's a pack of grampass
getting too close to that life sign. I want ramming speed, and a
quick turn at the last second, Corporal."

"A quick turn? Aren't you going to shoot from the doorway?"
Estes argued.

"We won't get there in time." She turned and squirmed
toward the side door, switching to V'Dan. It took her a moment
to find the words she wanted to say. "Uhh . . . *Ni-holl vassa
v'gista, zamma-vi'doulie. Jalak! Kei'il suloc julak!*"

The muddied, shivering survivors nodded and clutched at
whatever they could find, from the brackets that had held the
seats formerly occupying the back of the hovervan, to the seat
restraints still dangling down the side walls. Ia checked the
latches on her knife and pistol holsters, probing the timestreams.
One of the younger men, half pressed against her thigh, gasped
and looked up at her. Ia tightened her shields.

"Estes, I'll need another c-clip!"

"E-clip, hell! Take my p-gun!" Fumbling it free with one
hand, steering with the other, Estes offered it over her shoulder.
Ia stretched and snatched it before one of the civilians could
mishandle the projectile weapon. "Blow out its brains!—Holy!
There are *ten* of them?"

Ia grimaced and checked the safety before shoving it down
the back of her pants. What she *needed* was the electrical energy
in that spare e-clip. Projectile cartridges would do her no good,
later on. *So we do this the hard way. Great.*

Something rumbled in the distance. It wasn't thunder. "I think the dam just broke. Don't stop now! Fast turn to the left, on my mark! Three . . . two . . ."

"Ia, I can't . . ."

". . . *Mark!*" she shouted.

Estes sloughed the hovervan sideways. It rocked from inertia, several of the occupants inside yelping and tightening their hold on the interior and each other. The van darted off to the side, escaping the knot of predators. Ia, however, used the original momentum of the vehicle to fling herself out, leaping straight at the back of the first of three dinoid predators. A wrenching flip drove her feetfirst instead of headfirst, allowing her to clear the hump of its spine and snap her boot heels into the base of its long, long neck.

The grampass *gronked* with pain, staggering. Ia tumbled and wrenched again, grabbing for the gun at the small of her back and the one at her right hip. A flick of her thumbs released the straps. A second shoved the safeties off. Landing on her feet, flinging water everywhere, she continued her cartwheeling spin and fired.

A shot to the head of the grampass whose back she had broken. A shot to the head of the one rearing over the man wielding his shotgun at the crest of the rock outcrop. A shot at the one stabbing with that long-necked head at the woman frantically rolling back and forth, trying to protect both herself and her pet. A fourth at the one lunging now for *her*, diverted from their original pair of prey. Shot after shot, as fast as she could fire them.

Even with two of them being used, the pistols couldn't reload fast enough. They could only fire single shots. The man with the shotgun, doing his best to stave off the pack, screamed as a toothy head clamped onto his leg, dragging him down with a scream. Ia lofted her pistol and lashed her hand down to her waist, spinning with heavyworlder speed. Her knife *thocked* deep into the overgrown carnivore's eye socket, but she had already completed her spin and was grabbing the falling pistol again, whirling and firing at the rest.

The grampass grunted and dropped its bleeding prey, dead. Its companions, faced by so much whirling, confusing injury and death, *kerwhonked* at each other and beat a hasty retreat. They splashed into the mud and dove, swimming away. Panting, Ia safetied the guns and shoved them back in place. Scraping the water from her face, she hurried to check the fallen farmer. His leg was pumping blood. Not yet fatally, but it was bad.

Light lanced through the rain, sizzling and steaming as it zapped through the water. Estes had managed to get the hovercar swung around and was firing her laser pistol through her side window at the retreating predators, further encouraging them to flee. Yanking her knife free of the dead beast, Ia stabbed through her left sleeve, ripping the fabric free. Lashing the scrap around the man's leg at midthigh, she pulled it tight enough to make him grunt with pain. That stopped the flow of blood, but it was a temporary solution at best.

Beside her, Estes steered the hovervan to an approximation of a landing on the tilted stone outcrop. "Get everyone on board, Corporal!"

Helping hands pulled the battered, bruised woman and her pet inside. More hands helped take the man from Ia when she carried him to the open side door. Only when he was lying across the laps of the others did Ia cut off the tourniquet. She quickly grabbed the hand of one of the other colonists, forced it into a fist, and pressed it to the farmer's inner thigh. "*Sii-sek! V'tukol'eh!* Put pressure *here*!"

The man blinked, clearly uncomfortable at his hand being so close to the other man's groin, then nodded. He leaned, applying enough pressure to stop the arterial blood from flowing. A tourniquet cut off too much blood all over a limb, both into it and out of it, but pressure on the femoral artery would still allow blood flow to and from the rest of the leg via the other, lesser vessels.

The hovervan lurched, thrusters whining. Estes tried again, cycling the controls. She tried five times, then looked back at Ia, hazel green eyes wide with fear. "We . . . we're too heavy! I can't take off!"

Ia looked at the scared faces of the men, women, and children crowded into the van with them. Estes struggled with the controls, but couldn't lift off.

"*KerHONnnk!*" WHAM!

The blow knocked Ia out of the opening. Estes swore as the hovervan rocked and bounced up four meters. "Dammit! *Ia!*"

Ia knew her weight would drag the car down. "I'm too heavy for the van! Go!"

"Ia, dammit—!"

"Get out of here, Corporal! *GO!*"

Cursing audibly through the open side window, Estes lurched the van into gear. A rooster tail finally started to form, allowing Estes enough momentum to angle off to the left, back toward base. Behind Ia, the rumble was getting louder.

Ia yelled and waved her arms, distracting the grampass that had returned, hoping to still snag a two-legged snack. It stared after the sluggishly moving van, sagging dangerously low on the water as Estes did her best to pick up speed, then dove for Ia. She had her weapons drawn and a pair of cartridges slammed through its muzzle before it could finish opening its toothy jaws. Dodging as the dead beast fell, Ia watched the van, anxious to make sure it picked up enough speed. Wisely, Estes had pointed it straight down the valley in a dead run.

She turned just in time to see a second grampass rising up out of the murk . . . and then *gronk* and slosh right past her, half galloping, half swimming for the shoreline. Ia wished she could flee with him. The churning, frothing, debris-laden wall sweeping down the valley was a terrifying sight to see.

The grampass wouldn't make it. Ia had no choice; she *had* to survive. Closing her eyes was the hardest thing Ia had done since Basic. She shut them, drawing in a deep breath and letting it go. A second deep breath allowed her to drop straight into her own timestream. She would have at most a few seconds of pre-echoed future to find and follow, if she was to survive. She had trained for this, as best as her brothers and cousins and friends could help her to train . . . but this wasn't dodging flung objects and climbing stationary obstacles.

Eyes flicking open, she ran to the left of the floodwall. A deep-kneed spring flung her up high in the colonyworld's relatively light .92gs. The wave struck as she came back down, boots slamming into a tree trunk, only to bounce her body upward again. Mind and Time linked as one, Ia moved with a fast, faltering rhythm, thrusting off of a chunk of masonry here, a roof beam there, the dead back of an herbivorous suker, and even part of a bathtub. She leaped and spun, skipped and skimmed. Nothing existed but the next foothold and the next after that.

Lurching backwards across the face of the flood wave, Ia finally landed on her target: a chunk of corrugated metal, formerly part of a shed roof. A twist of her hips, a digging of her heels, and the front end lifted up out of the muck before it could complete its tumble. It was broad, and it was awkward, but it was long. Long enough to form a makeshift surfboard that could ride the front crest of that churning brown wave.

She knew seconds before something heavy *slammed* into the roof. Knew in time to leap high, and to press down and around with her mind, spinning the section of roof so that it landed just flat enough to accept her falling weight again. A twist of her hips, a thrust of her legs, arms spread for counterbalance, and the roof slashed sideways across the muddy, foaming waters. That forced her to squeeze her eyes tight against the murk, but she swiped at her face and opened them again on the far side of the broken crest.

Here was a moment of relative calm, in this stretch of the front wave. *Relative* meaning she had fewer tree chunks to dodge. Enough time to spare to flip open her wrist unit and punch the emergency transponder, activating her pickup signal. She had just enough time to grab her laser pistol and yank out the e-clip, letting her damp hand press into the contact sockets and suck out the precious juice inside.

She was cold, wet, exhausted, and in dire need of more energy for the next phase of her rescue from death. Her headset sputtered briefly with static, then cleared.

"Sir!" she heard Soyuez shouting on her headset, broadcasting on the Platoon frequency. *"I'm getting a signal! It's Corporal Ia—her transponder went off! Requesting permission to deviate and search!"*

"That dam water is racing down the valley, Private," Lt. D'kora argued back. *"Estes reported she had to abandon the corporal to the flood."*

"Sir, we have a light load, we can stay above the floodwaters— at least we can track where her body goes, sir!"

As much as she wanted to tell them that she was still alive, Ia didn't have the time. She was about to lose her surfboard to—the flood, as it crashed into a series of buildings and houses. The small town had already been evacuated, long since submerged to those upper windows by the initial flooding that had diverted not only the *Liu Ji* as the nearest source of manpower, but Battle Platform *Hum-Vee* as well, following in their wake as fast as its mass could move, bringing the sentientarian supplies it carried on board.

Sprinting forward, scrambling over the rooftops before they could be crushed by the waves, she leaped from building to building until she was several seconds ahead of the incoming fury. Panting, Ia positioned herself by a plexcrete chimney and slapped her comm link on.

"Soyuez, get your asteroid out here!" she shouted into her headset.

"Ia? *Gods alive! You're actually—*"

She didn't hear the rest of the lieutenant's exclamation. The crackling crashing smashing wall of mud and debris had caught up with her. Once again, she leaped high and hard, and scrambled from wall to window, carnivore to chair, table to tree.

". . . her transponder, sir! Speeding to her location!"

The flood reached the floating logs that had once been a paper mill farm of transplanted Terran trees. Now it was as much a matter of luck and telekinesis that kept her leaping from branch to trunk, rather than slipping and falling, perhaps impaling herself, perhaps simply drowning and being crushed under the flood.

"Holy shakk*! She's . . . I've never seen anything so . . . !"*

"Get over here!" Ia yelled, activating her comm link with her mind, since her hands were too busy flinging this way and that, correcting her balance and providing extra momentum for each dodging leap. She slipped as one of the logs underneath her feet lurched upward unexpectedly, and was forced to thrust with her tired mind, "climbing" with faked steps that finally made actual contact.

"On our way!" she heard Soyuez promise, and aimed for that intersection point in his space and her time. She thrust off the end of that sapling, only to leap from pole to lurching, tumbling pole. Squinting against the sting of the rain, she finally spotted the dark shape of the borrowed hovervan swooping up from her right. She could also see Estradille in his Marine Browns gesturing out the open back doors . . . but he wasn't her goal.

There was too high a chance the recoil of her falling weight would knock *both* of them out of the van. Dodging left, leaping right, Ia scrambled up one of the larger chunks of tree farm debris and jumped high and hard. Her feet skidded on the very back edge of the van, catching purchase just long enough to propel the rest of her body forward. She slammed into the roof, palms slipping uselessly on the rain-slick surface, and felt something *crack* inside her chest. Pain stabbed through her nerves, already stretched tight by her harrowing need to survive.

Stunned, breathless, she lay sprawled on the roof, muscles hunching protectively. That made the pain even worse. *Oh . . . God . . . I think I broke a rib.* Aching, struggling for air, Ia twisted awkwardly onto her side. Away from the hard metal ridge housing the van's traffic transceiver.

"She's still moving!" Estradille shouted, both in her headset and aloud. *"I think she survived!"*

"Well, we won't if I don't get us out of here, pronto! Time to bounce, meioas! Hang on!"

Curling her hand over the same ridge that had injured her, Ia clung to the top of the van as it swayed and picked up speed, angling away from the valley and its flooded, churning debris. If she'd had the energy to spare, if she'd gotten Estes' spare e-clip, she would have healed her broken rib. Instead, she would have to wait for the medics back at their makeshift base camp to get around to fixing the bone later tonight.

It would be painful, but she would endure. Ia focused on clinging and breathing, letting go of the cold, cold waters of her own timestream. She had survived. This time.

That was all that mattered.

———————

So much for sleeping.

Gripping the side of her cot, Ia rolled herself onto her elbow, then carefully levered her body upright. Bending over to reach her footgear had her biting her lower lip in the effort to contain her grunt. It escaped as a hiss, one thankfully quiet enough to avoid waking the others sharing the tent serving as their temporary shelter. A last few drops of rain from the passing storm still pattered on the plexi roof, and the sides rustled, flapping in the night breeze. The noises covered the soft hisses she made as she tugged on socks and laced up her boots.

Ia hadn't bothered to remove the clean, dry Browns she had donned after seeing the medical staff sent down from the orbiting *Liu Ji*. Her cracked rib had been declared a "nonemergency," whereupon she had been wrapped with rib-tape and given an

injection of bone-setting medicines right next to the break.
They then told her to go sleep it off and perform light duties at
best for the next two or three days until the tenderness healed.

None of that precluded the rolling waters of time, however.
Nor her need to channel them. Identifying her portable writing
station and her rain slicker by touch, Ia took them with her out
of the dark tent, wrapping herself in the latter and protecting
the former under its folds. The makeshift camp, cobbled
together with equipment and food from the *Liu Ji* and goods
salvaged from the colony's flooded emergency supplies, was
currently lit by two things: the chemsticks tied to the guy ropes
at the corners of each tent, and the static crackle of the tall
force field fence erected around the perimeter, flashing like
miniature lightning whenever a particularly large raindrop
skidded across the field's otherwise unseen surface.

The members of the 3rd Platoon patrolling that perimeter
in their half- and full-mech did have lights mounted on their
shoulder sockets. But those were aimed mostly outward, looking for the planet's various local predators, large, dinosaur-like
beasts, which had been forced to seek out the same patch of
high ground for safety. The camp itself was mostly dark and
quiet, everyone hiding inside a tent, bundled up in thankfully
dry blankets. Except for her, and her upcoming problem.

One of the tents along the western perimeter was little more
than a makeshift awning with two tarps for sides. They blocked
the prevailing wind, which wasn't strong but was still damp
and cold all the same. Someone had taped chemsticks to the
poles, and set up some folding chairs and a couple of plexi tables.
The tables were littered with random items, a soggy doll, a plexi
toolkit, a muddy towel, and other odds and ends salvaged from
the flood, but Ia didn't need the space. Instead, she pulled two
of the chairs into facing each other, seated herself in one, and
put her feet on the other, propping the writing board on her lap.

Flipping up the screen protecting the keys, she laid her fingers
over the machine, but didn't press down. After three months of
practice, she was getting better at electrokinetically typing. Not
that she was going to print anything right now, but she could at
least store a few more prophecies for later. If she could peer
through the fog cloaking most of the waters around her, that was.

She stared at the faintly glowing keys, at the document blank and ready on the screen. *Funny, how everything on the time-plains is so much clearer from a distance, yet so many parts become blurry close up . . .*

Her rare sense of humor quirked her mouth into a smile, after a moment. *Maybe Time is farsighted, and just needs an eye-correction?*

Unfortunately, she didn't know how to do that, yet. She didn't even know if there was some sort of psychic optometrist who could make it easier for her to peer at the future. A probabilities specialist, she knew about, and could tap into. It was one of her side-lives, the ones she could've led in an alternate reality, the kind where she knew who her father was and had only one mother. Difficult to reach, but not impossible.

Thankfully, tonight's mist wasn't all-encompassing. Focusing her thoughts on her homeworld, on the futures of her people, Ia was able to submerge herself in those streams and find the key points to write about, to direct long after the point where she personally would be dead. Because of the fluid nature of time, she couldn't write things out logically, sequentially.

Start at point A and write prophecies for B, C, D, and E, onward through Z? Not possible. Something that easy would be lovely, but time flowed like a river, one with individual streams that tangled together like the aftermath of a hundred hyperactive kittens let loose in a yarn shop. Another mental image that made her want to smile, even as it made her want to frown. Letting out a heavy sigh, Ia dipped into Sanctuary's most probable futures, letting the words form and scroll silently up the screen.

Somewhere between the ceasing of the rain and the twists of the twenty-seventh century, Ia jerked her head up, instincts twinging with fear. Slapping her writing pad half-shut, pinching her thumb in the process, she scrambled to her feet, grunting out a rib-twinging, "Sir!"

Lieutenant Ferrar nodded at her, barely visible in the fading glow of the chemsticks taped to the awning poles. The mist obscuring the local timestreams hadn't given her any warning. Heart thumping, she studied him, wondering what, exactly, would happen in the next half hour. She knew *something* significant would happen here and now, involving him, but not what.

"At Ease, Corporal. I came to talk to you about what the

mayor's planning for tomorrow," he stated. "That was her younger son you saved, the one bitten by the dinoid."

"Planning, sir?" Ia asked. She knew what would happen *if* she navigated this moment in time just right . . . but how to navigate it, she had no clue.

"An award ceremony, for you and some of the others. You were all big heroes today. Sit down," he added, nodding at the chair behind her.

Nodding, Ia turned to reach for the armrest. She couldn't sit quickly with her ribs still sore, and needed—Ferrar leaned over and snatched the portable workstation out from under her arm. Shocked, Ia grabbed for it, but her injury made her slow, and his grip was strong. For a moment, they tugged. The narrowing of his eyes warned her what would happen if she kept resisting. The ruination of her military career. Ia let go; she didn't have to be a precog to see that much.

Not that she could see much. The fog had descended in full, obscuring everything around her. Heart in her throat, she watched him lift the writing pad. If it hadn't been for the fog clouding this moment, she would have seen him snatch her pad in advance, and switched the display to something far more innocent, such as her homework for her correspondence degree. But it was too late for that. Ferrar waggled the pad at her in admonition.

"You know, your teammate has told me this is your one quirk. That you're constantly writing something, but that you haven't said what it is. And, like clockwork for the last three plus months . . . you have been shipping locked storage boxes stuffed full of your writings. Some back to your homeworld . . . but others to the Afaso Order. I can only conclude you're sending them reports of some kind." He pried open the lid, balancing the device on his palm, shifting his gaze from hers to the screen. "I don't know what sort of spying you're doing for either of them, particularly since the Afaso have never shown interest in the military, but . . ."

In the dark of the night, any electrokinetic changes she might have made would have been seen, opening up the risk of this exact same problem: the revelation of her psychic abilities. In the faint green glow of the chemlights, she could see the puzzled frown furrowing his dark brow. He stared at the screen, looked up at her, then looked back at the screen, tabbing through her most recent efforts with a few flicks of his thumbs. Realizing she was holding her breath, Ia forced herself to take slow, steady breaths. Being uncovered at this point in her career was a very, very bad thing.

She couldn't even take him onto the timeplains with her and show him what his actions were jeopardizing; that would screw things up even further. Some people could be converted to her personal religion. Most, however, couldn't handle it. Not discreetly enough. Ferrar would be one of the ones wanting to do too much, to help too much.

Ia wouldn't be able to stop him. Right now, she had no reputation, no power, and no control . . . except for one saving grace. Maybe. If she could get him to listen.

"Bloody Mary." The shaken whisper was not meant to be her nickname. It was an exclamation, for all there was hardly any sound behind it. Ferrar looked up at her again. "These are . . . Unless this is a story you're writing, this is . . ." Before she could seize on that option, he shook his head. "This is no story. Either you're delusional or . . . But the detail! The accuracy—what the *hell* is going on here, Corporal?"

"Keep your voice down, *soldier*," Ia murmured, shifting closer. Her cold words, as if she were *his* superior, shocked him. Using that shock, she plucked the writing station from his hand. "I see I'll need to figure out how to encrypt all of this." Snapping it shut, she gestured at the chair she had used for resting her boots, shadowed silence between them. "I suggest you sit and *listen*, instead of standing there and shouting at me."

"You don't give me *orders*, Corporal. You don't have the authority!" Ferrar growled, grabbing for her workstation again.

This time, she was prepared. This time, Ia was faster, catching his hand in her empty palm with a *slap*. The move strained her tender side painfully, but she didn't flinch. *"Two words*, Lieutenant. They give me all the authority I need in this matter. Just *two* words." Hefting the closed device, she tipped her head at it. "Given what you just read on this, I'm surprised you didn't remember that little legality."

He frowned at her, tugging his hand free. *"What* two words? Not even a 'Sorry, sir' could get you out of the deep *shakk* you just dove yourself into. I have *every* right to bust you—"

"Vladistad," Ia warned him, lifting her forefinger. Then her middle as well. "*Salut.* Now, sit. Sir."

He glared at her, and didn't move. Didn't speak, but didn't move. Ia backed up a step, feeling the edge of her own chair brushing against the backs of her knees.

"In case you don't remember, sir, I am referencing *Johns and Mishka versus the United Nations.* It was the single most important ruling regarding the legal rights of verifiable precognitives," she reminded him quietly. The plexi tarps sheltering them rattled with a renewed spate of rain and wind. "Giorgi Mishka was a crucial testimonial witness in an international effort to bring down a certain Russian cultist-cum-mafioso named Mikulo 'The Impaler' Vladinski, the Terror of Vladistad. A city which had been founded by his family line, and ruled with a cruel fist.

"Mishka refused to testify," Ia continued. "He did so citing that, as a precog, he could foresee something terrible happening if he did. Everyone laughed him off. Nobody believed in real psychic abilities back then. His government put pressure on him to testify anyway, even though he steadfastly refused."

"I remember that case from my history classes. He testified anyway," Ferrar pointed out. "Just as he was *ordered* to."

"Not until he cut a deal that would get himself and his family *out* of town on a certain night, three weeks later," Ia countered. "Not until *after* he put his sealed prophecies into a time-locked vault. Only then did he testify, stating for the record that he was being coerced to tell what he knew . . . and stating to the prosecution, on the record, '*You* force me to do this. *You* are demanding that I do this, against my will. This blood is on *your* hands. Not mine. *You* will have to make amends for what you are about to do.'

"The prosecution thought that he meant the blood of Vladinski's execution," Ia reminded her commander, holding his gaze. "Three weeks later, not more than fifteen minutes after Mishka and his family flew out of the region in secrecy . . . and just five minutes after Vladinski died at midnight in the maximum detention facilities just outside the city where his trial and execution were held . . . Vladinski's followers broadcast a message to the world. *Two words*, Lieutenant.

"With those two words, they detonated a nuclear bomb that slaughtered over one *million* six hundred thousand people, both from the initial blast and from the firestorms and radioactive fallout. Hundreds of thousands more burned, irradiated, injured. An entire region laid to waste, with radiation that lingers even to this day . . . all because of just two words.

" 'Vladistad. *Salut.*' "

A trickle of rain ran off the sagging edge of the awning over their heads, splattering onto the soggy ground. Ia held Ferrar's gaze, mindful of the passing of time.

"When the time lock ended on the sealed vault, they opened it up and read what Giorgi Mishka had written. That prophecy said, 'I would have kept my secrets to the end of time, knowing that the words you forced out of my mouth would lead to so many dead. But you would not stop. This is what you have done to the world, because you would not believe that my testimony would be far worse than what The Impaler had done. Now. You have about five seconds from the end of this note before the doors to this bank open and a lawyer arrives. He and I are suing all of you for my right to keep silent, in the future. Mr. Johns and I have almost two million clients to represent, because you wouldn't let me stay silent. Their blood is on your hands because of what you demanded, in your ignorance and disbelief, and it cries out for amends.'

"As I said, Lieutenant, I have just two words. Vladistad," Ia repeated quietly, easing herself down into the folding chair behind her. She tucked the writing station into the inner pocket of her slicker. "I suggest you sit down, and listen, before you *salut.*"

He studied her a long, long second, then sat. And waited.

Ia glanced at the chrono on her wrist unit. "I have . . . just over five minutes before I have to move and go do something important. I will tell you this only once, Lieutenant. I am not here for fame, glory, medals, or honor. If anyone else thinks I have earned them, that's fine. They can hand me whatever they want tomorrow, I don't care. I am not a glory-hog, and I am not a real-estater. Medals and coffins do not interest me. I am here to do one thing, and one thing only. Save lives."

"Is that what today's showboating was all about? Saving lives?" Ferrar asked her quietly. "*Surfing* the crest of a flood wave? The infrared sensors on the weather satellites we dropped into orbit picked up what you were doing down in that valley, you know."

"No, actually, I didn't know," Ia retorted lightly. "It wasn't important, so I didn't bother to look it up." Even in the gloom, she could see the dubious look he gave her. "Never mind. Everything I know is on a need-to-know basis only . . . and you don't need to know. Vladistad."

Ferrar leaned forward, bracing his elbows on his knees. "That's not good enough, soldier. You are a wild card in my Company, and I—"

"—Have no need to know what I know. You interfere, you blow up a *hell* of a lot more than one old Russian town. Do you know what future Giorgi Mishka saw after serving those papers, sir?" Ia asked her superior. "He saw the whole damn planet so *outraged* at what Vladinski's followers did to 'avenge' their leader's death . . . they *united* to track down the monsters responsible." She pointed out at the darkness beyond them, at the sleeping colonists and soldiers, the patrolling bodies, the force field keeping them safe. "*Johns and Mishka versus the United Nations*, the single most powerful legal case dealing with the rights for precogs to keep their mouths shut. If a precognitive decides it is best to stay silent, they have that right.

"That single decision, to allow the disaster to happen, was a drop in the *flood* of events that followed. Those events led to the unification of Earth's multiple governments under one leadership. Which led to the old United Earth government becoming the United Terran Planets when we colonized the other planets in our own star system, which led to our being a single voice and a single power when we first met up with the *rest* of the sentient races out there . . . which led to us being *strong* enough to enter the first Salik War, and win it. Which led to the Blockade, which led to the mess of the *Clearly-Standing*, which led to this moment in time. All of which were events that unfolded, not over days or weeks, or even decades, but *centuries*.

"Mishka certainly could not have foreseen all of that. In fact, what little he did see was too little, too late. He just saw that the fractured governments of Old Earth would unite to go after the monsters responsible for the mess caused by what he was being *forced* to do . . . and which he himself said he would rather have died than reveal if not forced to do so. I'll remind you, *he* didn't know before the fact that the world would be a slightly better place . . . and he died with the deaths and sufferings of two million people on his conscience."

A glance at her chrono showed her time was up. Pushing herself upright with a grunt, Ia gestured at the force field fence several meters away.

"You can come with me, or you can stay . . . but if you say one word to your superiors about me, one word to the Special Forces, or worse, the PsiLeague . . . the damage you do will make Vladistad look like a drop in the floodwaters I faced today. The flood that *I* faced, and survived. *You* would not survive, if you tried to interfere. Out of respect for you, I tell you these things, so that you *will* live. The rest . . . you don't need to know."

"*Not* good enough, Corporal!" Rising, Ferrar followed her out into the drizzling rain.

Ia walked only a few yards before squatting and digging through the branching, reddish, local version of grass. Cupping the rock she needed in her fist, she straightened with another grunt and a press of her free arms to her ribs. Without a word of explanation, Ia strode on, letting him catch up to her. Only when they reached one of the makeshift lanes between the rows of tents did she stop. Stop, and point at the ground.

"Wait here. Right here. Don't move."

"Corporal—"

Ia held up her empty hand, silencing him. "Right. Here. Don't interfere."

He subsided. It was enough. Moving back several meters, she reached into the timeplains. The fog was still there, still cloaking the way out, but this one vision she had pre-explored, and knew exactly where to find again. As before, she tapped into the waters. Prepared herself with two deep breaths. Rock in hand, she drew in a third and sprinted back toward the Lieutenant. Back toward the force field *zapping* and *fritzing* between the rows of pylons standing twelve meters high. Pain didn't matter, only the rock in her hand and the timing of her cast.

Arm circling hard and fast, she whipped her weapon back around and up. The fast-flung, underhand cast soared up high, clearing the half-seen, static-sparked top of the fence. Those static sparks illuminated the muddy, pale stone briefly, still rising as it vanished from view.

Ferrar opened his mouth to speak. Ia held up her palm, keeping him silent. Waiting, and listening. Mere seconds later, something *gronked* in the distance. It squealed and broke into a gallop that shook the ground, even from this far away. Several others honked and hooted in reply, and the gallop became a rumble of not-weather thunder.

Ferrar drew in another breath. Ia shushed him, palm still raised. She counted slowly, silently, to fifteen—and they both flinched as the retreating herd ran into yet more life-forms, ones which *skreeled* and *gronked*, growled and hissed, clashing in thudding blows that trembled through the ground and the air alike. Spotlights from the Marines on patrol lit up the woods beyond the perimeter fence, though no weapons fire was heard. Whatever battle was taking place out there, the soldiers on patrol were apparently going to let happen without them.

Pleased, Ia allowed herself a grin. Facing her superior, she gave him a slight bow. "As you can see, I know what I'm doing."

"See *what*?" Ferrar demanded, hissing the words at her. "What the hell did you just do, out there?"

"If you hadn't chosen to follow me, sir . . . no one would know what I just did." Closing the distance between them, she lowered her voice, mindful that the carnage in the distance could very well wake up some of the civilians sleeping around them. "Alone in the dark, with no one to witness, and no one to ever know about it . . . save for you and I. As for what I have done, I have just saved approximately sixty to seventy civilian lives, and another ten to twelve soldiers, if not more."

"How?" he challenged her, lowering his voice to match hers. His finger poked her in the chest, thankfully on the side opposite her battered ribs. "And *don't* give me any *shakk* that I don't have a right to know!"

"B Squad's the one patrolling on the west side tonight," Ia started to say, only to be interrupted.

"Tell me something I *don't* know," he shot back, impatient.

"I'm *trying*, sir," she retorted dryly. "Fifteen or twenty minutes ago, they let a small herd of about fourteen sukers graze a little too close to the perimeter. Sukers get scared off by a little light and noise, so they probably thought a single Marine could shoo them away if they came any closer. What they didn't realize was that, with the prevailing wind coming from the east, a sextet of grampass had slunk up the side of the hill, and were tracking their favorite, house-sized prey.

"That rock I flung?" Ia offered. "I aimed it—and timed it—

to hit the love-nodes of the lead bull suker, specifically when he was facing *away* from the camp. Those grampass were approaching from the far side of that herd. If I hadn't scared the lead bull and stampeded the rest into running with him, running in the direction he was facing, *away* from this camp . . . the grampass would have come up on their far side from us, and they would have bolted *this* way. Away from their main predators.

"Now. You tell me, sir. Do you really think that force field would've been able to withstand fourteen frightened sukers stampeding this way? Let alone a single Marine with a handlight?" Ia asked. She didn't have to see his wince to know it was a rhetorical question. Sukers were larger than the hovervans Estes and the others had driven earlier. So were their chief predators. Still, she drove the point home. "The sukers would have broken through the force fields and tramped through all of these tents. The grampass would have followed . . . and it would have been a slaughter of *us* instead of the sukers."

She pointed in the direction of the noises still echoing up through the woods, the combat still going on between the ram-horned herbivores and their long-necked, sharp-toothed foes.

"*This* is what I do. Not for glittery, and not for glory. If we had just talked about the mayor's ceremony tomorrow, if you hadn't grabbed my writer from me . . . that would have been fine. You would have gone on your way, I would have come out here, thrown my little rock, and gone back to bed with no one the wiser. If you hadn't stayed where I asked, if you had interfered . . . the suker bull would have continued to turn, ruining my one shot. Maybe I would've cast my stone well enough to get him to run sideways . . . but the six grampass tracking the herd would have come close enough to see the Marines out there, and smell the civilians in here, and maybe brought them our way anyway . . . and the force field still might have fallen, leading to an unnecessary loss of lives."

"Unnecessary?" Ferrar repeated. "But what if they were necessary? You said it yourself: Vladistad is what led to the United Earth reformation movement. Which led us to *this* moment."

"Are you willing to take that risk?" Ia countered, pointing at the now quiet forest. "I could show you what the future would be like if you interfered, sir, but you couldn't even *see* the bull-suker, right here, right now, hidden in the local equivalent of trees. Yet I still hit him, and I stampeded the herd away from this camp. You can go out and look for yourself in the morning. This drizzle will stop in about two more minutes, so the tracks and the carnage will still be there. Think whatever you like, but don't you dare do anything about what you saw and heard tonight until you go out there and have taken a good, long look at everything. Anything *else* I tried to show you, you wouldn't be able to see . . . so there's no point in my trying."

Ferrar snorted. "That's presuming you can see as much as Giorgi ever did."

Ia spread her hands, feeling the drizzle tapering down to a mist. "Giorgi was standing in the middle of a forest on a dark, stormy night, sir. By comparison, *I* stand on a wide-open plain at high noon, under a cloudless sky lit by a binary star system."

He started to argue the point, but the comm on his arm unit squawked. Lifting his forearm, Ferrar activated the link. *"Ferrar. Go."*

Ia listened as Sergeant Pleistoch's voice came through the unit's speakers. *"Sir, this is Sgt. Pleistoch. We just had a pack of sukers stampede straight into a clutch of grampass. If they hadn't run that way . . . I think they might've been scared this way, sir. As it is, most of the dinoids ran off to continue fighting elsewhere, thank God, but we have a lot of blood on the ground. Requesting permission to torch the scent from the zone so it doesn't draw in any more predators, sir."*

Ferrar studied Ia for a long moment, then spoke. *"Permission granted, Sergeant. Everything else is too wet to burn out of control. And keep the local fauna further out from camp from now on, Sergeant."*

"Understood, sir. Pleistoch out."

"Ferrar out." Shutting off the link, he lowered his arm, still staring at her.

Ia, uncertain and uncomfortable from the mist still obscuring the way out of this moment, squared her shoulders and stared back.

"What am I going to do with you, Corporal?" he finally asked.

"Sir?" she queried, unsure of his meaning.

"You are one of the best damned soldiers I have ever seen. If you aren't *shakking* me, if those . . . specifics you wrote down," he added, lifting his chin at the rectangular bulk of the writing pad sheltering under her rain slicker, "are in any way accurate . . . what the hell am I supposed to do with you?"

That was a good question. Drawing in a deep breath, Ia let it out slowly. "Well . . . if you ask me if I can do something, and I say yes, then it'll get done, sir. You have my word on that. If you ask me and I say no, then it cannot be done . . . whether or not it technically could be done."

"Is that so?" Ferrar challenged quietly.

Ia looked down at her muddied palm, then back up at his face. "I have exactly one rock to throw, sir. I'm aiming it at a suker bull located three hundred years from now. Between then and now, I have a hell of a lot more lives to worry about than a couple hundred civilians . . . or even a couple million. If I told you, if I *showed* you what I am trying to do . . . well, you're a very strong-willed man. You'd be tempted far too much into trying to take matters into your own hands. You'd be trying to fire a Heck at the enemy, only you're blindfolded with your ears plugged, compared to me, and the enemy is holding far too many lives hostage. The damage would be too great.

"I can only tell you this: if it can be done, sir, I will do it. You have my Prophetic Stamp on that . . . and you don't need to know anything more than that. I wish I *could* tell you more," Ia murmured. "But I cannot and will not take that risk. I'm the only one who can throw this rock, the only one who knows what to do. And how. And when."

He drew in a breath to speak, then paused and looked up, lifting one of his own hands for a long moment. "The rain has stopped. Like you said it would."

Ia didn't bother to look up. She was more grateful for the view down, and in. Whatever he was now thinking, whatever she had said to convince him . . . the mist had lifted from the timestreams.

So instead, she quipped lightly, "We'll have mostly clear skies with a few scudding clouds by ten hundred hours local, sir. Bright, clear skies by midafternoon, and temperatures rising into the mid-twenties. Humidity will be around ninety-five percent, though . . . but this region will have no more rain for the next five days, and only scattered light rains after that for the following three weeks."

He looked at her sharply. She gave him a lopsided smile.

"You'll note that I didn't *have* to tell you the weather report, sir. But there was also no reason *not* to tell you." She gestured with her clean hand off to the left, back in the direction she had come from. "Mind if I request permission to go back to bed, sir? My ribs are still hurting a little, and I'm tired from all the hard work I did today. At least now I know I can sleep in peace. Now that my work is done for the day."

He looked down at his arm unit, out across the now quiescent force fields, then back at her. Slowly, he nodded. "Permission granted. For now. But if I ask you to do something . . ."

"If I can do it, it'll get done, sir. The rest . . . you don't need to know." Dipping her head in politeness, she turned to walk away.

"You do realize there's still the little matter of your insubordination to a superior officer," he called after her, pitching his voice a little louder. "You don't give the orders in my Company."

Ia spun on her heel, giving him another wry smile as she backed up the muddy, makeshift lane. "In this one matter, Lieutenant . . . legally, I outrank you. In all other matters, you are my superior, and I will do my absolute best to follow any orders you give me. You have my promise on that, too. I never give less than my best, sir."

"I'll hold you to that," Ferrar warned her. He looked up at the cloud-strewn sky and sighed. "Fine. We have four more days of flood cleanup to wade through before the *Hum-Vee* brings in the Army to relieve us. I'm not going to put your insubordination down on your record . . . but I'm not going to let it slide, either. You're going to get stuck with the dirtiest, nastiest jobs you can manage with those cracked ribs of yours until we head back up into space, soldier. Unless you're going to try and claim that there's some special psychic voodoo out there that says otherwise?"

"Sir, no, sir. That was the last time-sensitive task on this planet, sir," Ia admitted freely, nodding at the fence in the distance. "The only hell you'll catch is from the medical team if you overwork me, sir. In the meantime, you should probably get some sleep, Lieutenant," she added. "As you said, we have four more days of cleanup ahead of us."

"Get some sleep yourself, Corporal," Ferrar told her. "You'll need it."

"Sir, yes, sir."

CHAPTER 16

I earned the trust of my commanding officers the same way as anyone else. By earning it with steadfast service, accuracy, efficiency, and not giving up when I believed we could win a particular fight. I'm no psychodominant. If I were . . . my life would've been slightly easier. I could've imposed my will on everyone around me . . . but I'm not.

I won their trust with logic and tangible results. No trickery, no sleight of hand. And I tried my very best not to lie while doing so. That's one of the Fatalities, you know.

~Ia

FEBRUARY 15, 2491 T.S.
RESEARCH DOME THREE
OBERON MINING & REFINERY CONSORTIUM
OBERON'S ROCK, GS 138 SYSTEM

Even knowing her mechsuit was fully sealed against the external environment, Ia's lungs still ached with the need to cough. Dust and debris choked the air, pounding with each bright yellow orange flash from the industrial lasers searing through the air. Her coolant system dealt well enough with the heat of supercharged particles slamming over and over into the metallic ores which comprised most of the chunk of planetoid they were on, but she knew that relief wouldn't last.

None of the members of 2nd Platoon dared to poke a weapon around the corner, not even to take a wild potshot at the laser pods. The pirates who had seized this research facility had rigged them to fire at anything metallic, and at anything containing ceristeel. Which included their mechsuits and weapons. Estes had already lost her Heck in the experiment of trying to take out those makeshift guns, the barrel melted into brittle slag.

Each rapid-fire *zwwowwp* was followed by a pattering shower of increasingly pulverized debris. Even with her external pickups muted, the sound was a nonstop pressure. A glance to her left showed D'kora gesturing in her own half-mech armor, though her argument with whomever wasn't being broadcast to the rest. Ia could guess, though. She waited patiently for the discussion to conclude, and through the several seconds that followed.

"Ferrar to Corporal Ia."

The broadcast came on a private channel, just the two of them. Ia didn't move. *"Ia here. What can I do for you, sir?"*

"Well, now, isn't that the question? You once swore to me, if I asked you if something could be done, you'd tell me whether or not it could be done. So. I am asking you, Corporal . . . can you get the 2nd Platoon through that stalemate? We're taking heavy casualties on the front and side doors. We need that back entrance busted open. Without blowing up the dome and venting everyone to space. So, I am asking you . . . can you get that back door open, Corporal?"

"Sir, yes, sir. I can get it open. It won't be quick, though. And I'll have to do some scouting farther up, to make sure the rest of the way is clear. I'm not taking the 2nd into any death-traps."

"Your concern is appreciated, Corporal."

She smiled wryly. *"Thank you, sir. Please explain to Lt. D'kora that I have an idea, and that you've authorized me to implement it. Stress that no one else is to follow unless and until the lasers stop. We don't dare risk any other lives."*

"Tell me something I don't know."

"You're an uncle."

"I said something I didn't know. Ferrar out."

Ia smirked. *An uncle . . . again,* she thought. She didn't try contacting him a second time, though. Half a minute later, D'kora contacted her.

"The Lieutenant says you had an idea, Corporal. You didn't bring it to me," her Platoon officer stated bluntly, darkly.

"I figured that, given the risk, you'd say no, sir . . . but we need this stalemate broken. I think I know how. If I'm right," she argued, *"we can crack open the back door and ride to the rescue. If I'm wrong . . . I'll be the only casualty, and the rest of you can go join the others. Now, I'm willing to take that risk, sir. I know what I face if I'm wrong, and what's at stake if I'm right."*

"Permission granted. Tell me what you need."

Ia moved away from where she crouched by the tunnel wall. She worked her way back down the line, and tapped Buck Sergeant Jung Baker, the new sergeant of A Squad, on his ceristeel-plated, gun-toting arm, switching to external speakers as well as her comm. "Sergeant!" she projected through the noise of the laser drills. "I need your medic kit!"

"What, are you injured?" he shot back, though he did swing open the compartment on his full-mech thigh, revealing the gear packed inside. Some of the gear was designed to be used by servo fingers, but for this, she needed greater dexterity.

Blink-coding the shutdown sequence for her armor, Ia opened the lower panels, freeing first her p-suited feet, then her hands. Straining, she reached for the goods in the sergeant's thigh compartment. He shifted a little closer, lifting one leg on servos that whined faintly compared to the thundering of the makeshift cannons up ahead. Digging through the supplies, she fished out a pair of dust masks and a roll of paper tape. Ripping the metal strips off the nose sections, she balanced the masks on his leg, and quickly unsealed the o-ring of her p-suit from her mechsuit helmet.

Ducking, eyes squeezed shut and breath held tight against the dust filtering through the air, she fumbled the mask into place over nose and mouth, and taped it to her face, sealing it in place. Quick movements sealed the second one over the top of the first. Only then did she breathe. The metallic compounds being vaporized around her were dangerous to inhale in large quantities. They wouldn't do her eyes much good, either. Then again, neither would the heat of the rock underfoot. Ia reached for the seals of her p-suit.

"What are you doing?" Baker asked her.

She ignored him, stripping out of the rubbery grey suit. Underneath, she wore nothing, not even underwear. For a pressure-suit to work at its most efficient, it had to cover as many pores on a wearer's skin as possible. In an emergency, they could be pulled on over clothing, but preparing for battle usually meant having enough time to do things properly.

A couple of the others catcalled and whistled via their suit speakers, peering through the dust at what she was doing. Ia ignored them as well. Grabbing one of the rolls of bandaging in Baker's medic kit, Ia balanced first on the toes of one foot, then the other, stripping off the booties for the suit and replacing them with wads of cotton gauze that she taped in place. It protected her bare skin somewhat from the heat of the rocks, but this was several meters away from those lasers.

Once she was safely balanced on her wrapped toes, she unlatched her wrist unit and held it up to the silver-faceplated sergeant. "Keep track of this for me!"

He accepted it reluctantly. Ia quickly wrapped her hands in gauze mittens and awkwardly taped them in place, then stored everything back in his full-mech thigh compartment.

D'kora made her way to Ia's side. She flipped up her blast shield, though she kept her suit sealed. For the first time since Ia had met her, the other woman asked her an actual question. Demanded it, rather. "Corporal . . . what the *hell* are you doing?"

"Metal, sir! Those lasers are aiming at anything metal!" she shouted back. The heat was beginning to make her sweat, which made the dust cling to her skin. "Even a p-suit has metal on it! They might also have motion sensors, so I'm going to have to move very slowly. The scanners can't tell much about what's up ahead; the dust and heat are screwing up the sensors. But we do know the drill emplacements are about twenty meters up the corridor. Give me twenty minutes to get to them, and . . . I don't know, another ten to figure out how to kill their power switches. If they don't stop firing in half an hour, find another way in without me!"

"Corporal, you are currently bare-asteroid naked!" D'kora argued.

Glancing down at her torso, naked curves and muscles smudged in pulverized dust, Ia spread her taped hands, letting her rare sense of humor out to play. "Well, I guess I am. Enjoy the free show, sir! Now, if you'll excuse me, I need to go break this stalemate."

Leaving the lieutenant to stare after her, Ia slipped between the other mechsuited soldiers. Some of them grinned, some of them rolled their eyes, and some kept their silvery grey blast plates down, their expressions hidden. She didn't care. The closer she got to the corner where the lasers were still searing away, the hotter the floor and the air became.

This really was the only way in for the 2nd Platoon. Posing as merely a metallurgical refinery, the Oberon Consortium was actually a military contract facility. In a way, it was ironic, even poetic, that she should be the one to help keep its secrets out of the wrong hands, given how those secrets would eventually end up in hers.

Dropping to hands and toes, she flexed her muscles in a modified push-up stance. Slowly, carefully, as low as she could go without burning her bare skin on the floor, Ia crept around the corner. The laser drills were targeting anything above knee-high that moved or had metallic components. Unfortunately, nothing in a mechsuit, even half-mech, could hunker down that low.

Centimeter by slow centimeter, she worked her way around the corridor, stalking with the patience of a sloth. Oberon's Rock, a mineral-rich, air-poor world, was only slightly heavier than Earth's gravity, 1.14gs instead of 1.01. The slow movement was more of a strain on her patience than on her muscles. Eventually, she managed to get her whole body around the corner, and up the corridor by a full meter, beyond any safe viewing range by her fellow soldiers.

She took a moment to rest her body, still sprawled in a modified push-up position. Now it was time to let her mind go to work. Sweating muddy, metallic droplets, she pushed static energy out from her body. That caused the swirling dust clouds to shift and scatter, but it also obscured what little the others would be able to detect with their scanners. Then, she focused her thoughts forward, on the electrical pulses and programming guiding the lasers firing over her head.

"Ia! Are you still alive?" she heard Estes shout.

I am not here . . . I am not here . . . you do not see me . . . you do not detect me . . . there is nothing here, along the right-hand wall . . .

"Corporal, report!" That came from D'kora.

The trio of cannons shifted their fire ever so slightly, avoiding the right side of the corridor. Pushing upright, Ia sprinted forward, skimming along the narrow path she had cleared for herself. She wasn't her biological father; she couldn't take a laser beam as powerful as one of these drills and hope to survive.

Her goal wasn't the drills or their controls. Yet. Ignoring them, Ia raced up the corridor, flinging herself down a side passage and up a long flight of stairs. Every turn, she already knew. Every step, she had already practiced in her mind.

Flinging herself into the third storage room on the left at the top of those stairs, she grabbed shoulders and snapped necks. Vertebrae crackled like broken kindling under her fingers. Two, three, five half-naked men died. The sixth managed to pull off of his victim and grab for his rifle. She grabbed his wrist just as he brought it around and slammed her other palm into his elbow, inverting the joint with a sickening *crunch*. Before he could do more than gasp at the pain, she broke his neck as well and dropped his half-naked body on top of the rest.

The battered, bloodied woman sprawled on the table tugged on the tape binding her wrists and knees to its corners. "Oh, God, I'm rescued! Help me! Get me free!"

Ia closed her eyes. As the brunette struggled to free herself, Ia probed the timestreams. Precious seconds ticked by while she searched for any other path. Any other way.

There was none.

It was a terrible choice to have to make . . . but not her first, and not the worst.

"Aren't you going to free me? Get me off of this thing!" the woman demanded, shaking the table with her struggles. Ia sighed and peeled off first her hand wrappings, then the dust-caked double-masks.

"I'm sorry." Approaching her side, Ia leaned over the woman. Met her wide, green stare. "But any children you have . . . *any* descendants . . . they will sabotage the future. You might *or* might not have been killed, had I not broken through . . . but I did, so that makes me responsible for anything you or your descendants do. I cannot allow them to exist. I'm sorry."

The woman blinked up at her through her puffy, swollen eyelids. "What . . . ?"

Reaching down and in, Ia compressed two key arteries inside the woman's mind. "Sleep," she murmured. "Sleep."

The woman struggled, then slowed. She slumped. Ia kept the pressure in place until she felt the other woman's kinetic energy spike, then fade . . . in an eternal sleep.

". . . Maybe heaven will let you know just how sorry I am."

Mindful of the ticking of time, Ia turned away. Grimly, she grabbed the discarded shirt of one of the dead woman's rapists and scrubbed the dust, sweat, and the threat of tears from her face. *I don't have time to cry. I can't take the time. I have too much to do to waste my time on . . . on regrets . . . and choices.*

I am damned for what I must do. I accepted that a long time ago. I had to.

Ia scrubbed as much of the dirt from her body as she could spare time for. Stripping two of the men to get the right sizes, she donned socks, boots, trousers, and a T-shirt. The lack of undergarments chafed a little, but it was better than the alternatives. Particularly since some of them had died messily as their muscles abruptly relaxed. Hurrying, she checked the time. She didn't have her chrono with her, but she could and did dip into the timestreams.

I have . . . twelve minutes to spare, before I have to get back. Sorting through the weapons, she snatched up two laser pistols and a pair of knives. The pistols were over-clocked, illegal models jury-rigged to fire double-intensity beams in the infrared zone. They would hit almost as hard as a military rifle could, if at less than half the usable e-clip life. The focusing crystals in the pistols weren't military quality . . . never mind Obcron quality.

Time to go wreak some havoc with the Lyebariko. Darting out the door, she headed up one more level and pelted down a long corridor. The hardest part, running full-tilt in such light gravity, was keeping herself from hitting the ceiling with each bounding stride. Most of the civilians had been rounded up and herded into the storage rooms she was passing, trussed hand and foot and locked inside. She didn't dare take the time to free them just yet; if anyone who later survived noticed her at this point in time, comparisons might be made on just where and when she was located.

Using her momentum to half leap, half run up a wall next

to a ladder way, she grabbed for the rungs and scrambled up through the open hatchway. This was an escape ladder, designed to take personnel from the biodome up above all the way down into the basement levels of the settlement. Flinging her mind ahead of her, she unlatched and opened each hatchway electrokinetically, saving the time needed to do it manually.

Even in such light gravity, she was nearly breathless by the time she reached the roof of the building she wanted. Sucking in deep lungfuls, Ia crouched on the grass-lined roof and pulled one of the pistols stuck into the waistband of her pants. Panting, she carefully braced it on the raised edge of the building and searched for her targets.

This wasn't a military-calibrated rifle with a sniper scope. This was a jury-rigged handgun aimed by eye and mind. She would have just enough time for three crucial shots before having to run back. Off to the right, she could see plumes of smoke from where the tech raiders were holding off the 3rd Platoon at the edge of the dome. Both sides were trying to be careful about shooting too high; neither wanted to pierce the triple-layered, strut-latticed bubbles protecting them from the vacuum of space. The raiders, because they didn't have any protective pressure-suits on hand, and her fellow Marines, because they knew the civilian hostages in this dome didn't have any suits, either.

There! The reinforcements! The group responsible for this raid, certain members of an undergalactic crime organization calling itself the Lyebariko—which translated as *Library* in some half-forgotten Terran language—had prepared well for this siege. Their makeshift troops were hauling another trio of jury-rigged laser drills off to the right, visible intermittently between the office-like buildings and the trees of the biosphere's central park. Scraping the butt of the pistol slightly along the roof edge, Ia aimed and pulled the trigger, spearing a bright yellow light down at that distant street.

And missed.

Swearing under her breath, she aimed at her second target, the first now obscured again by the park. Slowing her breath, she concentrated, firing between heartbeats. On to the third, letting the brief slash of orange light lance through the trees . . . and a dip into the timestreams, firing blindly through the foliage at her first target once more.

Success.

The laser drills were now damaged at critical points. Two had slagged power buttons, and the middle one had a damaged conduit socket. When they tried to plug it into a power source, the drill would explode. Sparing just enough time to use a bit of rumpled bandaging to erase evidence she had used the gun, Ia tossed it over the edge of the building and jumped back down the ladder way. Hands flying, feet flicking, slapping and tapping the rungs to control her descent, she "fell" all seven floors back down to ground level, then through the chute another four levels to the basement where she had entered.

Increasing each slap to a grab slowed her drop enough to land without hurting herself. From there, it was a sprint back down the long hallway, a leap down the stairs, two turns and another turn. Back into the heat and the dust . . . which she had forgotten about. Hastily hauling her borrowed shirt up over her nose and mouth, Ia squinted against the debris and aimed her second pistol at the middle drill, burning into the machinery's housing with its over-clocked, clip-draining beam.

Too many damned things to keep track of, today . . . Whirling, she crouched, ducking a mere second below the flying debris as the drill's crystal matrix cracked and shattered. The blast knocked her onto the overheated floor, but none of the parts slammed into her. The explosion also knocked the other two drills into the walls, damaging them. One spat sparks and smoke, but no more deadly beams. The other continued to fire, but now that it was wedged at an angle between floor and wall, it could no longer aim at anything.

"*Corporal? . . . Corporal Ia, is that you?*"

The mechsuit-amplified shout sounded a little tinny. It was also accompanied by a faint ringing. Rising, Ia shook her head and focused inward, on healing the damage from her ears. Within seconds, the tinnitus stopped, allowing her to shout back, "The drills have been disabled, Sergeant! You're free to move up—and bring me my wrist unit! Someone also needs to shoot this last drill to shut it up. I'm almost out of juice."

She flicked the safety on the laser pistol and tucked it back into her waistband. Unlike the other one, this one's e-clip had started out nearly full, not nearly empty. There was still more good she could do with the confiscated weapon.

Sergeant Baker eased around the corner, followed by Estes. There was enough room for a full-mechsuit to move without worrying about anything but the occasional chunk of debris; the tilted, immobilized drill was busy trying to dig a new, shallow-angled path in the side of the stone corridor. Seeing the way was free, the pair moved up to her position. Ia retreated quickly, taking refuge behind Estes' half-mechsuited bulk, in case anything else exploded. A steady shot from the permanent cannon mounted on the sergeant's armor silenced the firing drill, then killed the one still spitting sparks on the other side.

Double-E and Harkins moved up and the four Marines quickly moved the remainder of the drills out of the way, allowing the others the room to approach. Baker offered Ia her wrist unit, clasped in the delicate tips of his servo hands. "You gonna crawl back into your armor, soldier?"

Ia shook her head. "I have dust in places I don't even want to think about, Sergeant. I'd rather not grind it in deeper with the pressure of a p-suit, and I definitely don't want to gunk up the gears if I put my mechsuit back on without one." Clasping the unit onto her left forearm, she glanced briefly at her olive drab clothes and gave him a wry smile. "Besides, the few insurgents I saw while looking for a weapon, they were all wearing this army-surplus stuff, and not all of it was clean.

"Cover up my too-white hair with a hat or a handkerchief, and I figure I could blend in enough to do a little enemy infiltration. After all, they're expecting the Marines to show up in ceristeel mech armor, guns blazing, not strolling along the streets in Army Greens," Ia pointed out, plucking at her borrowed fatigues.

"Good idea, Corporal." That came from Lt. D'kora, who had moved up between the haphazard ranks. "You must have done a little bit of scouting, to get that gun in your waistband. I'll trust you also made sure no one reported your little foray to the rest of the enemy."

"No, sir. I didn't give them a chance for that, sir," she promised.

"Good. Show us what you found."

Nodding, Ia turned and headed up the passage at a trot. Behind her, the others followed, their mechsuited weight making the ground tremble. It wouldn't take long to show them the first storage room and its plethora of bodies. Nor would it be all that difficult to "hear" the stirrings of the trapped colonists in the other chambers. She knew D'kora would assign D Squad to give them escort back down the tunnel, sending the civilian researchers and workers back toward the other domed settlements scattered over a fifty-kilometer radius on this corner of Oberon's Rock.

Better for them to be well out of the way if and when the Lyebariko's raiders decided to counterattack. Or grab more hostages to hold off the military. Things which Ia intended to prevent. Once the civilians in this sector were freed, she would be free as well. Free to head deeper through the dome city, and the heart of the problem occupying it.

Free to wreck yet another set of lives.

———————

The trio of guards at the entrance to the office building eyed her warily when she jogged up. Hand pressed to her side, panting from what looked like a long run, she nodded at them. "Berrimoon. I need to report in. Kittrick got his hands on . . . a military unit. Figured the boss'd want to see it right away."

The lead guard eyed her warily. She had liberated a long-sleeved shirt to cover up her arm unit, as well as a scrap of cloth to wrap around her distinctive, if gritty, hair. "I don't think I know you."

Ia lifted her chin, sassing back, "I don't think I know *you*, either. This *is* the Fisk Building, on the corner of 5th and Pleiades, isn't it?" she asked, still breathing hard. Or at least faking it. "If it is, this is where Kittrick told me to report . . . and I see the name Fisk on the front doors, there."

"You're supposed to report in person?" the female of the three guards countered. "Why not use our commis?"

"Because the damned Marines have tapped into our frequencies. Half of us got caught in a trap because of it. We got our hands on a military unit," Ia explained patiently. "You know, and I know, that the boss would kill *you* to get her hands on it. Now, are you gonna let me through, or are you gonna at least send someone up to report our findings to the boss?" she asked, lifting her chin at the upper floors of the white-walled structure.

"I don't let through anyone I don't know," the leader of the trio growled. He shifted his weapon toward her, a black surplus projectile rifle with who knew what loaded into its c-clip. "And I don't know you."

His two companions did likewise, pulling their attention from the perimeter of the building. That was the moment she was waiting for. Ia spread her hands up and out. "Then send up my report!"

Deep red zapped in from three angles, triggered by her gesture. Ia snapped her hands down and across, shoving the muzzle of the lead guard's rifle away from her stomach. The move pressed the trigger guard into his hand, rather than pulled it away . . . which helped prevent his spasming finger from tightening too hard on the trigger. The weapon didn't fire. Ia sighed in relief, sidestepping the falling, skull-charred bodies. That had been her biggest concern at this step.

Projectile weapons had been chosen for this post because the cartridges were noisy when they exploded, and that would have alerted the people inside to her attack. Knowing in advance that the raiders themselves had accidentally damaged the surveillance system for this building was a bonus; it allowed her to step into the foyer without hesitation. Foreknowledge also had her choosing the correct emergency stairwell, the one the invaders hadn't booby-trapped.

It was, however, barricaded. Someone had tapped into the building's security measures and activated the force fields built into each doorway. They were meant to slow any intruder trying to break in and make off with any sensitive information. Since it was impossible for her to logically know the pass code without revealing how—though she could have just checked in the timestreams—Ia simply put up her hand to the doorway and leaned on the near-invisible barrier. Leaned, with both body and mind.

Static crackled into her palm. Up the bones of her arm. Down into her stomach, where it coiled and burned. The field shorted out. Ia ducked through and bounded up the stairs. This building was the structure where the critical research information was being stored for Oberon's military contracts. In specific, the contracts covering the composition of the focusing crystals for Terran laser weaponry, and in very specific, the hottest, hardest-hitting starship cannon crystals available.

Several years from now, she would need what this company

was striving to create. She didn't dare let it fall into the hands of criminal masterminds. This seemingly simple mining company was on the edge of a major breakthrough in refraction materials science. If she hadn't been assigned to Ferrar's Company in specific, she would have had to manipulate events to affect the outcome here anyway. Having the Grandmaster of the Afaso meddle so effectively in her initial career path had saved her a lot of stress and worry.

Mindful of the Marines rushing toward this building, she finished the last two flights at a full run, unfastening her wrist unit. Slapping her empty hand on the field surface, she drained it to the point of collapse as well, and touched the controls to open the door panel. Then flung up her hands in a "surrender" pose as the quartet of gunmen on the other side aimed their weapons straight at her chest and head. She didn't move. Neither did they.

"Who the frag are *you*?" one of them demanded. He was wielding a laser rifle instead of a projectile weapon, but his rifle looked like it had been ripped off of a full-mechsuit, or maybe a small armored vehicle. He was also quite muscular, almost as much as her half-twin, Thorne. Ia didn't let the comparison rattle her.

"Berrimoon, from Kittrick and the backside Squad. I blew up a Marine and managed to get the wrist unit off her arm. Kittrick told me to bring it straight to the boss," Ia rattled off quickly. "He thinks it's a command unit. Said she'd want to see it right away."

"How'd you get up here?" he demanded, inching forward. "Nobody called up."

"Someone was talking with Tubrik when I came up. Said something about the comm channels being compromised. But he knew who I was, and told me how to get through—"

The building rocked from an explosion somewhere below; her fellow Marines had picked the wrong stairwell door. Ia didn't let herself wince. Knees flexing to keep her balance, she unleashed the energy pooled inside her body. The shock wave of electricity burst from her body like the tendrils of a plasma ball, zapping the quartet of men even as they staggered and tried to recover from the unexpected quake.

Pain slashed through her left shoulder, making her drop the wrist unit. Ia hissed, twisting too late to avoid the last-moment firing of the leader's gun. Smoke billowed upward, along with the scent of burned meat. "*Sonova* shakk!"

Teeth bared, she slapped out the flames of her shirt with her right hand, grunting with each agonizing blow. Her body ached from collarbone to trapezium, and her left arm half-dangled at her side, too many muscles and tendons charred down to the bone. Gritting her teeth, she stooped and snatched up the wrist unit. Being shot had *not* been a part of her plan, not when it had been less than a two percent chance at best in the most dire of her calculated probabilities. Eating the energy like a full-blooded Feyori could, even in matter-form, was out of the question; laser fire was too hot, too fast, too much for her to handle.

Great. Can't do Plan A, Ia thought, hissing under her breath as she reclipped the thin plexi unit onto her left forearm. *Can't do Plan B, especially since I can't lift a two-handed gun right now. Plans C and D are out as well; they'd see me grabbing the gre-nade, and I cannot afford to let anyone know I can do that, right now.* Ia tugged her shirtsleeve back into place over the device, wincing as each move hurt her burned flesh. *Somewhere up there, God is eating snacks, pointing, and laughing at me, I swear.*

That left Plan F, since she didn't have a Plan E. Somewhere down below, projectile fire rang out in staccato bursts of noise too loud to be muffled even by the most modern of construction techniques. The 2nd Platoon had encountered resistance.

Eyeing the walls, Ia quickly searched for what she needed. A fire alarm went off, but the sprinklers didn't burst into action on this floor. Yet. Several doors hissed open up ahead. The rush of bodies that poured out aimed various weapons her way, but haphazardly. Pointing their weapons in other directions as well, it was clear they were busy looking for a mechsuited enemy after those explosions, not one more body among the many in shades of green.

"You! What happened in here?"

That was the voice she needed to hear. Lilian van Trijkell was a trusted lieutenant of the Lyebariko, the "Library" of forces that ruled the undergalatic elements, and a crime boss in her own right, specializing in selling arms and armor on the black market. Clad in a simple, tasteful dark skirt-suit with a white blouse underneath, the dark-haired woman looked like she should have been one of the office workers—and in fact had been, having infiltrated the Oberon Consortium personally in order to pull off this tech theft.

Ia staggered and slumped up against the wall, doing her best to look dazed. Under the cover of cradling her arm, she flicked her comm unit's recorder on with a subtle press of the outer buttons through her borrowed sleeve. "Uhh . . . Marines . . . force fields . . . They're in the building."

"Tell me something I don't know. Slap some sense into her," Lilian ordered one of the others. "And get ready to take me hostage. I will *not* have this operation fail completely!"

Sagging against the wall, Ia palmed the knife she had stolen and slid downward. Just to her right was a power socket, the kind meant to be used by the cleaning crews at night. Reversing her grip on the steel blade, she eased the tip into the recessed opening just as one of the men stooped and peered at her face.

"I don't recognize this one."

"Yeah, I keep hearing that a lot," Ia muttered.

The unnamed thug frowned and lifted his free hand to her head.

She shoved the knife into the socket just as the man yanked off the fabric covering her scalp. Electricity crawled up her wrist, soaking into her flesh. Off-balance already from the pain in her shoulder, Ia hissed in another breath from the sharp stinging in her bones and focused on containing it. This was a *lot* more energy than two static force fields being drained nice and slow and easy; this was a live power conduit that tapped directly into the trunk line supplying energy to the entire floor.

It was also the wrong amperage, and that meant setting herself up for the conversion. She didn't want to kill anyone if she could prevent it, just render them helpless. One innocent woman's death was more than enough to regret, plus the six who had been violating her.

The man peering down at her squinted, then grabbed her head, scrubbing at her hairline with his thumb. He scraped off more of the grit remaining from her jaunt past the laser drills, and frowned.

"Wait . . . *white* hair? *Shakk*, this isn't one of ours! It's that goddamn white-haired Marine!" The thug hastily stepped back out of range, no doubt in case Ia attacked after having been revealed. Ia, however, didn't move. She was right where she needed to be for Plan F.

"Kill her!" Lilian snapped.

"Already on it, boss!" He raised the over-clocked laser pistol.

Ia unleashed the energy in the tapped conduit. Arcing it between herself and the man in front of her, she shoved it through the air, leaping it from body to body, weapon to weapon faster than conscious thought. She screamed as she did so, not because it was a battle cry, but because it hurt like hellfire. Electrokinetically transforming the current so that the amperage wouldn't kill anyone in the hallway meant that she had to suffer the leakage flux inside her flesh.

Triggered far too late, the thug's laser shot went wild, scoring the wall and ceiling well off to one side. Bodies twitched and slumped. The lights directly overhead and down the hall exploded and shut down, but the ones in the rooms beyond the hall continued to glow, protected by capacitors and circuit breakers.

Panting harshly, heart pounding from too much energy coiled too high, Ia locked it back down with sheer force of will and yanked out the knife. Letting the blade drop, she carefully cradled her left arm in her lap, taking some of the strain from her shoulder, and thumbed off her recorder. Some of the tech raiders continued to shudder, bodies spasming from the electrical attack. Others fell limp, though several moaned, letting her know they were still conscious, if in no condition to notice anything other than the racing of their own blood and the screaming of their own nerves.

What she needed was in one of the rooms farther down the hall. Thankfully, she had a way to convert the excess energy crackling through her nerves from electrokinetic to telekinetic. As the men and women around her groaned and tried to regain their senses, Ia cast the last of the excess energy outward, and back again. Catching the silver and white egg that zigzagged through the air toward her, she fumbled it around until she found the trigger, and thumbed it with her good hand. A harsh burst of white static light *pzzzztsed* outward, washing down the hall.

The electrosonic shock added yet another layer of pain to her injuries. It took her a few moments to realize the salty metallic taste in her mouth was blood: Ia had bitten through her lip. Letting the egg clatter onto the floor, Ia gingerly touched her mouth and stared at the crimson stain on her fingertips.

Lovely. Yet more pain to endure . . . No more than what I deserve, though.

. . . Thoom thoom thoom.

The stairwell she had used shook with the sound of approaching mechsuits. Grey silvered figures darted into the hall, crouching and taking up firing positions in rapid progression before easing back up onto their feet. She rolled her head against the wall, looking at her fellow Marines. She spotted Estradille's name embossed on his shoulder plates. "Hey, Estradille. Took you long enough."

"What the *shakk* happened up here?" he asked, stepping over a couple of the fully unconscious bodies. Behind him, the others made way for Lieutenant D'kora.

She had her breath back by now. "Stunner grenade. See the lady in the navy blue suit?" Ia added, lifting her chin. "Don't be fooled. She'll probably come awake protesting she's just another civilian hostage, but she was giving a lot of orders to these creeps. One of 'em called her 'boss.' I think I got it recorded on my wrist unit. I don't know, though; the grenade might've damaged it."

"Yeah, right. If a stunner grenade went off up here, then what are *you* doing still awake?" she heard Hooke asking from her spot by the stairwell door.

D'kora replied, sparing Ia from having to say anything. "In case you haven't noticed, Bloody Mary here has a few oddities up her sleeves. This isn't the first static shock survival trick she's pulled in her career." Though the lieutenant had her blast shield down, Ia could tell by the body language of her mechsuit that the older woman was sizing up the needs of the situation. "Sergeant Baker, get up here. Seems the corporal here needs your med kit again.

"The rest of you, strip and zip!" D'kora ordered, meaning they were to strip the prisoners of any and all gear, and lash their ankles and wrists together with zip ties. "Anyone who isn't in a mechsuit . . . excepting Corporal Ia . . . you are to presume is an enemy. You will presume they are dangerous even when disarmed, and you will secure each and every one accordingly. The Justice Department can pay a psi to tell the real hostages from the fake ones. Our job is just to strip and zip, today."

The others hurried to comply. Ia dragged her feet into a cross-legged position, giving them more room to work around her. She wasn't in a hurry to move. Now that the worst of the battle was over, her adrenaline was beginning to crash. Baker thumped up next to her and flicked up his blast shield, peering at her through the crystal of his inner helm plate. She could just make out the tufts of blond hair above the brown headband circling his brow, and the light blue of his eyes.

"Report, soldier," he ordered, activating a light on one servo hand so he could shine it in her eyes.

Ia did her best not to flinch. "One of 'em tagged me in the shoulder. Hurts like a sonova, Sergeant . . . can't move the arm much, but I'll live. And I bit my lip. Obviously."

"That . . . is one ugly wound, soldier. But I'd still take a laser burn over a bullet hole any day," he muttered, opening up his thigh compartment again. "So would the docs on board the ship. This stuff, Doc Keating can regenerate without needing to stitch everything back together. Of course, you'll be stuck in a goo tank for days, and carrying a goo pack on your shoulder for weeks."

He poked around in his supplies with his flexor-glove-controlled digits and grimaced.

"*Shakk.* There's dust all over the compartment. I think you'll just need a sling to keep that shoulder immobile, though. Move it around, and you might crack open the burn and start bleeding from more than just your lip. That'd be bad. There's still a lot of fighting left to do."

"Tell me something I *don't* know." That was the other reason she hadn't tried to attack her would-be killer. The less damage she did to her shoulder now, the more quickly she would be back in action again. Oberon's Rock wasn't the only battle the *Liu Ji* would be seeing this week. Nor was today's little war the only fight they would see in this particular system.

With luck, the Lieutenant will now be open to any suggestions I have on subtle little schedule changes. He'll be calling me in for a private, off-the-record debriefing, and if I steer the conversation right . . . ow, dammit . . . he'll wind up asking for a weekly "Anything you want to tell me, soldier?" briefing . . . Plus other, larger alterations to our future plans.

Not that I'll hold my breath, given how badly I miscalculated this hit, she thought, eyeing her black-charred flesh. Then sucked in a deep lungful and held it, trying not to grunt as her Squad Sergeant bent her elbow and started wrapping the bandaging around her neck and forearm, forming a makeshift sling.

Ow, dammit . . . Okay, maybe I'll hold my breath a little.

CHAPTER 17

The incident on Oberon's Rock—the first one—earned me the trust of my commanding officer, and the respect of my peers. I'd had some respect from the very first battle, but I guess it was my fellow Marines seeing me charge into a fight just about bare-handed, putting my life on the line without any protective armor, and without any hesitation, that gave them the faith to put their trust in me as well.

Shortly after the incursion on Oberon's, I was granted my second . . . well, technically my third promotion, if you count my First Class stripes right out of Basic. I was shifted up to Squad Sergeant, our current sergeant got passed over to B Squad, and Pleistoch got promoted to Platoon Sergeant. Hooke was shuffled around to be Estes' teammate . . . and an old friend from Basic wound up replacing her as Knorrsson's teammate on A Squad Epsilon, a rather colorful fellow by the name of Spyder—one of those surnames where you didn't have to earn a military nickname to stand out. Then again, he's always been quite colorful. And a good soldier.

He earned a promotion, too, replacing Estes as lead corporal, who in turn opted for planet-side duty when the end of her six months came up. I, of course, opted to stay on board. The DoI and my psych evaluations said I could handle it, so on board I stayed.

Lieutenant Ferrar earned a promotion to Captain, while Lt. Cheung cycled out, and we got a new 1st Platoon leader, Konietzny. Captain Davanova was replaced by Captain Sudramara, and other faces came and went, both in the Company and on the ship. The border was heating up. You didn't have to be a precog to know Something Was Up . . . and it wasn't just the Salik trying to break through the Blockade seventy or so light-years away.

~Ia

JUNE 14, 2491 TS
BATTLE PLATFORM *HUM-VEE*
ALBEDO ICE STATION, SJ 723 SYSTEM

"Hey, Sergeant." The redheaded chaplain jogged a couple steps, catching up with Ia. She smiled and nodded at the younger woman. "How's the shoulder?"

Ia flexed her right shoulder. "Back in its socket, and cleared for combat, sir."

Bennie grinned. "No scars again, I take it?"

Ia shrugged. "Nope. Still none. I heal too well. Doctors think it's the high metabolism and high cellular density working overtime together."

"And how are you sleeping at night?" This time, the chaplain's tone was softer, yet more pointed.

She didn't dissemble. "Lousy. The burn-out survivors on that catalyzed domeworld were bad enough, but . . . the ones that didn't make it . . . The people I couldn't save are haunting my dreams again." The two of them waited a moment for the next section seal to cycle them through, then Ia continued. "But I'm cleared for all activities again. That'll help."

"And you're quite good at it. Are you going off-ship on Leave?" Bennie asked.

Ia shrugged. The movement didn't make her shoulder so much as twinge, which was a relief. Popping it out of its socket had not been a pleasant experience, and a dumb move on her part. Lieutenant D'kora was half the heavyworlder she was, but the woman could certainly move on a combat practice mat. "For an hour or two. The Captain wanted to see me for a chat, first."

"Anything up, this time?" Bennie asked.

Ia mock-clawed her fingers. "He's secretly a zombie, and wants to pick my braaaaaaiiinsss . . ."

She laughed. The chaplain gave her an odd look, then chuckled softly as well. Bennie also shook her head. "You have a very strange sense of humor, Ia."

Shaking it off, Ia sighed. "Just the usual weekly review of the troops under my purview."

"Good luck with that. Maybe I'll see you down in Frostie's?" the chaplain added, stopping with Ia as they reached the lifts.

Ia raised her brows at the news. That hadn't been a high probability. It might make things interesting, if the chaplain saw her in action. "You're going down there?"

"Chaplains know no Branch boundaries. So I'm allowed to go into a Marine Corps haven," Bennie quipped. She hung back as Ia tapped the button. "That, and I heard the chaplain from the *Alvin York XVII* will be there, overseeing a birthday party for a pair of Marines who share the same natal day. I haven't seen Delilah in a while, and thought I should go."

Stepping into the lift, Ia shrugged. "Then I guess I'll see you there."

Wondering what else could go odd with her day, Ia rode the lift up to the same level she had first visited. The front office was the same, though the clerk wasn't. Ferrar didn't look that much different, either, save only for the twin silver bars on his collar points. His skin was still a rich brown, his dark hair close-cropped to his head, and his gaze was still direct. This time, as he had for the last handful of months, he merely gestured for her to sit rather than exchange a formal set of salutes.

"Report," he ordered.

"Spyder got 'Happy' Harkins to smile." That lifted his brows. Ia smirked. "Twice, no less. I think he's ready for a promotion to Lance Corporal soon. Serving with Gaskins' GroPos settled him down from the recruit I knew, and I think he's finally getting the hang of command. Double-E and Knorrsson should be promoted as well."

"What about Guichi and Cooper?" Ferrar asked, making a note on his workstation. "I could use another full-mech sergeant. I'd like to pull from my own ranks before sending out a requisition for more personnel, though."

Ia shook her head. "They're both content with their rank and pay grades. Especially after that last evaluation raise. You might want to consider Private Adams in C Squad. He's quick, he adapts well, and he can get the others in his Squad to cooperate. They listen to him."

"He's not exactly an asteroid-buster," Ferrar pointed out, glancing briefly at her.

"No, but it's a skill set. It can be learned." She waited while he made a few more notes.

"Anything else, *for* the record?"

"No, sir. A Squad is doing fine. So is the rest of the 2nd, as far as I can tell."

Nodding, Ferrar signed off his workstation and shut it down, lowering the screens into the desk. Leaning back in his seat, he laced his fingers over his brown-uniformed stomach. "And off the record?"

Ia looked past him, skimming the timestreams. "I foresee you getting another 'hunch' and passing it along to Captain Sudramara. Shake up the patrol schedule, big-time. And keep news of the change confined to this ship."

"I'd wondered about that." Sighing, Captain Ferrar rubbed at his forehead. "Changing the schedule without reporting it in will skim us very, very close to insubordination. But . . . it does feel like we have a leak somewhere in the system. If the *Ackbar* hadn't suffered a tank leak and been forced to backtrack to the closest system for repair and refueling, they wouldn't have caught that clutch of raiders forcing the fueling station to refuel their ships. That was a nasty firefight."

"I know." At the Captain's sharp look, Ia shook her head. "It's not what you think. I'm just agreeing. The *Ackbar* came out of that one with a bad limp."

"Right. So . . . the patrol schedule. Any clues on how we should shake it up? Or is the future a big ball of misty possibilities?" Ferrar asked sardonically.

Mist wasn't her problem, usually. Seeing *too* much was the usual headache, unlike most other precogs. Ia looked past him at the wall, skimming delicately through his and the captain of the ship's timestreams. ". . . I just get the feeling we'll be near Oberon's Rock again in two days. Two and a half days, actually."

Ferrar leveled a look at her. "We just *came* from Oberon's

Rock, Sergeant. That's on the *Triskelle*'s patrol route, and they'll be passing through in just under two days."

"I know, sir." She held his gaze steadily. "I just get the same feeling thinking about it, like what I got when I heard about the *Ackbar*."

"That someone knows all our exact patrol routes, and is drafting in right behind us the moment our back is fully turned?" he asked. She didn't answer, because it was a rhetorical question. Ferrar knew it, too, and slowly nodded. "For such a simple-seeming mining consortium, Oberon keeps attracting a lot of attention, doesn't it?"

"That it does, sir." Sensing the meeting was over, Ia flexed her hand, thoughts already on the coming confrontation.

"Right. I'll bring up the *Ackbar* and the fact that we've already thwarted a couple of other piracy attempts to Sudramara, and aim for arriving in that system a few hours after the *Triskelle* leaves. Anything else, off the record?" he asked.

She shrugged. "Nothing really worth noting. Except for the nagging feeling we're beginning to piss off whoever is so interested in a simple mining company."

"I don't have to be a psychic to know we're pissing them off, Sergeant," Ferrar stated. "Frankly, I don't give a damn. They can't do a thing to us. There is no criminal organization that will ever match the TUPSF Marines, let alone outnumber us. They'd be suicidal to try."

She seized on that opening, smiling slightly. "On the record, sir . . . if they ever do try something, do I have your permission to 'chastise' them appropriately?"

Ferrar chuckled. "All by yourself? Not even *you* are that good of a soldier. This is the work of some very well-connected, very large crime syndicate—if you do ever have to go after them, then yes, you have my permission. Just make sure to bring the rest of the Company along for the ride. That's on the record. Whoever these people are, I want them shut down. If you get any 'ideas' on how to do that . . . then by all means, follow through."

"Sir, yes, sir."

"You're taking your Leave on the Platform, right?" Ferrar asked her. She nodded. He grinned. "Good. You've been trading too many Leave hours for voluntary guard duty—I know you're a long way from your homeworld and you want to save up enough time to be able to travel there and back, but you also need to relax once in a while. So. Buy me a drink at Frostie's?"

"Yeah, right. When are you going to buy *me* a drink?" she shot back, rising from her seat.

"When you outrank me, *Sergeant*."

"If I ever do, I'll hold you to that." Nodding politely, she headed for the door. "I'll see you down there as soon as I change, sir."

———————

"The pilgrim, on his knees on the road, then clasped his hands together," Chaplain Delilah Smithson recited. The others lounging around the table listened avidly to the short little tale. "And to his surprise . . . so did the bear! Greatly heartened by this, the pilgrim then began to pray. 'Oh, Heavenly Father, *please* let this be a Christian bear! I don't want to be eaten by those evil nasty devil bears!'"

". . . And?" Lieutenant Nguyen asked, polishing off the dregs of his beer.

"And the bear, to the great shock of the pilgrim, began to pray, too!" Delilah told the mix of noncoms and officers from three different ships crowding one of the longer tables in the brick-walled pub. "Kneeling there on the side of the road across from the pilgrim, paws clasped together, the bear prayed, 'Oh, Heavenly Father! For this meal, which we are about to receive . . . we give thanks.'"

Laughter roared across the table from her listeners, Ia included. She hadn't heard that one before.

Delilah smirked and saluted the others with her scotch on the rocks. "I told you it was an oldie, but a goodie! That one predates the Industrial Revolution."

"That's worth buying you another round," one of the sergeants from Delilah's ship quipped.

"I'll get it," Ia offered, rising from her seat.

Ferrar looked up at her, a pretzel halfway to his lips. "You'll buy *her* a drink, but you won't buy one for *me*?"

"She tells a better joke than you, Captain." Grinning as the others laughed and Ferrar mock-scowled, Ia headed for the bar. Halfway there, she heard the catcalls from one of the tables closer to the entrance.

"Lookit the civvies! Think they're lost?" "They gotta be, to wind up in here." "A business suit, in a dive like this?" "This is Ma-*reen* country! Not some fancy wine cellar!"

Swerving their way, Ia swept the enlisted snickering into their drinks with a quelling look. "This is an open, public bar. It is *not* exclusively Marine country. And you will *not* insult Frostie by driving away more potential customers. Is that clear, gentlebeings?"

Most of the Marines at the table knew who she was, by now. There was only one woman with chin-length white hair who ever showed up in bloodred clothes at Frostie's Tavern. Ia had had the white hair since birth, and was clad in a bloodred vest and matching silk pants. She had also earned their respect through her Bloody Mary reputation by now. The men and women at the table stopped their catcalling, burying any further comments in their drinks.

The gentleman who had been hazed strolled over to her. Lifting her left hand in his, he smiled, brown eyes gleaming with humor. Bowing over her fingers, he pressed a kiss to her knuckles. "My heroine. I thank you for such a gallant rescue. May I buy you a drink, lovely lady in red?"

"Whoa! Somebody's gonna try t' melt the Snow Princess?" Coughing on his drink, a private from Ferrar's 3rd Platoon rasped out, "I'd pay to see if he succeeds!"

"Shut it, Han," she retorted. "Don't make me bust you back down to recruit."

"Oh, I think I can handle this, my lady," the businessman stated, smiling pleasantly, if darkly. With his long, dark hair pulled back into a braid and a ring in one ear, the smile made him look more like a corporate raider than a mere corporate man.

"With respect, *I* can handle this," Ia told him, holding up her other hand. "I have a reputation in here. You don't."

"Oy!" Detaching himself from another table, Corporal Spyder swaggered her way, beer in hand. "Ia, izzis meioa botherin' you?"

"Not really, no." Ia glanced briefly at another man entering the bar. Clad in plain civilian clothes, his light brown hair a rumpled mess and exuding an odd, almost entirely un-minty odor, he brushed past Spyder brusquely, nearly making the corporal spill his drink. Mindful that time was running out, she looked back at the man still holding her hand and gestured with her free one at the bar. "Why don't you tell me your name, meioa, and we'll see if it leads to that drink?"

This time, it was Spyder's turn to choke on his beer. He followed at a slight distance, coughing and grinning. Ia had cultivated a friends-only attitude all this time. She knew her old Basic Training teammate was amused by the thought of her actually wanting to date anyone.

"Well, my name is Darroll Rekk-Noth, and I am an independent businessman. I only have a couple of ships in my admittedly small fleet, but I do a fair amount of intersteilar trade. I specialize in rarities, antiquities, and . . ."

Ia held up her hand again, forestalling him.

"Not right now, Drek," she murmured, her gaze on the other man who had entered. That man was muttering in dark tones at the chief waitress, Rostie. She shook her head and hurried to the next table, but the fellow followed.

". . . I *said* I don't want you working here! Get back home, now!" the newcomer ordered the waitress.

"And I said I'll work anyway. I *like* working here." Lifting her chin, Rostie indicated the door. "My shift's up in six and a half hours. Go find something to do until then."

". . . So you recognized me?" the man at Ia's side murmured into her ear. He touched her shoulder at the same time, making the gesture look like a caress. "I wanted to meet the meioa responsible for so much of my business success."

"Of course I did. I knew you'd be here," she murmured back, eyes on the other tableau. She lifted her chin at the man following Rostie, still bothering her. "The same with him."

"So you know I'm here to . . . renegotiate your terms?" her would-be suitor asked.

The man pestering Rostie grabbed her upper arm, jerking her around. "You are *not* going to parade yourself in here like a filthy little bar slut!"

Ia wasn't the only one who moved forward at that, but she was prepared for it; the other Marines were still scraping their chairs back and shoving to their feet when she reached the blue-haired waitress's side. Rostie tried to shrug free. Her spurious boyfriend squeezed harder, making her wince.

"I *said*, go home!"

"And *I* say, get your hand off her," Ia warned him coldly as more of her fellow soldiers stood. "You're in a bar full of big damn heroes, mcioa. Think *carefully* before you do anything else, today."

"You think I'm afraid of *you*?" he snorted, looking her up and down. In her sleeveless vest, the curves of her arm muscles were quite visible. His eyes were bloodshot, his face reddened. "You're nothin' but a slab of unnatural, unfeminine beef!"

"You heard the Sergeant," one of the Marines behind him ordered. "Get your hands off Rostie, and walk away."

Another one leaned in close, sniffing the man. "*Shakk* . . . I know that smell. You're hyped up on poppers! My cousin tried to get me to take that *shova*!"

"Poppers is a one-way ticket to a prison-patch, for a Human," a third Marine stated darkly, cracking her knuckles. "Particularly on a military base."

Purpling with rage, the man released Rostie. His hand darted into a pocket and whipped out again. Ia got there first, stopping his punch with her palm. Ice-cold pain screamed up her nerves from her hand to her brain, followed by a searing hot ache. Even knowing it was coming, despite being willing, it took her a moment to get past the shock of the impact. Blinking, Ia sucked in a slow, unsteady breath.

Her attacker blinked as well. He looked down at their hands, joined at rib-height. Looked back up at her face. Blanched as she met his gaze without flinching.

Teeth clenched against the pain, gut tight against the urge to grunt, Ia slowly curled her fingers down around his. "Let. Go. I will *not* ask you twice."

Brown eyes met amber. Short as they were, Ia dug in her nails. The move put pressure on the wound, causing more pain and more blood to trickle free, but the sting of her warning did the trick. Feeling his fingers relax and release the blade, she lifted her arm a little, displaying to some of the others what had just happened.

The blade, with the curved tip of a bone-knife culled from some kitchen, stuck out of the back of her hand. The hilt had sunk all the way to her palm. Dark crimson dripped down her forearm. The others in the pub hissed and hastily grabbed him. He struggled, trying to throw them off. Ia fisted her fingers around the hilt, squeezing out another trickle, and brought the bloodied blade up in front of his face.

"Either you go with these meioas, nice and quiet . . . or I will backhand you. Yes. With *this* hand. It's your choice, meioa-o. Choose wisely."

"Let's not give him one," growled one of the men holding the idiot. "C'mon, let's haul this *shova*-sack out of here and hold 'im for the Platform Peacekeepers."

Several willing hands hauled him backwards and lifted him up overhead with just a few muttered grunts for coordination. Wending their way through the scattered tables and chairs, they carried the idiot outside to await pickup. Others clustered around Ia, eyeing her hand. A couple grabbed napkins and offered them. She accepted, mostly to wipe up the blood dripping down to her elbow, but shook her head at offers to remove the blade.

". . . I'll let the Platform docs do that. I'd rather not bleed freely from here to the hospital, thank you—and I can make it all the way to them just fine. I'm not about to pass out, trust me." Nodding at her fellow soldiers, she made her way toward the front door. The businessman, Darroll Rekk-Noth, followed her. So did her commanding officer.

As soon as they were outside the tavern, Ferrar lifted his chin at the idiot still being held firmly overhead by the Marines who had carried him out. They had his arms twisted behind his back and crossed his legs, limiting how much the idiot could struggle. "There'll be a trial, of course. Technically, he damaged government property when he struck you. With a lethal weapon, no less. Five to ten years on a penal farm, at the very least."

"I don't care what happens to him. I just want him off this station. If the military wishes him sentenced to a penal farm-patch far, far away, that's fine by me," she quipped as she kept walking. Her attention was more on bracing her hand with her other palm so that the knife wouldn't jostle and injure her any worse. It hurt, but in a different way from a dislocated shoulder, a broken ankle, or even having her shoulder charred halfway through her collarbone. More bearable, in some ways. But it hurt. At least she had managed to twist her palm just enough so that the knife blade had shoved between the bones, limiting the overall damage.

To her relief, Ferrar reversed course as the Peacekeepers arrived. He waved her onward, letting her know in a brief flick of hand signs that he'd arrange it so she got medical aid first before being interrogated over her part in this mess.

"Is your life always like this?" the suited man pacing at her side asked her. "Getting into knife fights with random strangers?

Acting tougher than tough? Or was this just something you staged for my benefit?"

"It's not acting, and it's not staged. I will do whatever it takes to protect innocent lives. Even if my methods aren't . . . orthodox." Mindful of the stares she was garnering from the other personnel, military and civilian, they were passing on their way out of the public sectors, she lowered her voice. "As for any attempt at renegotiation . . . I advise *you* to think carefully, and choose wisely. This is not the worst thing I will backhand you with, if you betray me . . . and I will know in advance and be ready for it. You have my Prophetic Stamp on that.

"You will do as I say, when I say, how I say . . . or I will expose everything you do, and destroy you. I have enough evidence on you, they *won't* sentence you to a pea-patch."

"I have more than enough evidence to implicate *you* as well, meioa," the disguised Drek the Merciless growled back, though he kept a pleasant-seeming smile on his face. "How would your precious military react if I told them what *you* have been up to?"

"I have two words for you, meioa, that give me all the legal freedom I need to do what I need to do. The first one is 'Vladistad.' I'll let you have two guesses as to what the second word is. I'm feeling generous, tonight." She slanted a look at the supposed businessman at her side, and smiled. "Think carefully, meioa. Everything you do at *my* command gives you that legal freedom, too. Even more freedom, since you just have to point at me, and let *me* bear the brunt of explaining it all. Unless you're an idiot, and throw it all away. In which case, I'd have to backhand you with a laser cannon in hand."

The rapid thud of footsteps approaching them from behind warned her someone from the tavern was catching up to them. "Oy, Ia! Y' need an escort?" Spyder trotted up beside her, then twisted and walked sideways a few steps, eyeing the floor. ". . . Or p'raps a mop?"

"I'll be fine. It hurts, but it's not bleeding too much. Ah . . . Spyder, this is Darroll Rekk-Noth, a businessman. Darroll, this is Corporal Spyder. We went through Basic together, and now serve in the same Company." She lifted her chin in lieu of gesturing with a hand, and lengthened her strides. "If you're going to come along, do try to keep up, gentlemen. I'd really rather be safely in the Platform's hospital before I pass out from pain or blood loss."

"Wot, from that little scratch?" Spyder teased her. He grinned when she gave him a dirty look, and matched her stride for stride. He also craned his neck, giving Drek a curious look. "So, why're you walkin' along wi' us?"

"I want to make sure the lovely lady, here, will be all right. And to see if I can do anything to distract her from her pain, once she is patched up." He eyed Ia, his smile never once slipping. "At least, I hope we will be able to see more of each other. She is . . . extraordinary. Don't you think?"

"That's our Bloody Mary, arright," Spyder agreed. "Literally bloody, at times."

The man on her other side gave her a wry smile. "So I've noticed."

Ia kept her mouth shut. Grateful the timestreams had settled firmly in her favor, she concentrated on carrying her hand without jostling it. Drek had seen and heard enough to change back his attempted change-of-mind. He was too important to her plans to let slip out of her grasp. Even if he was a murderous, thieving pirate and would-be crimelord, she needed him.

OCTOBER 25, 2491 T.S.
SUBSURFACE EMERGENCY TUNNELS
OBERON'S ROCK

Ia paused just long enough to swipe her forehead over her red-clad bicep. It smeared the dirt around, but did reduce the amount of sweat beating on her face, threatening to drip into her eyes. Not that the tunnel was warm, but her exertions were taking a toll.

Face more or less dry, she went back to heaving rocks, working steadily despite the dust and the darkness hampering their efforts. Beside her, eight of the twelve trapped in the emergency tunnel with her grunted over the effort to move the larger stones, and hauled away the smaller ones. Behind them rested their three wounded.

Hunters and Mitchell, both of them from the 3rd Platoon, had broken bones. Their limbs had been crudely straightened by hand and left to lie on the floor for lack of any splints. Hmongwa, from the 2nd Platoon like Ia, had a badly sprained ankle and a concussion; he couldn't see out of one eye and couldn't really focus with the other, so he was resting with the other two. The remaining men and women were from the 1st Platoon; they were battered and bruised, but they were alive and mobile.

Their supplies were limited; the emergency sirens had sounded the alarm pattern for an imminent dome breach, and everyone had scrambled to get underground. Like Ia, the mobile ones were digging without pause in the hopes of unburying themselves. They had no food but for a couple napkins filled with hors d'ouvres, no water but a couple of plexi cups that used to hold beer, and no equipment beyond the small spotlights built into their wrist units. Unfortunately, the metallic content of the local rock was playing havoc with their attempts to call for a rescue.

So all they could do was dig. They almost hadn't had Ia to help them. She had a bruised head and several scrapes down her arms and back from having raced through the falling debris even as the first of the bombs had struck, but she was here.

No one but Ia had known the attack, or rather, counterattack was coming. The *Liu Ji* had arrived in time to thwart another attempted invasion. The colonists, grateful for yet another rescue, had organized a party for everyone. It had just about ended when the raiders came back from wherever they had fled to just eight or so hours before. This time, their intent was to strafe and shatter the research domes. Mass murder, venting the air inside to outer space, would allow them to pick through the debris at their leisure.

She knew, though no one else did, that the Lyebariko had planned for this in case their latest attempt was thwarted yet again. With the *Liu Ji* orbiting in a loop that had taken them to the far side of the planetoid's surface, they no doubt thought the Terrans had moved on to their next patrol spot. They hadn't. Not because Ia had warned Captain Ferrar, but because Oberon's governor insisted on throwing a party for the meioas who kept coming back and saving their hides.

The only thing she had done about this potential disaster was electrokinetically trigger the dome sirens about eight minutes early, saving thousands of lives. Everyone was safely tucked underground when the first enemy missile struck. Well, safely, except for this lot.

"Keep digging," Ia urged them. She kept her tone matter-of-fact, aware just how close most of them were to despair. The noise of the bombardment had stopped hours ago. She knew it was because the *Liu Ji* had been joined by another warship, driving away the Lyebariko's smaller, less heavily armed fleet. The others didn't.

Private Gunga stumbled on a patch of grit and dropped the rock he was carrying. He cursed and hopped, then sagged to the ground. "Gods . . . I'm so tired . . ."

"We just need to dig far enough to get to the next air pocket," Ia urged them. She knew exactly where it was, and that it wasn't far away, now. She also knew it connected to a functioning lifesupport bay, which would supply them with just enough air to stay alive until the others could find and dig them free. "They have oxygenators all over the place in these tunnels."

"Just not in the patch *we* picked," Hunters grunted, briefly lifting his head. He gasped and panted, holding himself still. "Goddamn collarbone . . . goddamn arm . . ."

"Think of something else," Ia urged.

"Like what?" Lok'tor asked. The corporal was from the 1st Platoon, and sweating even more than Ia. "Like the fact I'm gonna have to piss in one of those cups in a few more minutes, just so I don't bust my bladder? And then, what, drink it?"

Gunga chuckled, gathering himself to get up again. "Won't taste any worse than that piss they called beer." He regained his feet with a grunt, only to stagger and drop. "Ugh . . . I don't feel so good . . ."

"Hold it together, Gunga," Ia told him. "This is no worse than Hell Week, and you know it."

"Hell, this *shova*'s *easier* than Hell Week," Mitchell muttered from her position on the floor next to Hunters. Her legs were broken and swollen, though at least neither of them had compound fractures.

"Yeah, you just get to . . . uhn! Lie on your back, while we do all the work," Lok'tor grunted. She staggered as well, stumbling back against the wall. ". . . Oh, that's not good. The . . . air is getting thick in here."

"Keep working, Corporal," Ia ordered, forced to pick her way up and down the rock pile now that two of them were taking a break. "We only had three strikes that sounded like they hit close overhead. The damage to these tunnels can't be that bad."

"Says you," Gunga grunted. He tried to push up again, only to sag back down. "Permission to . . . to pass out, Sergeant?"

Ia didn't stop working. She could feel the air growing stale, too, but knew they needed to keep shifting the rubble between them and the oxygen they needed. "Permission denied, soldier."

". . . *Shakk* you."

She didn't take offense. She slid a large rock halfway down the slope, ignoring the thumps and bruises of several smaller rocks rattling down around her ankles. Like the others, she was clad in civilian clothes for the party, though she at least had been forewarned enough to wear pants and calf-length boots. Heaving the stone up, she carried it to the far end of their patch of tunnel and let it drop with a cracking *crunch* on several of the others.

Turning back, Ia played her wrist unit light over the faces of her fellow soldiers as she strode past. The beam wasn't very strong, but it was enough to make them flinch. "Marines *do not* give up. Marines *do not* leave anyone behind. Marines *do not* lie down and die. And so long as *I* am your ranking officer, I will do *everything* in my power to make sure you survive.

"We just need to dig far enough to reach the next pocket of air."

"Hey! I think I found . . . something . . . Oh . . . oh, God." Davisson, Gunga's teammate, scrabbled at the debris shoved aside by Ia's falling rock. Gunga shoved off the floor and Lok'tor off the wall, joining them in digging out the dusty shoe he had found . . . and the foot it was attached to. And the leg. "Oh . . . God."

Ia joined them. In grim silence, they unburied the crushed corpse of Private First Class Paul McDaniels, 1st Platoon C Squad Beta. Once he was free from the debris, the others slumped to their knees, heads bowed. Ia bowed her head for a moment as well, then stooped and picked him up.

"Marines don't leave *anyone* behind, if we can help it," she murmured. "We'll bring him out with us, and anyone else we find."

"Gods damn you to the foulest depths of Gehenna!" Gunga half shouted, half panted. "We are *not* getting out! We are going to *die* down here!"

"Is that what you believe?" Ia asked calmly. The smell of dirt and blood and worse made the air thicker than she wanted to breathe. Turning away, she carried McDaniel's body to the far end of the pocket that had saved most of them, and knelt to lay him in state.

"What kind of fairy tale do you live in, Sergeant?" That came from Lok'tor. "We're trapped down here. We can't get a signal through, we're running out of air . . . *nobody* knows we're down here!"

"I don't live in a fairy tale. I just refuse to give up." She laid the battered hands at their owner's sides and murmured a benediction. "May whatever god you prayed to have compassion for your soul, Paul . . . and give strength to your fellow Marines to carry on."

"Carry on where?" Mitchell asked. She coughed and panted, watching Ia rise and turn toward her and the others. "The air's . . . so thick . . ."

"That's because you're lying down where the carbon dioxide is piling up. Tang, Davisson, shift those rocks and make a platform. We'll move Hunters and Mitchell up above the worst of it. And then we will keep digging," Ia told them.

Nobody moved. She tipped her head slightly, studying them, until her gaze fell on Lok'tor.

"You may all want to lie down and die . . . but if we die, then I will be found still trying to dig us out. Still doing *my* duty." She slapped her left palm on her breastbone and left it there, illuminating her face in the dim glow of its miniature spotlight. "*I* will be found still trying to save your lives.

"Now. Get up, piss in a cup, and get back to moving those rocks, Dinea," she ordered Lok'tor softly. Implacably. "*You* still have lives to save, too."

Lok'tor stared back.

Hmongwa, blinking and not quite focusing on anything, shifted on his hip. He scooted closer to the end of the tunnel they had been trying to uncover, scraping grit with each hitch. "I can't stand . . . and can't exactly focus . . . but I'm not worn out. I can't carry anything anywhere, but you prop me up there, Ia, and I'll pass you the rocks. The others can rest for a while."

Lok'tor shifted her gaze to him. Watched him *shuff* closer to her end of the tunnel. Slowly, she moved. Pushed from her knees to her feet, and turned back to the remainder of the pile they had shifted, rock by rock, from the far left to the far right for far too long. Davisson met Ia's gaze only briefly in the dim, patchy light before he, too, turned back to work on the rubble. Tang followed him, murmuring suggestions as the pair shifted one of the large pieces into a base for a makeshift ledge.

Stepping up to Hunters, Ia crouched and met both his and Mitchell's worried looks. "This is going to hurt like hell when we move you, but it'll give all of us a little more time."

Mitchell, both of her legs broken, nodded in understanding. "I'm not ready to die."

"*Shakk!* Watch it, meioa!" Davisson swore, dodging down and back as Lok'tor's actions shifted the rock pile.

Lok'tor started to slide down with the rocks she had dislodged, then jerked and scrambled upward. That sent more debris scattering down, but the sound of her dragging in a deep, ragged lungful of fresh air made the dangers of her precarious perch not matter. She did it again, silencing everyone.

"Oh, God—air! I can't *see* anything, but . . ." Another lungful and she slithered back down. "I'm smelling fresh air!"

The other mobile members surged forward, abandoning building the platform in favor of forming another rock-toting chain. Lowering her arm, hiding her face in the darkness, Ia smiled. She'd known how close they were, more or less.

"Work carefully," she cautioned the others. "Now is *not* the time to break something from carelessness. A Marine never gives up, and a Marine never makes a mistake if it can be helped."

Gunga grunted and swiped the sweat from his own brow. "Ugh . . . the air's not clearing fast enough. I still feel like I'm going to pass out, here."

"Permission still denied, Private," Ia quipped, moving forward to join them in widening the gap. "Besides, Marines *don't* faint. We engage the floor in mortal combat."

The others laughed. They coughed and strained to move large chunks of broken bedrock, but as the gap and its trickle of fresher air widened with each effort, they laughed.

CHAPTER 18

Was there any resentment in the troops when I was jumped up from mere Squad Sergeant to Company Sergeant after Sergeant Pleistoch was reassigned? Not in Ferrar's Fighters. And not from anyone else who knew me on the Hum-Vee/Johannes circuit. I had earned their trust, and their faith in my abilities. I stayed with the Captain as one year became two, testing psychologically sound and thus fit for continued combat duty. Not everyone can, but in my case, I could, and the military wisely wasn't going to waste my abilities at a desk job.

Once they moved Battle Platform Johannes into the same system as Oberon's Rock—I'll admit, at my suggestion and Captain Ferrar's formally worded request—it silenced the tech piracy attacks. Of course, that ended up causing other problems down the road in turn. But it wasn't as bad as it could have been. I did have the faith of the men and women both in Captain Ferrar's Company, and on board the Liu Ji. With their faith, we were able to accomplish great things.

~Ia

MARCH 29, 2492 T.S.
OBSERVATION STATION *IVEZIC*
ZELJKO 17 BINARY SYSTEM

The setup was perfect.

With Battle Platform *Johannes* relocated by a couple days of travel, their patrol route had been altered to include *Ivezic* Station, located more toward the nadir of the galactic plane. It was more of a combination of refueling depot, mineral refinery, and astronomical research facility than a bustling port of call, but they were pleased to get the contract to service and support the Terran Space Force. And they were pleased to show that, backwater-ish though they were, they were still quite cultured.

Particularly when one of the companies sponsoring the stellar research also sponsored a touring musical production, nudging it into swinging by *Ivezic* for a series of live performances. They also gave the entire crew of the *Liu Ji* and its Marine Company free tickets. Not that the entire crew and Company could fit into the station's modest combination of auditorium and performance theater at one time, but—as Ia knew they would—Captain Sudramara and Captain Ferrar decided the Marines would attend one show and the Navy the other.

As a special treat, the acting company issued invitations to the officers and noncoms to party with them in the theater's greenroom after the performance. Flattered by the invitation, Ferrar ordered his lieutenants and sergeants to attend both the performance and the party in formal Dress Blacks.

Ia couldn't have been more pleased than if she herself had lent a hand in setting it all up. Not with such irresistible bait. Not so pleased that she had to pin all of her medals and honors to her dress jacket, with its satin black color and brown satin stripes down the sleeves, but that everything was proceeding exactly as she had foreseen.

Right down to the need, halfway into the party, to visit one of the restrooms. Concluding her business and washing her hands, she lingered at the mirror over the sink. Lingered, and waited, fussing minutely first with her snow white hair, which had been recently trimmed into a neat, uniform bob cut ending just below her ears. Her hat was still back in the greenroom, which had grown a bit warm from the press of bodies. Once her hair was smoothed enough, to kill some of the intervening minutes, she fussed with the medals pinned to her chest.

By now, she had accumulated several honors. Nine Honor Crosses for exemplary conduct above and beyond the call of duty. Eight Skulls, and twenty-three Crossbones, for taking out or capturing known enemy commanders and noncommissioned officers. Three Target Crosses for exemplary sniper fire, and a Scout Cross for exceptional scouting—that one, she had earned on Oberon's Rock, along with one of her three Vanguard Stars, and the rarely granted Civilian Award of Merit. It was one of the highest peacetime awards a soldier could earn from a local civilian government; Oberon's governor had bestowed it upon the members of Ferrar's Company for their consistent, repeated rescues, not just Ia.

Her jacket also bore six White Crosses, one for each incident involving the rescue of wounded or trapped comrades, and of course her eight Purple Hearts. The one ribbon bar she wore was striped in the purples and greens patterned to represent the Border Patrol she still served, but it held four tiny bronze stars on its surface, representing the four six-month tours of duty she had undertaken so far.

The left side of her jacket therefore literally glittered, even down to the snaps on the lower half of her left sleeve, which could be unsnapped so that she could access her arm unit freely. Dress Browns, she would have worn just one of each type of medal. But this was a major touring show; the lead performers were some of the most current, famous faces in the Alliance. Ferrar had insisted on Dress Blacks, which included her formal black cap, the polished sword stowed in its baldric-supported sheath at her hip, and the full, glittering array of her honors and merits.

Unpinning one of her Purple Hearts, she carefully re-pinned it, fastening the clasp just so, then checked the fit of the blade sheathed at her side, loosening it just a little bit. Some of the others had set aside their caps and their blades for the party, but she hadn't. Particularly not this blade. Her brother had shipped it to her all the way from Sanctuary, where it had waited in one of her storage lockers. It wasn't a standard issue Marines saber, for all she had commissioned an artist to coat the blade and hilt in silver gilt, making it look normal. Instead, she had crafted it three years ago to look like a schläger, a thin, straight-edged dueling sword.

This blade was about to save her life.

Footsteps approached the unisex bathroom. The door hissed open behind her; the soft sound was followed by the *phunt* of an air gun. At the same moment the door opened, Ia spun, hand snapping out and back in again.

Two years of practice had honed her abilities, both in combat and in battle precognition. Mind linked with the timestreams, her fingers snapped down on the shaft of the tiny dart, stopping it before it could strike through the fabric covering her opposite shoulder. It would have lodged in her back if she hadn't been prepared.

The foremost of her three assailants widened his eyes. He glanced between her and his gun, and fired again. She caught that tranquilizer with her left hand. The other two started to reach for their own weapons, then quickly spun to the left as someone else approached.

"Hey, Ia," she heard D'kora call out. "You're taking too long. You're missing a . . . the hell . . . ?"

Ia flung the first dart as the first man started to turn as well. He slapped his hand to the back of his neck, hissing in pain, but it was too late. He sagged even as the others whipped around again at the noise he made.

The pair exchanged quick looks. "Right," one of them said, giving the other a brief, significant look. "Plan B."

Once again, they grabbed for the weapons concealed in their clothes. Ia moved, too. Plan B was "kill them all" and there was no way *that* was going to happen. Gritting her teeth, Ia jumped and slammed her palm down onto the edge of the porcelain sink next to her.

It *cracked* off the wall, startling both of the remaining two men. They looked back just in time to see her grabbing the edge of the sagging sink and ripping it off its plexi pipes with the brute force of arm and mind. Water splashed as she flung it at them. They dove out of the doorway, but not completely in time. The sink basin *thumped* into one of the men, knocking him over and sending his gun flying.

Behind her, an alarm started buzzing, warning the station's personnel of the break in the pipes. Ia lunged through the doorway, flinging the other dart at the downed man, who was struggling to get back to his feet. He slumped back down with a curse, fumbling briefly at the tiny cylinder poking out of his bicep before dropping slack. Whatever drug was in those darts, it was powerful.

The third had already encountered the confused but not helpless D'kora. His gun was still clattering to the floor as she blocked his follow-up punch. She was fast and strong; Ia heard bones crunching. So was he; D'kora *oofed* and staggered back from his retaliatory kick. He was also not alone; two others came running up behind the lieutenant.

Ia drew her sword and lunged, gritting her teeth for what she knew came next. D'kora whirled to face them, giving one a roundhouse kick. The man between her and Ia grabbed the lieutenant from behind, one arm wrapping around her chest and shoulder, the other wrapping around the brunette's head. Even as Ia swung, closing the distance between them, his shoulders flexed. D'kora's neck *crunched*. He released her and swung around to meet Ia's attack.

Time was not on D'kora's side. There was nothing Ia could do for the lieutenant but fling out her free hand, cushioning the older woman's fall with a fierce pulse of her will, preventing her death. But Ia could slash her blade through the assassin's neck. That didn't *crunch* so much as *thock*. Droplets of blood *thwapped* against the corridor wall as the sword followed through. A shove of her free hand toppled body, upraised arm, and head to the floor in three separate pieces.

The two newcomers widened their eyes and backpedaled hastily, to avoid both her advance and the blood gushing across the floor. One hastily raised his gun, a familiar style of overclocked laser pistol. Ia snapped her blade up. Bright, yellow orange light struck the silvered weapon. Acrid smoke hissed up for a moment. He fired again, backing up another step. Again, her blade caught the beam . . . guided by a touch of her mind on *his* hand, making sure the laser and the sword would properly connect. Not even she could dodge the speed of light, after all.

Not in a flesh-and-blood body.

He tossed the gun down and turned to run. Ia lunged low, slashing hard. He screamed, collapsing, thighs no longer attached to his knees. The other one swapped weapons and fired at her with his projectile pistol. Again, her blade snapped into place; the bullet *tinged* off the flat. The sword bounced in her hand, almost slapping her shoulder, but she didn't lose her grip. He fired again. She flicked her blade, and deflected the second shot.

The last of her attackers stumbled farther back. "*Shakk . . .* that ain't natural! You ain't real!"

"*I* am Bloody Mary, the herald of death. And *I* will be the last thing you see, unless you tell me *everything* I want to know."

Eyes widening, he hastily re-aimed his gun. Not at her, but at the two men slumped by the doorway of the bathroom.

And now we're up to Plan C. Kill anyone on their own side to stifle chance at an interrogation. Ia blocked both shots, scattering more droplets of blood, then flicked the too-sharp blade across his wrist as he lifted the handgun to his own head. He gasped and dropped the gun, tendons and veins severed.

Grabbing his wrist with her free hand, Ia slammed her hilt-bearing fist into his face, stunning him. A second blow, not too hard, knocked him out. Most of the man dropped to the floor, save for the arm still caught in her grip. Applying pressure to the bleeding wound she had made, Ia tugged apart the snaps on her left sleeve and thumbed open the comm link on her arm unit, balancing the sword awkwardly as she worked.

"*Sergeant Ia to the* Liu Ji. *Code India Alpha! I repeat, India Alpha! Lieutenant D'kora and I have been attacked by unknown assailants, Section 5, Deck 9, outside the auditorium green-room on* Ivezic *Station. I repeat, Lt. D'kora and Sergeant Ia have been attacked by unknown assailants, Section 5, Deck 9, outside the auditorium greenroom. D'kora is down, and badly injured. She's breathing, but I think her neck is broken. I have three prisoners, two of them unconscious from tranquilizers, and one of them about to bleed to death if I let go. India Alpha, all available personnel arm and get to the station greenroom. I have no idea who else is involved.*"

"*Acknowledged, Sergeant, code India Alpha, copy. The Navy is responding with all dispatch to your distress call. We are contacting the station Peacekeepers as well. Keep this link open, Sergeant. We'll get there as fast as we can.*"

"*Acknowledged. I, ah . . . made quite a mess defending myself and the lieutenant,*" she added, looking down at the blood seeping across the floor, at the dark spots dampening her dress uniform. "*Be prepared. Ia on standby.*"

Not wanting to let go of her captive, but needing to clean her blade, Ia wiped it against his arm. She wrinkled her nose at the patches of translucent gold that showed through the silver gilt, seared away by the laser fire. She made several passes, getting the blade as clean as possible, then slid it home in its scabbard.

"Liu Ji to Sergeant Ia, we are unable to hail Captain Ferrar, Lieutenant Konietzny, or Lieutenant Nguyen. Their wrist units appear to be in the greenroom but are not responding. Can you confirm their location and condition?"

"Negative. I am currently keeping watch over my three prisoners in a side corridor near the bathrooms, and am not in the actual greenroom."

"Acknowledged. Routing Master Petty Tanaka and his team to the greenroom direct—ah, we have Sergeant Spyder on the comm; he's en route to your location as well."

"Acknowledged. Ia on standby." Fingers still clamped around that bloodied wrist, she waited for the rest of the events to unfold. Ia already knew Spyder had escaped because he'd walked out of the greenroom with a lovely lady from the stage crew a few minutes before she had gone to the restroom. They had retreated to a dressing room on the far side of the theater for some privacy, so it wouldn't take him long to reach her side; a couple of the others had retired early from the party, but Spyder was closest. The man dangling from her hand mumbled and shifted, rousing slightly.

Oh, no you don't. Time for you to repair some of the damage you did to the lieutenant. Dragging him over, fingers still clamped around his wounded wrist, she crouched and very, very gently touched D'kora's face. Her biokinesis didn't extend well to others, but she could give some help to the other woman. Namely the transfer of some of the life-energy of the idiot in her grasp. A faint, burning warmth flowed up through the nerves from her left hand, and poured cool and calm down through her right. The idiot sagged, dropping unconscious. D'kora lay there and breathed, motionless.

"Stay with me, D'kora. Don't try to move," she warned the woman. Not that D'kora could move, but Ia knew she was partially conscious, and wanted her to know to keep still. "You're badly injured, but you will pull through. They're going to have to use an immobilizer on you, since I think your neck is broken, but the docs on the *Liu Ji* are on the way.

"Don't you worry. I've got your back. We all do."

Easing back on the flow, Ia eyed her prisoners. By now, the Captain, lieutenants, and other sergeants had been dragged off down a service corridor, knocked unconscious along with every-one else in the greenroom party by hidden, timed stunner grenades. They would be hauled on board an OTL, other-than-light, courier shuttle that would undock right about the same time that the *Liu Ji*'s crew arrived at the greenroom, and vanish through a hyperrift long before the next scheduled patrol ship, the TUPSF *Havelock*, arrived.

On board the *Havelock* was not only an Army Company as well as the usual Navy crew, but an Army lieutenant general, Vestoc Sranna. At his rank, he was technically a member of the Command Staff, capable of overseeing any Branch of the Space Force in an emergency. Sranna would therefore be her next-nearest superior, once D'kora was declared unfit for duty. Between now and then, both Ia's prisoners and D'kora had to survive. She would make sure they did.

The latter didn't necessarily have to survive in good shape, though. Their fates were already sealed. Footsteps hurried up the corridor, slowing quickly as Spyder encountered the edge of the mix of blood and water slicking the floor. Picking his way forward, he wrinkled his nose at her.

"Oy, Ia, you sure like t' keep yer nickname fresh, doncha?" he managed to quip, though he swallowed at the carnage scattered around her feet.

"Only if I absolutely have to," she muttered back. "Don't touch Lt. D'kora—her neck's probably broken. See what you can find to strip and secure those two," she added, nodding at the intact bodies on the floor behind her. "They had an accident with a pair of trank cartridges, but I don't know how long they'll stay out."

"I'm onnit," he agreed, picking his way across the slippery floor.

Bathed and changed into fresh camouflage Browns, her sword re-slung at her side, Ia hurried to keep up with Major Keating, chief doctor on board the *Liu Ji*. The woman had tended to several of Ia's own wounds with aplomb in the past, but it was clear D'kora's condition had her worried.

"She's insisting on talking to you before we put her into the goo for the first round of regeneration treatments." Keating stated, striding up the corridor from the lifts to the Infirmary.

Ia suppressed the urge to snicker. Most of her fellow grunts referred to the blue gel as *goo*, but it was amusing to hear a medical professional doing the same. However, this was not the best moment for her rare sense of humor to surface.

"I'm not sure if it'll be enough to stop the swelling currently putting pressure on her spinal cord. She may need surgery, but my specialty isn't neurology. My best hope right now is to get her stabilized enough for transport. But to do that, she has to go into the goo . . . and to do *that*, she wants to talk to you, first. Brace yourself."

Ia nodded. She knew what was coming. They stopped outside one of the treatment wards and sterilized their hands under the scrubber rays stationed next to the door. Stepping inside, the chief medical officer led Ia up to the humming, monitor-equipped bed. D'kora had been strapped into something that looked more like a medieval torture device than modern medicine. But it cupped the older woman's forehead and shoulders, and looked quite sturdy. Immobile, which was what the injured heavyworlder needed.

"Lieutenant D'kora, Sergeant Ia is here." Gesturing for Ia to lean over the portable bed so she could be seen by the prone officer, Keating moved back out of the way.

Ia stepped up, taking her place. She had to place her hand on the hilt of her sword as she did so, to keep it from banging into the bed. "Lieutenant."

"Sergeant." The words were quiet, nearly a whisper. She couldn't consciously draw in a lungful, but had to pause between autonomous breaths. Ia leaned closer, concentrating as D'kora spoke. "They gave me . . . a report. Three prisoners."

"Sir, yes, sir. They've been stripped, tended, and locked in the *Liu Ji*'s brig. I'm on my way down to interrogate them after reporting to you, sir," she said.

"And the rest . . . captured."

"Twelve of the sergeants in attendance, the other two lieutenants, and the Captain, yes, sir," Ia confirmed. "None of the actors, director, or theater crew in attendance were injured, other than a few bumps and bruises when they fell down. More than that . . . they came prepared with tranquilizer darts. They *knew* I'm resistant to stunner fire, sir, and knew in advance."

"Whoever they are . . . they have their hooks into . . . the military. Spies here, or on the Platforms. Don't . . ." D'kora paused, gathering her strength. "Don't go to our immediate superiors. Go straight to the nearest Command Staff. That's an order."

"Sir, yes, sir." Just as she had anticipated.

"Major Keating . . ." D'kora flicked her eyes to the side, indicating what she wanted.

"Doctor?" Ia asked, looking over her shoulder. The major moved around to the other side of the treatment bed.

"I'm here, Lieutenant."

"Record . . . these orders, Major," D'kora ordered.

Ia watched as the major flicked open her command wrist unit and pressed a couple buttons. "Ready when you are, Lieutenant D'kora."

"My last act as surviving . . . senior officer, I am . . . promoting First Sergeant Ia . . . to Acting Lieutenant Second Class. Battlefield promotion. She is in command of . . . A Company, 3rd Legion, 9th Battalion, 3rd Brigade, 2nd Cordon, Terran United Planted Space Force . . . Branch Marine Corps, effective immediately." D'kora fixed the other woman with a look that lacked strength, but lost nothing in significance. "Confirm and copy that, Doctor. *Then* you can remove me . . . from active duty."

"About *time*, you stubborn meioa," the chief medical officer muttered. She cleared her throat and spoke clearly, letting her words be recorded. "I, Major Keating of the Space Force Branch Navy Medical 5th Cordon, and medical auxiliary to the Branch Marine Corps 2nd Cordon, hereby concur and concede the elevation of First Sergeant Ia to the rank of Acting Lieutenant Second Class and acting commanding officer of the designated Marine Company in question."

Lifting her unit, Keating nodded at Ia, who hastily raised her own. The orders were synched, then the doctor nodded at her wrist unit.

"I'll imprint an official chip with the transcript and file it with Captain Sudramara. He'll probably add his own agreement. You just go out there and get the sonovas who did this to her, Acting Lieutenant Ia. And get your superior officers back. In one piece, and alive," the doctor added. "That includes yourself, you know. I'm getting tired of patching you up."

"Sir, yes, sir. I fully agree, sir," Ia said, saluting her. Keating saluted back, then shooed her out of the ward.

———————

General Sranna was short, balding, and stocky, a fellow heavy-worlder. Not from Sanctuary, of course, but from Eiaven. Ia had contacted him with the message that there was a Situation on board the *Liu Ji* and her superior officer had requested that he handle it.

The first thing he did after coming aboard and being briefed on the situation was to visit Lieutenant D'kora. She was sub-merged in goo from shoulders to scalp, sedated not only to keep her from injuring her neck, but because of the incisions on the back of her neck, in the hopes that the regenerative fluids would reach her injuries without requiring complicated neurosurgery. She didn't respond to his presence.

After viewing her recumbent, torture-device-wrapped figure in silence, the lieutenant general quietly insisted on being on hand when the prisoners awoke. So did Ia. He didn't object. She spoke up when they reached the brig. "Do you wish to take the lead on these interrogations, sir?"

"No. Not at first," he amended. "I checked your file. It's become rather sticky with several DoI fingerprints. I want to see how you handle an interrogation, Acting Lieutenant. If you mess up on the first prisoner, I'll step in on the next. If not . . . it's your show." Sranna nodded at the guards she had ordered into place. "So far, I like the security precautions you're taking."

"Thank you, sir." She nodded at the nearer of the armed pair of Marines stationed opposite the brig door. "Open it up, Private Gunga."

"Sergeant, yes, Se—er, sir, yes, sir!" he corrected himself. Stepping across the corridor, he typed in the command key for the door controls. His teammate, Davisson, aimed his stunner rifle at the doorway. The panel slid open and another Marine poked a white and black muzzle out the opening. Both held their fire long enough to confirm identities, then the one inside resumed his inward-pointed stance, echoing his partner. Ia and Sranna stepped inside, letting them seal the door shut again.

Captain Sudramara was already inside, talking quietly with the Navy brig officer. The swarthy, blue-uniformed man nodded at the green-garbed general. "General, sir."

"Ship's Captain Sudramara of the *Liu Ji*, this is Lieutenant General Sranna, 3rd Cordon Army," Ia introduced briefly. She surveyed the trio of doors with red-glowing "occupied" lights, and panned her finger back and forth for a moment. "I'll interrogate *this* one. Open it up, Ensign."

She picked the door in the middle, which contained the man whose wrist she had slit. Captain Sudramara nodded at the brig officer, who saluted and moved to open it up. General Sranna cleared his throat. The ensign hesitated, glancing back at the lieutenant general.

"Lieutenant Ia, your weapon?" Sranna asked. "Aren't you going to remove it, first?"

Both of the Marines *snerked*. The brig officer struggled to smother a smile. Captain Sudramara outright snorted. "You're talking about Bloody Mary, sir. Medical says the man's a lightworlder. Even if he wasn't bound down, he'd never get to it first, and certainly couldn't pry it out of her hand."

"You didn't see the mess she made of their bodies with that blade, General," the Marine who had met them at the door stated. "The one in that cell is still recovering from what she did to him with it. The others are all very dead, sir."

Captain Sudramara frowned at Ia. "How *did* you manage that, anyway? The security vids were at a bad angle and didn't catch everything, but they did show several unbelievably clean, straight cuts. Plus the fact that you threw a sink, among other things."

"Let's save that for the coming interview," Ia quipped, lifting her chin at the middle door. "Open it up, Ensign."

The young man hesitated again, glancing at his captain and the general. When both nodded agreement, he pressed his thumbprint to the scanner. The red light by the door shifted to green. Ia stepped up to it and palmed the door open.

Inside, the man whose wrist she had severed sat on the plain, air-cushion-lined cot. He was naked, stripped of all his clothes, and his wrists were shackled and held apart by a spreader bar. That bar was kept from being lifted higher than abdomen level by a set of chains attached to manacles at his ankles and to the foot and the head of the bed. His right wrist was wrapped with a short length of lumpy bandaging tape strapped just above the metal cuffs; the lump was actually a small regen pack, sealed over the stitched-together wound on his wrist.

"Naked?" Sranna asked. "With that . . . thing holding his hands apart?"

"It's to keep him from picking open the wound and bleeding to death. He can't move more than two feet in any direction, bound like that." Ia stated, stepping inside. She met the glare of their captive with a slight smile. "Their clothes were taken away, their hair checked for garroting wires, their digestive tracts scanned, and even their teeth examined for poison capsules. Which is ironic, since we discovered each already had been dosed with a specific poison. If they didn't receive the antidote within half an hour after attempting their attack . . . well, they would have died about twenty minutes ago."

Their prisoner frowned at her, his jaw dropping.

Ia smiled. "Yes, you've been sedated that long. I suspected it when I saw you trying to kill your two companions and yourself, when your attack against Lieutenant D'kora and me failed. While your friends were sleeping off the tranquilizers, and you were anesthetized for surgery on your wrist, the medical staff ran all those tests. They determined what you'd been doped with, and concocted antidotes for all three of you . . . since each of you had been dosed with something slightly different from the rest."

"Clever," General Sranna praised from behind her. "Both of you. A means to ensure no one can tell tales if they're captured . . . and the wit to realize the possibility and stop it."

"Oh, this idiot didn't devise it. His masters did," Ia said dismissively. She stepped into the cell. The prisoner dipped his gaze briefly to the hilt of her sword and back. Ia smiled slowly. "I see you remember me. Did you like seeing your companions cut down by my blade? Their deaths were swift and merciful . . . well, as swift and merciful as dying from severed limbs and massive blood loss can be. But then, I am Bloody Mary. It's an occupational hazard around me."

He curled his lip in a sneer. "Do you think you scare me? You don't. You have no idea who you're dealing with. You're nothing."

"At the moment, I am dealing with a little *pissant* nothing who is naked and bound in a military brig. If you mean your masters, they're not here to whip you to death." She planted her hands on her hips and shrugged, tapping into the timestreams. "I guess that means I'll have to do it."

He snorted, glancing at the blue-and-green-clad officers watching the two of them from beyond the open cell door. Straining against his bonds, he leaned back against the wall on the far side of the cot and lifted his chin at her. "You can't do anything to me."

Her right hand snapped down, slashed out, and flicked back again. Touching blade tip to scabbard mouth, she slid the sword home again. Behind her, the general, captain, and even the ensign all sucked in a sharp breath. Ia kept her gaze on the prisoner.

He blinked, and tried to lift his hand to his scalp. The chain and the stretcher bar wouldn't let him. Hesitating, he finally shook his head a little . . . and stared as a couple tufts of his thumb-length brown locks drifted down over his shoulder and chest. "What the . . ."

Ia snatched her sword out of its scabbard again, this time flourishing it on the other side of his head. Whirling it back to the sheath, she slid it back into place. Again he blinked, and again a moment later, hesitantly shook his head. More locks fluttered down.

If he hadn't been leaning against the wall as he was, chained so firmly in place that he couldn't really move much, she wouldn't have dared. While she had taken the time to repaint the flaked-off spots silver again, her blade was still what it was beneath the gilt disguising its nature: deadly sharp.

He swallowed and lifted his chin again. "I'm not scared."

Again, she smiled slowly. "You should be."

"Of what, a big-asteroid razor?" he countered.

This time, she drew her sword slowly. Bringing the pointed tip of the schläger down on the spreader bar resting in front of his shins, she tapped it with a *ting-ting-tinngg*. "This bar— indeed, the whole setup confining you—was crafted for us by the station's machine shop while you were unconscious. It's made from solid steel."

Whipping the blade around, she whacked the bar with a *TANG* that echoed through the cell and out into the rest of the brig. It bounced against its bindings with a clatter of loops and eyelets . . . and something else *ting-tinged* onto the floor. With the point now hovering close to his throat, pinning him in place without a word, Ia slowly bent and scooped up that sliver. Eyes locked with the prisoner's, she rose and displayed the slice of metal. It was nearly ten centimeters long, slightly oval, and pointed at both ends. Her blade descended, tapping the spreader bar once more.

"Solid. Steel."

The bar looked like it had been flattened in a narrow, pointed oval roughly ten centimeters long. Brown eyes wide, he stared at the shaved section between his knees, the sword in her right hand, the sliver in her left, and her face. Back to the bar, to the blade, the sliver . . . and her face.

"What the *shakk is* that thing?" he whispered, watching the tip of the blade rise with visible fear in his gaze.

"You know, I'm really not quite sure," she quipped, tucking the sliver of metal into her shirt pocket. "I just like to call it the Reaper's Blade . . . for it will cut down anything, and anyone, that gets in my way."

"So, what does that make you?" her would-be assassin challenged, regathering some of his attitude. "Death?"

Ia shook her head at the sneered word, her tone soft, almost gentle. "No. I am not Death. I am merely Her herald. I stand before you now, ahead of the coming of Lady Death, singing a warning to all to get out of her way. And you," she murmured, tapping the tip of the blade very, very lightly against the flat section of the bar in between each phrase, *ting*, "—are in—" *ting*, "the way."

Ting . . . ting . . . ting . . .

The slow, rhythmic tap was barely audible. Quiet enough, they could all hear the ventilators whooshing faintly, feel the faint *thrum* of the ship's generators. Sense the soft intake and exhale of each person's breath. Like a wind chime in the distance, it seemed almost sweet, each tap somewhere between metallic and crystalline. She kept tapping the bar, tap . . . tap . . . *ting . . . ting . . .* and stopped.

Silence stretched. Her eyes never wavered, though her eyes itched with dryness from holding his gaze.

"Ohhh, Death. Ohh, ohhh Death. Ohhh Death . . . The herald came, the herald said, Death is comin' to claim Her dead. No wealth, no weapons, no silver nor gold, nothing will stop Her hands so cold . . . Ohhh Death," she sang softly,

quietly, paraphrasing an old Appalachian dirge. Bracing her knee on the edge of the cot, she stared him down, and pinned him down, with the ancient melody. *"Will She spare your soul another year?"*

Ting.

Ting.

Ting.

The blade stopped striking the bar, suspending sound, song, and everything for a long, long moment.

"I am Her herald," Ia whispered, lifting her free hand toward his face. "And *your* death is near."

Her fingers skimmed over his skin. Slid. Stayed.

Ia dragged him into the future, and forced him through Time itself. Force-fed him just a sip of the vast and bitter brew she herself endured, in a fraction of the time he needed to consciously comprehend.

His breath hissed inward in a long, pained inhale, then hurled outward again in a scream, body bucking to try and get away. An unending, repeating, breath-catching series of screams. She jerked her sword arm back and away, as much to keep her two startled superiors out of the room as to prevent the prisoner from injuring himself. Her left hand stayed glued to his cheek, riding through his frantic thrashing.

"Enough!"

The shout came from General Sranna. Gentling her touch, Ia hauled her target's mind out of the timestreams. She mentally shook his dripping, chilled soul dry, and settled him back into his body. Pushing off from the cot, she released the prisoner. He shuddered and panted, eyes blinking rapidly without seeing. Ia waited patiently while he recovered.

Finally, he focused on her with a last trio of blinks. Ia tapped the spreader bar with the tip of her blade, once more sending that cold, cold chime ringing through the cell.

Ting . . . Ting . . . Ting.

"You will tell me . . . everything. And you will tell it to me before I open the gates to hell." She let the implications otherwise sink in, blade shifting but not quite touching the partially carved bar. "Who your masters are." *Ting.* "Why they stole our soldiers." *Ting.* "Where they were being taken." *Ting.* "What is to be done to them." *Ting.* "And when it will be done."

Ting.

"Everything," she commanded, and spread the fingers of her left hand, not quite reaching for his face.

Pale and shaking, swallowing hard under the implacable weight of her gaze and the unspoken threat of her touch, he complied.

"How the *hell* did you do that, soldier?" General Sranna demanded as soon as they were outside in the corridor. At least he had waited until both cell and brig doors were shut, but this wasn't the place for that question.

Ia held up her right hand, stalling his own interrogation. With her sword re-sheathed, she was free to do so. The sliver of steel was still caught in the fingertips of her left hand. "With respect, sir, I'd rather wait until we were somewhere private?"

Sranna looked at Sudramara, who lifted his chin at the nearby lifts. "My office."

They held their silence all the way up to Deck 3 and into the captain's quarters. Only after Sudramara ordered the petty officer on duty in the front half of his office to hold all requests and sealed the door to the back half of his office did Ia speak.

"You wanted to know how I got him to talk?" she asked both men. Sudramara nodded and gestured for them to take a seat in one of the quartet of chairs grouped in the corner across from his desk. Sranna nodded and spoke.

"That, and how the hell you cut off a chunk of solid steel with a flimsy little blade," the lieutenant general stated, settling into one of the seats. "Unless you prepped it somehow beforehand, like a magician readying a stage trick?"

Sudramara gestured toward the caf' dispenser in the corner of his office. Sranna nodded. Ia shook her head. She remained on her feet as Sudramara fetched two mugs of the hot drink. As much as Ia wanted to claim it was just a trick, she knew she had to be honest with her superiors. Lying outright in this moment would come back to bite her on the backside a few years down the road. Even if technically she was protected by precog's law, she knew she had to tread a lot closer to the truth than that.

"For the first part . . . you heard what he said," Ia reminded them. "This 'Lyebariko' has been gathering information on the TUPSF's actions in this corner of space, and specifically on all the ships involved in thwarting their attempts at taking over the Oberon Mining & Refinery Consortium. They knew enough, and were powerful enough, to bait their trap not only with the best and brightest in live entertainment, but they came *prepared* for me.

"The fact that I am resistant to electrosonic shocks, including stunner grenades, sirs, is buried in my military file. Deep in my files," Ia emphasized. "At the insistence of the Department of Innovations and the Department of Military Security. They don't want that information out in the general public, as much to give the Marines an ongoing edge as to keep people from taking random potshots at me with other weapons. Yet these people tracked me down with an air gun loaded with tranquilizer darts. Not with a stunner pistol, or another stunner grenade. They came after me with tranquilizers.

"That flunky came into this *knowing* my reputation. Or rather, having heard about it thirdhand." She shrugged her shoulders, hands resting lightly on her hips. "Hearing about it, and being faced with the reality of it, are two different things. Even in the criminal undergalaxy, it's rare to be surrounded by literally a body's worth of spilled blood. Never mind the blood from two bodies. I just . . . used that reputation. Played psychological games with him, which I reinforced with the tapping of my blade. Sort of a . . . a death knell sound effect, if you will."

"And the screaming when you touched his face?" Captain Sudramara asked.

Ia smirked. "My hands can sometimes get a bit cold and clammy. Particularly when I'm nervous. It was an important interrogation. I used it, hoping that those lines about Death's cold hands reaching for his soul would still be lingering in his brain. Which they apparently were. Between the song, the sound effects, the fact that I am one scary-crazy bitch by reputation . . . it all combined into one pure punch to his gut via psychology."

"Either you are one lucky meioa, or you really *are* one cold, crazy, calculating bitch." Sranna saluted her with his mug. "Not bad, soldier. Not bad at all. If you ever want to change Branches, the Special Forces just might want to snatch you up for their Intelligence Division."

"I'd rather indulge in a clear-cut fight, General. More blood upon my hands, but less blood upon my soul. Speaking of which . . ." Drawing her sword, she carefully balanced the blade between her hands. Turning to first the captain, then the general, she let them have a close enough look, but pulled the blade back before Sranna could touch the edge. "Please don't touch. It's far sharper than you think."

"It looks like it's cheap, chrome-coated plexi up close. There's even some chipping in the metal coating a short distance from the tip," Sranna observed.

"That's because it *is* coated." Shifting her grip carefully, mindful of the double, sharp edges, she scraped her fingernail over the blade, peeling back some more of the paint. The patch she revealed was an odd transparent gold, as if the blade were made of glass. "Silver gilt, to make it look like plain steel."

"What lies underneath?" Sranna asked.

"We don't know, exactly," she hedged. At their chiding looks, she shrugged and straightened, blade still cradled lightly in her hands. "It's a native mineral on my homeworld. Geological, mineralogical, and chemical scientists have been trying to make heads or tails of it since the planet was first accidentally discovered by its colonists. They were supposed to be headed for a heavyworld of 2.73gs, and ended up at Sanctuary instead. Since Sanctuary has an atmosphere, and their original plans were for a dome colony, they decided to settle there instead. That's when they found this stuff.

"The planet is dusted with patches of giant crystal sprays. Most of them grow in octagonal patterns, with many of the shafts looking almost square and growing as thick as a Human's thigh or head. But a rare few grow these thin, diamond-shaped shafts. Some of the locals call them Devil's Sticks, but the official term is *crysium*."

Sranna blinked. "I believe I've heard of that stuff. It replaced the compound trinium lonsdaleite as the hardest known substance by . . . what, twenty times? Plus there was something about how they couldn't actually break off a sample, and had to chip off an entire spray to ship it to a lab?"

"Oh, you can break it. You just have to apply pneumatic pressure in excess of several thousand tons to a very, very thin crystal shaft." Ia hefted her sword. "This is one of the few shafts they broke off when they discovered that. My family acquired one and had it set in a hilt as a sword-blade when they found out I'd been promoted to Company Sergeant—this is why I've been diligent in keeping up my sword practices along with my other fighting skills, Captain. More Afaso than Marines-style swordplay, of course," she added with a shrug. "But then I know more about Afaso style sword-fighting, obviously."

"And the silver paint?" Sudramara asked, draining his caf' mug.

"Well, it's not exactly a standard-shaped Marine saber to begin with," she said. Touching the tip to the mouth of her scabbard, which had a hidden lining of more crysium to prevent the edges from cutting through the sheath, she slid it home. "I can't say anyone has figured out how to bend the stuff, yet. As far as the mineralogists are able to tell, each shaft of crysium is a monocrystal . . . a single, solid, flawless crystal . . . and this particular variant has two very acute, monofractal edges."

"Monofractal?" Sranna asked.

"The crystalline structure is pretty much flawless and uniform in all of its properties, down to the molecular level. Whatever it's made out of, it's as strong at the microscopic level as it is at the macroscopic . . . and it is very, very sharp. Put enough force behind a blow, and it will cut through just about anything. Except another crysium blade, but there's only a handful of those, and the rest are all back on my homeworld," she allowed. Ia added, shrugging, "Hiding the truth of this blade under the silver-gilt paint is like hiding my native resistance to static shocks. It's meant, literally, to give me an edge in combat."

Sranna snorted. "Bad pun, meioa."

Ia let her sense of humor show through, twisting up the corner of her mouth. "I'll take any amusement I can find in a situation as grim as this one, sir."

Sudramara sighed. "Tell me about it. They've carted off the lieutenants and sergeants by OTL courier to Zubeneschamali. The far side of Terran space from here. Other-than-light travels at about two seconds to the light-year. FTL an hour to the light-year. We won't get there in time."

"Actually . . . we just might. I have some, mm, unusual friends," Ia offered, spreading her hands a little. She clasped her fingers together in front of her belt, enjoying the bemused looks on the two men's faces. "One of them managed to get from a sector not far from this one all the way to Zubeneschamali, in an FTL ship, in under five hours. Mind you, it was a somewhat smaller ship than the *Liu Ji*, but it is possible."

Captain Sudramara scowled. "Impossible! That's hundreds of light-years away!"

"Impossible . . . if you don't know the secret to Solarican interstellar travel. Which my friend discovered," Ia returned calmly. Unbuckling her baldric, she settled into the nearest seat and leaned her sheathed blade against its armrest.

Sudramara gave her a sardonic look. "We *know* the secret to Solarican-style travel. The TUPSF's researchers are working on it. We just don't have the *technology* to locate and access natural hyperrifts. That . . . and I'm not sure my ship can take it. There are patrols that regularly visit the Zubeneschamali System, and half the Special Forces between here and there. I hate to say this, but *they* can track down the captain and the rest far better than we can."

"Track them down, yes . . . but get them back? I don't think so." Ia shook her head. "Wherever this Lyebariko is taking them, you can bet it'll be a fortress. A veritable castle, with the drawbridge lowered and the portcullis raised by invitation only."

"Castle walls can be breached," the Navy captain reminded her. "Pull in enough firepower, and their walls will go down. Nobody messes with the Space Force."

"I would rather not risk my commanding officers being destroyed in the middle of a bombardment, sir," Ia countered flatly. "I barely lived through one of those myself, and I wasn't the prisoner of a bunch of madmen at the time."

"You sound like you have a plan," General Sranna interjected before the *Liu Ji*'s captain could argue the matter further. "Let's hear it."

"My, ah, friend knows how to calculate the location of *one* natural hyperrift. It travels from Gliese 226, which is about seven, eight light-years from here, to the outskirts of Zubeneschamali. He and his crew can pinpoint the mouth of the hyperrift for us, and give us the field specifications to wrap our ship in an FTL warp bubble with the right frequency to 'grease' the *Liu Ji* through the tube. He is also . . . the sort of person who could earn an invitation into the enemy's fortress," Ia hedged, tipping her head in acknowledgment of the activities being left unsaid. "*If* he comes bearing the right gift in hand."

"Gift?" the stout general asked, offering his mug back to Sudramara for a refill.

She shrugged, spreading her hands. "Me. Obviously D'kora can't go, so it would have to be me. These people went to a lot of trouble, which is now public knowledge, to get ahold of us. My friend could stage a kidnapping of me, and offer me as a 'gift' to the underlords of the known galaxy," Ia told them. "Given his, ah, well-established professional interests and avowed ambitions . . . it's quite believable that he would offer a prize like me in exchange for access to the Lyebariko, just for a shot at future business dealings with them."

"And then what?" Sudramara asked, coming back with both mugs freshly refilled. He handed one to the Army general and sat down with the other. "You're good, Ia. I've seen you pull off a lot of things over the months since I took over. But you're *not* a one-woman army—whatever the recruitment ads might say."

"No, but for the right compensation, my friend and *his* crew could open the castle gates from the inside, while this 'Library' of criminal masterminds is busy looking me over. One of their specialties is infiltration and sabotage," Ia revealed. "Corporate warfare can be just as physically ugly as any military engagement, and the Lyebariko is just one more business conglomeration to these people."

"What consideration did you have in mind?" Sranna asked, sipping at his mug.

"If I were you, I'd give him a choice. Upgraded engines and military-class weapons for the ships in his fleet . . ." She had to pause while Sranna choked on his caf'. He coughed and accepted the napkin the captain fetched for him. As soon as he could breathe again, Ia finished her statement. "Or a full and unconditional pardon for every illegal activity he and his crew have ever committed, up to the moment Ferrar and the others are freed and returned to the Space Force . . . and granted on the sole condition that everyone makes it out alive. Provided they're all still alive when the rescue operation begins, of course."

"Of course," Sranna rasped, rapping his knuckles against his barrel-broad chest. "You, Acting Lieutenant, have the biggest pair of planetoids I have ever met. Male or female."

"Thank you, sir. All we have to do is have the military waiting for the castle gates to open. Even if it's just a sally port, to continue the analogy," she acknowledged, "a few on the inside can open things up so that the rest can come pouring in. If we pull this off, we rescue the Captain, the lieutenants, and the sergeants . . . and take down or at least thoroughly disrupt and chastise several arrogant crimelords who think they can mess with the military.

"If we can't pull it off . . . at worst, you'll lose myself, the Captain, lieutenants, sergeants . . . and a handful of criminals," Ia reminded them. "On the bright side, if things go system nadir, you'd still have the military lurking in wait, armed and ready to knock down those castle walls. But no matter what, sirs, we *have* to show these crimelords that they cannot mess with the Space Force and get away with it. I would just prefer to extract their prisoners *first* before cracking open their thick heads."

Sranna mulled over her offer. He sipped at his caf', finger slowly rubbing his chin. "Can we trust this so-called friend of yours? You've admitted he's as much a criminal as these Lyebariko fellows."

Rising, she crossed to the caf' machine and fetched a fresh mug from where she had seen Sudramara fetch the others. "He owes me too much to back out. Plus, I have too much dirt on him, so he *can't* back out."

The general nodded. "I want to meet him."

"That can be arranged," she agreed, returning to her seat. "He's not too far away. Half an hour at most, in a courier ship . . . but he won't meet us midsystem. It's too dangerous. I suggest we head out like we're going back on our regular patrol, send somewhat edited information on the attack on to the rest of the Space Force—because it's obvious there's a huge security breach somewhere in the system—and then detour once we're well beyond the system's scanning range to TZL 11818."

Sudramara frowned. "That star's a little brown dwarf not even half a light-year from here. Hell, it's practically a *black* dwarf, it's so cold and dead. That system doesn't even have any planetoids, just a few chunks of loose-floating rocks. Which we won't see until we're practically on top of them."

"Which makes it ideal for a rendezvous," Sranna stated.

"More importantly, it's not that far off from our patrol route. We can still get to our next port of call on time, which is *Tasket* Station. At that point, I go ashore as if on Leave, I get kidnapped, my friend whisks me off, you give chase . . . and we meet up again in the depths of untraveled space. He sets up the meeting with the Lyebariko to deliver his gift, you bring his courier on board, squeeze it in next to the shuttles, and we head for Gliese 226," Ia summed up. "We take the wormhole, drop out at system edge, and dump him out with me on board—the amount of travel time the *Liu Ji* would spend in transit would probably be roughly the same time it takes for a courier to get there, what with the pauses to recover from OTL hypersickness—and then just wait for the hook and bait to do their job."

"And then we just wait for the Trojan Horse to open the fortress gates and be rolled inside." Saluting her with his mug, Sranna nodded. "This might actually work. They did their damnedest to take you, too, so you should be the bait we need."

"What if your 'friends' can't get the gates open quickly enough?" Sudramara asked her. "What if they torture you, or the others?"

"They could be doing that right now to Captain Ferrar and the rest," she pointed out in return. "It's a risk we all have to take. The Lyebariko has declared war on the Space Force—specifically, on Ferrar's Fighters. I want to prove to them, and to the rest of the undergalaxy, that they made a very serious mistake."

"I don't know," Sudramara murmured. "The few cases of FTL ships falling into natural hyperrifts often ended with those ships badly damaged by the end. Your world's colonists being a case in point. They had no choice but to pick your planet, because they couldn't get back out of the system again, and I think, what, couldn't use the hypercomms until they were repaired a few months later? I don't know if I can risk that kind of damage happening to this ship. As much as I want Captain Ferrar and the others brought safely back, it'd be *my* career on the line."

"Well, there is one more, and a very important, factor to consider," Ia murmured, knowing she had to have the conservative captain on her side to pull this off. "The morale of every man and woman remaining on this ship. Navy as well as Marines. Your crew *likes* our Company. You know we'd be riding to your rescue if they'd struck *you* down during your greenroom party. Both halves of this ship know it."

Sudramara wrinkled his nose. "Don't remind me. *We* were supposed to go see the second show. Now it's been canceled." He sipped at his caf', then sighed. "Unfortunately, you're right. My crew would mutiny if they knew about this chance for payback and heard I'd turned my back on it. Provided *you*, sir," he added to General Sranna, "are willing to cover my paycheck on any repair bills to this ship. And we're going into this on the Zubeneschamali side with as much backup as we can muster. Discreetly muster."

"I'll cover this mission, and see what help we can get," Sranna asked. "Discreetly, but you'll need whatever help you can get."

"I'm happy to hear you say that, sir," Ia muttered, draining her own caf'. "I know very well I'm not a one-woman army. I'll go set things up for that meeting. The sooner this gets done, the better off we'll be."

CHAPTER 19

The incident involving the kidnapping of Captain Ferrar and the others has been exaggerated in many ways. Some things were correct, however. Did I consort with known criminals in order to get the job done? Yes, because it caused many more known criminals to be put out of business. Did I cut some of my foes literally into three pieces, like the song suggests? Some of them, yes, but they were trying to kill me at the time, so I figured it was only fair. Did I rip off the leg of a K'katta and beat him to death with it? . . . No comment.

The whole operation was a gamble, and we knew it going in. It helped that we released the falsified news that our captives had died without revealing any information, made sure the touring cast was safe, and supposedly took off on the rest of our patrol. Being captured at the next station, well . . . that was staged to look quite real. A little too real in some ways, but it did work as intended.

~Ia

MARCH 30, 2492 T.S.
SYSTEM EDGE
GLIESE 226 SYSTEM
. . . NOT TZL 11818

The first thing on her mind when she woke up was the nasty taste in her mouth. The second thing was the words that came out of that mouth. "Did you *have* to use that particular drug?"

Heddle, Drek's medic, shifted to the other bed in the cramped cabin, his attention on the hypospray he picked up from the tray on the counter by the door. "That particular drug can be counteracted quickly. In fact, it wears off naturally after OTL transit, which we have just finished achieving. The shot I gave you should clear your mind. Other choices . . . would have delayed your mission."

"Could I get a bottle of water, please?" Ia asked, hauling her lethargy-filled body more or less into a sitting position. Her brain was muzzy, and she had to duck to avoid the underside of the bunk over her bed. Fighting off her mental sluggishness, she reached for the timestreams, dipping briefly into her own stream to make sure everything was lined up for the future.

What she saw there made her wince. Betrayal was a high probability. The little addition to their plans would complicate her correction of the problem. *Oh . . . stupid, stupid . . . stupid.*

"I am curious about the strange bracelet on your right wrist," Heddle murmured. "We of course had to leave your military unit behind so you couldn't be easily traced, but this other thing . . . it has me curious. Particularly as we could find no hinges, catches, or seams."

"Be curious all you want," Ia said dismissively. She smacked her mouth and grimaced, then lifted her chin at Drek. "How soon until he's on his feet?"

Still not looking at her, he applied the hypospray to his boss, who was dressed to look like conservative, polite businessman Darroll Rekk-Noth, occasional, casual date of Sergeant Ia of the TUPSF Marines over the last several months. "A minute."

The bald-headed medic—not quite a doctor—returned the hypo to the tray on the counter near the door and busied himself with some minor tidying. Within moments, Drek groaned softly, and shifted a hand to his head.

". . . I hate that drug. Water," he ordered, lifting his hand from the makeshift exam bed.

The medic fetched him a bottle of water from the cooler, but not one for her. That confirmed what Ia had read in the timestreams. The crew already knew.

She needed to clear the drugs from her system, some of which were not the same ones Drek had received. But discreetly. Glancing around, she spotted a power socket at the head of the bunk. Sighing, Ia stretched out, draping her right arm over her head. That conveniently placed the thick, golden-clear bracelet cuffed seamlessly around her right wrist right next to the conduit outlet. "Can't wait for my head to clear . . ."

"Oh, clarity will be achieved soon," Heddle murmured, smiling to himself. No doubt he was enjoying the irony of his words. Ia sighed and relaxed into the bedding. But only her body, not her mind.

Her bracelet shifted. The movement was subtle, a thinning of the thick, broad, glass-like substance. The edge nearest the outlet molded into a pseudopod, oozed into the socket, and brightened a little bit. She kept her wrist in the alcove, hoping the medic wouldn't notice anything, and spooled out more of the bracelet, twisting it into a thin coil.

It had been a while since she had practiced this in any depth. Crysium was near-impossible to bend, break, or shatter. It shrugged off heat, ignored cold, and devoured electricity. But above all, it was still the equivalent of Feyori *shakk*. Energy-infused matter. Biocrystalline, not just crystalline. It wasn't just a property of the crystalline structure that made it so impervious; it was the life force still lingering inside, the energy feeding it and keeping it whole.

Created from the residue of living energy manipulators, only those who could manipulate energy themselves could reshape it. Using electrokinesis to pull *out* the energy naturally stored in the bracelet meant softening and reducing that impermeability to the point of pliability. Telekinesis—or even plain old physical effort—could then be used to shape and mould the almost plexi-like result. But that was the trick; no one had thought of using psychic abilities on the seemingly impervious stuff. No one else would for another two centuries, either. Except Ia, of course.

While it was a truism that a psi never had just one gift, not all of those gifts were strong enough to be developed beyond the most basic levels of awareness. Of those that did have more than one strong, trainable ability, cross-channeling energy was still often difficult for the majority of them. For Ia, if she didn't include her precognitive and postcognitive abilities, her ability to manipulate electricity was next-highest on the list; biokinesis, the ability to heal rapidly, consciously, was farther down. But she could transform and channel the energy from electricity down into her other gifts, empowering them.

She did so now. Not just into her biokinetic self-healing abilities, but into her pyrokinetic, heat-inducing ones. Literally burning out the drug he had injected into her.

"Is she asleep yet?" she heard Drek ask.

Heddle moved to the side of her bunk, crouching to lean into the alcove. She had her eyes closed, but she could feel his presence, and his voice was close at her side. "Meioa Ia, are you awake?" His fingers brushed against her cheek. "Odd. She feels feverish."

"Well, she can't come down with some sort of deadly plague. They won't pay nearly as much for a dead gift. Fix her, Heddle. We jump again in twenty minutes. I want to be long gone from anywhere near that ship of hers."

Ia heard Drek getting up from the other bed, and flicked out her mind. The cabin door did not hiss open. She heard him thump the controls with his fist, then jab the comm button a couple of times.

"What the . . . ?"

Heddle touched her face again. Ia seized his mind and dragged him down into the timestreams. She was not gentle about it, though she wasn't nearly as brutal as she had been with the Lyebariko assassin. It wasn't easy, balancing the needs of his sanity versus the purging of her system. Her heartbeat increased, racing uncomfortably, unsteadily if she focused too much on him instead of on her health. Heddle twitched a little, threatening to scream if she focused instead on the toxins in her bloodstream. An awkward balance, keeping herself alive and him silent.

"Heddle, open your comm link and . . . Heddle?" Drek briefly returned to the bed. "Holy . . . She looks *very* feverish—

Drek to the crew!" He moved away again. "If you are monitoring us, why the hell did you lock us in here? Several of the rest of you handled her, in bringing us on board! If she's infected, you are, too!"

There. The last of the drug was purged. Lifting her hand to capture Heddle's fingers, keeping him on the timeplains, she sat up on the edge of the bed. Now her attention had to be split between the medic and his employer. Drek turned and looked at her.

"What . . . ?"

"I told you: if you ever betrayed me, I would be prepared." She still felt feverish, but the flush of heat was something she was now free to channel into other areas. Tipping her head, Ia gave the pirate crimelord a small, cold smile. "I'll admit the second drug you dumped into my system was low on my list of expected events. But it has now been dealt with, and I will be just fine. You, however . . . are perilously close to making me mad."

Drek backed up, eyes widening. He glanced again at the kneeling medic. "Heddle?"

Heddle shuddered and sobbed. Ia eased her grip on his mind, gentling his suffering. The trembling man blinked and looked up at her, hazel eyes watering. Ia brushed her fingers over his scalp, stroking the smooth-shaved skin. "Will you serve me?" He nodded, too choked with emotion to speak. Ia nodded as well, giving the medic one more pat. "Then everything will be made right . . ."

She looked up at Drek, who was leaning back against the cabin door, trying to subtly pat down his clothes for a weapon. He fished out a small holdout laser pistol. Ia leveled him a look somewhere between patient and chiding.

"Do you *really* think a one-shot gun is going to stop me, Drek?" Leaving Heddle kneeling by the side of the bed, she rose . . . and found her wrist still tethered to the socket. Wincing in self-disgust, Ia snapped her wrist, flexing her powers. The pseudopod recoiled, absorbing back into her bracelet. Which used to be her sword, hilt and all.

"What the hell is that thing?" he asked, distracted.

The gun dipped a little in his distraction. Ia didn't lunge for it. She didn't even move, yet, other than to lower her arm at her side. "What it is, is none of your business. *Your* business was to carry out *my* business," she chided him. "The only mistake you *didn't* make was telling them that this was supposed to be a sting . . . but I suppose that was as much to save your own hide as anything. But as far as obeying me goes, you failed."

He lifted his chin, and the pistol, aiming it again. "I don't work for *you!*"

Now she moved, lifting her hand. His weapon jerked out of his fingers before he could fire, sailing across the two meters between them. She caught it deftly, no longer lethargic from the second set of soporifics, and studied her wide-eyed, would-be captor. "You know, I really need to figure out an easier way to do this . . . because I *am* only one woman. I cannot be everywhere at once.

"Unfortunately, though I know I do eventually figure it out, *how* is a big blank grey spot I cannot foresee. Yet. In the meantime," she muttered, tossing the gun on the bed, "I guess I'll have to do this the hard way. Don't struggle. I out-muscle you, and I'd really rather not break anything I might need, soon."

"Heddle—grab her!" Drek ordered. The medic, sniffing hard to clear his nose, pushed back to his feet.

"No." He fixed his employer with a hard look. "I would rather help her. It's the only way things can be made right."

Drek looked between Ia and his formerly loyal crewmember. "What the hell did you do to him?"

Three steps brought her within easy reach. Lifting her hand, she cupped his face, following him as he tried to dodge. "Come find out *why* I need you on my side. Come see all the lives *you* are destroying."

He froze, stiffening in shock as she plunged him, too, into the timestreams.

This really is getting tedious, she thought in a private corner of her mind, dragging him through the soul-shaking waters. *I cannot personally take* everyone *into the timestreams over the next three hundred years. Even if they are stubborn, blind, self-centered fools . . .*

He begged. He had more presence of mind than Heddle did, enough to think somewhat past what he was seeing. Ia had no mercy. By the time she was done, Drek was pale and sweating, as if he was the one recovering from an inexplicable fever.

"Now," she stated softly as he wiped a trembling hand over his eyes. "You will go to your crew, and tell them we're not jumping for a few more minutes. Then you will send each one, one at a time, into this cabin. Make up the excuse that you want to give each of them a chance to mark me up a little or whatever while I'm unconscious. As soon as your bridge crew has seen me, then they will jump us to rendezvous with the *Liu Ji* . . . and the future will proceed *exactly* as I have planned and outlined to you."

He bowed his head. "Yes . . . I'm sorry, Prophet. I didn't understand."

Ia patted his cheek lightly, just enough to sting a little. "Snap out of it. You *are* still Drek the Merciless. Recover that side of your nature. I *need* it. You will return to being every bit of the bastard budding crimelord and businessman as ever. You will just work for *me* now. Think of this as the biggest combination of con and heist of your entire career."

"Yes, Prophet," Drek murmured, breathing deeply.

"Drek . . . don't call me Prophet," Ia ordered, sighing roughly. "*Particularly* in front of anyone else. Call me Ia, call me bitch, call me a pain-in-the-asteroid or something like that, but not Prophet. Heddle, go with him and fetch that pilot of yours. We need to get back on schedule as soon as possible, and that means Kells has to be on the same page as the rest of us."

"Yes, Proph—sorry," Drek apologized. He started to turn toward the door, then looked back at her. "Ah . . . two things. First, did you lock this thing?"

"Of course." A flick of her hand followed the flick of her mind, unlocking the electronic controls. "And the second thing?"

"If I hadn't tried to betray you just now . . . for all the wrong reasons, I can see that, now . . . would you have ever considered dating me for real? Not just as a cover for our little business deals?"

Heddle glanced between the two of them, lifted his brows, and quickly turned to the counter by the door, blatantly focusing his attention on his tray of hyposprays and drug vials.

Ia shook her head. "I'm sorry, Drek. No matter how attractive a man may be, I literally do not have time for romance in my life."

He nodded slowly, accepting that. Then lifted a brow. "But you *do* think I'm attractive?"

She twisted her mouth in a wry smile. "When you're not being a selfish, self-centered, uncaring, murderous bastard . . . yes. But I wouldn't have you any other way. So long as you obey my prophecies, that is. Now. Go fetch the pilot of this courier ship," Ia ordered, dragging him back onto task. "We're losing time I cannot waste, and I'd rather not have to dodge any awkward questions as to why we're running late."

"Of course, Pr . . . ah, Ia. I'll get him here immediately." Opening the door, he left. Heddle escaped in his wake. Once the door had slid shut again, Ia moved to rest against the counter, far enough from the opening that anyone entering the room would not immediately see her. That would give her time to strike.

I really have to find a better way to convince people to do everything I need. Words and the proof of my prophecies can only go so far. Particularly for all the times I myself will not be there.

TZL 11818 SYSTEM

"You're late," Captain Sudramara stated, the moment the courier ship's airlock hissed open, revealing Ia, Drek, and his crew.

"We had engine troubles," she stated. "Permission to come back aboard, Captain?"

"Granted. But I wasn't born yesterday; I do realize 'engine troubles' is a common euphemism for groping your . . . boyfr . . ." Sudramara stopped midword. Stared. The sextet of men in the airlock were worth the interruption.

Drek, Heddle, the pilot Kells, the engineer, and two gunners had all switched from business suits and ship suit coveralls to their version of battle attire. From boots to gloves, pants to fitted jackets, it consisted of deep shades of purple and black plexleather studded with bits of metal. Some of the metal wasn't even weaponry. They had also braided their hair, and in Heddle's case his beard, donned several barbaric-looking piercings, and streaked dark war paint across the visible portions of their skin.

". . . The hell?" the captain of the *Liu Ji* asked, glancing between them and Ia, who had moved onto the gantry the docking crew had extended to the cylindrical courier's side. "*These* are corporate raiders?"

Drek smiled. His canine teeth looked pointed, thanks to false caps. "Sometimes we like to emphasize the 'raider' half. A large part of any successful business dealing lies in the establishment of an effective reputation, and a memorable corporate image. This is all just part of that image. It allows us to resume normal clothes and normal lives when we're not on the clock, so to speak. Now. Permission for my crew and I to come aboard, Captain?"

Again, Sudramara looked between Drek and Ia, eyes wide. "*Armed?*"

"Captain, the deal includes the fact that they will behave themselves in a lawful and respectful manner while on board this ship," Ia pointed out. "That does not, however, include disarming them."

Drek placed one gloved hand on his chest and gave Captain Sudramara a half bow, smiling with a few too many teeth. "I would never do anything to upset my lady . . . but I *never* go into a business deal unarmed. We come aboard as we are . . . or we leave, and we take the information you need with us."

Sudramara looked between them a third time, then pointed his finger at Ia. "If anything happens while they're on board, it's *your* head on the chopping block, *Acting* Lieutenant."

"I take full responsibility for their actions while on board, sir," she returned, unfazed.

"Permission, Captain?" Drek asked again, this time smiling with just his lips.

"Granted. Keep your 'boyfriend' on a short leash," Sudramara ordered Ia.

"He knows how to behave, sir. As for the 'engine troubles' we had," Ia added, pulling out and displaying a datachip from her shirt pocket, "it involved the conversion factors between his FTL ships and military vessels, and not some euphemism. I was having to work out a lot of this stuff from memory of just what shape the *Liu Ji*'s hull actually is, and where the warp panels are distributed around it. This datachip has specifications for field intensity variations, thruster adjustments, and energy requirements. You *did* fill up every single tank and spare water container on board while I was off getting kidnapped, correct?"

Sudramara took the chip from her and started up the gantry ramp. "We did. But that's assuming this ship will still be intact enough to need all that fuel for a firefight at the far end of the hyperrift."

"We will. You won't get the Marines and anyone else we pick up along the way past the orbital defense grid without at least the threat of being able to knock it out. Drek's engineers stole the specs straight from the Solaricans, and worked the conversions for his own little fleet. All the hard work has already been done for you," she stated, following the captain.

Drek and his crew followed Ia. At the end of the ramp, two pairs of soldiers, one set Marines and the other set Navy, joined them, giving Drek and his men wary looks. She addressed Sudramara's concerns as they headed for the lifts.

"We'll have to be running at minimal internal power to save the hydrogenerators from strain, but Drek's engineers know what they're doing. I gave him specs that would err on the conservative side of caution."

"I am uncomfortable with you giving *criminals* sensitive military information," he growled.

"We already knew most of the needed specifications," Drek stated, earning him a hard look. He shrugged. "Mostly for things like insystem speed, FTL capacity, and other general, public knowledge. Fuel capacity and total available energy output weren't things we knew. Nor the placement of the field generators, since you disguise them so well on your hulls."

"With good reason! I don't like—"

"Captain," Drek interrupted, catching Sudramara's sleeve and halting them. He let go immediately, for which Ia was grateful, and spoke bluntly, directly. "I have *never* targeted the military. That is suicidal. Most of us are smart enough to leave you alone. The meioas you hunt, however, are far more powerful, and far more arrogant than you realize. They believe they *can* withstand the might of the Terran military. This is something I believe is a big enough mistake, I am willing to help you correct it. A mistake that, if not corrected immediately, will spill over onto all of the rest of us. *That* is why I am here."

"Well, maybe that's a good thing," Sudramara shot back. "Maybe it *should* wipe out the lot of your kind."

"*Captain.*" This time it was Ia who cut him off. She met

his frown with a cold stare. "You do not work for the Branch Special Forces. You do not have any training in the intricacies of covert operations . . . and it seems as if you have forgotten your Academy training on diplomacy at the moment. Your opinions on this matter are immaterial. The Navy flies fast, shoots hard, and carries others into and out of combat. That is your assignment. Carry it out."

He stepped forward, tall enough to look down at her by five or six centimeters. "And *you*, *Acting* Lieutenant, forget your place! You don't give orders on my ship!"

She didn't back down. "And you forget *your* place, Ship's Captain. *You* are in the Navy. *You* do not have the rank to give *or alter* the orders given to the Marine Corps. That includes *me*. *I* take my orders from *my* duly appointed superiors, up the chain of command in that Marine Corps, all the way to the Command Staff. Of which, General Sranna is a lawfully designated substitute superior. *He* has been given training in understanding the needs and requirements of covert ops. *He* has authorized the presence of these men on board the *Liu Ji*, because *he* has the authority to speak for operations across *all* four Branches.

"*Shova* the *shakk* all you want, Captain," Ia stated, not quite poking him in the chest, "your *orders* are to cooperate in helping the Marine Corps rescue its missing soldiers. *This* is the fastest way to do so, in the manner least likely to get Captain Ferrar and the others killed the moment we try. Take some comfort in the fact that this is *my* mission, and therefore *my* head is on the block, if these 'special agents' get out of line. They are not the Navy's problem; they are the Marine Corps' problem, and most specifically *mine*.

"Fly fast, shoot hard, and get *all* of us in and out of there. Alive. *Do* you have a problem with the orders a member of the Command Staff, one of your lawfully designated superiors in the Navy's chain of command, has given to *you*, Captain?" she asked, her voice hard but quiet.

A muscle ticked in Sudramara's tanned cheek. "No. I do not."

"I'm glad. We'll need to send a time-delayed message to Battle Platform *Justicar*, so they'll know we'll be needing reinforcements as soon as we show up in the system. Any sooner, and word might get back to our targets," Ia added. "I'd like to get everyone in and out in one piece, without any further betrayals of our plans to the enemy."

"Don't worry about my crew and me on this job, Captain," Drek stated quietly, catching Sudramara's attention. Drek dipped his painted head in Ia's direction. "You and your threats don't mean a damn to us . . . but *she* scares the *shakk* out of us. You have my word as a businessman and a fellow captain that we will not step out of line."

"Good," Ia snapped, glad he hadn't gone so far as to give her game away. "Your orders are to be polite, respectful, and cooperative on any matter relating to this operation." She turned back to Sudramara. "Drek has sent the message that he has captured me and is willing to deliver me in person for a tidy fee. I am hoping that this means they'll wait until they have me in their hands before they carry out their intentions toward the others, but we don't know what this Lyebariko intends to do to our missing soldiers. We have to assume the worst, and that means time is running out. You know Drek already. These are his best engineer and his best pilot from his fleet. Gentlemeioas, introduce yourselves."

"Captain Sudramara, I am called Zipper. I am the closest you'll get to an expert at Solarican style star-hopping without actually being fuzzy," the tallest man in the group stated politely, if wryly. "Engines producing the balance of power to the warp fields need to be monitored carefully by someone with experience in surfing a natural rift. It is as much a matter of sound as it is of scanners, so I would like to be escorted to your engine room. I shouldn't need to touch anything, but I do need to know that my advice will be heeded, or the rift will buck us back into realspace. In pieces, if we aren't careful."

"And I'm Kells," Drek's pilot stated, smiling and holding out his hand. He dropped it when Sudramara just stared at him. "Your *Liu Ji*, here, is a sweet ship, but she needs to be piloted by someone who knows what is normal behavior and what is dangerous. I'm the best at surfing the rifts, so that means I will actually have to touch the helm controls." He tipped his head and flashed Sudramara a grin. "But if it makes you feel better, you could always have a pretty girl hold a gun to my head while I fly this ship. I like a little spice in my life. Makes things interesting."

The look Sudramara aimed at him was a disgusted one, but the captain turned away without saying anything more, including any protests. Ia sighed and followed, mindful of how closely she had skimmed the legalities in what they were doing, and how closely she had just walked the line of military protocols, too.

MARCH 31, 2492 T.S.
SIC TRANSIT

"Harder!" Ia ordered, straightening back up. She staggered in the next moment, but so did the man in front of her. As did the men and women watching this fight.

Most of them were fellow Marines, members of the 1st Platoon who were supposed to be exercising as they bounced their way through hyperspace wrapped in a tenuous FTL bubble that could break at any minute. One of them was Drek, who leaned against the mirrored wall with his arms crossed over his plexleather-covered chest. Not that anyone could see much, since most of the lights had been shut down to conserve energy, but they were watching the two of them.

Spyder raised his fists again, but hesitated. They were covered in clunky rings that didn't quite fit his fingers even over the thin exam gloves he wore to keep his genetics off the silver. "I'm not exactly comf'rable doin' this. *Sir.*"

"You're under my orders, Sergeant. It's all perfectly legal." She gave him an impatient look when he hesitated. "I need *color*, Spyder. Cuts, bruises, all of it. And it has to have time to age by a few hours. Everything has to look real. It's completely realistic for me to have woken up and fought my captors, and for them to take out some of their frustrations on me. But it's *not* legal for Drek or his men to hit me. I don't intend to give the captain of this ship any excuse to lock them in the brig. Now, *hit* me."

Sighing heavily, he swung. This time, one of the rings caught on her cheek, digging hard enough to scratch and draw blood. The welt stung painfully, but she smiled. Half smiled, quirking up the opposite side of her mouth.

"That was better." She leaned in close and murmured into his ear. "But remember, you're senior-most among the sergeants who retired early from the party. *You* have to have the guts to follow your orders, and the will to lead these meioas into combat. Hit me again. Hard."

He swung again, and stomped on her foot, bruising it near the ankle. Ia hissed in pain and hopped a little, but regained her balance. Only to stagger again as the ship bucked around them.

The intercom beeped, and projected a message from the bridge. Spyder checked his next swing as they all stopped to listen. *"Attention, all hands. Once again, this is Kells, your guest pilot for the evening. We are coming up on the next big bump on our path in approximately . . . three to eight minutes. After that, we should have a three-hour stretch of minor scrapes and contusions, nothing too much worse than what we've recently experienced. Provided our football-shaped field integrity holds.*

"Once we're past the bump, I'll be passing the helm to your friendly, helpful helmsmeiva, Ensign Fresco-Vadrakka, for two and a half hours of that. Major bump in three to eight minutes, all hands brace for impact, lock and web. I repeat, brace for impact, lock and web. If you don't secure it, I'm not paying for it. Kells out."

"This mean I get t' stop?" Spyder asked her as the other Marines scrambled to get everything stowed and themselves strapped into the nearest acceleration couches, which were little more than straps that could be extended out of the padded wall opposite the mirrored one.

"It means you get a few minutes of reprieve. You heard our pilot, meioas!" Ia ordered the others, raising her voice. "Lock and web! Get those straps pulled out and hooked up, move it or lose it!"

Considering how hard the last "bump" had struck the ship, resulting in half a dozen crew members being sent to the Infirmary with injuries, no one hesitated this time to strap themselves into a sitting position against the cushion-padded wall opposite the mirrors.

Somewhere outside the ship, the warp panels were straining to project an elongated, cylindrical, extremely close field around the otherwise lumpy ship. A flexible field, rather than the normal stable one. Because the *Liu Ji* was wrapped in a warp field, they weren't experiencing hypersickness from the distorted acceleration forces that normally plagued OTL travel, but the sheer size of the vessel dragged it very roughly through the edges of the hyperrift.

Two and a half hours is enough time for a nap, Ia decided, buckling the acceleration restraints around her torso. *As soon as Spyder gives me a few more decent hits, I think I'll go hide in my quarters.*

APRIL 1, 2492 T.S.
BETA LIBERTY RESORT, BETA LIBRAE V
ZUBENESCHAMALI SYSTEM

"Ready?" Drek asked her.

"Yes."

"Are you sure you can break free of all those restraints?"

"Yes."

"Absolutely sure?"

"Drek, you are a calculating, uncaring bastard. *Be* that uncaring bastard. *Go.*" Hanging as loose and limp as she could get herself to relax, Ia let the engineer, Zipper, and one of the gunners drag her zip-tie-wrapped body out the airlock of their courier ship, their hands hooked under the cream bands spanning her frame.

The plexi ties binding her body had been strapped multiple times around her wrists, forearms, elbows, shoulders, thighs, knees, calves, and ankles. Her long-sleeved shirt and long trousers had been artistically ripped, her boots scuffed, and her hair mussed. With the welts and contusions now in full, colorful bloom on her face, she looked like a battered, subdued wreck. The trick right now was to seem unconscious, so she let herself dangle in their grip.

"Halt!"

She couldn't, daren't open her eyes to see what was happening, but knew it was the security guards for the backside entrance to the pleasure-dome colony of Beta Liberty.

"We'll take the prisoner," the guard stated.

"That was not the deal I arranged with your employers," Drek stated calmly. "The deal is that I bring her in person directly to your board of directors."

"Deals change."

Ia strove to stay limp as she picked up the distinct whine of energy clips charging.

"True, deals can change," he acknowledged. She heard the

plexleather of his outfit creak slightly. "So can the off-button on this bisthmite grenade. I can always turn it on, and blow up the back half of this installation."

"You're bluffing."

"I am called the Merciless for a very good reason, meioa. I don't bluff. I do not fear death, and I do not go into a business meeting unarmed. Our deal is a personal audience, with a hand-delivered package. I am here to deliver it by hand. If you are smart, your masters will receive what they requested. If you are too cautious, there is simply no deal; we get back on our ship and fly away. With our little package. But then you will have to explain to your superiors why their little gift was taken away. The third choice, which will happen if you are too stupid, is a very short but *very* bright death for a lot of people."

Ia couldn't see anything with her head dangling down and her eyes shut, but after a few seconds, she heard a soft rustling.

"You choose wisely," Drek praised, his tone sardonic. "You just might live to see a pay raise, at this rate."

Again, she was hauled forward by the hands holding the straps wrapped around her elbows and chest, feet scraping down a flight of steps. Courier ships were small so that they could conserve energy during transit; their correspondingly light mass made it relatively easy for them to land and take off from planetary surfaces. That had meant passing through a series of airlocks and parking the ship on a landing pad a short distance from the complex proper. It also meant a long walk for the two men dragging her along; she didn't blame them for letting the muscular weight of her legs scrape along the ground.

Several minutes of tedious hanging and dragging later, she heard Kells ask, "Are we almost there yet? Or can we stop for a few minutes? I'd like to pause and kick her a few times for being such a heavy bitch."

"You already had your fun," Drek told him. "As soon as we get paid, it'll be our hosts' turn to play with their prize."

More dragging. The hissing of doors, the shifting of gravity from an elevator lowering them down somewhere. Ia occupied her time with reaching out, seeking, and tapping into each of the electronic systems they passed. Some she sampled and let go; others, she hooked into and carefully altered.

It wasn't Drek and his men who would sabotage this place

enough for Ferrar's Fighters to enter. They wouldn't have enough time to do it themselves, for one. For another, because they were being kept from openly opposing the Lyebariko, Drek and his organization would be scrutinized carefully but determined to have had nothing to do with the coming disaster. That would leave him free to join the Lyebariko a few years from now. At least, join the other members; only a few of those present would escape from here. The key to the Lyebariko's long-term survival was carefully never exposing all of its members to the same dangers at the same time.

The light pressing against her eyelids faded as they passed from well-lit corridors into a deliberately darkened chamber, one large enough to echo slightly. Checking the timestreams, she risked opening her eyes. The flopped angle of her head was wrong to see much, but she did catch a glimpse of a long, dark brown, oval table illuminated by a single bright light carefully focused to shine down only on that table. The image was broken up by the silhouette of high-backed chairs ringing the near side, some turned at angles to face their inbound visitors.

She quickly shut her eyes again, lolling limp and unresisting as they neared the table. A single pair of hands clapped, loud and staccato, bringing Drek and his men to a halt.

"Well played, meioa," a smooth baritone voice stated. The owner's voice filled the chamber without strain. "An actual, functional bisthmite hand grenade. Our scanners say it has enough explosive power packed into that little sphere to crack open this chamber all the way to the surface. Your calling card is quite impressive."

"It has its uses," Drek returned calmly.

"No doubt it has opened many doors of opportunity for you. Including this one. Though you take a great risk in your insistence on personally hand-delivering our prize."

"Some business contacts are best secured in person."

"You thhinnk you have ssskills *we* would sseek?" a lighter, Tlassian-feminine voice hissed from somewhere off to the left a little.

"I have acquired that which you could not," Drek replied.

"A fffluke," the Tlassian scoffed.

"A carefully calculated series of actions, meioa-e," Drek corrected her. "When it became apparent to me that your organization was taking a particular interest in a particular mining organization . . . and that said interest was constantly being thwarted by a specific Marine Company, I deliberately altered my usual territory so that I could find and insinuate myself into the life and trust of one of their members.

"At the time, I had no idea you would seek to kidnap the command structure directly, but I knew that having inside access would eventually pay off. As you can see, it did," he admitted, his plexleather creaking faintly in what had to be a shrug. "I like to study a situation carefully and lay my plans accordingly for the long term, meioas. My skills would be an asset for any Library staff."

The chittering of a K'katta proved there was more lurking in those shadowed chairs than just bipedal sentients. The meioa's translator box kicked in after a moment, speaking in cultured Terranglo over the clicks, whistles, and hisses of the alien's natural speech. "You are an assassin, a kidnapper, a saboteur, and a tech thief. We have plenty of those at our disposal."

"Plenty, if you enjoy enduring all that incompetence. I also dabble in information, speculation, and acquisition of otherwise unattainable rarities. As I said, *I* have acquired that which you seek. Gentles, deliver the meioas their package. Consider this a gratuity on my part, gentlebeings. A gift, and my calling card as you said. The next one will not be free. I am a businessmeioa, after all."

Zipper and the gunner heaved Ia's legs off the floor. Grunting, they threw her up and forward. Even knowing it was coming, the *thud* of landing on that sturdy, solid, broad table knocked the wind out of her. Coughing, Ia struggled for breath.

"Thank you, meioa. Beyond this, however . . . your services are not required." That came from one of the Human-sounding females lurking in the shadows.

"Are you absolutely sure there is nothing else you want from me?" Drek asked.

"Absssssolutely." That came from the Tlassian.

"Well, then. Since you are so *determined* to do without my services at this time," Drek stated coldly, "that is *all* that you will get from me. The rest, at your insistence, is no longer of any concern. Do with her whatever you will. We'll leave now. Call me when you change your minds . . . because you will."

Ia pressed her cheek into the polished surface of the table, resisting the urge to smile. She had coached him to state it exactly that way, so that he could cold-bloodedly point out that they *had* essentially ordered him to walk away without asking him if he knew of anything else they might want or even need to know. Like the Marines, Army, and Special Forces operatives currently infiltrating the perimeter of the resort, bypassing system after electrokinetically sabotaged system.

The doors hissed quietly shut behind Drek and his men. The same first voice spoke again. "Well. Shall we fetch the others, and have ourselves a little celebration?"

"Gloating is dangerous," a new female voice said.

"Oh, but *so* much fun," the male countered. Something clicked, and he stated, "Bring all of the toy soldiers to the boardroom, and fetch my red case."

"Yes, sir," someone replied on the other end of the connection.

"I personally have lost too much in our ventures not to extract my pound of flesh," the shadow-cloaked man stated.

She didn't have to see his face to know who he and the others were: Siddhartha of the powerful, influential Tycho Interstellar holding combine. Sllaish of the centuries-old Tlassian Longspitters crime clan. A Gatsugi with the nickname Black Eyes who had yet to speak. The second female was a Solarican named Purtzen, while the K'katta held the nickname of Webmaster in the Lyebariko. Most of the other races couldn't pronounce his real name . . . but it didn't really matter. Like the others gathered around the table, the nine sentient beings in this room were forgettable. Dangerous, and therefore eminently expendable, but forgettable.

Not that they'd see it that way themselves, she thought wryly, lifting her head from the table. She made a show of blinking and peering into the darkness, then of testing her bonds.

"No, no, don't struggle, Sergeant. Or, wait . . . *do* struggle. The futility and frustration are so amusing to watch," Siddhartha Tycho murmured.

Roughly four minutes to the arrival of the others, give or take. Lyebariko staff don't dawdle, but it's not like they're being held in the next room, either.

Twisting around, Ia sat up with a wrench of awkward effort.

With her arms bound behind her back, her balance wasn't the best, but she managed. She craned her neck, looking in the approximate direction of that voice. "First of all . . . I'm not frustrated, gentlemeioas. A little disappointed to find out that Darroll was so willing to sell me out, but not frustrated."

The K'katta chittered briefly. The neutral-male voice of his translator box stated equally briefly, "It speaks."

"And I can also sing and dance," Ia quipped. "But not right now." She glanced down at her bonds and smiled slightly. "It seems I'm a little tied up with other things at the moment. Now, as for being a sergeant, your information is out of date. I've been field-promoted to Lieutenant. After all, you successfully wiped out everyone superior to me in my Company. Somebody had to take charge, and that somebody was me. I suppose I ought to thank you for my promotion, come to think of it."

"You're welcome," the second female stated sardonically.

"A pity that promotsssion will nnnot lasst lonng," the Tlassian female hissed.

Ia dipped her head, acknowledging the Tlassian's point. "War always carries the risk of not making it back. Unfortunately, this applies to all of you as well as to me. Your second error, you see, was declaring war on the Space Force Marines."

Her eyes were beginning to adjust to the shadows beyond the pool of light gleaming over the table. She could pinpoint who among the Lyebariko snickered at that, and who snorted or scoffed.

"Your third error," she stated flatly, cutting through their mirth and disbelief, "was in thinking my efforts here were futile. While we are still alone, just the nine of you and I . . ." She paused while a few of them jerked slightly in their seats, startled that she knew their exact count, despite the twenty seats ringing the table. "I will give you fair warning. I know this session is being recorded for posterity's sake, so I know the rest of the Library will end up hearing it as well:

"Beware the Blood of Mary. Get in my path again, and you *will* go down. This warning stands for three hundred years, guaranteed . . . and for a thousand more," she added, ignoring the scoffing noises that snorted from a couple of the shadowed crimelords surrounding her. "Interfere with *my* war plans, meioas, and in the end the Jack of All Trades will burn your

Library to the ground. Beware the Blood of Mary. You have been warned."

On the side of the room opposite the entrance she herself had been dragged through, a new door opened. Through it came several bipedal figures, carrying in a total of fifteen bound, gagged, and blindfolded Humans, males and females alike. Their arrival cut off any reply the Lyebariko members would have made. The door slid shut for a few seconds, then opened again. Someone pushed a scarlet-enameled tool cart into the chamber, then the door slid shut and darkness descended once more.

"Time to have some fun," Siddhartha quipped. "Anyone interested in joining me as I torture my way through our little toys?"

Ia thought it was ironic his parents had named him after the historical, first Buddha. This Siddhartha was not a man of peace, and he definitely didn't intend to alleviate anyone's suffering tonight. A few of the others accepted, and a few demurred. The rest remained quiet.

"Come get this one," he ordered, raising his voice to the figures lurking in the near-darkness. "Then chain all of them to the walls, so that we may begin."

Bodies moved, padding across the floor. Two burly, neck-hooded Tlassians leaned over the table, grabbed Ia by the feet, and slid her off the surface. They worked so smoothly and efficiently, hooking their sharp-nailed fingers into her plexi bindings, she didn't even crack her head on the polished edge, let alone gain a scratch. Between one breath and the next, she was hauled off to join the other soldiers bound and waiting in the darkness.

CHAPTER 20

How difficult was it to escape the situation at Zubenescha-mali? Compared to some situations I've been in, not all that difficult, really. Not in terms of danger, by my standards. But complicated, yes. It was definitely complicated at points.

~Ia

Mindful of the Gatsugi watching her being carried into the darkness, Ia focused. Doing this at a distance wasn't easy, but absolutely necessary. Gatsugi had large, dark eyes which absorbed not only the visible spectrum most aliens saw, but also partway into the infrared. So it was absolutely necessary to blind the crimelord Black Eyes.

The trick of it was to ignite the very air right in front of his face, hard, hot, and fast.

"—Iiiiiiihh! Iiiiiiihh! Iiiiiiihhhh!" Flesh slapped flesh as the alien smacked at least one set of hands over his singed face—which only increased his screams, not the smartest thing anyone should have done to a serious burn wound like that.

Still, his scream was her cue. Sucking in energy from the crysium bracelet circling her right wrist, she reshaped it even as she flexed her muscles, snapping the plexities supposedly holding her in place. Twisting as she dropped, she landed on her toes and free hand, absorbing the impact of her fall with a soft *slap* hidden beneath the shrieks of the blinded alien.

Thrusting upright as the cables pattered to the floor around her, Ia whipped herself and her re-formed sword through first one Tlassian neck, then the other. Launching out of her spin, she attacked the next nearest set of guards, tapping into the timestreams so that she didn't miss. Her faintly glowing blade whistled through the air. Bodies thumped to the floor behind her. Metal *ting-chinged* as she slashed up, then down, severing the bindings holding First Sergeant Likkety's wrists and ankles together.

"What the *hell* is going on in here?" she heard Siddhartha demand. It was too late; Ia was already hacking her way through the third pair of guards. Behind her, she knew Likkety was scrabbling to rip the blindfold from his face and remove the gag from his mouth, and cut through Buck Sergeant Lok'tor's bindings with another chime of crysium versus steel.

"Lllightsss!" Sllaish demanded, hissing the command harshly.

Snapping her eyes shut, she squeezed them against the explosion of brightness and spun into the fourth set of guards, the ones holding Lieutenant Nguyen. Not to cut them, but to shove the Humans back from their captive. This time, she cut his bonds first, *then* slashed the thin, frail-seeming blade through both men's torsos. Grabbing one by the upper arm, she finished the move by giving herself an extra spin, hurtling the dying man's upper half at the hastily drawn weapon being aimed her way by the nearest Solarican crimelord.

She did so with a scream, an impromptu war cry. *"India Alphaaaa!"*

Snatching up the next body part, she flung it at the Choyan, who was pulling out a holdout pistol of her own. Not bothering to wait and see it hit, Ia sprinted to the next guard on her list. A dodge behind him shielded her from the weapons being drawn by the other Lyebariko employees; she cracked her hilt up into his nose, stunning him and staggering him back, his hands instinctively going to his bleeding face. He gasped in the next second, shot in the back by one of his fellow guards, robbing her of her cover. It had been just long enough, however, to cut the bindings on the next sergeant, and shove the guard over the kneeling man, knocking him into his partner.

"Ia?" Likkety gasped, his blindfold tossed aside and his brown eyes blinking, adjusting to the light flooding the chamber.

"Hoo-rah!" Ferrar yelled, thrusting upright and to the side. Bound as he was, the sudden surge from his kneeling position battered aside his captors. The others followed suit, staggering on bound-together ankles, but doing their best to knock over the guards trying to aim at her.

Her own eyes had finally adjusted, allowing her to snatch at the falling guard's arm. Her blade slashed up through his armpit. Blood splattered everywhere, adding to the mess on her clothes, the gore on the floor, but her impromptu missile struck Siddhartha in the face, sending his laser shot wild. Whipping the blade back down, tapped into the timestreams, she smacked the blade into a laser shot from one of the guards. He was body-checked in the next moment by Nguyen, who punched the other Human in the throat and wrested the gun from his grip.

Her blade hadn't caught all of the beam. A thin slice of over-clocked yellow streaked across her side, scorching through her clothes. It was nothing like the laser cannon shot she had once taken; it hurt, but it didn't slow her down. Other weapons fired, as the men and women she had freed so far wrestled with their captors and confiscated weapons.

The Lyebariko members were taking refuge behind the chairs on the far side of the table, and firing back. Likkety screamed hoarsely, taking a shot in his back. She knew he wouldn't die and thus ignored it, cutting through another set of guards, another set of chains, and another.

Ferrar was now free, and those still bound had scraped their blindfolds off their eyes, allowing them to see and thus fight. Blakely had her bound legs wrapped around the throat of a knocked-over guard, choking him between her knees, her wrists still caught behind her back. The most athletic of the sergeants, Vin, was hopping around, head-butting everyone not on his side. Somehow, he was keeping his feet, making her want to laugh. Unfortunately, the rest of their situation wasn't a laughing matter.

Their luck wasn't going to hold. Beheading the next guard, Ia snatched the gun from his hand, spun, and fired. The yellow-hot beam speared into the back of one Lyebariko member fleeing through the door she had been brought through. Ia turned and cut through more flesh and steel, then whirled back as three more crimelords fled. This time the bolt smacked into the control panel. The machinery spit sparks and smoke, and the door hissed shut, sealing the remainder in the room.

Carrying through her spin, she fired at the other door—and was struck from behind. Not on her gun arm, which fired steadily, destroying that entrance's control panel as well, but on the elbow of her sword hand. The blow hit her on the nerve, numbing her fingers and fumbling her grip. Ia snatched at the blade as it fell, barely catching the hilt as she was yanked backwards.

The Tlassian's other arm hooked around her chest and shoulder, bending her over with a *hrrruk-hrrruk* sound. Abruptly she had a bigger worry on her hands. Dropping blade and gun, she wrenched herself around, twisting into his chest. Hooking her left arm between his legs, she heaved the moment he spat, lifting him too high. Acidic venom spewed past her shoulder. She wrenched muscles in the move, for he was larger and muscular, but the venom missed.

Thank you, Grandmaster, for teaching me to recognize that sound! The fervent thought was all she could spare, though. Tossing him to the floor, she spun back and dove for her sword— and slipped on the blood coating the floor. *Oofing* at the impact, Ia slapped her hand down on the blade anyway—and hissed as one of the remaining guards grabbed the hilt, cutting up into her fingers. He laughed and tensed to thrust, but it was too late.

A shift of energy, a flow of force, and everything was reversed. Suddenly, *he* was holding the now slightly cloudy, pink gold blade in his abruptly bloodied hand, and *she* had the hilt. Thrusting and slashing up even as he blinked in shock, Ia scrambled to her feet, cutting through him from gut to shoulder. Spinning to find her next target, she stumbled and slipped, dropping to one knee.

She didn't have to attack, though; Sergeant Vin hopped over to her side, distracting the next guard long enough for Ferrar to kidney-punch the other man, then reach up and break his neck just as the Human reached for the still-bound Marine to do the same. Grabbing Vin by the arm, she spun him around and snapped her blade through his wrist shackles, then whacked through his leg chains, setting him free. Sergeant Gilvers, still bound, was taking a beating from two of the guards, so she shoved Vin in his direction and moved to release the next captive.

Those who were already free had managed to disable most of the other guards. Two more of the Lyebariko were dead. Unfortunately, with most of the guards down, there wasn't enough confusion and milling of bodies for the remaining three Lyebariko to hesitate about firing. Her fellow Marines were using the lumps of bodies on the floor as best they could for their own cover, since they didn't have the chairs the Lyebariko did.

Except, Ferrar and Nguyen didn't crouch for long; instead, they grabbed one of the dead guards and spun the body around in tandem by his heels. They let go, flinging it at the table and its cluster of chairs. That not only broke the crimelords' line of fire, it smacked apart their cover. Injured though he was, Likkety opened fire, dropping the Choya female with a cry. Someone else picked up a severed head and threw that as well, disrupting Siddhartha's aim.

Blood was everywhere, a sea of metallic-scented crimson. For once, she wasn't the only one coated in the stuff. Even Siddhartha, crouching once again behind a pair of chairs, was splattered and soaked in spots. A *bang, bang, bang* on the door the others had been brought through disrupted the battle. Siddhartha shouted as the Marines paused, looking around for the newest threat.

"Ha! Here come my reinforcements! You're going down! *No one* gets in our way!"

Ferrar shot at Siddhartha's feet with a projectile pistol, sending the crimelord scuttling back, dragging his chair with him.

"We're the *Marines!*" he retorted, shout echoing through the hall. "*You* picked the wrong fight! *Eyah?*"

"*Hoo-rah!*"

Someone else threw another body part from the side, disrupting Siddhartha's next shot. Shaking off her unsettled fascination with the scene, Ia scrambled across the bloodied floor, reaching Blakely. The other woman was down, but merely to take cover behind the lump of the guard she had strangled into unconsciousness. Dragging her over and snapping through her chains, Ia hurried on to the next sergeant in need of his freedom.

The door to her right started to glow along its edge. Ferrar fired two more shots at the retreating Siddhartha, then tossed aside his weapon and cast around for another one. Ia dipped into the timestreams again, and bared her teeth in a frustrated hiss. The probabilities had shifted to the lower scale while she wasn't looking; the soldiers coming as their reinforcements were bogged down. Someone needed to stop what was about to break through that back door, but they also needed every single Marine free.

"Captain!" she shouted, and heaved her sword at him, throwing it just low enough that it landed with a *tang* and skittered, chiming, through the blood at his feet. "Deadly sharp!"

He dove for it with a roll of his eyes. "I *did* notice, Sergeant!"

She didn't bother to reply. Dodging through the body parts being flung at the crimelord by the others, she reached the door just as armored hands shoved it open. Catching the black-and-white canister in her left hand as it sailed through, Ia dropped it to her right and flung it back low, between the mechsuited legs of the Lyebariko's private army. The sonic grenade went off, scattering static energy over the quartet of crimeworld soldiers in the corridor.

She ducked and grabbed the edge of the door despite the lingering, burning heat. Breath hissing in pain, Ia hauled the overheated edge into the mechsuited guard's forearm and the holdout gun popping up out of the armor plating. It bent with a *crunch*, not designed to take a sideways blow like that, and the arm retreated. She shoved the door the rest of the way shut, hoping the guard beyond wouldn't be able to get his much larger servo-fingers into the gap where he had burned out the locking mechanism.

Something was wrong. Ferrar wasn't moving. Struggling to keep the door braced shut, her muscles versus the mechsuit's servos, Ia yelled at him. *"Captain!"*

He was still on his knees, staring at the peach-hued blade in his hands. A blink and a twitch startled both of them—Ferrar's arm flicked the crystalline blade between himself and Siddhartha. The move successfully intercepted the bright orange beam aimed at the Lieutenant's chest by the crimelord. Stunned, Ia stared at both of them, not sure she could believe her eyes.

Ferrar whirled and flung the blade back at her. "Blakely, Vin, get the last ones free! Nguyen, Lok'tor, get that table over! Everyone, behind it and retreat to the far wall! Ia, rearguard!"

Lunging forward, Ia caught the sword by the curved strips serving as the swept-style knuckle guards. Flipping it around, she snapped her fingers around the hilt and whirled back in time to slice off the muzzle of the mechsuit-sized laser rifle being aimed her way. The blade *clanged* with the blow, jolting her hands; unlike flesh, ceristeel was a lot harder to cut through.

There was no way she was going to be able to cut open a mechsuit like a man. Ia quickly changed tactics, switching from slashing to stabbing. *That*, she could do. Dodging the swipe of the armor guard's arms, she put her full weight behind her thrust. The tip punctured with a chiming rasp, and the man inside twitched, stabbed through his ribs.

"What the hell is this furniture *made* out of?" she heard Vin exclaim. "Why isn't he going *down*?"

Not quite the right angle, dammit. Foot planted on his thigh, she shoved as she pulled back, scraping the blade free. That meant she tumbled onto her back, but Ia was ready for it.

"Don't argue, Vin!" Lok'tor shouted back. "Not when it's giving *your* asteroid cover, too!"

She grinned and launched herself back at the doorway, thrusting hard, but with better accuracy this time. This time, the tip of her blade penetrated the mechsuit's power pack. The suit didn't even spark; all of that power drained straight into the blade, and from the blade, into her. She flushed some of it through her biokinetic gift to her injuries, healing them, but the rest swirled into a giddy sense of euphoria. Giddy enough, she found herself staring right at the easiest, quickest way to cheat.

All she had to do was block this entrance just enough to keep the Lyebariko's reinforcements from getting through in the next ten minutes. And all she had to do, to do *that* . . . was pyrokinetically ignite every explosive and power pack being carried by the remaining three mechsuited guards, and the lightly armored but heavily armed sentients lurking behind them.

She had enough energy for it right now, too.

Yanking her blade back out of the dying man's armor, she spun around and sprinted for the far side of the room with a scream, mind giddily and gleefully stabbing backwards. *"FIRE IN THE HOLE!"*

The explosions—series, really, but rapid-fire—flung her off her feet. At the last second, she realized Nguyen had stood up to take advantage of Siddhartha's hasty sideways scuttle, dragging his chair into the left-hand corner. Wrenching herself midair, she brought her sword around so that it wouldn't accidentally cut him. At a cost. She *cracked* arm-first into the wall instead of feetfirst and dropped with a scream, landing behind the long, oval table the others were using for shelter.

The overhead lights flickered and dimmed, as much from the thick, black smoke billowing out from the far side of the chamber as from the disruption to their power. Rubble pattered down. Panting, Ia flexed her telekinesis, straightening her broken bones with an *urk* of pain. A second flex melted the sword, flowing the biocrystal up under her blood-soaked sleeve, until it hardened into a makeshift cast. Now that the euphoria was fading, she knew it had been a damn fool move. Successful— very successful, since no one else in this room would be injured—but foolish.

"Ha! *Die*, you bastard!" Nguyen shouted, crouching back down.

"You got 'im?" Ferrar asked. At the lieutenant's nod, the Captain sighed. "Good work, everyone . . . *Shakk*, what a mess. At least they're not getting in *that* way. Keep an eye on that other door, meioas. Anyone injured?"

A list was quickly compiled. Some minor gut wounds—laser fire, so they were self-cauterized at least—scrapes, cuts, a couple of projectile wounds to arms and legs, a shot in the back, a chest wound, both in nonvital spots, and her broken arm. Everyone would live, provided reinforcements arrived soon. Satisfied, Ferrar shifted to sit beside Ia as she sat up, cradling her arm carefully in her lap.

"So, Sergeant . . ." he murmured.

"Acting Lieutenant," Ia corrected. "D'kora promoted me as senior-most before Doc Keating shipped her off for treatment. Broken neck, but she'll live."

"Good choice. I trust you have *some* sort of plan to back up all of this madness?" he asked her. "Like a way for us to get out of here? You did shoot the other door in the control panel."

With her arm stabilized in its crysium cuff, the ache was bearable. Painful, but bearable. She dipped briefly into the timestreams, checking the progress of Spyder and the rest. "Right now, sir, I'd say . . . just sit tight and wait for the reinforcements to arrive."

"Reinforcements?" Ferrar asked.

"I allowed myself to get captured so we could track these bastards down. Right about now, Sergeant Spyder should be leading the vanguard of an invasion force into . . . aaand there he is, right on time," she murmured, grinning as they all heard an explosion off in the distance. Specifically, one behind the nearby door. It wasn't nearly as strong as the one that had reduced the far wall to smoldering rubble, but it was an explosion nonetheless.

"Yes, I remember him chatting with that meioa-e and walking her out the door, back at the party. I hope he gets here soon . . . but we should be safe until then," Ferrar agreed, sighing. Ia knew he was taking her literally at her word, that Spyder and the rest were temporally on time. There was just one thing wrong with his statement, something she had to correct.

"Safe, yes . . . except for the K'katta clinging to the ceiling," Ia stated. Ferrar wasn't the only Marine to give her a sharp look. Lifting her uninjured left arm, she pointed up. Vin, Nguyen, and Blakely bounced back onto their feet first, aiming upward. They were followed by the others who had snatched weapons from their fallen captors.

Chittering echoed down at them. The translator box snapped the alien's words, sophisticated enough to convey feeling as well as meaning. "*How* did you know, Human? You didn't even look up!"

"You keep underestimating the Marines, meioa! It's a simple case of xenopsychology, the kind you get in Basic Training," she catcalled back, peering up into the shadows. "Humans rarely look up because we evolved on the plains, but the K'katta evolved in the forests, and your kind always flee for the trees!" Struggling to her feet, she stepped forward, shifting far enough that she could catch a glimpse of the shadow of a shadow that was the multilimbed, spider-like alien. "Now. I am going to give you a *choice*, meioa. You can be smart, come down here and surrender, and you will not be harmed. But if you are *stupid*, if you make me come up there after you, I will *rip* off your own legs and *beat* you to death with them!

"*Choose.*"

Her threat echoed off the walls. The shadow hesitated, then moved. Dangled. Dropped, flipping just enough to extend all ten legs and cushion most of the alien's landing. The twelve-meter drop wasn't that dangerous for him, despite the *thump* of his landing; like Ia, he was a native-born heavyworlder. All of his species were heavyworlders: K'katta had evolved with a dual skeleton, sturdy bone on the inside and chitin-armor on the outside, allowing them to attain two-meter leg-spans as well as brains big enough for sentience.

"How very smart of you, meioa," Ia told him as the K'katta crimelord drew up his legs close to his body, his posture an alien version of surrender.

"Chun, Vin, go look at that cart they brought in, see if it has anything to bind the meioa with," Ferrar ordered. "Nguyen, take Blakely and Lok'tor, and make sure all the guards are dead or bound."

Lok'tor choked on a laugh. "You think some of 'em are still alive? After the mess our Bloody Mary made?"

"Hey, I only knocked *mine* unconscious," Blakely countered, keeping her gun trained on one particular target as she picked her way around the table. "With my luck, he's just faking it."

"I don't even *want* to look at the mess she made," Lieutenant Konietzny muttered. He was one of the ones shot in the leg, and couldn't stand. Someone had dragged him behind the oblong table when the retreat had been called, though the act had left a literal trail of blood leading all the way from the puddles staining the far sections of the floor. Some of it was his; most of it thankfully wasn't.

Ia returned to the wall, sagging down it to sit on the floor. She had passed off her injury as a greenstick fracture, though it was actually a full pair of breaks. The lie was enough to get her out of having to work, though, and that was good enough for her.

"Speaking of messes, Ser . . . Acting Lieutenant," Ferrar corrected himself, looking back at her. "Where is that sword of yours?"

"I can't say right now, sir. I lost track of it in the explosion."

He gave her a dubious look. She flicked her eyes ceiling-ward. Twice, when it looked like he was going to speak. Subsiding, he eyed his own blood-splattered clothes and grimaced. "Bloody Mary . . . you've coated even us in your crimson mess. I should make you clean it all up."

Another explosion, this time much closer, trembled the stone wall behind them. Ia rested her head back against that wall, smiling. "Don't be silly, sir. I'm an officer, now. Officers don't clean up messes. They make the enlisted do that."

Ferrar wasn't the only one who busted up laughing. He recovered enough to give her a dirty look. "Then I'll bust you back down to Private!" He sighed, losing most of his humor. "These *shakk-tor* told us they were going to torture and kill us, once you arrived. Thank you for riding to the rescue."

"You're welcome, sir. But thank the others," she added, lifting her chin at the still-intact door off to the side. "They're the ones fighting off the rest of the Lyebariko's private army. Without them, we wouldn't be able to get out of this room alive."

Nodding, he relaxed against the wall beside her. "I'll keep that in mind."

CHAPTER 21

. . . Okay, fine, since you won't let it go, I did not beat that K'katta to death with his own limbs. I just threatened him. I guess the threat was so amusing to the rest, they just kept retelling it and retelling it, until it took on a life of its own.

For the record . . . if he had forced me to climb up after him? Yeah. I would have beaten him to death with his own limbs. You don't mess with the Marines. Hell, you don't mess with any Branch of the Space Force. But the moment he surrendered, he became a prisoner of war. I didn't touch him after that point.

~Ia

APRIL 2, 2492 T.S.

The door beyond Ia's desk hissed open. Despite her field promotion to Acting Lieutenant, she was still the Company Sergeant, and that meant filling out paperwork on the battle that had just passed. Filling it out with one hand, since her right arm was now firmly secured in a sling-supported cast while the bone-setting enzymes did their work, but working on it all the same.

"Could I have a moment of your time, Ia?" Ferrar asked her.

Nodding, she keyed the workstation to save her files. Even without the timestreams, she could guess what he needed to discuss right now. It was something that had bugged her since the fight on Beta Librae V two days ago.

They were still in the Zubeneschamali System, handling some of the cleanup details from the fight, but mainly just waiting for Battle Platform *Justicar* to finish reaching the system. The *Liu Ji* could still fly, but she was definitely battered from her trip through the natural rift, and would need several repairs before being redeployed anywhere. The Platform would have the equipment and supplies needed to get them moving again. The rest would be taken care of at the shipyards in orbit around Mars when they swung by on the way back to their regular patrols on the Terran/Gatsugi border.

Entering his office, she closed the door behind her and took the same chair she had first used roughly two years before. Ferrar seated himself, shut down his workstation, and rested his elbows on his desk.

"Now. About your sword," he stated flatly.

She settled back in her chair. She couldn't quite fold her arms, given her cast, but she could and did hook the fingers of her left hand into her belt. "Yes, about my sword. You acted rather strangely when I tossed it at you. I was hoping you'd go and cut the last of the others free, but you didn't, sir. Why didn't you?"

"When I picked it up, I saw things. Flashes of things."

Ia sat up a little at that. ". . . Things?"

He gave her a significant look. "*Future* things. The next few moments in time. I know . . . because you took that sword and did exactly what I saw you ended up doing. And that we needed to get behind that table for cover, when the corridor blew."

Her jaw dropped. It took Ia a few seconds to realize it was sagging. She snapped it shut, sitting up fully. "You . . ."

"You said you lost that sword in the explosion. But I remember seeing you flying through the air with it in your hand," Ferrar stated. "And it wasn't in the mess we left behind in our little makeshift foxhole. So. Where did it go?"

Mind racing, Ia pondered the implications. *If he could see the future . . . why could he see it when he touched it? Crysium does have some mild precognition-projective abilities, but only in large masses back on Sanctuary. I know it's the source of the Fire Girl Prophecies . . .*

"Ia, I asked you a question," her commander stated quietly. "I'd appreciate an answer."

"Shhh, I'm thinking," she murmured.

"Ia. The sword. Now," Ferrar ordered flatly.

Sighing, she shifted and bent over, tucking her fingers up the cuff of her pant leg. When she pulled them out again and lifted her hand up into his line of view, she was holding the sword. It gleamed in her hand, sharp and transparent pink gold.

"I . . . am not going to ask where you were hiding that," Ferrar muttered, eyeing the long, thin blade warily. "You told General Sranna it was some mineral from your homeworld. But *that* is no natural mineral. Which means you lied to a superior officer."

"Technically, I didn't lie. It is a real mineral native to my homeworld. I simply didn't reveal *all* that this stuff is," Ia replied. "As for *what* it is . . . you don't need to know. I am, however, curious about your reaction to it back in the Lyebariko's lair."

Reversing the blade, she offered the weapon to him on her palm. Ferrar hesitated a moment before wrapping his brown fingers around the hilt. Lifting it carefully, he . . . froze again. Blinked. Stared, and carefully set it down on his desk.

"That . . . is something I am not meant to know," he finally murmured, staring at the gleaming, crystalline schläger.

"No, sir. You're probably not. But I would like to know what you saw."

He looked up at her, mouth twisting wryly. "More of the near future. We have about four, five minutes before Sudramara pays me a visit. Put it away . . . wherever you were hiding it."

Nodding, Ia tucked it back below the edge of the desk, drawing and reshaping it into an innocuous ankle-cuff.

"Anything you *can* share with me, Acting Lieutenant?" he asked.

"No, sir. But . . . I'll have to figure out what this means. You shouldn't be seeing the future like that." Ia shrugged. "Something happened. Something involving my sword. I'll have to give it some thought. If I can harness this . . . inadvertent precognitive ability in someone who has shown absolute zero ability before now . . ."

"That's a dangerous-sounding power," Ferrar warned Ia.

"As much as I or any other commander would love to be able to see even a few glimpses of the future, particularly on the battlefield . . . the future is fluid. I don't even know how you can navigate all of the possibilities with such accuracy. The rest of us would have far worse luck steering the currents. Not to mention if that power fell into the wrong hands . . ."

"Oh, trust me, I want to avoid that possibility even more than you," Ia promised him quickly, fervently. "I'll save experimenting with it until I get back home. Until then . . . well, sir, I lost track of my sword in the battle, and that's the story I'm sticking to."

"Good. That's an order, by the way," he added, pointing at her. "A standing order, until you hear differently from me. That way you *can* lie about it and still avoid that particular Fatality. The responsibility for this particular lie will rest on *my* shoulders . . . and I'm protected from it by the fact that a precognitive told me I couldn't tell anyone else."

"Sir, yes, sir," she agreed, smiling slightly.

"Good." Lacing his hands together, Ferrar studied her. "In the meantime, we have something else to discuss. Lieutenant D'kora will be months recovering from her injuries. That leaves me without an officer in charge of the 2nd Platoon. I have assembled the paperwork to permanently approve your Field Commission. All it requires is your authorization . . . temporal or otherwise. That . . . glimpse at the future tells me that this is a power I do not want to mess with."

Well, at least something *good came of that, if it's convinced him not to rush ahead. Maybe I can harness that for everyone else I need to convince,* Ia thought. *If I can only figure out how.*

"So. Do you want the field honor? And, more importantly, can you handle it?" he asked her, giving her a pointed look.

She nodded. "Sir, yes, sir. I can handle it. But I'll want to take off for an Academy when my current duty posting is up. Actually, I'll be required to, by military law. All field-promoted officers still have to go through Academy training at some point. Preferably within the first year."

"That's in, what, three months?" Ferrar asked. He nodded. "Granted. By then, D'kora should be back on her feet, or if not her, the Corps will be able to assign me another junior officer to take her and your place."

His door chimed. Thumbing a control on his desk, Ferrar opened the panel. Captain Sudramara stepped inside. He nodded politely at both Marines.

"Captain . . . Lieutenant. We just received word. Battle Platform *Justicar* will be in the system within an hour. Repairs are estimated to take three days, then we'll be under way. The Command Staff has authorized two weeks of Leave while we're at the Deimos dockyards," Sudramara revealed. "You should be getting your official orders shortly."

Ferrar nodded. He glanced at Ia. "Are you going to finally take some extended Leave, Ia? Or are you going to continue to volunteer for yet more work?"

"My homeworld is on the backside of Terran space, sir. The far backside, by about seven hundred light-years," she reminded him. Their one-day stops at Battle Platforms didn't exactly count on the vacation roster, though she had stood guard duty a couple of times in the past year-plus. "The more off-Platform Leave I can accumulate, the more time I'll have to spend on *getting* home . . . and actually having some time to visit before I'll have to spend the rest of it on coming back. I'll probably take it between the end of this duty posting and heading for an Academy. Sort of a break before beginning the next phase of my career."

"Make sure you do come back to that Academy, Lieutenant Ia," Sudramara stated, surprising her a little. He lifted his chin. "You stood up to me and shot me down in front of my own crew. But you were in the right, and you did it within the lines. You'll make one hell of an officer someday. Of course, my ship is battered and barely spaceworthy, but those friends of yours behaved themselves and cracked that fortress wide open for our side."

"Just don't go around thinking I can pull it off a second time, sirs," Ia warned both men. "Drek's debt to me has been repaid, and I don't exactly have a lot more 'friends' like him wandering around the galaxy at the moment."

"I just wish I knew who leaked enough information for those bastards to set us up like that. But, with luck, we've bloodied the noses of these so-called crimelords hard enough, they won't come back looking for more," Ferrar said. "You can work guard duty on the ship while it's undergoing repairs at Mars. There'll be a brief stop at Earth first, however. The Command Staff wishes to recognize the acts of valor and courage so many of you displayed in riding to our rescue."

"Just doing my job, sir," Ia demurred. She rose from her seat. "Speaking of which, I still have a ton of paperwork to wade through. At least, until you can get a Company Sergeant to take over for me. It's a different enemy, but it still needs to be vanquished."

"By all means, get to it, soldier," he allowed, waving her out of his office. "Better you than me."

"Sir, yes, sir." Nodding to both officers, Ia took her leave.

APRIL 6, 2492. T.S.
SIC TRANSIT

A blue-clad body clipped a tray of food onto the galley table next to Ia's, and slipped into the rotating, permanently affixed empty seat next to hers. Reaching for the salt and pepper shakers in their clip-holders, Bennie nodded politely at Ia. "Lieutenant."

"Commander," Ia quipped back.

Exchanging titles had become something of a joke between the two of them. Despite the large part of herself that wanted to hold back from making friends, particularly when she could learn all too easily when and how each person around her would die, Ia considered the chaplain to be one. Or rather, something of one, since not even Bennie knew about her various abilities.

"You have any plans for our two weeks' Leave?" Ia asked, picking up her second sandwich somewhat awkwardly with her left hand. Pulling that stunt back on the planet had been a damn fool move because it left her fumbling her way through life one-handed for well over a week.

"More plans than you do," Bennie snorted, digging into her salad. "I heard you picked up guard duty again."

Ia chewed and swallowed. "Someone has to stay and help oversee the repairs. Might as well be me."

"Service junkie," the chaplain accused under her breath.

"You're damn right," Ia retorted, chuckling. "But I'll finally have enough Leave accumulated to go home for a couple of weeks, plus travel time."

"Make that three weeks."

Ia looked at the older woman. She knew it was coming, had planned for it, but still managed to look at least a little surprised. Lifting her brows, she repeated, "*Three* weeks?"

Bennie nodded, chewing her food. She sipped from her glass of milk before responding. "The way I figured, you have the longest way to go home of just about any soldier out there, period. Probably *the* longest, since you're the only one who enlisted from your homeworld that I've heard about. So, I very carefully and firmly pointed that out to your higher-ups. With a clue-by-four for my sword and the authority of God as my shield. I may not wade into a bloodbath up to my hairline like you do, but I do fight for what is just and right, in my own way."

"Thank you." Ia smiled. She scraped together the falling-apart bits of her sandwich and lifted it one-handed again. Then had to drop it and patiently scoop the food back into a manageable pile. "I really miss my family, you know? I'm looking forward to finally seeing them again."

"We all do," Bennie allowed. She speared another forkful of greens, then asked, "So, how are you sleeping at night?"

"Actually . . . pretty good, lately," Ia found herself confessing after a moment's reflection. "Particularly after rescuing the Captain and the rest. It was a good day's fight."

Bennie nodded slowly. "Yes, I think it was. They're showing Old Earth 2-D films in the forward boardroom, Deck 3, starting in an hour. Marines and Navy are both invited. You coming?"

She shook her head. "I have letters to write." Ia started to bite into her sandwich again, then glanced at the redhead and smiled. "Particularly if I get to have an extra week's Leave back home. I'll have to warn them I'm staying extra long. Thank you, Bennie."

The chaplain dipped her head. "My pleasure, Ia."

APRIL 11, 2492 T.S.
THE TOWER, ALOHA CITY
EARTH, SOL SYSTEM

This time, the sword at her side was a standard-issue Marines saber. The crysium currently formed a cuff around her left ankle, the safest place to hide it. Her Dress Blacks had been cleaned and re-pinned with her full compliment of glittery, and her brown-piped black cap sat squarely on her neatly trimmed hair. Her arm was still in a sling—black, to match her uniform— and would be for another four days, but otherwise she was ready for what was about to happen.

This time, the occasion wasn't a fancy greenroom party with acting celebrities, but a large auditorium at the Tower, the sprawling complex which housed the Space Force's headquarters just outside the Terran United Planets capital, Aloha City. Civilians as well as soldiers filled the tiers of seats. Not quite a full house, but close to it.

". . . We award you the Vanguard Star, for leading the invasion of the kidnapper's underground complex with great courage and valor. You were a great inspiration to the meioas under your command," General Culpepper Brandestoc stated, gripping and shaking Spyder's hand once again before handing over the commendation box. "And finally, at the request of your superiors, it is my pleasure to bestow upon you the rank of Staff Sergeant, and all the commensurate pay and responsibilities thereof."

"Sir, thank y', sir!" Spyder shook his hand one last time, accepted the box with his new pips, then saluted.

Once it was crisply returned and he was dismissed, Spyder about-faced and walked off the platform to the accompaniment of applause from the audience, and cheers from Ferrar's Fighters and the crew of the *Liu Ji*. He was escorted by the aide who had carried in the platter bearing Spyder's array of medals, directing him down the steps at the side of the platform. While he and the others who had been awarded their commendations had started out in a row of seats on the stage, each one had retreated afterwards to one of the seats in the audience. With Spyder's departure, Ia was the only one left in the chairs a few meters from the podium.

The foremost general of the Space Force Marine Corps faced the podium again, his voice projected by the discreetly placed pickups. "Our last soldier worthy of tonight's commendation ceremony is, in a word . . . extraordinary."

Ia tried not to blush. The actual wording of this speech had varied quite a bit, so she hadn't paid much attention to it in the timestreams. General Brandestoc wasn't a man for overplanned speeches.

"She will protest in her roundabout way that she is normal. Ordinary. Extra *ordinary*, in fact. That any Marine who puts in the thought and effort that she does is equally capable of such feats of heroism and bravery. However, while most of her claim is true, and we have had the joy of recognizing several others in this Company perform outstandingly well as fellow Marines . . . her superiors, the Command Staff, and myself all choose to disagree.

"Moreover," the black-clad general stated, "the extraordinary, and not just extra-ordinary, actions of this one particular soldier have caught the attention of more than just the military. While it would be my great pleasure as head of the Space Force Branch Marine Corps to award the following commendations to the soldier in question . . . my authority in this matter has been superseded by the Space Force's direct superior.

"Meioas, I give you Sindra Multalla, Secondaire of the Terran United Planets Council." With a slight bow, the general backed away from the podium, giving ground to the woman who approached from the wings of the stage.

Clad in a long, dark purple gown, her dark hair piled elegantly on her head, Secondaire Multalla claimed the attention of everyone in the hall. She did so with almost all the grace of a politician born and bred. Her only flaw was that the smile she bestowed on General Brandestoc and the others was a genuine one, openly pleased and thrilled.

"Thank you, General. Greetings, meioas, soldiers of the Space Force, and the civilians who know, support, and love them," she stated, sweeping her gaze over the hall. Her accent was faint at best, holding only hints of her origins in Persia Province on the other side of the planet. "While the Space Force does report directly to the Council, specifically to myself as Secondaire and then to the Premier, who is *my* superior in the military's final chain of command . . . there are literally billions of men and women and other meioas serving in our Space Force. We rely heavily upon the officers of the Space Force to notice and commend particular individuals on our behalf.

"With so many acts of heroism and service happening around our interstellar empire, it is rare that one particular soldier is singled out and brought to the Council's attention.

But this particular soldier's actions merit that attention." She turned sideways a little, facing Ia. "Acting Lieutenant Second Class Ia, please come forward."

Rising from her seat, Ia approached. With her right arm still immobilized for a few more days, enzymes busy healing the breaks in her forearm, she saluted instead with her left hand. "Secondaire, sir!"

The pickups projected her voice around the hall. Secondaire Multalla managed a very credible return salute, and glanced over her shoulder. Another aide strode up from the far side of the platform, carrying a silver salver bearing a pile of small black boxes. She smiled at Ia and gestured at the tray.

"As you can see, we have reached certain conclusions after carefully reviewing your actions in the incident involving Captain Ferrar's Company, Acting Lieutenant." Turning, the Secondaire addressed the hall. "The military, like any branch of the government, runs on paperwork. After every deployment, whether it is a deadly engagement with a vicious enemy, or a desperate battle against nature and the elements when giving sentientarian aid to a new colony, everyone in the military has to write up a report on it.

"When we first reviewed Acting Lieutenant Ia's personal report on the incident in question . . . it was very dry, bland, and boring. A straightforward recital of facts. The words of her superiors, fellow noncommissioned officers, and the enlisted under her command, however . . . were positively loquacious by comparison." Multalla smiled wryly. "It is like the difference between what history records about Caesar's actions in Pontus, and what he himself wrote. When everyone else was writing scrolls upon scrolls about the battles in northeastern Europe, filling in the details for folks back home in ancient Rome . . . he simply wrote 'Veni, vidi, vici.' 'I came, I saw, I conquered.'

"Admittedly," she allowed, tipping her head slightly, "Ia does write down a few more words than that . . . but the flavor is the same as Caesar's. Bland. Like a cracker. According to those who witnessed her in action . . . she is more like a curry-stuffed chili pepper when in action. Given the sheer number of concurring accounts, plus visual recordings for confirmation regarding some of her actions . . . the Council's Military

Oversight Committee and I were forced to agree that the curry-stuffed pepper version is the most accurate one, and not the plain cracker she would have us believe."

Her recital earned a number of chuckles in the crowd. Multalla dipped her head in acknowledgment, then turned to the salver-bearing aide, gesturing him to take up a place between her and Ia, slightly behind the two of them. Facing Ia again, she picked up the first box, opened it, and displayed it first toward the audience, then toward Ia.

"For the wounds you bravely received in combat during the actions both at Observation Station *Ivezic* in the Zeljko 17 Binary System, and on Beta Librae V in the Zubeneschamali System, I award you the Purple Heart. May you not have to receive another one, though none of us are free to hold our breath on that count."

The audience applauded politely. Ia nodded and shook her hand, accepting the award. Secondaire Multalla picked up not one, but two boxes, next.

"For the act of personally removing or capturing the equivalent of at least two enemy noncommissioned officers, I award you with two Crossbones. Taking out the chain of command is important to sowing confusion and inefficiency among the enemy, and we recognize this fact." Multalla offered her the boxes in her hand.

Ia still had the first one in her grip. Snapping it shut, she debated putting it into her jacket pocket, then gave up and stuffed it into her sling. There were too many boxes still waiting on the salver, compared to the number of pockets available on her Dress Blacks. Accepting the other two, she shut them and stuffed them up her sling as well, then shook the Secondaire's hand.

Multalla smiled wryly, and picked up the next two. "Also, for the act of personally removing or capturing two enemy officers . . . so to speak . . . we award you a Skull for each confirmed personal conquering on your part of a major crimelord who dared to declare war upon our Space Force and its soldiers."

"Thank you, sir." Those boxes went into the black folds of her sling.

"Next, we have three White Crosses. The White Cross is for rescuing wounded or captured comrades from either a dangerous situation, or enemy hands—as with the others who have received White Crosses tonight, we decided that one awarded per soldier rescued would be too many," the Secondaire stated, "so one is for rescuing your fellow sergeants, one is for rescuing your fellow lieutenants, and one is for rescuing your commanding officer, Captain Leonard Ferrar."

Ia didn't have to glance into the audience to know Ferrar was blushing and sinking a little lower in his seat. He hated his first name and never used it if he could get away with it otherwise. Personally, she thought it was a nice name, but then she wasn't him. Instead, Ia carefully kept her attention on the Secondaire, accepting the boxes with a handshake and a nod.

"The White Heart, on the other hand," Multalla stated, picking up the next box, "is awarded for rescuing *yourself* from enemy hands. Which you did most . . . *extraordinarily* . . . as General Brandestoc pointed out."

She did not mention that Ia had flung herself willingly into her own capture. A good thing, in Ia's opinion; that kept Drek's own actions from being scrutinized too closely. Multalla waited for the applause to die down, then continued.

"In reviewing your actions during the incident in the Zubeneschamali System, the Military Oversight Committee discovered an exceedingly rare level of valor, bravery, and action. You have, by your efforts, earned not only the Vanguard Star, for leading the attack on your captors in a most . . . lethal fashion . . . but also the Rearguard Star, for heeding your commander's orders to guard and defend the rest while they retreated to a more defendable stance while awaiting reinforcements. First in is often deadly enough," the Secondaire stressed. "Last out, usually even more so. But you flung yourself into combat both times without any hesitation, and with only the goal of saving others' lives in your mind.

"It is a distinct pleasure to award these two commendations to you in person, at the same time . . . and *not* have to hand them to your next of kin, as is so regrettably often the case."

Ia accepted the boxes solemnly. "I lead from the front, sir. Even if I have to fight facing backwards."

Multalla's mouth twitched up on one side. "That's good to hear. The next award . . . is very rarely assigned. For all that these crime bosses declared war upon the Space Force, the battle still took place in an era and a venue of peace. You join a very rare few who have put everything on the line and then some just to do what a soldier is meant to do . . . and you have surpassed all expectations, all hopes, and all dreams by your efforts to save others' lives. So, after a great and lengthy review, but very little following debate, it is my honor to award to you the Terran government's highest peacetime honor: The Star of Service."

Applause burst from the crowd. Even a number of cheers. Not the polite clapping for the various earlier awards.

"Sir." Ia squared her shoulders and saluted. Despite knowing it was coming, hearing the words pricked at her emotions. It wasn't the medal itself that moved her. It was hearing that her efforts were recognized, appreciated. Deliberately manipulated via the timestreams or not, her efforts *were* real. The intention behind them, her sanity-saving drive to save lives, was very real.

This medal, the Secondaire did not hand over in its box. She pulled it out, snapped the empty box shut, and tucked the black velvet container into Ia's right sleeve with a small, mischievous grin. Sobering in concentration, Multalla carefully pinned the blue and silver Star of Service to Ia's left lapel below her temporary Lieutenant's bar, which had been pinned above her First Sergeant's stripes and rockers, indicating she was still merely an Acting Lieutenant at the moment.

Nodding, Multalla stepped back and finally returned the salute, allowing Ia to drop her left arm. "Lastly . . . it is the firm belief of the Oversight Committee and myself that the temporary promotion from First Sergeant to Acting Lieutenant Second Class was not only necessary at the time, but has since been thoroughly earned by your ongoing display of inherent leadership skills throughout your military career.

"It is my final pleasure to officially confirm your Field Commission Honor to the rank of Lieutenant Second Class of the Terran United Planets Space Force, Branch Marine Corps. Attendant with this elevation in rank come all of the rights, responsibilities, pay upgrades, and headaches thereunto pertaining. Congratulations, Lieutenant Ia. You have earned this rank. Do not let down the confidence and faith your superiors have entrusted in you."

"Sir, no, sir. I will do my absolute best, sir," Ia promised, helping stuff the last box with her official brass bar into her sling. There were now so many, the velvet-wrapped containers were threatening to slide back out.

Multalla smiled wryly, if warmly. "From the look of things so far, I have no fear you'll do anything less."

Ia smiled and saluted—and hastily fumbled at the shifting boxes as they tried to escape her sling. Multalla chuckled and helped her stuff them back in, then gave her another credible salute.

"Dismissed, Lieutenant." Turning back to the podium as Ia hurried off the stage, left hand holding everything in place, the Secondaire addressed the waiting crowd. "I give this message to the rest of you as your commander, and as one of you, having served in the Space Force Navy for four years in my youth. The military runs on efficiency, discipline, regulation, and praise. We try our best to be efficient, so we do not waste our valuable resources. We drive ourselves with discipline, so that we are the saviors of the innocent, and bring no harm to the harmless. We enact various codes and laws to regulate our actions and efforts into uniformity, which in turn promotes the efficiency and the discipline we need. But it is the praise that is most important.

"To my fellow citizens, I ask that you take the time to thank any military personnel you may meet. Thank them for being willing to place themselves between you and whatever may harm you. To the soldiers of the Space Force, I ask that you take the time to thank each other, as well as watch out for each other . . . and to make sure you fill out a little bit more on your reports than just 'veni, vidi, vici.'

"Not *too* much more, because there are literally billions of these reports circulating around, and somebody has to read them," she joked lightly, earning a few, final chuckles. "But if you see someone beside you exhibiting great acts of courage, honor, skill, and compassion . . . please, report it to your superiors. These acts need to be brought into the light, so that we may all draw the strength and inspiration needed for our own moments of valor.

"Aloha, meioas, and good night," she finished. "Thank you for coming."

Every story has a beginning. Even Time itself. This story was how I began my military career.

Why the military? Couldn't I accomplish my goals any other way? Not really. Not and stay sane. It was just like I told Chaplain Bennie: I could not stand aside and watch others drown in the icy waters of the swirling flood of events I knew were about to descend upon us all. Not when I could wade in and help lift them out.

Someone else might've been able to stand aside. Others might've looked for a rope to throw to the victims. But not me. I knew a rope would never be enough. I knew it would take risking my skills, my weapons, my knowledge, and even my life if need be, to stand between the innocents of the galaxy and everything rising to threaten them.

Would I do it all over again? Go through all of that trouble and pain? In a heartbeat. Now, as for why . . .

I am a soldier. That duty is mine.

~Ia

TURN THE PAGE FOR A SPECIAL PREVIEW OF

THEIRS NOT TO REASON WHY:
AN OFFICER'S DUTY

BY JEAN JOHNSON

AVAILABLE IN AUGUST 2012 FROM ACE BOOKS!

"This is so exciting!"

Ia glanced over at the woman settling into the next seat. The orbital shuttle was nearly full, and the crew were urging passengers to take their places. The woman who was Ia's seatmate fished for her restraint straps. Her efforts at pulling the three-point belt into place were somewhat hampered by the added bulk of her gravity weave. Nudged a few times by the woman's elbow, Ia rolled her eyes and held out her hand, silently offering to latch it.

"Oh, thank you. Wait—where's *your* gravity weave?" the woman asked as Ia slotted the tab into its latch. "You're taller than me!"

Ia's rare sense of humor surfaced. Since she was clad in camouflage Browns, the speckled, mottled uniform of the Space Force Branch Marine Corps, she flashed a brief smile and stated, "I'm a Marine. We don't *need* gravity weaves."

The woman blinked, her brown eyes widening in shock.

Ia rolled her eyes. *Really, some people will believe* anything *about the SF-Marines.* "I'm also a native. Born and bred on Sanctuary. I'm coming home on Leave."

"Ah. Um . . . thank you for serving," the weave-wrapped woman finally offered.

"It's an honor to serve, meioa," Ia murmured in reply. Now that her seatmate had settled in, her mind was elsewhere, busy going over her schedule for the next three weeks. Some things would have to take place at exactly the right moment in time, while others would be more fluid. Like the problem of her tainted sword-turned-anklet.

The crew finished checking and securing the cabin. The woman at Ia's side said nothing for a long while, paying dutiful attention to the safety procedures lecture. Then, as they detached from the space station with a slight bump, the woman muttered once again, "This is so exciting!"

Sensing the woman was one of those sorts who just had to talk or burst, Ia sighed and asked the most obvious question, rather than dipping into the timestreams. "Is this your first trip to Sanctuary?"

The woman nodded quickly and smiled. She also held out her hand. "Amanda Sutrepya. And yes, it's my first time to your homeworld. I'm here on a missionary trip. And you are . . . ?"

"Lieutenant Ia." Ia shook the other woman's hand as briefly as possible. The closer she got to her homeworld, the more she feared her precognitive gift would turn unpredictable again. Plus there was the fact that physical contact always enhanced her ability to read another sentient being's plethora of potential futures. The combination held too much danger to risk it, though there wasn't much else she could do to avoid brushing up against someone in such crowded conditions. At least the other woman was wearing a purple, long-sleeved shirt under the lumpy web wrapping her limbs.

"Missionary trip?" The question came from the short, balding man on the other side of the aisle. He gave the woman, Amanda, a derogatory look, snorting, "Great. Another godless heathen," before returning his attention to the book pad in his hands.

"Excuse me?" Amanda asked, her tone and her expression both taken aback. "I am *not* a godless heathen, I am a Christian!"

The man gave her a look somewhere between disdain and pity. "Even worse, then. A deluded *polytheist.*"

The woman started to protest. Ia quickly reached over and touched her sleeve. "Don't."

"But he—"

"Just don't," Ia murmured again, cutting her off. "See the

corona pin on his jacket lapel? He's a member of the Church of the One True God."

"I . . . don't understand," Amanda muttered. She glanced back and forth between Ia and the man, finally settling on Ia. "Aren't they Christians, too? I thought their worship was based on the same general beliefs. One loving God, Abrahamic teachings . . ."

"So are Muslims and Jews, if you measure it by that method . . . but no, they are not Christians, they are not Muslims, they are not Jews," Ia told her, flicking up one finger per listing. "In fact, if you must get technical, their dogma actually began as an offshoot of *The Witan: The Book of the Wise*."

"We are *not* an 'offshoot' of anything. *We* are on the *true* path," the man across the aisle corrected tartly. His eyes were on the text of his book pad, but his ears were clearly listening to his neighbors. "Not my fault if the rest of you have been misled by the sweet-sounding poison of the Devil's books. The Bible, the Koran, the Torah . . ."

"Well, I never!" Amanda gasped, visibly upset.

"Meioas."

Ia's tone, more sharp than actually loud, cut across the missionary's sputterings, and caused the Church man to look up at her once more. A few others in the nearby seats glanced her way as well, but they didn't protest. Ia kept her eyes on the Church man. When she was sure she had his attention, she had her own say, leaning forward slightly while she held his gaze.

"I am on Leave from two years' worth of fighting on the far side of the known galaxy." That was a slight exaggeration, but she wasn't going to bother with the full truth. "It has taken me three weeks of travel to get this far. I have exactly three weeks, one day, and four hours from the moment we land, precious, precious days and hours to spend with my family, before I have to go back. I would therefore like to finish this last, tedious leg of my journey in peace and quiet."

"You'd be better off spending those three weeks on your knees in Our Blessed Cathedral, confessing the sins of spilling blood on some godless heathen's orders," the balding believer retorted.

Ia gave him a not-smile. "And I say unto you in reply, from Book Nine, The Righteous War, Chapter Three, verses four and five: 'Succor the weary and wounded soldiers who claim Sanctuary and take shelter among you. Give them rest and peace, and honor them for the sacrifices they make for the betterment of all.' "

He reddened a bit, having his own holy words flung in his face.

"*I* am a weary soldier of Sanctuary," Ia reminded him, speaking softly, but with enough point to cut to the bone, "and I am here to take shelter among my people. Give me my rest and peace, and honor me for the sacrifices I make . . . or spend your weeks on *your* knees, for failing to follow through on God's Own True Words."

Holding his gaze, she stared at him until he backed down, subsiding into his seat. He refocused his attention on his book pad. Only then did Ia settle back in hers. Just in time, too; they hit the atmosphere with a jolt and a rattle that made her grateful for the cushioning supporting and sheltering her body. Several jolting minutes later, the cabin screens lit up, showing the smiling face of their pilot.

"This is Captain D'Sall. We are currently traversing the edges of the local early-evening thunderstorm, so a bit more of this mild in-flight turbulence is to be expected. Please remain in your seats with your restraint belts firmly fastened. However, our flight will be short, as we will be landing at Our Blessed Mother Inter-Orbital Spaceport in approximately twenty minutes.

"As a reminder, all passengers wearing gravity weaves should have their weaves set to Adaptive Gravimetrics on the Low Strength setting so as not to interfere with the integrity of the shuttle. Do not adjust them back to Full Strength until we are fully on the ground and the Gravity Weave permission sign has been turned on. If you need help fighting the gravity to do so, please remain calm, press the button on your armrest or alert your seatmates, and the cabin crew will be by to check on you shortly. Once we land, only the flight crew are allowed to move about the cabin until we have reached the terminal, so please remain seated.

"If at any time you experience difficulty in moving, breathing, or even thinking, or feel like you are going to black out during your visit to Sanctuary, these are the primary symptoms of the onset of adjustment sickness, which can lead to more serious complications. If you suspect you are about to be ill at any point during your visit to Sanctuary, contact the emergency nets immediately, and go straight to the nearest medical facility to be checked out for the possibility of gravity sickness.

"The government of Independent Colonyworld Sanctuary wishes to remind all visitors and returning natives that it assumes no liabilities, fiscally or legally, for the complications of gravity sickness or any related injuries. Neither does Gateway Inter-Orbital Transit, of which you were advised before boarding this flight. However, we thank you very much for flying with us. We hope you'll have a safe time while on Sanctuary, and wish you a good day."

The shuttle jolted again. Ia winced as the woman next to her grabbed at her forearm.

"God Almighty!" Amanda exclaimed, bouncing in her seat with the next jolt of turbulence. "*This* is *mild*?"

Prying the woman's hand off the sleeve of her brown camouflage shirt, Ia pressed it to the armrest and tucked her own hands into her lap. "Since we're due to arrive at the equivalent of near-sunset, yes, it's just one of the mild, daily thunderstorms. If it were a *real* storm by Sanctuarian standards, the pilot would have delayed the flight. This one isn't nearly as risky as you'd think."

". . . Oh."

The other woman started to relax, then yelped a little as the ship bucked again. A flash of light and a not quite muffled *boom* beyond the porthole windows made her yelp a second time, along with a handful of the other passengers. The rest were either too busy enduring the ride, or like Ia and the balding believer across the aisle, weren't fazed by the local weather. Certainly this turbulence wasn't as bad as some of the planetfalls she and the rest of Ferrar's Fighters had made, riding to the rescue of various colonyworlds.

Now I'm riding to the rescue of my own world, in a way. Though my efforts won't bear results for a few more years at the earliest. Enduring the bouncing with stoic patience, she absently rubbed her left hand over the hard cuff hidden beneath the mottled Browns of the opposite shirtsleeve. *Presuming all my speculations on the trip out here are in any way accurate, that is . . .*

I wonder what my brothers are going to think when I ask them literally to shed their blood for me, this week?

Thorne was the easiest of her family to spot. He stood literally head and shoulders above everyone else waiting on the far side of the Customs Peacekeepers, as tall as a local doorway and as broad as a tank. His dark brown hair had been trimmed with bangs in the front since she had last seen him in person, though it looked like it was as long as ever, pulled back in a ponytail.

She'd seen the change in the timestreams, but seeing it in person was another matter. It struck her just how much everything had changed back home. How much she had changed, even though Ia had known it would happen.

His hazel eyes met hers within moments, drawn to her thumb-length white locks and mottled brown uniform. There were other tall-by-comparison people arriving, mostly visitors from light-gravitied planets who were wrapped in gravity weaves, but she wasn't lost in a crowd; the others had spaced themselves out so that their personalized repelling fields, now set to full strength, wouldn't conflict and cause each wearer to stagger off balance.

The only thing that made her want to stagger was the full resumption of her home gravity, which she hadn't felt in over two years. Weight suits and artificial gravity could compensate somewhat, but she could tell she was out of shape by home standards. Until she saw her mothers.

Aurelia Jones-Quentin had gained a few fine worry lines between her brows and at the corners of her eyes, but her straight, dark brown locks were as grey-free as her son's. Amelia Quentin-Jones had picked up a few more streaks of silver among her lighter brown curls, but no extra lines on her face. They were clad in the same soft pastels the two women had always favored, and both their faces lit up with the same delight as they spotted her in the queue. Just the sight of her parents banished most of the annoying drag of the planet on her body. Gravity could not stop the lifting of her spirits.

As soon as she cleared the last checkpoint, Ia hurried forward. She dropped her bags to the plexcrete floor as her family moved up to meet her, and swept both of her mothers into a hug. Both of the older women laughed and sniffled and hugged her right back. She'd forgotten how stooping to hug them could put a crick in her back from the awkward angle, but Ia didn't care. Given everything that had happened since she had left, the pain was an old, revived pleasure by comparison.

For a moment, she let herself be a young woman again, saying good-bye to her family before heading to her destiny. Then one of her brothers ruffled her hair; from the downward pull of his palm, it was Fyfer, too short to have been seen immediately, compared to their elder brother.

"Look at that hair, all short and ugly, now!" Fyfer crowed, ruffling it again.

"Fyfer!" Aurelia scolded.

As her mothers released her, Ia pushed his hand away, then pulled him into a half hug and rubbed her knuckles over his brown locks. He squirmed and spluttered a protest, then twisted into her grip and pinched her inner bicep in the spot she had taught him. Even toughened up by her life in the military, it hurt like hell. Grunting and flinching, Ia released him. Then *oofed* as he flung his arms around her ribs in an enthusiastic hug.

Chuckling, Ia hugged him back. Unlike their elder brother, Fyfer was normal for a Sanctuarian. Naturally muscular, but short and not nearly the brick-walled body that Thorne was. So she squeezed and sort-of picked him up. Just a few inches, but enough to prove she was still stronger. He *oofed* in turn, then laughed and slapped her on the back.

"Slag, Ia! You used to pick me up higher than that! What happened to you in the Army?" he joked.

"It was the *Marine Corps*," Ia shot back, dropping him gently onto his feet. "And I've been living in lesser gravity. Working out as heavy as I can get it for several hours a day, but still *living* in lightworlder spaces."

Releasing her younger brother, she faced her half-twin. They had different mothers but the same father, both of them born barely half an hour apart. Both were anomalies in a world of gravitationally challenged heights. Thorne just held open his arms and Ia walked into them, nestling her head on his shoulder and her arms around his waist. He didn't threaten her ribs, just hugged her back.

"*Mizzu*," he murmured, his voice a quiet bass rumble. *I missed you*. The word was the shorthand speech from their childhood, raised like full-blooded twins, treated like twins, thinking like twins, until her gifts started developing in earnest.

"Mizzu tu," she agreed. *I missed you, too.* She hugged him, relaxing for a long moment . . . until her skin crawled, warning her that her precognitive gift was trying to open, trying to read all the possibilities of his future. Thankfully, the moment she shifted back, he released her. It might have been two years, but he still remembered how touchy her abilities could be.

"You okay?" Thorne asked her as she stepped back. He wasn't the only one giving her a concerned look.

Ia nodded . . . then shook her head. This was more than just the timestreams prickling at his proximity. Holding up her hand, she squeezed her eyes shut and focused on strengthening the walls in her mind. *No. Not right now. Not here and now, among all these people. I will not succumb to the Fire Girl Prophecy right now* . . .

Pushing it away, resisting, she breathed hard for a few moments. Someone else screamed, making her jump and snap her eyes open again. It wasn't a member of her family that had collapsed; instead, it was a familiar, purple-wrapped body. The Christian missionary, Amanda Something-or-Other, had dropped to her knees.

"Fire!" Amanda screamed, startling the mostly Human collection of tourists into wide-eyed, wary looks. "Fire! Birds in the sky! A girl—fire in her eyes! Fire in the world! A . . . a cathedral—a wall in the sky—aaaaaaah!"

Those who were native to Sanctuary looked at her, too. They, however, weren't confused by her outcry. Instead, they were broken into three groups. A few concerned-looking spaceport personnel hurried forward, mostly to ward off the few concerned tourists who were about to touch her—never a good idea, since the Fire Girl attacks tended to spread on contact more often than not. The rest were either blasé about the attack, looking for a few moments in curiosity before shrugging and moving on, or they hastily backed up, sketching corona-circles on their foreheads and muttering under their breath, no doubt prayers warding off any evil influence from the "demonically possessed."

Since it looked like the missionary would get some of the help she needed, a sketchy explanation of the phenomenon and suitable reassurances from spaceport staff, Ia herself settled into the non-Church category of natives and ignored the poor woman's plight. Stooping, she picked up her kitbag and the locked travel case stuffed with her writing pad and all the postdated letters she had printed out during the journey home. "I'll be fine. We have a lot to do. Move out."

She didn't miss the look her mothers exchanged, nor the glance they shared with Thorne, but Fyfer immediately started chatting about all the things she had missed, his graduation half a year early and subsequent enrollment in an acting school, Thorne's fast-paced progress in his space station governance degree, and of course questions on what her own last two years had been like. Ia did her best to listen and respond, but Fyfer didn't cease the steady stream of chatter until they were at the family ground car, and he finally noticed that Ia wasn't moving to put her things into the vehicle parked on one of the tiers of the spaceport's garage.

Instead, she had stopped, closed her eyes, and was simply breathing. Deep, steady breaths, the kind that sought to fill every last corner of her lungs.

"Hey," Fyfer admonished her. "Are you falling asleep already? I thought you Marines were tough!"

"I'm not *that* tired. I'm just enjoying the smell of home. You don't get ozone like this on other worlds, unless you deliberately go around creating sparks. Or the dampness, or the flickering of lightning pressing through your eyelids like little feathery touches . . ." She sighed and opened her eyes, smiling wryly. "It's just not the same, elsewhere."

"So what *is* it like on other worlds?" Thorne asked her, taking her bags and tucking them into the back.

She held up her hand and gestured for the others to climb into the car, then took the front passenger seat, her preferred spot so her gifts didn't trigger. Thorne took the driver's seat; with his broad, muscular shoulders, it was either let him drive or be squished in the backseat as he took up half of the space usually meant for three people. Once they were moving, Ia answered his question.

". . . What's it like on other worlds? Bouncy, until you get used to the gravity. The air can smell like a million different things. Recycled and dusty if it's a mining domeworld. Slimy and moldy if you've set down in a rainy spot on an atmospheric world, like that planet where we helped out the flood victims.

And then there's the recycled air of a starship, with cleaning products and sweating bodies in the gym, lubricants and hydraulics fluids in the mechsuit repair bays . . . and of course the greenery in lifesupport, but they limit access to that part of the ship. The Motherworld didn't smell bad," she added. "Lots of flowers and green growing things. Not enough thunderstorms, but not bad."

"Ooh! Tell us about the Motherworld!" Amelia interjected.

"Yes, please," Aurelia urged Ia. "What's it like? I've always wondered."

Smiling, Ia complied. "My first view was from orbit. It's really not that much different from Sanctuary, except the nightside glows with a million cities, and not from crystal fields and the few settlements we have. And only so many lightning storms can be seen, and only so many aurora curtains and sprite jets . . . You can't really see the lightning on Earth from space unless it's in a really big storm. And then of course my first stop was Antananarivo, on Madagascar Island. It's very tropical in the lowlands, but where I was, which was up in the hills, it's a bit cooler. More like around here."

"That was at the Afaso Headquarters, right?" Thorne asked her, directing the car into the flow of traffic skirting the capital city.

Ia nodded. "That's right. Grandmaster Ssarra says hello, by the way. They have a lot of land, much of it established as a nature preserve as well as farmland for self-sufficiency. There are *lots* of green plants there, compared to here—yes, the grass really *is* greener, on Earth." That made her family laugh. Enjoying their humor, Ia smiled and continued. "They have none of the blue plants like we have, not even as imports, and very few that look even vaguely purple. There are some yellow ones— grass when it's dry, for one—but the first impression you get of a non-desert landscape on Earth is of a million different shades of green . . ."

———

A door opened down the hall. It was followed by shuffling footsteps which were not quite lost under the soft, rhythmic grunts coming from Ia as she measured out a set of sit-ups, toes hooked under the living room couch for counterbalance. Her biomother, Amelia, squinted at her in the light from the reading lamp.

"Gataki mou?" Amelia shuffled a few steps closer, her bare feet tucked into worn pink slippers and her body wrapped in a fuzzy green bathrobe. "What are you doing, child?"

A little distracted by being called her old, Greek nickname of *my kitten*, Ia struggled to finish the set. Uncurling her stomach after three more crunches, she relaxed on the springy, rubbery floor, breathing hard. "I'm doing my morning calisthenics . . . and I'm really out of shape. I did what I could on the flight from Earth, but . . . I had to leave my weight suit behind. It would've cost too much to transport all that mass."

"Well . . . can you keep it down a little?" her mother asked. Behind her, the door opened again. "And maybe not start so early? I know we changed the beds in your old room so your brothers could have a little more room, which means you have to sleep out here, but . . . well, the floor here in the living room kind of squeaks, and . . ."

"Have you lost all sense of common courtesy?" Aurelia demanded, coming up behind her wife. Being slightly taller, she glared at Ia over her partner's shoulder. "It's five in the morning! Not even your brothers get up until seven at the earliest, and only because Thorne's first class is at eight this quarter!"

"Sorry." Sitting up, Ia shrugged. "I'll go for a run or something."

"In this neighborhood? At *this* hour?" Amelia asked.

Pushing to her feet, Ia arched her brow, looking down at her mothers. "Would *you* mess with someone as tall as me, who can comfortably jog in *this* gravity?"

"No, but we're not talking about vagrants or gang members," Aurelia reminded her daughter. "The Church has been moving more and more converts into this area. They're not going to look kindly on some . . . some solitary weirdo jogging around the block at this hour. Anything that isn't in Church doctrine, they won't like it."

"And they'll let you know," Amelia agreed.

Rolling her eyes, Ia swept her hands over her hair, raking back the sweaty locks. "I *do* know, Mother. But I'm going straight into the Naval Academy after this, and they'll be expecting me to stay in shape even while on an Extended Leave."

It didn't matter which one she was addressing. Amelia was Mom, Aurelia was Ma, but both were forever *Mother* to all three of their kids, and usually addressed as such when the pair were tag-teaming said kids.

Aurelia lifted her finger. "Don't sass us, *gataki*. If you're going to go jogging, then go. But go *quietly*. Your mother and I need our sleep. We closed the restaurant for your homecoming yesterday, but we'll have a busy day of it today, since it's the end of the week."

"I'll go put on my cammies," Ia offered, holding up her hands. "Even Church members have seen the occasional episode of *Space Patrol*, so they should know what a soldier looks like . . . and I'm just as sure that, by now, everyone who came into Momma's Restaurant in the last month knows that you've been expecting me home from the military."

"I suppose that'll have to do," Aurelia muttered. She pointed a tanned finger at her daughter. "And no more getting up at 'oh dark hundred,' you got that? That's an order." She folded her arms across her chest as Amelia turned to eye her. "A mother *always* outranks her little girl."

There were several retorts Ia could've made to that, but she refrained. Her mothers were trying to reduce her to the little girl they knew and loved—and they were succeeding to a point—but Ia's universe had changed. It was an uncomfortable, unhappy realization, acknowledging that her parents were no longer the center of that universe.

Instead of replying, she sighed and grabbed her kitbag, tucked at the end of the couch where she had been sleeping. Fishing out a set of camouflage Browns, she headed for the bathroom. Amelia and Aurelia let her pass, then returned to their bedroom.

Her parents had never had much room in their apartment above the small but popular restaurant: just the two bedrooms, a bathroom, an office, the living room, and its small nook of a kitchen, which was rarely used to cook any meal other than breakfast. Sleeping on the couch wasn't any worse than sleeping in a tent, and she was already in the habit of tidying her bed, so folding up the blankets right after waking and rising hadn't been a problem.

It was the getting up part that seemed to be the problem. *I forgot to adjust my hours to Mom and Ma's hours, not*

Sanctuarian hours, on the trip out from Earth. I forgot they don't get up until almost 9 a.m. and don't go to bed until midnight—though I'd think I would've noticed last night how "late" everyone stayed up, catching up with all the gossip I never bothered to scry for in the timestreams . . .

Speaking of which, I should check the timestreams, see what I need to do versus what I should do, while waiting for my family to wake up again. Better yet, I'll take my writing pad with me and work on jotting down yet more prophecies electrokinetically while I jog, she decided, slipping out of her plain brown T-shirt and shorts. It was a little chilly outside, the weather more autumn-like than late summer, so jogging in long pants and a long-sleeved shirt wouldn't be too warm. *Three hundred years go by awfully fast when you're dead and can't tell anyone how to stop a galaxy-wide war.*

JULY 20, 2492 T.S.

"How much longer?" Fyfer asked, his tone bored.

"If I can put up with Mom and Ma throwing that surprise welcome home party for me at the restaurant yesterday . . . and then making me wash all the dishes afterwards," Ia muttered half under her breath, "*you* can put up with a little drive into the countryside this morning."

"The question is, how far of a drive?" Thorne asked her. Once again, he was driving, guiding the family ground car over the ruts in the unpaved, barely graded road they were following. Hovercars strong enough to counteract the local gravity were too expensive for most settlers on Sanctuary to afford, but that didn't mean the government sank a lot of money into high-quality back roads, either.

"Yeah, you said you're looking for a crysium field, but we've already passed three," Fyfer added, shifting forward as far as his safety restraints would allow, bracing his elbows on the backs of their chairs.

"One where we won't be interrupted. What I'm about to do, no one outside of the three of us is to ever know about . . . and I do mean *no on*e—turn left up ahead," Ia ordered Thorne.

He complied, carefully turning between the red-barked,

purple-leaved trees. The side road she picked wasn't even really a road, more like a leafer-path. Aquamarine grass had sprung up in the leafer's wake, along with small bushes, making him slow the car. "How much farther? I am not damaging Ma's car on one of your quests if it can be avoided."

"Quarter klick, no more. There's a small clearing of crystals off to the right. Up there," Ia added, pointing ahead at a gap in the growth. "You can just turn around right there. Point the car outward."

"Ia . . . pointing the car *back* the way it came is the new version of the archaic handkerchief-on-the-doorknob trick," Fyfer warned her.

"All the more reason the few who might make it this far will back up and find another spot," Ia countered.

Thorne sighed and carefully jockeyed the ground vehicle around so that it faced back toward the dirt road. "At least with a path this wide, the leafer isn't likely to wake up until late winter at the earliest."

"Another thing I'm counting on." Disentangling herself from the restraints, Ia opened her door and faced the other way. The partially recovered path ended about a hundred and fifty meters away in what looked like a brush-choked, grass-strewn slope, a modest hill that rose a good twenty-five meters at its crest, twenty or so meters in width, and probably extended for five times that in length. But a leafer was no hill.

Thankfully, it wasn't a carnivore, either. Instead, it was the largest land-based herbivore in the known galaxy. If the beasts could have been tamed and trained, the government of Sanctuary would have done so, but the few times they had tried had proven too disastrous. Leafers were too dumb, too interested in the recyclable plastics and elastics known as plexi—a common prefab building material—and too prone to torpor and months-long hibernation after only a kilometer or so of feeding, depending on the size.

Her brother's assessment was fairly accurate; a quick probe into the local timestreams showed that it wouldn't bother them, so long as they didn't try to climb up and dig a hole through the outer patina of dirt hosting all those bushes on its back. Closing the car door, she looked over at the field bordering the leafer-path. Rocky outcrops poked up through the ground to the east, a rugged clearing too stony to permit the growth of many trees. A few bushes did their best to cling to pockets of soil, but there was plenty of evidence that this little meadow flooded whenever a heavy rainstorm came through. The back-and-forth cycle of dry-and-drowned kept most plants away from this area, making it the perfect zone for a different sort of growth.

The real growth, slow as it was, came from the sprays of crystals dotting the field, pastel and glowing faintly, just bright enough to be seen even in the light of midmorning.

The predominant color among the shafts was transparent gold, not quite amber, but here and there, other hues could also be seen. Mint green, aquamarine, lilac, and rose. All of them were clear enough to see through. They also ranged in sizes from tiny, sharp-edged sprays no bigger than her head, to towering, conifer-like shapes four times her height. Heading toward them, Ia stopped when her younger brother gasped, dropping to his knees.

"Fire!" he yelled, clutching at his head, eyes wide and focused on things that weren't there. *"The Phoenix rises! The cathedral on fire—golden birds covering the sky!"*

The attack startled her. She hadn't felt anything building up around her. Normally, those who were the most psychically sensitive suffered the most from the phenomenon, and her brother Fyfer was about as mind-blind as any second-generation resident of Sanctuary could possibly claim to be. Slightly more sensitive than the rest of the Humans in the known galaxy, but only slightly.

Thorne rolled his eyes and aimed a kick at his brother's rump. "Get up. Your acting isn't *that* good."

Laughing, Fyfer dropped his hands and pushed to his feet. He grinned at his siblings, brushing the dirt from his knees. *"You* know I've been practicing . . . but I'll bet I had *her* fooled!"

"If I weren't so sensitive to the buildup of precognitive KI— or rather, the lack of it this time—then yes, I would've been fooled," Ia agreed. "You were good in every other detail I could see."

"Annoying is more like it," Thorne snorted, eyeing his younger brother. He returned his attention to their sister. "So, why are we out here? I'm supposed to be studying for my second big test in Economics."

"We're here to experiment." Ia removed the cuff from her right arm. Not the left one, which was her military ident unit, but the one hidden under her right sleeve. Molding it with a touch of electrokinetic energy to soften the material and a nudge of telekinesis to shape it, she formed it into a round, pink peach sphere. Unlike the sprays, it wasn't completely transparent, as the pink infusing the gold seemed to cloud the material. She held it out on the palm of her hand, displaying it to her siblings. "Do you know what this is?"

"A holokinetic illusion?" Fyfer asked, dropping his jester's attitude with a shrug. Underneath the charming jokester, he was quite bright for such a young man. "Or maybe some sort of psychic gelatin? At least, I'm presuming it's one or the other, either holokinesis of something that doesn't exist, or telekinetic manipulation of something that does. Except the last I checked, you weren't a holokinetic."

Thorne, for all that he looked like a walking mountain of muscle, frowned at the sphere on her palm, then looked at the sprays. "It sort of . . . That *can't* be . . . can it? Is that crysium?"

Ia drew out energy from the sphere, making the solid ball sag. She poured energy back into it, enough that her palm crackled with miniature lightning, and the ball crystallized. Literally, it grew crystals, turning into a miniature version of the much larger, cone-spoked spray around them. Both of her brothers swore under their breath, eyes wide.

"How . . . ?" Thorne managed.

"Special abilities," she said dismissively, carefully staying vague even in front of her own siblings. "The next person to be able to do this won't come around for another two hundred years . . . and she will *be* Phoenix, the Fire Girl of Prophecy. The thing is, *this* stuff isn't your standard crysium."

Drawing energy out, which destabilized the otherwise tough mineral, she reshaped it as a ball, then tossed it at Thorne. He caught it on reflex . . . and stiffened and stared at nothing. Blinked. Breathed. Blinking again, he focused on her. "You . . . this . . . what . . ."

She crossed the few meters between them and plucked the sphere from his palm. "What did you see?"

"The . . . time moved. The day sped up and raced by. The evening lightning storm came by . . . but I *knew* I was still standing here in midmorning," he finished, confusion creasing his brow. "Ia . . . I saw the *future*."

She nodded, and held out the ball to Fyfer. He quirked one of his dark brows but took the crystal ball—and sucked in a sharp breath, as real as the previous one had been faked. He didn't drop to his knees, but he did shudder. Taking pity on him, Ia took it back.

"What did *you* see?" she prodded him when he just blinked and breathed.

"Uh . . . the crew, the other students from school . . . they're going to call me on my wrist unit . . . ask me out to dinner with the group," he revealed.

Ia probed the future, and nodded. "Go ahead and accept . . . but tell them you plan to shift majors at the end of the semester."

"Shift majors?" Fyfer protested. "Why would I want to shift majors? I'm great at acting! I actually enjoy it. Besides, *you* told me to go into acting school."

She pinned her brother with a firm look. "Because I also told you that you would need to shift majors. You're going to start studying law—"

"Law!" he protested, throwing up his hands. "Why me? Why law?"

"And politics," Ia finished. Sphere cupped in her right hand, she ticked off three of the fingers on her left hand. "Rabbit is studying sociology, psychology, and behavioral sciences. Thorne is studying economics, business management, and logistics. *You* need to study law, acting, and politics. I've *told* you this, Fyfer. Over and over and over.

"Rabbit will be in charge of organizing the Free World Colony and its resistance movement. She can write a very moving speech, but she is *not* a public speaker, and thus not a public motivator. We all know that the adults wouldn't take her seriously just because of her size. Thorne will be in charge of the FWC's physical needs, making sure the cities are well-planned and well provisioned, with strategic defenses, housing and feeding, powering and cleaning needs all carefully considered and arranged. *You* will be the face of the Free World, but you need to be *more* than just a face to motivate people. You need to know the difference between wrong and right, just and unfair, and that means studying acting, politics, and law."

"Only Church slaves study law and politics. All those classes at Thorne's college are filled with forehead-circling fanatics." He wrinkled his nose in disgust, then mockingly scribbled his finger on his forehead, making a face.

Ia gave him a disgusted, sardonic look. "How *else* did you think the Church was going to take over the government? They're going to do it *by the book*, Fyfer. The Church's leaders have been planning this since they *funded* their half of the push to find a new heavyworld to settle. It may have been a cosmic accident that they ended up on *this* world along with the saner contingents from Eiaven and the other heavyworld colonies who contributed, but they are here, and we have to deal with them. *Your* job will be to stave off the too-rapid degeneration of Sanctuarian society from within the political, social, and legal framework."

"Isn't there some other way?" Fyfer protested, throwing up his hands. "*Any* other way? You're supposed to be able to see all the twists and turns for a thousand years! Isn't there some other way than . . . than to turn me into a Kennedy, or a Mac-Kenzie, or some other historically big-named *politarazzi*?"

She wished there was. Ia clenched her hands and closed her eyes. She searched on the timeplains, the great, amber-hued prairie of existence crisscrossed by a thousand million life-streams. What she *needed* was a way to show him what his best future path could be, without the trauma of actually dragging him into his own timestream and holding him there. Fyfer had the grace to stay silent while she dipped into stream after stream in rapid, practiced succession, but pouted when she opened her eyes and shook her head, fingers tightening on the ring in her grasp.

". . . I'm sorry, Fyfer. But I need you to do what I'm telling you. You're very charismatic and quick-witted when you want to be, and you know how to skirt the fine line between believability and showmanship. *You* are going to save a lot of people from slipping into the madness of believing the Church's doctrines and dogmas in the coming years." Ia held his gaze, though she softened her expression. "I *need* you, Brother. I need you to do what I myself cannot.

"*Everyone* on this world needs you . . . and they will need you to study law and politics, so you can *use* those as your sword and shield in the fight against the fanatics of the One True God!" She flung out her left hand in the direction of the city . . . and realized her right hand was no longer clutching a sphere. Instead, it now held a pink peach bracelet, a wrist-sized torus of rippling, stiffened crystal shaped something like either a turbulent stream or a fluttering veil. Confused, Ia stared. She hadn't consciously tried to shape it . . . or . . . had she?

Acting on impulse, Ia grabbed Fyfer's wrist with her free hand and dropped the torus-bracelet-thing on his palm. He shuddered, eyes widening much like they had when it had been a mere sphere, but this time he dropped to his knees as well. Sagged, more like it. Thorne hissed and shifted forward, ready to catch Fyfer in case he didn't fall safely, but Fyfer ended up merely kneeling. Rather than touching his brother, Thorne stopped next to him, glancing up in confusion at their sister.

Unsure what was happening to Fyfer, Ia extended a finger and brushed his temple very lightly, intending to use her minor telepathic skill to probe his thoughts. What she got instead was swept onto the timeplains next to her brother, who stood waist-deep in the waters of his own stream, his gaze fixed on the surface as scene after scene rushed past. Hissing, she hauled herself out and snatched the overgrown ring from his hand, freeing him as well.

Fyfer sucked in a deep breath and let it out again, coughing a bit. "God! God above!" He blinked and looked up at her. "Is . . . is *that* what you always see? Like a series of 3-D movies, snippets of . . . of moments . . . ?"

Wary, Ia merely asked, "What, specifically, did you see?"

"I . . . saw myself going to law school. It was hard—I could see myself hating you at times, but . . . then I saw what you were talking about. I was in a debate over some council position . . . and I turned some Church woman's arguments upside down and in her face and . . . and I was winning, and it was a rush to win . . ." Fyfer shook his head. "I *never* would've thought I'd like politics. Politics are . . . ugh! But, this?"

Patting him on the shoulder, Ia left him to deal with whatever it was he had seen. Whatever it was, it hadn't harmed her cause. Turning to her other brother, she held out the bracelet. Thorne backed up, hands raised out of accepting range.

"No, no, not me; that's not necessary," he protested. "Honest. I remember all too well my last visit into your timestreams."

"And normally I wouldn't subject you to that again," Ia promised. "But unlike Fyfer, you *know* what that's like . . . and I need to know if *this* is like *that*."

Holding it out, she waited. He shifted, clearly uncomfortable, then wrinkled his nose and held out his palm. Dropping the bracelet onto his skin, she waited. He, too, gasped and sagged to his knees. His eyes blinked, flicking this way and that, no doubt viewing the same timestream images that Fyfer had seen. Or maybe not. After several seconds, her curiosity overwhelmed her, and Ia touched his forehead as well.

What she found shocked her. He *wasn't* seeing his brother's life-choices. Some of them, yes, but only from his own perspective, wherever their lives crossed. Most of what he was seeing were his own possible paths. Since they would continue to live and work together, the two stepbrothers' lives intertwined quite a lot, but the perspective was purely from Thorne's life and its choices. Plucking the bracelet from his hand, Ia waited while he shuddered and recovered.

"Okay . . ." Fyfer finally murmured, head nodding slightly. "*How* did you do that, Ia? You weren't even touching me, yet you put all those images in my head!"

"That's what I'm here to find out," Ia confessed, shrugging. She eyed the bracelet on her hand, then set it on the grass-trampled ground. As soon as she released it, the ever-present lurking of the timestreams in the back of her mind diminished just a little bit. Barely enough for her to notice, but it was just enough to detect. Picking it up again, she could hear the faint, psychic "hum" of the crysium, and could once again feel the timestreams crowding a little closer than usual.

Whatever she had done to the bracelet had changed it. This wasn't a brief look into the immediate future by a few minutes, or a few hours. This was a look into the future by months, even years.

The strange, semi-alive biocrystal already defied logic. It was literally the discarded matter of the Feyori. The only sentient race to have evolved as beings of energy instead of matter, they were the only race in the known galaxy who could manage to convert energy to matter and back at the squared speed of light.

They did so by traveling faster than the fastest spaceship, whether it traveled through normal space by greasing the laws of physics through faster-than-light panels, or by siphoning itself through a hyperrift via other-than-light travel. Because the transformation from one form to the other was never one hundred percent complete, it was the Feyori who had introduced psychic abilities—using energy to manipulate matter, rather than the other way around—into the sentient races they had secretly bred with over the millennia.

The converse was also true. When they shifted back to energy-based bodies, the Feyori took a little bit of matter across with them. The easiest way to shed it and "purify" themselves was to find a world with a high enough gravity to pull it out of their bodies. By preference, they preferred high-energy worlds where they could "snack" at the same time. Sanctuary, with its churning core of both molten iron and gold, had a natural electrosphere as well as a natural magnetosphere. Lightning was nothing more than candied popcorn to the Feyori, making it a favorite dumping ground.

That dumped matter, discarded in the form of dust, combined itself with rainwater and the constantly generated energies from the storms plaguing Sanctuary every day. Seeded on bare rocks like the ones scattered through this field, the solution crystallized into sprays, with growth dependent upon just how much energy each shaft received. It was too tough to be cut, too difficult to break in all but the thinnest of shafts, and too bizarre for anyone to figure out how to use . . . unless they knew the secrets of both its origins and its strength, as Ia did.

But what to do with it? How to do it?

"Ia?" Thorne finally asked, catching her attention. She looked down at him. He shrugged. "What's going on?"

"I'm not sure, but . . . I *think* this is the solution to my not being able to be in two, or three, or five hundred different places at once. Follow me," she ordered, tucking the bracelet into one of the pockets on her brown military pants.

Without looking back, she headed into the middle of the field. Selecting one, she touched the shaft. This time, the humming resonance was louder in her mind; this was a full-sized shaft on a spray twice as tall as her body. She only needed some of it, however.

Concentrating on the flow of energies, she siphoned off just enough to pull away a chunk barely the size of her head, then carefully reshaped the end of the shaft so that it looked whole and untouched. Only someone who intimately knew each and every shaft would be able to tell this one was now shorter. Settling on the ground, Ia prepped the lump she had separated. Carefully dividing it into eight fist-sized chunks, she shaped them into balls with a thought, then looked up.

Fyfer and Thorne had followed her, thankfully. She held out a sphere to each of them. Both hesitated. At the arch of her brow, each of her half brothers settled on the ground across from her and took a clear pink sphere.

Tense, they waited once again to be dragged under the rough waters of the future.